THE ONLY THINGS HE WAS GOOD AT WERE FLYING AND KILLING. WHAT WOULD HAPPEN WHEN HE COULDN'T KILL ANYMORE?

Bear was an ordinary man who happened to be a damned good chopper pilot. And flying a Huey gunship happened to entail killing. Somehow he managed not to think about that until the day he had to retrieve the bodies of the men he'd just killed.

What can you do when you meet the enemy and he is you? And how can you save your buddies' lives—or your own— when that means doing the one thing you can never do again?

"[HOLLAND'S] ABILITY TO MAKE VIVID THE PARTICULARITIES, THE ATMOSPHERE, OF THIS AERIAL WAR IS AWESOME: THE HELLACIOUS DIFFICULTY OF FLYING THE HELICOPTERS, THE DARING TOUCHDOWNS AND EVACUATIONS— ALL THESE ARE ENTHRALLING AND SHARP AND TERRIBLE. AND IF THE HELICOPTER IS TO VIET- NAM WHAT THE TANK WAS TO WW II, [IT] FINDS ITS APOTHEOSIS IN THIS FICTIONALIZATION."
—*Kirkus Reviews*

LET A SOLDIER DIE

WILLIAM E. HOLLAND

A DELL BOOK

Published by
Dell Publishing Co., Inc.
1 Dag Hammarskjold Plaza
New York, New York 10017

For information address Delacorte Press, New York, New York.
Dell ® TM 681510, Dell Publishing Co., Inc.

ISBN: 0-440-14977-0

Reprinted by arrangement with Delacorte Press
Printed in the United States of America
First Dell printing—October 1985

For my parents

ACKNOWLEDGMENTS
I wish to thank Dr. George Acton for the many hours he
spent enlightening me about combat medicine. And thanks
to Rhoda Weyr for continuing to believe.

The helicopter slid slowly, slowly from the sky, as if reluctant to touch the darkening earth. In the glass-smooth air no thump of its blades announced its coming: it sighed from the sky in a long, slanting glide. As it neared the earth, the last weak sun, fighting through gathering evening haze, blazed the cross painted in dull red on its door. It crossed the line of surf where the South China Sea broke on the coast of Vietnam, on the rocks and reefs at the foot of the cliffs of Ky Ha. It skirted the seaward edge of the parking apron, checkered with revetments where the ships of two assault helicopter companies stood. In a last flurry of blades it settled on the helipad at the field hospital sprawled on the southernmost cliffs of Ky Ha.

The big side door of the ship slid back, and a corpsman got down and walked to the hospital; but no one came to meet the ship. It stood on the pad, the engine whistling, the big blade swishing softly, until the pilot shut off the fuel and the engine expired with a final sigh. The blade continued to turn, but more and more slowly, until at last it teetered to a halt. The copilot climbed out then and, with a long hook, caught the eye at one end of the blade, pulled the blade down to the tail strut, and tied it there by the cloth band tied to the hook. The pilot still sat in the ship.

The copilot walked to the pilot's door. "You coming, Trung-úy?" he asked.

"Go on ahead," the pilot answered. "I'll wait here till they come."

After the copilot had gone, the pilot climbed stiffly down from the ship. He sat down in the open side door at the feet of the two bodies lying across the floor of the ship.

One of the bodies wore black-embroidered aviator's wings above the left shirt pocket and a major's oak leaf in dull gold thread on the collar. The other was covered from waist to chin by the armored chest plate of a helicopter pilot. The plate was cratered in the center where a bullet had struck. This body lay closest to the pilot as he sat in the door. One of its boots was missing. The pilot, sitting there, laid his left hand on the stockinged foot. He grasped the foot roughly and shook it, then shook his head. He stood up and walked a little way from the ship to wait.

It was dark when the graves-registration truck jolted down from the hut at the end of the cliffs. The blackout lights of the truck made hardly a mark on the night. The truck groaned to a halt beside the helicopter, so close that the driver and his assistant had no need to take even a step to transfer the bodies.

The pilot would have helped them lift the bodies onto the truck, but there was no room, so he stood back and watched. When they had gone, he slid the big door closed. Its rumble echoed down the silent ramp, among the revetments where the helicopters stood. He stood a long time, holding the handle of the door. Then he, too, went into the night.

1

The early afternoon sun of the dry season baked the fuel pits at Landing Zone Baldy. The fuel pits were a broad stretch of olive-drab pierced steel plank littered with thousand-gallon rubber bladders of jet fuel. The air above the planking shimmered with heat.

Among the bladders two helicopter gunships were running their blades up to operating speed.

Spec-Four Cripps dragged the fuel hose away from the lead ship and stepped gingerly back across the planking, which burned at the soles of his jungle boots. He climbed into the back of the ship, plugged his helmet cord into the intercom, and picked up his machine gun.

"You up, Cripps?" the Bear asked over the intercom. He was lounging in the right front seat, fanning himself.

"Up, sir," Cripps said.

"Okay. Think you can get us out of here at this weight, Cov?"

"That or die trying," the copilot, Warrant Officer Covington, answered.

"Don' say that, sir!" This came from Sergeant Handy, the door gunner, who sat in the right rear door, opposite Cripps, also cradling a machine gun.

"You know this isn't the strongest ship in the world, Handy," Covington said. "If you'd toss off a hundred pounds of that ammo, we might have a chance!"

"Hey, don't insult Cripps's ship," the Bear said, looking into the back with a grin. "This is a good ship, right, Cripps?"

"I didn't say it wasn't a *good* ship," Covington pointed out. "I said it wasn't a *strong* ship. Old ninety-seven back there"—he motioned with his head back toward the second ship of the fire team—"can get off the ground easy at this weight, no hotter than it is today, even with no wind at all; but *this* ship . . ."

"Give it a try," said the Bear.

Covington made an elaborate show of settling himself at the controls. He simultaneously stretched out his legs, resting his heels on the floor with the balls of his feet just touching the pedals that controlled the tail rotor; took in his left hand—the "power" hand—with an elaborate curl of his wrist the collective-pitch stick that angled up from the floor at the left side of his seat; and gently settled his right hand—the directional-control hand—against the grip of the cyclic-pitch stick, which rose from the floor between his knees. He paid particular attention to his right hand. His right forearm rested on his right leg. He flexed the fingers of that hand as if he were a pianist preparing to play. He took the grip of the cyclic delicately between the thumb and fingertips.

"Great style so far," Bear said.

"I learned from a master."

Twisting the motorcycle-style throttle on the grip of the collective stick, Covington brought the engine and blade speeds up to the bottom of the operating range, then nudged them up to flight speed by thumbing the governor button at the end of the collective stick.

He pulled up on the collective stick, at the same time pressing the left pedal to counteract the increased torque that would try to spin the ship around to the right as it came up off its skids. The skids slanted so that, at rest, the ship sat slightly nose down. As Covington pulled in pitch, the ship rocked slightly back and rested on the heels of the skids. It danced there, just touching the steel planking, ready to fly.

"You set?" Bear asked.

"I'm ready."

The Bear was slouched back in his seat. He was preparing Covington to become an aircraft commander, and so he was not going to follow through on the controls, however heavy the ship

2

was. He keyed the radio with the foot switch beside the pedals: "Two, are you ready?"

"We're ready," came the answer from the second ship.

"Wolf Lead coming up." Bear held out his left hand to Covington, thumb up.

Covington pulled the collective even higher, at the same time easing forward the cyclic, to keep the ship from skidding backward, and pressing the left pedal farther forward.

The ship rose straight up, maintaining its heading without a quiver. But it stopped a foot above the ground.

"She's not gonna do it," Covington said. "A foot's all she has in her." As he had lifted the ship from the ground, the tachometer needles had sunk from its normal sixty-six hundred rpm to sixty-four hundred. For a normal takeoff the ship was supposed to hover at three feet above the ground; but the higher the hover, the more power required; and this engine had no more power to give.

Covington concentrated all his effort on holding the ship, trying to will it to rise higher. Sometimes, with Bear at the controls, he had thought that Bear's will alone was what made the ship perform. He willed the ship to go higher. But it went no higher.

"If you can get her to translational lift, she'll fly," Bear suggested.

"And if cows had wings, they'd fly, too, Bear. But translational lift happens at eighteen knots, and we're standing still." Translational lift was the sudden increase in lift that would occur when the airflow through the rotor rearranged itself, when the ship changed from a fast hover to flight.

"Maybe you could bump her off."

"Maybe. Or maybe I could catch a skid shoe in the PSP and turn the ship over."

Pierced steel planking had a way of catching skid shoes in its perforations. Being snatched sideways was unpleasant in a ship carrying eight hundred pounds of jet fuel and six hundred pounds of ammunition and rockets.

"You want me to take it?" Bear asked this without looking at Covington.

"No." Beads of sweat formed along the line of the helmet, above Covington's eyes. He could do nothing about those, but he flexed the fingers of his right hand to relax them, without disturbing the cyclic stick still resting lightly between thumb and forefinger.

He eased the cyclic forward—a half inch, no more.

The ship moved forward. As it moved, it descended, gliding off the cushion of air that helped support it at a hover. A heavy ship could sometimes be coaxed to translational lift by easing forward off the ground cushion, bouncing off the ramp, using the resulting altitude to get a little more airspeed, and so on in a series of bounces until she flew—or didn't fly.

In a ship less heavily loaded, Covington would have pulled up the collective, increasing the power to hold altitude, while simultaneously adding left pedal to counteract the increased torque. Today, the ship had nothing more to give. And so Covington held the collective steady, gave back the altitude, kept the ship pointed straight ahead. He did not even glance at the airspeed indicator. It would not register speeds this slow. If he got to translational lift, he would know it. If not . . . With a great grinding crunch, the ship hit the PSP and lurched to a halt.

"Way to go, Lead," said the radio.

"Don't mind us," the Bear answered. "We'll figure this thing out yet."

Covington looked at his aircraft commander in resignation. He was not embarrassed. He had given it a good try. The ship could not be got off. "You want to take off some ammo?" he asked the Bear.

"How about if we pump out some fuel?" Sergeant Handy suggested. Handy hated to give up any of his ammo.

"We can't spare the fuel," Bear said. "We'll be short of time on station as it is, even if the Mustangs aren't as late as usual."

"*You* gonna try it, then, sir?" Handy asked, addressing the Bear.

"Let Cov give it another try," Bear said.

"Bear, this sucker is *not* going to fly at this weight!" Covington said. "Not even for you!"

"Probably not. But what the hell . . . let's give it a try." The Bear laid his hands and feet on the controls. "I got it."

"You got it." Covington shrugged, and sat back to watch.

"Let's see if I can remember what old Tate showed me in flight

4

school," Bear said. He picked up the ship delicately but without hesitation, bringing it straight to a hover a foot and a few inches above the ground. He did not test the controls, did not bring them to one position and then ease them to a final setting. He moved them to a position, and there they stayed. He got no more power from the engine than Covington had, but the efficiency of his movements took the ship an inch or two higher than Covington had taken it.

He moved the cyclic forward, three-eighths of an inch exactly. At the same time he brought the collective up another eighth of an inch and added a sixteenth inch of left pedal. The ship bowed forward; the tachometer began to ease back down through the green arc—the blade was slowing because Bear was asking for more than the engine had to give. But the ship settled more slowly than it had for Covington. It gathered speed. It kissed the steel of the ramp, bumped into the air, settled again, but moving faster. The low-rpm warning pinged through the pilots' earphones.

"Better set her down, B.," Covington said, but the Bear held steady. The ship bounced again, rose again, moving still faster.

There was that sudden, wonderful, carnival-ride lurch to the pit of the stomach, and the ship began to climb.

The Bear felt the lift come in. The low-rpm warning was still pinging. He lowered the collective a fraction of an inch to let the blade start winding back up to operating speed while not giving back the altitude he had gotten. They needed five feet to clear the concertina wire surrounding the LZ: they had five feet, but nothing to spare. The ship flew with the jerky wallow of a bicycle ridden too slowly. He gave up a foot of altitude, outside the wire, to build up airspeed and rotor rpm. The controls smoothed out. The ship felt alive again. He eased back the cyclic. The nose came up, and they were climbing.

"Hoo ha!" said the Bear happily.

"You son of a bitch!" Covington said.

He said it with admiration.

Handy and Cripps lounged knowingly in the back.

Number zero nine seven, the stronger second ship of the fire team, lifted out of Baldy without fuss and slid into position a quarter mile behind the lead ship and an equal distance to the side. Its pilot called, "Wolf Lead, two is up."

"Roger, Two." Bear turned to Covington. "You ready to take us to the LZ?"

Covington got back on the controls. "I've got it."

"You've got it."

With Covington flying, Bear leaned back in his seat and closed his eyes. He looked, to Covington glancing over at him, less like a bear than like a seal asleep on a beach. His mustache bristled as he unconsciously puffed out his upper lip. But Covington knew that the Bear was not asleep. He was concentrating on the feel of the ship, to see what was new in the way it flew.

The ship had the same shuffle-bump as always, resulting from a chronically out-of-track blade. Bear opened his eyes and studied the instruments. They showed one auxiliary fuel pump out, as usual. Everything else was operating. At length Bear took out a map from the case beside his seat. The map covered a hundred and fifty miles of the coast of South Vietnam, from Da Nang to Qui Nhon, with a breadth of fifty miles from the coast. Bear had pasted it up by hand from a dozen separate maps. It was much folded and marked with the notes of a hundred missions.

"Do you have the place in mind?" Bear asked Covington.

"Yup."

"The slicks will be coming in from the south." A slick was a helicopter without the external weapons of a gunship dragging in the wind—a "slick ship." Today the slicks would be carrying troops. "Let's fly over the inbound track, and then check out that village to the north of the LZ. You know the one?"

"Yup."

"What's it called?"

"Van Tay."

"You're a good man, Cov."

The name of the village didn't matter. The landing zone was specified by the map coordinates, and not one pilot in a hundred would show any interest in the name of the village a mile away. But Bear was pleased that Covington knew the name. It showed respect, to know the Vietnamese names for places. After all, it was their country.

6

"Someday I'll be able to fly this thing, besides remembering names," Covington said.

"Mr. Covington," Handy said from the back, "there ain't a pilot in the country who could of got this turkey off the ground back there, except for the Bear."

"Hey, don't call Cripps's ship a turkey." Bear grinned. "Right, Cripps?"

"Yes, sir," Cripps said.

As Covington flew, Bear tended to other business. He studied the ground for likely cover or concealment where Charley might have installed a weapon. He did not expect anything: after months of flying this area, he knew where trouble was to be found. It wasn't at Van Tay, or en route there. Division was even using the area as a training ground for brigades new in country, before those soldiers went on to harder stuff. But still Bear was cautious and tended to his business. Some pilots felt that the business of gunships was to kill people; but to Bear, his business was to keep his slicks from being fired upon. So he studied every paddy dike tall enough to hide a dug-in machine gun, every clump of palm trees, every peasant following a buffalo and plow.

Tending to business did not prevent the Bear from enjoying the ride, however. Bear loved flying; but, unlike many pilots, he also loved riding, as long as he was up front where he could get his hands on the controls in a hurry if things got hot. Like all pilots, he hated riding in back, where even the best pilot was only another piece of cargo—a "pack," as helicopter pilots referred to live freight. On a day like this one, though, even riding was a treat.

It had been a hot, dry day in the fuel pits at Baldy; but as they flew nearer the coast, a sea breeze rose from the northeast—a cool breeze promising rain, not today, but sometime in the future. The northeast monsoon—the wet monsoon on the Indochina coast—had been teasing for weeks, blowing up intermittent showers and then dying away in a series of Indian summer days in whose afternoons the peaks of the Annamite chain dwindled away into the blue distance in the west, while to the east the South China Sea burned like a blue jewel clasped in the curve of silver beach. The land seemed to wait breathless for the seasons to rearrange themselves, for the breathing of the whole Asian continent to alter, to settle into the winter rhythm that brought rain and life to the coastal plain east of the mountains, the plain which had parched while the highlands only fifty miles to the west had been inundated with the summer rains borne up from the Gulf of Thailand on the southwest wind.

Bear slid back the armor plate at his shoulder, the better to look out the window of the ship. Because the ships were traveling, not hunting, Covington was flying at fifteen hundred feet, above the top of the Dead Man's Zone where small-arms fire was effective.

The plain was alive in the sunlight. On Route One long chains of trucks crept on the highway. Motorcycles dodged among them, scattering peasants on foot or on bicycles but giving wide berth to the water buffalo swinging their curved horns on the margins of the road. On both sides of the highway the plain was subdivided into irregular paddies separated by low narrow dikes. All but a few of the paddies were dry now, awaiting the coming monsoon, their soil red as though rusted from disuse. Some paddies were tiny, no more than a few square meters in size; some stretched for half a mile and would have held a thousand helicopters.

The plain was not a patchwork of squares and rectangles, as it would have been in a younger land. Instead the paddies grew in rings and swirls, starting from small villages, from single farmhouses, or even from nothing at all. From the air they seemed to be cross sections of living creatures that had spontaneously burst into life and added layer on layer of flesh until their growth was checked by collision with a growing neighbor. These cellular patterns fitted into one another in complex mazes that took up the whole of the plain between Route One and the sea, except where they eddied around the shoulders of isolated rolling pastures, or where ragged clusters of palm trees marked a village.

The landing zone for the mission was a broad open paddy on the south side of a low rise. The rise was topped by a pasture holding a few scraggly cattle. At the very top was an old graveyard with narrow vertical Buddhist gravestones crowding among more ancient round stone tombs. North of the rise the palm tops of Van Tay stretched in an arc three-eighths of a mile long and a hundred yards wide.

The mission briefing had been for the slicks to land north, to drop their troops, and to turn east coming out of the LZ so as to avoid flying over the village. There was plenty of room for the maneuver. Nevertheless, Bear waved Covington on toward the village. "Let's do a high recon. Villages make me nervous."

They flew the length of the village from west to east and back. There appeared to be no reason for nerves. There were the usual numbers of people, chickens, pigs, and dogs. Covington swung out over the paddies to the north. They were dry and empty except for one where a man was plowing behind a water buffalo. A tenuous trail of red dust followed him across the field, drifting slowly southward on the light breeze.

As Covington turned back south, Bear took the controls again. "Let's have a closer look at the village. I've got it."

The two gunships came down in a long, curving dive that ended ten feet above the treetops at the east end of the village. The boom of their blades sent pigs scuttling and chickens flapping wildly. A woman turned, startled, to stare at them, clasping her broad conical straw hat to her head as the two children behind her grinned and waved at the ships. Bear rocked the ship to them and grinned back. He wrenched the ship into a hard right turn and, at a hundred and forty knots, rocketed westward the length of the village. As he passed the far boundary ditch, he pulled the cyclic stick back to cash in his speed for altitude in a steep climb that took him back to fifteen hundred feet. There he nosed the ship forward again, pulling in power to get back speed without losing altitude. Satisfied, he rolled out on a southerly heading to set up and await the slicks. "If there's a weapon here," said Bear, "I'll eat it on television."

"There could be anythin' in that village," Handy said hopefully. "You could hide a elephant in there."

"Sure, Handy," Bear answered. "But who'd pull his trigger?"

Bear's laugh was a cackle which shook his belly and lit up his face. In the helicopter it could only be seen and not heard above the din of the machine itself, all flapping blades and screaming engine and whining gears; and even the shaking belly was covered by the ceramic armor plate strapped to his chest; but the mere idea of Bear's laugh, as much as the joke itself, sent Covington and Cripps into unheard laughter, until Bear finally grumbled, "Listen, why am I doing all the work here, anyway? Fly this thing, Cov."

Still laughing, Covington got promptly on the controls and went through the change-of-control ritual: "You got it?" "I have it."

Bear relaxed in his seat. "Anyway, Handy," he said, careful of Handy's feelings, "Captain Martin said he flew cover for two sweeps through here this week already, with the new brigade. Nobody's taken fire out of this place yet."

"We're flyin' cover for the Mustangs, don't forget, sir," Handy said. "They take fire from anyplace."

"Don't remind me," Bear said tiredly. "Those assholes would claim they were taking fire on short final for the officers' club. And they're worst of all when Baker's leading them." Captain Baker was a platoon leader in the helicopter company—a sister company to Bear's own—whose slicks had the call sign "Mustang." "But I'll guarantee you they won't get any fire out of *this* LZ."

At Bear's direction Covington set up a pattern to the west of the LZ itself, flying an elongated figure eight north and south so that the gunships were never turned completely away from the landing zone. With the second ship lagging a half mile back now, one of the two was always inbound. They paralleled the flight path the slicks would take on their final approach, where the slicks would be slow, easy targets for any nearby weapon. But it would take a brave gunner to open fire with two gunships on station. As his ship turned inbound at one end of the figure eight, Bear studied the number two ship coming toward him. It flew nose-down, like a tracking hound. Weapons hung heavy from its sides: on each flank a six-barreled machine gun on a flex mount, and below it seven rocket tubes in a bundle. Above these main weapons, in each door a crewman harnessed to the ship on a strap carried a machine gun, the crew chief at one door and the gunner at the other.

"Wolf Lead," the radio said, "this is Mustang Lead." Bear knew Baker's voice.

"Go, Mustang."

"Wolf, Mustang Lead with a flight of ten is, oh, three minutes out. How's the LZ?"

10

"Roger three minutes out. The LZ is cold."

Mustang made no response.

They flew the northbound leg of the figure eight again, and when Covington rolled out, the slicks were there below them.

To the Bear there was nothing so beautiful as a formation landing of helicopters—not only for the physical beauty of the formation's geometric order, but for the determination and purpose they showed, driving downward into whatever might lie ahead. He had felt it in the first company formation he participated in back in flight school, which seemed ages past. He felt it again, seeing the Mustangs cross below him, even though this was only a routine lift into a cold LZ.

There were ten slicks, flying V's of three in trail, with the tenth ship in the slot at the rear. They were in tight, so that the lead ship of each V slotted into the opening of the V ahead, making three perfectly linked diamonds. A slick driver was known by how closely he could hold a formation on a combat assault, and like every pilot in Vietnam, these intended to be the best. The main blades were slicing not five feet from the tail rotors ahead, even though the slightest touch between blades would surely knock one ship, and probably both, from the sky—if not half the formation with them.

There was no need for them to be so close: the landing zone would have held ten times their number. They could have flown fifty yards apart, and in safety.

And yet, because they were close, they were a beautiful sight, those ten ships driving down as one. The diamonds glistened, as the sun caught the rotor blades, like the pattern on a snake's back.

The diamonds wavered as the ships flared a hundred feet above the ground to bleed off speed for their landing. The noses of the ships came up: the whole formation shivered, seemed about to disintegrate, then consolidated again as the pilots adjusted. Bear could see door gunners and crew chiefs leaning out the open side doors, scanning the paddy for any sign of enemy fire.

As the ships reached fifteen feet above the ground, dust began to lick beneath the formation. The first wisps grew to a rolling cloud that enveloped the ships as they touched down. Troops were jumping from the doors.

11

This was the hard part, Bear knew. The slicks had to get on the ground, get the troops off, and lift out again before their self-created dust storm became so intense that the pilots could not see the other ships. The pilots were pulling pitch now: the red cloud of dust rolled around the rear half of the formation in dense vertical curls. Blades flashed through it, then became suddenly clear again as the ships burst up into clean air.

"They're up, Two," Bear said over the gunship radio channel to his second ship. Two answered with two clicks of his microphone switch, to show he had heard.

"Follow them when they turn east," Bear said to Covington. But the slicks did not turn east. They continued straight toward the village. *"Now* what the hell?" Bear muttered.

"Hey, they're putting down fire!" The voice was Sergeant Handy's.

The door gun of the ship on the right side of the first V was firing on the village. Tracer rounds arced down from it in short bursts, like tossed baskets of coals. Other ships began firing, by ones and twos, until within seconds the guns of half the formation were in action.

Bear was on the controls instantly and broke toward the village while Covington pulled down the flex-gun sight from its stowage clip above the windscreen. "Mustang," Bear called urgently, "where's your fire?"

Baker's voice came back: "Mustang's taking fire from the village. Request you suppress."

"Why is the horse's ass over the village?" Bear said over the intercom. Over the radio, he said, "Where's the source of the fire, Mustang?"

"Right out of this village!"

"Where in the village?" Bear asked.

No answer came back.

"I don't see a thing," Covington said. Bear had turned to fly along the south side of the village, to avoid drawing fire in the direction of the slicks.

"Two, do you have anything?" Bear asked over the gunship channel.

"Negative," came two's answer.

The ground troops Mustang had just inserted certainly were

taking no fire: they had stopped and were standing in the paddy watching the show.

Bear was not about to fire at random into an inhabited village. "We haven't located the source of your fire, Mustang," he called.

"Well, shit, it's from that village!" Baker responded. "Hose the whole place down, dammit!"

"Screw you and the horse you came in on!"

If radio silence could be shocked, the silence that followed was. It was broken after some seconds: "What did you say?"

"I say again," Bear repeated, "screw you *and* the horse you came in on. Sir."

"Wolf Lead, I'm in command of this mission, and I'm ordering you to suppress that fire!"

"And I'm saying I don't see any fire to suppress. Are you ordering me to fire at random on the village, sir?"

When Baker finally replied, his voice was shaking: "I'm ordering you to suppress enemy fire that my flight is taking!"

"Request again you identify the source of the fire," Bear said instantly.

By this time the flight was out of range of the village, and the slicks' machine gunners had all given up. When the reply came, it was: "Wolf Lead, I'll see you in the pits at Baldy."

"Roger that," Bear said.

Bear flew low over the village. There was nothing to be seen but palm trees and thatched roofs. Even the pigs and chickens were out of sight. But at least there were no bodies. Bear ranged out to the north. The farmer plowing behind his water buffalo had not even looked up as the slicks roared low over him, their machine guns firing; and he did not look up now. That was not unusual, either. For an unarmed peasant, safety was in not noticing.

Bear wished bitterly that he could land, could enter the village, and see what had happened there. *Had* there been a weapon? It certainly wasn't impossible: plenty of colder LZs than this one had suddenly turned hot. And pilots didn't always know from where they were being shot at. But Bear didn't believe it. None of the signs were there. It hadn't escaped Bear's notice that half of the slicks in the formation had not fired. Someone in the formation should have been able to tell Baker, if he didn't know himself, what they were shooting at. The troops on the ground should have shown some reaction. And Baker shouldn't have tried to weasel out of an order, if it was legitimate.

More important than the weapon, or lack of it, Bear wondered who had been hurt. Probably he would never know. The troops on the ground, when they swept the village, might learn there had been casualties, or might not. Either way the word would almost certainly never get back to the pilots of the gunships.

The Mustang slicks had already refueled by the time Bear's fire team made its approach to Baldy, but Mustang Lead was still there, his ship tied down at one side of the fuel pits.

Bear did not report to that ship; he led his flight directly to the fuel pumps and left the ship running as Cripps refueled it.

Mustang Lead, Captain Baker, came to the Bear.

He was a lean, stoop-shouldered senior captain with a Vietnam mustache and fire in his eyes. He stepped up on the gunship's skid at Bear's door and motioned for Bear to remove his helmet. Bear did so.

"I'm going to have your ass, mister," Baker said. "And that's not a threat: that's a promise!"

"You know what you can do with my ass."

This was not exactly what Baker had expected from a junior warrant officer, and he stepped back and, in doing so, nearly fell from the skid. He sputtered as he tried to find words for his rage.

"Careful, sir," Bear said solicitously. "You might hyperventilate."

Baker stood back in astonished rage. Fists clenched, he appeared to be considering inviting the Bear to step outside: but if he was, he thought better of it. At last he merely pointed a shaking finger at Bear. "Your CO is going to hear about this, mister!"

Even over the noise of the helicopter Bear imagined he could hear the steel planking ring under Baker's boots as he stalked away.

"Do you think that was a good idea, B.?" Covington asked after Bear had put his helmet back on. Handy and Cripps were wide-eyed.

"Probably not," Bear said. "Who the hell cares?" He had been

14

cool enough in his insubordination. Now he pounded the cyclic stick in rage and frustration. "Let's get the hell out of here." He pulled pitch and whirled out of the pits, not even calling to ask two if he was ready to depart.

What the Bear felt was often written on his face; but Covington could not at the moment interpret what he saw there. It was a striking face, though far from handsome, a broad face with heavy brows, a bristling wide mustache, and rolling, wild eyes which, together with the stout frame and muscular shoulders, had led Lieutenant Arp, their section leader, to give Bear his nickname. Bear could be morose, as Covington had just seen, and then he had a cutting tongue; but he was subject to fits of uncontrollable good humor. When he was in a happier mood his face was likely to creep through a range of animal imitations: he could look like any sort of beast, real or imaginary. Even at rest his face, with its bulging eyes and mustache bristling, had a walruslike expression. But now it had a disdainful look, as if the walrus had tasted a bad clam.

It took a long time for Bear's number two ship to catch up coming out of Baldy. Bear climbed out toward the seashore before turning south toward the company's home ramp at Ky Ha. He passed through a thousand feet, through fifteen hundred, and kept on climbing. The ships crossed the beach at three thousand feet and swung south, but still they climbed, higher and higher into the glassy air, until the beach narrowed to a thread below them, while to the west unsuspected mountains rose behind the coast ranges, muscular giants thrust from the silent forest. Among them slender wavering threads of smoke arose at wide intervals. Over a thirty-mile radius a dozen such columns were to be seen. Villagers near the farthest smoke might never have seen the sand and the sea above which the helicopters flew with such remote ease. Over that precipitous land it was a month's walk to cross the distance that, from the Bear's ship, was contained in a glance. But the smoke did not rise from any of the villages which dotted the maps of that area, small clusters of huts that flashed startlingly into view from low above the trees and vanished instantly. The mysterious whispers of smoke rose from unbroken green forest where even maps were silent. They were aloof utter-

15

ances of unknown men proclaiming only, but beyond mistake, "We are here," or "Here we have been."

Bear had climbed the ship with his eyes fixed on the land, studying the mountains that were on most days hidden by rain or a blue humidity haze, but which today sparkled as though new-minted for him to see. But wherever he looked there was smoke, there was distant burning, and no knowing if it were friend or foe.

But it was the sight that met his eyes when he turned from the land that tore a gasp from him. There on the left, the inverse of the ghostly smoke rising from the solid earth on the other side—like the reflection of a material universe in some fourth dimension, firmament rising from the emptiness where sea paled into sky without ever becoming horizon—an island hung, a rock in the void, a dream of peace removed from the burning land.

Its name was Cu Lao Re, and it was real. Though it was on his map, he had never seen it before, for haze and the distractions of war hid it on all but the rarest clear days. He was a mile above its highest peak, but it seemed to hang at his own level, for there was no horizon against which to place it. The sea, so fiercely blue below, paled in the distance to silver even as the blue sky overhead paled as the eye left the zenith, so that there was no meeting at all, no line of demarcation between the two, but an intermingling of sea and sky, of being and not-being, and in that space hung Cu Lao Re, the rock in the void, shimmering.

He felt a sudden dizziness, for his eye, bereft of the customary marks of up and down, high and low, led his brain into confusion. He had felt vertigo before. He knew—something of the pilot in him knew—he must tear himself away, seek a reference on which to orient himself. But he did not. He stared at the apparition, enchanted.

The voice on the radio brought him back. "Lead, if we're going to San Francisco, we could use some fuel first." His eyes snapped down to the gyro horizon on the instrument panel: the ship was in a left bank and turning out to sea.

Five thousand miles away, somewhere in the void in which the island hung, lay the continent of North America, with nothing between but the curve of the sea.

Bear turned his ship back down the line of the beach. He did so with a sigh which could not possibly be heard above the thousand noises of the aircraft; but he thought Covington looked at him strangely.

2

"Well, Martin," Captain Blood asked as they left the hospital, "what's your date of rank?"

"February," Martin said.

"This year?"

"Yes."

They climbed into the gun platoon three-quarter-ton truck. Martin had driven down to the hospital direct from the gunship ramp the minute he landed.

"What day?" Blood asked.

"What?"

"Your date of rank—what day?"

"I don't remember. Who cares?"

The truck ground and protested up the steep red-clay road. The road was dusty now, though rutted from past rain.

"What d'you think about Carlsen's hand?" Blood asked, bracing his own hand against the windshield frame to keep himself from being thrown against the roof.

"Couldn't tell much under all that bandage. I don't think he'll lose it, will he? You were there before I was. Did the doctors say anything?"

"Not to me. It don't matter if he doesn't lose it, though—he won't be back here, anyway. Carlsen is *short* in this country."

"It might matter to him," Martin said.

"Is it before the thirteenth?" Blood asked.

"What?"

"That's my date of rank—the thirteenth. Yours before that?"

"Christ, I don't know! What difference does it make?"

"Every Ringknocker knows his date of rank, Martin," Blood answered with a satisfied grin. "You can't shit an old trooper." His fingers, curled over the top of the windowframe, drummed slowly on the taut canvas roof.

Lieutenant Arp put down his tray on the mess-hall table and lowered himself into his chair, cautiously, with a simultaneous downward motion of his left hand like that made in lowering the collective-pitch stick of a helicopter to put the machine on the ground.

"A little rough," observed Warrant Officer Carter, who was sitting across the table, "but not a bad landing for a gunnie. Given some time and practice, you could do something with it."

"The aviator's art," Arp replied, "is in *flying* the machine, not sticking it into the ground."

"I'll remember that next time I try to get eight packs into that hole they call a helipad up at Three MAF. I'll fly over and boot them out at treetop level. 'Sorry, guys,' I'll tell them. 'The aviator's art is in *flying* the machine. But you're capable folks—you figure out the rest.' They'll like it."

Arp agreed enthusiastically: "Yes, by God, spoken like a true lord of the air! The earth is too lowly for the likes of us. Avoid it! Avoid it!" He turned to Warrant Officer Carlisle seated between them at the end of the table. "Apparently Cap'n John didn't avoid it far enough, Hitch. What hit him?"

Carlisle had been copilot in Captain Carlsen's ship when the bullet came through: through the door, through the cyclic stick, and through the middle of Carlsen's right hand.

"Hitch did the Blood a favor," Carter said.

"I didn't know they were such great friends."

"About as close to being friends as Carter is to being funny," Carlisle said. Unconsciously he passed a hand over his bare scalp that glistened under the mess-hall lights. At age twenty Carlisle was nearly bald, and, resigned to this, he shaved short what little hair he had left. For a while after he had joined the company he had been called Chrome, but Arp had given him the cognomen Trailer Hitch, now generally shortened to Hitch or T. H.

"Hitch put Captain John in front of a bullet," Carter said to Arp, "and now the Blood will be executive officer."

"God forbid!" The voice came from someone at the next table. Arp crossed himself and rolled his eyes theatrically ceilingward.

"God Himself couldn't keep Blood from grabbing for that job!" Carter insisted. "There's nothing to do but grin and bear it."

"Grin and bare his ass for kissing," Carlisle muttered.

Sensing some tenderness in Carlisle, Arp asked more gently, "How is Cap'n John, Peter?"

"Fair, considering that he's missing the middle of his right hand," Carlisle said without looking up from his coffee. It was not his favorite drink, but it gave him somewhere to keep his eyes.

"Jesus, it's not *your* fault, Hitch!" Carter insisted in quiet exasperation. "You weren't even flying the ship; and if you had been, you couldn't have done anything. If a bullet comes through where someone's sitting, he's going to get it! There's nothing you can do about it."

"Not unless your prayers are more combat effective than mine," Arp agreed. "The trouble with Carlisle," he said to Carter, "is that he doesn't see enough gore, being a slick driver. He hasn't had a chance to get used to it. We should send him out with the Bear a few times."

"I've seen enough blood," Carlisle said evenly. "I've brought in three dinged aircraft commanders in two months, and two were evacuated to Japan."

"Why, T. H., that's not *blood!*" Arp said. "I've *killed* more men than that in one pass! The Bear kills more men than that every morning before breakfast!" Although Arp pretended not to notice, the subject of this compliment had come through the mess line and was standing behind him.

"Not *our* men," Carlisle said.

"Well, not on his better days," Arp admitted. "There's no telling what he'll do when the ravenous mood is on him, though. Oh, *he*llo, Bear!" He gave a friendly pat to the Bear's belly as the Bear pushed past him. "Eat well. Keep the old fires stoked. Keep the blood lust burning."

20

"If Hitch wants to see some blood," the Bear said, "he should fly with the Mustangs."

"You et 'em up today, eh, Killer?"

"We didn't. But it wasn't for lack of readiness on their part."

"Again? What was their excuse this time?"

"When did they start needing excuses? Sir, Captain Martin's got to stop sending me out with those bastards!"

"Darn it, Bear, you're going to spoil all my efforts in building up your reputation! Who's going to believe you eat babies for breakfast when you come in complaining like this? What have the Mustangs been up to now?"

"It doesn't take a genius to guess that one," Carter put in. "If you have three companies flying an assault in the same landing zone, the Mustangs will be the only ones to take fire. Every damn time. So then they proceed to shoot up the surrounding country-side. Right, Bear?"

"There was this village over the hill from the LZ," the Bear said by way of answer. "On the way out one slick opened fire on it, and everybody followed. I didn't see anyone hit on the ground; but I didn't see any unfriendly fire, either. Mustang Lead asked me to suppress."

"And you said?"

Covington, who had come up behind the Bear, answered for him. "He said, 'Screw you and the horse you came in on. Sir.' "

"I told him there wasn't anything to suppress," Bear said.

"In your words, or Covington's?"

"You know how my memory is," the Bear said. "But I think there was a horse mentioned at some point."

"Oh, the old man's going to love you today," Arp said with a grin. "You do such a job of coordination with our sister compa-nies."

"I already told Major Hart," Bear said.

"And *he* said?"

Carter interrupted. "*He* said, 'That's easy enough to figure out. Whatever you think is right, Don.' Major Hart is okay."

"Someone's been tampering with Carter's rheostat again," Bear said. His eye scattered the accusation generally over the gathering. "You're a lot brighter than the average warrant officer, Carter."

"That's why you get sent out with the Mustangs," Arp told him. "Somebody's got to keep the wild beasts in line. To listen to your sob stories," he added, but still grinning, "a body wouldn't realize you were the most efficient killer since Typhoid Mary."

"That's all right, too," Bear answered, following Covington to an empty table.

Captain Blood would have given much to be known as the most deadly killer in the division. He could not envy the Bear: it was beneath the dignity of a commissioned officer to envy a warrant officer. But he knew that, given the chance, he could distinguish himself beyond anything done by the Bear. Blood yearned desperately for the chance to command the gun platoon and show what he could do. When he had arrived in the country five months earlier, the gun platoon had been under the command of a well-established officer, Captain Stoddard, and Blood had been given an airlift platoon. He took no satisfaction in commanding slicks. If the platoon was making combat assaults it might have been different, but this company's slicks were flying mostly administrative flights and "ash and trash"—resupply and other once-around-the-park things that brought no medals to the man in charge. Blood's ships helped other companies' combat assaults but flew none of their own. His leadership talents were water on desert sand, or so he told himself. The Bear's nonsense jingle ran in his head despite his distaste for the author: "Kill 'em dead'll win a medal." But Blood killed no one, and the Bear, a fat nobody who spent his free time chattering at the hooch-maids in what Blood doubted was Vietnamese, had two Distinguished Flying Crosses, while Captain Blood had none. So Blood watched the gun platoon commander like a hawk, and visited Major Hart regularly with recommendations for tactics, for operational improvements, for ways to improve the company's figures on hours flown, passengers carried, enemy killed. He laid snares for Glory, but always she continued to elude him.

"What do you s'pose Captain Blood is after today?" the company clerk asked, staring out the screened window of the orderly room.

The first sergeant looked up from the weapon he was cleaning,

22

a Chinese-made AK-47 assault rifle that one of the flight crews had brought in. He snorted at the clerk. "Now, I just don't know why the Blood would be comin' to see the old man on the very same day Captain Carlsen got his ticket back to the world. When Captain Stoddard got his orders, it took a whole day for Blood to get over here and work on getting command of the gun platoon. Either he's ahead of schedule, or he's making a social call. I leave it to you."

"I guess he's more desperate than he used to be," the clerk said.

Blood came through the door talking. "Hello, First Sergeant. Where'd you get the weapon?" Without waiting for an answer he took it from the desk. He would have given it a proper, squared-off military inspection, but he had trouble opening the bolt. As he fumbled, he asked, "Is it Chinese, or East European? The NVA get weapons from both places, you know." Blood had an answer for every unasked question on things military. He did not always waste them on noncoms, but Major Hart's feet were visible below the plywood screen separating his small office from the orderly room proper. As he continued to examine the weapon critically, Blood asked in an offhand manner, "Say, is the major in? Ow! Shee-it!" The bolt had slammed shut on his thumb.

"Yes, sir, he sure is, sir. Just go right on back. I think it's Chinese, sir," the first sergeant added as he took the weapon back. "It's got all these little chicken-scratches here on the barrel, you see. . . ."

Captain Blood departed sucking his thumb.

"Del, it's a sad day." Major Hart waved off Blood's salute and pointed to the chair beside the desk. "We lost a good man. Thank you for going up to see him. I just called the hospital, and he's resting now; but I'll get up there later this evening. Maybe you could get a few of his things together: we don't know if he'll be evacuated yet, I understand."

"Anything I can do to help, sir. Let's hope he won't go; but he don't look good. But you know how those Minnesota Swedes are. They'll get him to Japan, get some of that cold air on the wound, and it'll fix him right up. Not like us southern boys. Me, I'd do better staying right here in the heat—and in the hot of it."

"You think he'll be evacuated, then?"

23

"Well, he was lookin' a mite peaked, sir, as my momma used to say."

The major rubbed his short-cropped silver hair and pursed his lips in silence.

"Of course," Blood offered, "if it looks like they'll only send him to Qui Nhon, say, and he'll be comin' back to the company, why, I can come over and get out his paperwork anyway. Say, wouldn't that be great, if he *could* come back? Of course, it takes a while, after a fifty goes through your hand, before you're up to snuff. . . ."

"It's kind of you to offer, Del. There'll be time enough to think about what to do, once we're sure what's happening."

"We can't reckon on getting another XO in from outside," Blood supposed, with regret in his words and hope in his heart, "the way replacements have been running. Or maybe I should say, the way they haven't been running. The ol' pipeline has just about dried up, it appears to me, ever since the company got switched out of the Aviation Group and into Division. Twenty pilots came in last week, but *they* all went to other units."

"There's a lot in what you say, Del," the major admitted. "I expect we'll have to move somebody up. Tighten up the belts down below."

"It's a shame, but I reckon it's true, sir. Well, as I say, if there's anything I can do . . ."

"Believe me, Del," Major Hart said, "you'll be the first to know."

Captain Blood was whistling as he walked to the mess hall.

As he strolled with Covington across the parking ramp, evil muttering creatures appeared and disappeared on the Bear's face. He was reliving the afternoon's emotions, Covington knew. "Thank God for a night off," Covington said, hoping by pleasant anticipation to break his friend free from unpleasant memories. After four days on standby alert, awaiting the call from Division that would send them to anyone needing gunship help, for one night at least they could walk to their own hooch, air out their sweaty sleeping bags, get their clothes off, and sleep in their own beds, without having to tune one ear for the scramble horn.

"Praise Him," Bear agreed fervently. Covington smiled pres-

24

ently to see by the Bear's face that his storm-wracked thoughts had sailed into calmer waters.

Covington took off his cap and let the wind blow through his hair. In the middle of the ramp he stopped. "Tell me something, Bear," he said, "what were you thinking about, when you turned out . . . toward the island?"

"That wasn't me," Bear answered. "It was the prisoner in me, trying to escape."

"No dramatics, Bear. You were thinking how close we were to home, weren't you?"

"No. I absolutely wasn't. Or hardly any at all."

"I was. Home never seemed so close as right then, Bear. I was just thinking how to tell Pinky about it." He added after a moment, "There's nothing between here and home. Did you ever think about that? You could walk right down the beach and swim away, and walk up the other side in California."

"Nothing but the curve of the sea," Bear said. "And that's nothing at all."

"Nothing at all. I think I'm going to be homesick tonight, Bear. I almost wish I hadn't seen it."

"Those who fly too high get their feathers burned." He tried on the face of Icarus falling. All the way down he was thinking how different their impressions had been of their one transcendent flight: he and Daedalus.

Covington laughed at the face. He thought Bear was being a lobster.

The laugh was a cold plunge into the sea. "You're lucky to have Pinky to be homesick for, Cov," Bear said. "I hope I get a chance to meet her someday."

"Ah, she'll love you, Bear. When we get back to the world, you and I, you're going to come stay with us, and get a chance to know her."

"And she will introduce me to her equally delightful, stunningly beautiful, sexually incontinent friends. . . ."

"No, nothing like that. I want her to have a good opinion of you."

"Well, Cov, any wife who would send her husband's company a subscription to *Playboy* can't be *all* prudish."

"She's not prudish. She's . . . well, shoot." Covington thrust

25

his hands in his pockets and walked on in sudden, real, despairing homesickness for his distant wife.

The Bear, ambling beside him in rueful helplessness, could think of nothing to ease his friend, and as a consequence was left to rake the embers of his afternoon's anger against the cool bank of the vision they had seen together, if not shared.

Captain Martin smiled at the sight of the two coming toward him. Covington, a slender twig of a youth, feeding his straggly boy's mustache on serious thoughts and lover's yearnings; and the Bear, muscular but clumsy-looking, with his jigging walk like a fish fighting the line. He could not imagine how such a pair came to be soldiers, but soldiers they were. The Bear, this wide-eyed monster, filled a commissioned officer's position as acting gun section leader, and filled it as well as any man could.

The Bear, as he again raked over the afternoon's events, had begun to glower and gnaw the ends of his mustache. "What's the matter, Bear?" Martin asked, wanting to laugh at the procession of expressions across the Bear's face but successfully avoiding it. "Your after-action report says you drew a blank today. Is that it?"

"*We* drew a blank," Bear admitted. "No KIAs, no rounds expended. I wish I could say the same for our hosts, the horses' rears. But they're such rotten shots, they didn't kill anyone that I noticed." He added, as an afterthought of no importance, "I told that Captain Baker of theirs what I thought about it all. He didn't like my opinion."

Martin's face became serious. While he shared the Bear's opinion of the Mustangs' tactics, he could see only trouble from bringing it up directly. "And it was such a nice day, too." He sighed. "Okay. I'll let the old man know after I have some chow."

"I did that, sir."

"Major Hart was in Operations when we came in, sir," Covington said with a shrug. "He asked how we did, so we told him."

"Okay. Okay."

Bear saw that Martin was displeased. He said hotly, "Shooting up villages won't win any hearts and minds, sir."

"You don't need to tell me that, Bear. But we're supposed to be protecting *our* people, too. That's what you were sent along for."

"I always thought we've done a fair job of that, when there's anything to protect them from!"

"Yes. You have, Don. I can't complain about that. Well, I'd better check with Major Hart anyway."

Martin knew well that Covington and the Bear sometimes embroidered their tales of one another's adventures; but this all had the ring of truth about it. "Just go away and let me handle this," he suggested. "If there's any more, I don't want to know. It's hard to fabricate a good story when you're bound by a lot of facts."

Although a damp wind had come up, the evening pleased Blood mightily. He sat on the deck of the officers' club with his feet up on the rail, listening to the sergeant of the guard post the sentry in the bunker twenty meters below his feet. He could not hear the words, but the voices pleased him for their timeless exchange of confidence in duty, for their promise of peace in the night. There came the rapid rattle of a field phone being tested in the bunker. Then the sergeant and his little skein of guards passed on down the perimeter. Down the hill, beyond the double-apron fence that stretched along the military crest of the hill, beyond the ancient graveyard with its circular tombs like military earthworks, the lights of a village flickered in and out of sight as the wind moved the palm leaves. They came and went in silence like fireflies on Alabama nights. Beyond them lay the dark waters of the bay whose name Blood had never learned. Beyond that, Route One ran in the darkness up the narrow plain between the mountains and the sea. Both the island in the bay and the shore along the highway were heavily populated, but they were dark at night.

"Cô, where the hell is my drink?" Blood called even though he saw that the girl was bringing it. If he had not called, she would have been even slower. Even beautiful Vietnamese annoyed him, and this one was not especially pretty. She arrived with a rustle of her white *áo dài*, complaining querulously, "I come *beaucoup* fast. Too many officer here. Carry *beaucoup* drink, get *tí-tí* money."

"Cô needs *tí-tí* boot up her ass to make her move faster," Blood said scornfully. But he dropped a half-dollar tip—an undersize orange paper military scrip half-dollar—on her tray. It was more than the drink cost, but he enjoyed overtipping the girl. "You no

27

forget to change that before you go home, you hear?" He knew that if she could get off the post without changing it into piasters, she would.

He sipped at his Scotch and soda. He preferred gin, but he had not ordered that since a general's aide told him it was a plebeian drink.

As she returned to the bar, the girl nearly ran into Captain Baker, who had dismounted unsteadily from his barstool and was coming toward Blood's table.

Blood had known Baker slightly for years, as a result of their serving together on several posts without ever being in the same unit. He remembered Baker chiefly as a fixture in the officers' club bars. Blood had been careful never to be associated with club bar fixtures; but he was feeling expansive this fine evening. He waved Baker to a chair.

"That cunt will be buying grenades to roll under your bunk with that money, Blood." The years had not improved Baker, Blood noted with satisfaction. Blood was always most comfortable where he felt superior.

"She loves my ass, Baker. Just be firm with 'em, that's the secret with women. But you wouldn't know anything about that, would you? What are you up to—out seeing how the upper class lives?"

"Out trying to find out what makes this outfit you fly for so fucked up. I'll let you know, if I ever find out."

"After flying with the Mustangs as long as you have, Baker, doesn't fucked up just look normal to you?"

"At least we don't send out a gun escort just to fly around at a safe distance and let the other people take the fire."

"I didn't know that was SOP anywhere," Blood answered blandly, "although I can see where somebody might reasonably not want to risk his rear on a bunch of Mustangs."

"I'm beginning to think it's SOP in that rinky-dink outfit you people call an assault helicopter company," Baker returned scornfully. "You've been flying generals around so much, you get nervous if you have to do more than run up and down the coast delivering letters."

The indignation in Baker's voice departed so far from ordinary intercompany insults that Blood concluded he was serious. "You

28

really had trouble with our gunnies today?" he asked with sudden officiousness.

"I don't know why you call them gunnies. They didn't do much gunning as far as I could tell. That bug-eyed turd you people sent out with a fire team just stood off and bitched that we were goin' to hurt somebody! Who are we fighting this war for, anyway?"

"Baker, I'll report this to Major Hart, sure as hell." Blood took a notebook and pencil from his jacket pocket to reinforce the promise. The commanding general at his first post had demanded that all officers carry notebook and pencil at all times to write down whatever flashes of genius might strike them, and he had been known to stop young officers on the street and demand that these implements be produced for inspection. Blood had carried them ever since.

"Your Major Hart already knows about it," Baker told him. "I reported it the minute we got in, and the old man called Major Hart while I was in the office."

"What time was that?"

"I don't know—seventeen hundred maybe. Know what your major said? He said he'd talk to the men involved to find out what the deal was. As if he couldn't take my word for it! Christ, Blood, if any of our pilots tried a stunt like that, our old man would have 'em up for a general court before they could get their blades tied down!"

"Major Hart's had some other things to think about today," Blood said uneasily. He had seen Major Hart since seventeen hundred hours. As the new executive officer he ought to have been informed. But of course it wasn't certain yet that Carlsen would go—or at least Major Hart wasn't certain of it. "He might have put it aside for now because he was worried about other things. Our XO got shot up today, and things are kind of crazy."

"Who's that, Carlsen? Stopped a round, did he? Well, you can't make an omelet without breaking some eggs."

"Not quite *stopped*—it went through his hand. They'll evac him out of country. The docs haven't said so, but I was over to see him, and he won't be using that tater-hook for much. The old man was going up to see him—I reckon that's kept his mind off of other things." Blood could not forbear adding, "You'll see some

29

action on this gunnie thing tomorrow, I promise you. I'll remind the old man. A little push from the XO can't hurt."

"I thought Carlsen was being shipped out?"

"There'll always be another XO, Baker," Blood said.

His significant tone slowly penetrated Baker's mind. "And you're it, eh? Well, Blood, Christ, congratulations! Your very own company, almost, eh? Won't the shit fly now?"

"Won't it?" Blood laughed. Baker had a proper understanding of his abilities. He offered to buy Baker a drink. "O' course," he added, "it's not official yet. The orders can't be cut until Carlsen goes. But it's never too early to celebrate."

"Never too early to celebrate good fortune," Baker agreed. He shouted at the girl to bring him a gin and tonic.

On the ramp a gunship slouched complacently under the baking glare of a portable spotlight, enjoying the attention of a half-dozen mechanics and maintenance technicians who poked in and around the cockpit console and the clusters of rocket tubes on the flanks of the aircraft. The square clusters of tubes, twenty-four tubes to a side, were the only armament on the ship except for the crew chief and door gunner's light machine guns. A ship with that armament was known as a "hog." True to its name, even its indolence had a certain ferocity, as if it might willingly bite the hand that ministered to it. The technicians worked carefully around the rocket tubes as they raced to finish before the coming of the rain that the wind promised.

Martin, standing within the circle of light, did not see Major Hart's jeep stop behind the aircraft. The major did not disturb the work. Not until the technicians had begun packing their tools did he move down into the light.

"Tell Operations we've got another ship up, Sergeant Magruder," Martin said to his platoon sergeant. "And have them roust another crew out of the rack. It's a good night for business with Charley." He saw the major then. "I went to your hooch to look for you, sir; but you weren't home."

"No. I went over to see John."

"Had the shock worn off yet?"

"I don't know. He was pretty disturbed. To be expected, I suppose—he doesn't think he'll ever use his right hand again.

30

And the surgeons think he's probably right." He added, "I guess I'll have to ask you to do some packing tomorrow, Ben."

"Sure. I'll get his things together in the morning."

"I'd be grateful." Major Hart often treated acts which he had power to command as if they were personal favors. In another commander this might have seemed an affectation. In Major Hart it sprang from honest appreciation based on more years' service than he now cared to count as enlisted man and company-grade officer. But even as a second lieutenant he had never been able to convince himself that his power to send men even to their deaths was his by divine right. He still looked on it as a magical gift which might vanish if not cautiously used. "I didn't mean I wanted you to pack only his things, though," the major went on. "Pack yours, too."

"Mine, sir?"

"I'd like you to move into my hooch," Major Hart explained. "It's customary for the executive officer to room with me. Unless you'd rather stay where you are? You *do* have better quarters, I'll admit."

"No . . . it's not that, sir." In his surprise Martin fumbled for words. "But what about Captain Blood? Doesn't he have date of rank on me?" Despite Blood's doubts Martin *had* forgotten his own date of rank. And he had been willing enough to concede the position to Blood on that basis.

It would not have surprised Martin to be promoted over Blood, date of rank or no date of rank—he was convinced of his own egotism—but he knew that Blood had visited the major before dinner, and Blood's self-satisfaction since then could have meant only one thing.

Beyond that, Martin had not come down from Group staff only to sit behind another desk. The Army would see the change to XO as a step up, and Martin would take it if he had to take it. He was not in the Army to retire after twenty years with a tombstone promotion to colonel. But he did not want it badly enough to have trouble with Blood. Blood needed the boost. For himself Martin expected better things in due course. Egotism again, he told himself.

"No," Major Hart answered him. "Blood doesn't have an earlier date of rank. In fact, you both have the same date." He added, "I want you to have it."

The major was less innocent than he sometimes seemed, Martin reflected. He knew the bait to use. "All right, sir."

"Will you be needing the light, sir?" It was Harper, one of the electronics technicians.

"No, you can take it, Harper. Thanks. And good night."

"Good night, sir."

Under the light it had been warm. With it gone, the night closed chilly and damp about them. The wind eddied around the sand-filled steel plank walls of the revetment that protected the helicopter.

"I said I came up to see you. I wanted to talk to you about the Bear," Martin said, in the confidence of the darkness. He added with a laugh, "Maybe I should have done it before letting you offer me the job as XO."

"You surely haven't been having any trouble from the Bear, Ben?"

"No, *I* haven't. But I gather that the Mustangs were not so pleased with him today."

"So he told me. And then, I had a call from that . . . from their company commander. Isn't it strange how incoherent some folks get when they're upset, Ben?"

"What do you think ought to be done?"

"You realize I don't have power to dispose of the affairs of other companies," Major Hart said, "though God knows they need it. I don't believe there's anything to be done *here*. Unless you have a suggestion?"

"No, none at all."

"You're going to be an easy XO to work with," the major said. "Always give the old man his way."

"Only when he's right," Martin answered.

A crew arrived with a tug to move the hog to the arming pits. The ship was quickly jacked up on ground wheels and dragged off into the night.

"You'd better get some sleep on your last night of standby," Major Hart advised. "Tomorrow you're going to have to start working days. No more of this lying around all day, flying all night."

32

"Thank the Lord. And who gets the honor of commanding the gun platoon? Arp?"

"Blood," the major answered.

Although Captain Blood had purposely returned to his quarters early to receive the major's call, the coffee-grinder rattle of the field telephone excited him. He answered in his best military manner: "Blood here."

"Del, if you have a minute, could you come up to my quarters?"

"I'll be right up, sir."

The major's hooch was not very grand, Blood noted with a possessive eye. It was in fact not even comfortable. Captain Carlsen had brought in a television and a small refrigerator. Those would be packed and sent wherever it was he was going. There was an ancient civilian table left behind by the marines who had formerly occupied the building, and a spindly metal chair. Against the side walls were two metal wall lockers and two steel-frame bunks. Beyond those the building was starved of comforts. The skeleton of its studs and rafters threw shadows on the outer plywood skin and galvanized iron roof. Many of the pilots' hooches were finer. They were lined with flamed plywood and insulated with Styrofoam packing from rocket boxes. Some even boasted elaborate bars, bookshelves, and cupboards whose ancestry could be traced through the same line as the insulation, for on their days off from flying, officers with nothing else to occupy them turned housekeeper. But the commander's hooch had been occupied by only two men, and as the two had seven-day-a-week duty, the luxury of space remained mere vacancy. Nevertheless, it suited Blood. Important emptiness was a better thing than insignificant comfort.

The major sat on the edge of his bed, leaving Blood the chair, a soft-iron thing badly welded by a Vietnamese entrepreneur for sale to the Americans. "Del," the major began, "Captain Carlsen is going to be leaving us."

Blood began a sympathetic eulogy, but stopped at a wave of the major's hand. "I know you've been unhappy, tied down to a slick platoon flying ash and trash." The major would not hear Blood's objection, but went on, "I'd probably feel the same myself in your place—want a chance to do bigger things. Anyway, as you expect,

33

we'll have to make some changes because of Captain Carlsen. You'll be one of the changes."

"I can't say I wasn't expecting it, sir," Blood admitted. He tried to achieve just the right mixture of humility and self-confidence in his tone. "I can report for duty first thing in the morning, if you like."

"Good. Get together with Captain Martin and—"

"Martin, sir?" Blood asked, perplexed.

"Yes. You'll be taking over his platoon. You'll want to inventory the platoon property with him. And then get with Lieutenant Harris—he'll take your platoon for now. God knows if we'll ever get another captain." Seeing Blood's confusion, he added, "Don't worry. Martin has left you a good-working platoon. I'm sure there'll be no problems."

"No," Blood mumbled. "No. I'm sure there won't."

Martin came in the door carrying clothing in a parachute bag. Seeing Blood there, he excused himself and began to back out. The major stopped him: "It's all right, Ben. You live here, after all. I was just congratulating Captain Blood on having inherited your platoon. There are no secrets passing." If the major did know of any strain between his two captains, he looked over the top of it with the serene gaze that excluded any hint of awareness that there could be an objection to what he had ordained. He waved off the lingering salute Blood gave him in parting.

Blood's idea, when he first left the major's hooch, was to have a drink, perhaps many drinks. Not that he felt any need for alcoholic anesthesia. But, in the same way that habitual indulgence seemed to him improper in an officer, intoxication seemed the proper response now. Blood had never liked alcohol and never really desired it. He had had no contact with liquor until he joined the Army at seventeen. He took up liquor, as he had taken up the Army, as a manly way of life. But like many an unimaginative man he mistook his idea of the conventional response for a personal desire. He concluded that he wanted to be drunk.

For months Blood had tormented himself with thoughts of the glory that would be his if he were commander of the gun platoon. Now the plum had fallen into his lap, but, in that moment, he had stretched for something still higher. And when he found that promised to another, he returned to his old desire only to find it withered and worthless. The juice was gone out of it.

Strong drink was called for.

But then he recalled that Baker would still be at the club. Blood was not eager to provide a laugh for gin-drinking fools at his own expense.

Blood kicked angrily at the steel plank of the helicopter ramp. Martin was junior to him; but somehow Martin had cut him out. And Blood knew how: West Pointers stood together, the damn Ringknockers! He had once seen a West Point graduate jokingly knock his ring against a table and whisper across the ring: *Knock-knock. Calling Washington! Calling Washington!* They stuck together, and they knew which way was up. Somewhere up there another Ringknocker had heard Martin. Blood cursed and beat his fist against a steel revetment.

Martin was hanging his uniforms in the metal wall locker.

"You should have brought over that fancy wardrobe Stoddard left you, Ben," the major said, watching him.

"This is good enough, sir."

"I'm ashamed not to offer you better, after you gave up the big city for us."

"We had mildew in the closets there, too."

A metal locker was all Martin wanted. He had come down to the company from a staff job at Aviation Group headquarters. Most officers, if they ever reached that high, arrived at a staff position only after six months in a line company. Group staff, subordinate only to First Aviation Brigade and MACV itself, was the nearest thing to heaven that Vietnam offered. The higher headquarters sweltered in Saigon, out on the sticky mudflats of the Delta, while Group was headquartered in the old French resort city of Nha Trang on the central coast, on a site of stunning beauty between the mountains and the sea.

Martin had gone there at the beginning of his tour because the adjutant at Group knew him and wanted him there. The adjutant had been his company commander at Martin's first duty station after West Point. It had taken four months for Martin to convince the man, who meant well, that he really did want to go to a line company. "If I'm as good an officer as you keep telling me I am,

35

sir," Martin had argued, "I *should* be sent down. That's where the war is."

There certainly was no war at Group staff. Life at the staff level bored Martin, and angered him. Papers bred like rabbits in his desk at night. Reduce their offspring to manageable numbers in the evening, and by morning they were back to their old strength. And none of them mattered. Awards for meritorious service, PX thefts, even procedures for maintaining files, by God! When he was appointed files control officer for the Group, he knew it was time to get out.

His friends thought he had lost his senses. "If you're not getting a company, Martin, you're better off here. Command of a unit looks good on your two-oh-one file, but you're not going to get a command as a captain. You'll only get a platoon in the boonies someplace. Better stick here. The adj likes you. You'll get a great efficiency report."

Martin could not stick. Tennis at noon, Sunday afternoon on the beach, dinner at La Frégate—these were killing him slowly, but as surely as were the papers raging over his desk. It was not the way to run a war. Nor was a room in a beachfront villa, with a live-in cook, private bar, and rooftop garden where the Air Force nurses came to dance on weekend nights. Beach Road for five miles was lined with villas facing the broad bay. Once they had been filled with the families of French planters. Now they were occupied by American master sergeants.

Even in the boonies it was not always different. The grunts slept on the ground, true enough, but back at the home base the colonel had his trailer air-conditioned. Martin had told a colonel how to win the war once: "Put every man in the Army, from Westmoreland on down, in a tent, and tell him he's going to stay there until it's all over. Close the PXs and the clubs. Send every man's pay home to wait for him, except for the wages a peasant gets for farming his land. Send home the hooch-maids, the cooks, and the laborers. Besides saving the country's economy, it'll get us all home before Christmas." The colonel was outraged.

Martin tossed the empty parachute bag under his bunk.

"That's not exactly the most extensive wardrobe I've seen in country, Ben," the major said. The locker contained only the three issue sets of jungle fatigues and the khakis in which Martin had arrived in country. "Did you wear out your party clothes in the big city?"

"Those are my party clothes," Martin answered.

3

The northeast wind lunged landward out of the grey South China Sea, whipping the wild rain before it and pressing long rolling waves down a thousand miles of open sea to crash at last against the Indochina coast. All fluid elements conspired against solidity. The earth melted and ran in rivers of mud inch by inch toward the sea. The mountains were reduced, were ground by microns to powder, ran riverward. The plain was awash, with paddies brimful and their dikes sloughing off at the edges. But through it all, greenness endured in the sprouting rice, life struggling skyward even in darkness.

Out in the rain the gunships crouched. Their wet flanks glistened darkly in the revetments, glinting under the distant light from the hospital beyond the long, level ramp. The wind gusting over the revetments made them shudder like live things dreaming of the hunt. Because of the angle of the skids and the main rotor mast, they stood on the ground in the nose-down attitude in which they flew, with the tense readiness of tracking hounds.

Unprejudiced eyes might have found them less than handsome. They were C-model Hueys, with oversized tail-booms appended to short fat bodies, like mongoloid tadpoles. They entirely lacked the lean grace of their D-model relatives, the slick ships. And, like all helicopters, although they could be flown with great precision by a skilful pilot, they flew at all only by dint of the most frantic exertions, as when some fat barnyard fowl hoists itself aloft for a triumphant moment. A helicopter is a collection of moving parts each trying to tear off and throw away every other, and these could be coaxed to fly two days running only through the dedicated ministrations of a retinue of maintenance men. To control them in flight required the use of two hands, two feet, and singleminded concentration that through long practice finally became second nature, but could never be relaxed. Unlike other aircraft, a helicopter untended would not fly itself. It preferred to crash.

But, though clumsy on the ground, the gunships were hunters; and they were ready. Before night came, each had been lovingly prepared by its crew. Helmets now were plugged into the communications system and placed on the seats; shoulder harnesses were adjusted and laid over the seat-backs; searchlight and landing light were positioned and tested; weapons were tested, loaded, and safetied; the throttle was rolled to the starting position, the start fuel switched on, the rpm governor beeped down; the radios were set for departure frequencies; the panel light switches were on and the rheostat set to keep the lights to a dim glow; the position lights and anticollision beacon were switched on. All the electrical systems would come to life at a touch on the master switch. At a squeeze of the starter trigger, fire would rush through the turbine engine, and within sixty seconds from the time the cockpit door opened, the ship could be airborne.

While the ships stood in the rain, the crews waited in the alert hooch. The alert hooch smelled of sweat and mildew. It had been slept in by too many bodies in too many wet clothes on too many soaking nights. The plywood shutters that completely covered the glassless screened windows were down all around to hold back the driving rain; but every chink on the windward side leaked a constant fine spray. The two bare light bulbs dangling from the ridgepole glowed weakly through humid halos. Rain rattled like shot on the metal roof. Below the cliffs the ocean hammered the beach. The wind ripped at roofs, at shutters, at doors.

Cripps on his mildewed cot struggled through disconnected snatches of dreams, washing in and out of sleep like a body tumbling in the surf. From the end of the hooch under one of the light bulbs came the click of cards, murmured words, occasional

39

shouted oaths as the cards hit or failed. Players groped for their cards in the dim light. Through the darkness of lost years came the sounds, the sounds of his father's friends playing poker downstairs, and on the shingles the rain tapping. Rain on the metal roof, a ghost of the past asking to be let in. His mother writing to an aunt somewhere, somewhere up North where, they said, snow came, and stayed on the ground. Not rain. Her pen scratched over the hard shiny paper as he lay drowsing on the floor beside the table. "They're family, even if they are Yankees." Firelight flickering warm outside his closed eyelids.

The bare bulb danced as a gust shook the hooch. Through the slits of his eyes he could see the line of the filament. The horse-blanket smell of a too-much-used sleeping bag seeped from under his sweaty back.

Mr. Covington, on the next cot, was sitting with a book on his lap for a table, writing. He wrote to his wife every night. Married, and no older than Cripps was himself. Cripps smiled at Covington's serious face laboring over his work.

Beyond Mr. Covington, Sergeant Handy snored on his cot. Moisture glistened on his black face, below the hat he had pulled over his eyes.

Democracy reigned in the alert hooch. The assigned quarters might be segregated by rank; but here, where the gun crews spent half their nights, officers, NCOs, and enlisted men alike slept shoulder to shoulder, played cards, traded lies, dreamed their dreams.

In search of a better-smelling spot on his sleeping bag, Cripps rolled the other way. The Bear was seated cross-legged on the next cot like a khaki Buddha, hands folded in his lap. Their eyes met.

"You sleep beautifully," Bear said.

Cripps blushed.

"Cov, did you ever notice how beautifully Cripps sleeps?"

"Often," Covington said, not looking up from his letter.

"Hey, no, I'm serious."

"So am I. Cripps, you sleep more genteelly than any person I've ever seen in all my born days."

"Your sleep, Cripps, is something to behold," the Bear told

him. "The most pleasant smile comes and goes, and your nose twitches. I wish I had your dreams."

"You ought to," Atterburn said. He had come up the aisle from where he had been watching the poker game. "A good wet dream is as close as you'll ever get to any real stuff, Bear."

"Now, Atterburn, you know Cripps wouldn't have any dreams like *that!*"

"A stud like Cripps? Who are you kidding? Just look at him! A little scrawny, maybe, but . . ."

Cripps rolled facedown without answering, and closed his eyes. Cripps never answered, although he was frequently the butt of lewd pleasantries from Atterburn. Cripps did not like Atterburn. But he admired the Bear, and sometimes went so far as to hold a hurried conversation with him. Cripps would have died for the Bear, or done anything else short of holding an extended conversation.

Seeing that Cripps was not to be baited, Atterburn turned to Covington. "What's this? Letter to Pinky? You haven't written to her since noon. You must have a lot to say by now."

Covington did not reply. He had heard this before.

"You going to tell her how many Dinks you got today?"

Covington shook his head.

"Why not? Man, I'll bet she'd like to know that! Doesn't she want to know about your work?"

"Since I told her about the round that came through the floor and took the earphone out of one side of my helmet, back while you were still in flight school," Covington answered, "she doesn't want to hear any more about shooting."

"Well, hell, what else is there to write about? I don't see how you can fill up your three letters a day, Covington. Around here, you can't even truthfully tell her you went to town and screwed the bar girls. Excuse me, I forgot you were being faithful to Pinky."

"It's only fair," Covington said. "She's being faithful to me."

"So you say."

"She is."

"Well," Atterburn admitted, "if she's being *fair* to you, she is. Except for that doughnut dollie that was at Colt last week, I

41

haven't seen a round-eye in two months. I'm getting horny enough to ask Suzie for a little boom-boom."

"Suzie's been too old for that sport for fifty years," Lieutenant Arp put in from his quiet corner at the front of the hooch.

"Well, I'll ask Yan, then."

"You'll waste your breath," Arp said.

"Arp wants Yan for himself," Covington said to Atterburn. He had begun to copy the conversation for Pinky, and he wanted to keep it moving.

"If the major catches anyone making free with the hooch-maids," Arp said, "we lose them; and then you'll do your own laundry, or send it to town to be washed in buffalo piss. Besides," he added, "Suzie watches Yan like a hawk. You'll never catch her alone."

"The famous Bear has her alone in a corner every day he's off standby," Atterburn said. "Of course, he doesn't know what to do with her. He thinks 'good relations with indigenous person-nel' means talking friendly. One of these times I'm going to show her what really good relations are."

"It's a fat rooster that has a pecker as big as his crow," Bear observed.

The scramble horn blasted the reply from Atterburn's lips. Half-dealt hands fell on the card table. Covington stuffed his unfinished letter into his sleeping bag as Bear fumbled with the zippers on his boots. "Christ," Atterburn objected, "we're not going to fly in *this* shit, are we?"

"It's only a shower," Arp told him comfortably, settling deeper into his cot. He grinned at the gesture which was Atterburn's only reply. Arp's fire team was on secondary standby. Shower or storm, he would not have to fly in it for a while yet. After the rush had cleared the door, he pulled on his raincoat to go to Opera-tions and learn where the mission had gone.

Blood was first to the ships. He muttered one of his favorite military sayings to himself as he slung the blade tie-down hook under his seat and climbed in: "You got to lead from up front." He said it again as Atterburn piled directly into the left front seat and switched on and pulled the trigger: "You got to lead from up front, boy." The blade was revolving slowly while that on the Bear's ship in the next revetment was still being untied.

The low cry of the turbines spinning up carried only faintly across the wind to the Operations hooch. Arp hurried inside out of the rain and then stayed at the door, watching the steady flash of the red anticollision beacons. He checked his watch. "Not bad time," he said to no one in particular.

"Captain Blood ought to be quick." The duty sergeant laughed. "He makes me wait for him to locate the coordinates and get out the door before I can blow the horn for the rest of you. I think he wants you to get all the sleep you can."

The duty officer came up to the door beside Arp. "Think they'll get far in this weather?"

"I didn't notice any webbed feet on the ships."

"Blood had the hero lights flashing in his eyes. They're going someplace for sure."

Arp turned to study the large-scale chart on the wall.

Covington had already pulled the trigger when the Bear climbed aboard. The steady snap of the spark plug was slowly obliterated by the rush of the turbine, like fire in a distant chimney, that climbed steadily to a harsh whistle. The Bear fastened his harness and pulled on his helmet. His hands raced over the switches on the panel and the overhead console for a last check, and then he laid his hands on the controls. The ship was rocking rapidly as the main blade, which had begun with an almost imperceptible inching rotation, blurred toward invisibility. "I've got it." Covington released the controls and began strapping himself in. "You up in back?"

"We're up, sir," Handy answered.

Bear rolled the throttle fully on and touched his thumb to the rpm governor button to ease the engine to operating speed. He tested the controls gingerly, lifting most of the weight of the aircraft from the skids as he waited for the call to come on the radio.

Blood's voice came on the VHF, the radio on which the gunship crews communicated among themselves: "Two, are you up?"

43

"Affirmative," Bear answered.

Then Blood was on the UHF, calling the tower: "Ky Ha, Wolf Lead for hover and takeoff; request left break."

"Wolf Lead, clear for departure with left break. Winds zero-seven-zero at twenty-five, gusting forty."

Blood again: "Roger. Two, you copy?"

"Affirm."

"Lead coming up."

The slap of the blades rose to a sudden pounding, the unmistakable sound of a Huey coming to operating rpm. Arp came back to the door to watch the ships depart. They rose into the air and eased slowly backward from their revetments, turned, and bobbed delicately down the ramp three feet above the surface. The solid thump of the blades came as a series of physical blows to the chest. The ships rocked with the gusts but maintained a steady slow pace to the takeoff lane. Hovering across a strong gusting wind was an adventure in itself, for the ship fought continuously to turn its head into the wind, or to slip sideways into the immovable flank of a revetment.

At the takeoff lane the two aircraft pirouetted, made their obeisance to the wind, and, still head-down, battled forward in a flurry of blades and climbed rapidly out over the sea. Their lights winked out in the rain.

A mixture of rain and salt spray streamed over the windscreen. "Do you want wipers?" Covington asked.

"Yes."

The wipers hardly helped. The screen filled with rain faster than the wipers could throw it off. The lights of Blood's ship ahead were a cluster of colored blurs. "Get on the instruments, Cov," Bear said. "We may lose him before too very long." It took time to transition from visual flight to instruments. Close to the ground the crew could not afford to lose time in the transition. If they lost sight of the lead ship, which at the moment was the only mark on the darkness, they could be into the ground before they could reorient themselves. Bear could feel Covington's touch on the other set of controls.

Blood swung in a broad arc back over Ky Ha, and for a moment there was a visual reference again, with the ramp lights rain-washed below them. The powerful lights of the jet runway, only a mile distant, were not to be seen.

"Think he's going to tell us where we're headed?" Covington asked.

"That's Blood's little secret."

They climbed out over the hooches on the ridge, over the lights of the officers' club, bright but blurred by rain, and swung northwest over the coastal plain. As they crossed the Chu Lai perimeter, all lights vanished behind them. They had flown into the void.

Bear increased power to draw within twenty meters of Blood's aircraft and settled into a position close off the starboard quarter. "Put out the beacon," he ordered. The rotating beam was reflecting from wisps of cloud which they plunged through, obscuring the lights of the lead ship. With their own light off it was easier to keep Blood's lights in sight.

On most night missions the Bear would have flown several hundred meters back and well to one side of his fire-team leader. He would have flown lights out then, too, but for tactical reasons rather than for safety. At night slick ships flew with their beacons off, marked only by three dim position lights with the bottom half of the lenses painted out to make them invisible from the ground. Slicks huddled together in the darkness like chicks without a mother hen, so as not to lose one another. Gunships flew low and loose, the lead ship with lights blazing, arrogantly daring onlookers to fire. Those who go armed do not fear footsteps in the night, especially when they have a friend for security. The second ship, lights out, stalked the leader through the night, ready to rain fire on any attackers from the security of its own invisibility.

Tonight Bear huddled in behind his leader like a slick, so close to the lead ship that one burst of ground fire could destroy them both. But he could not risk losing sight of the other aircraft. Once visual contact was lost, they might be unable to find one another again, or risked finding one another so close at hand that a collision could not be avoided. A helicopter could take a few bullets without great danger; a collision was deadly.

They flew scraping the cloud bases. The puffs through which they plunged became larger and larger, turning to great walls of cotton that blanked out even the rotating beacon of the other ship for seconds at a time. "I don't like this one little bit," Bear said at length. They were being forced lower and lower as they went north. There was high ground downwind to the west. They could be drifted off course—what the course might be Blood still had not deigned to tell them—and into a mountain without ever seeing what it was they hit. "We're below five hundred feet."

They had flown in bad weather before, but never in ignorance. It was different, knowing where you were bound, and being able to watch the needle swing on the navigation aid which told you at least the direction to fly. Leading flights of his own, the Bear had always briefed the second crew on locations and radio frequencies, so that they could find their own way if the need arose. But he no longer led missions. Blood's first act as platoon commander had been to replace him as section leader, and now he followed Blood like a duck on a string. He did not especially mind that, so long as he knew where he was supposed to be going. But flying into nowhere was agonizing. Finally he radioed on the VHF: "Lead, can you share the ground frequency and destination with us?"

The answer came eventually in Atterburn's voice: a coded set of coordinates and a coded three-digit number that was the FM frequency.

"Nothing like being halfway supercareful," Covington said. He worked out the code on his clipboard. "That's forty-six point three on the Fox Mike. Ground location"—he took up a map from the map case at the rear of the central console—"outside Tam Ky. Province headquarters?"

Bear switched the FM in time to catch the tail end of a transmission by Blood: ". . . about five miles south, if we can get under these clouds."

A strange voice: "Roger. We've still got beaucoup Charlies coming at the wire. Arty has kept 'em outside so far."

Bear watched the directional needle on the FM homing device as the voice spoke. It hung slightly to the left of center. Because the aircraft were crabbed into a crosswind from the right, it meant that they were almost directly on course to the location of the ground station that was transmitting.

"Blood must have been homing on that guy for a while now,"

Covington said. "Nice of him to tell us. If he'd lost us in a cloud out here, we might have busted our rear ends on a rock."

"You talk like we were there already," Bear replied. "If that guy on the ground has artillery coming in on his position, we should have seen it by now. There's nothing ahead but black."

"You think there might be a little cloud between him and us, I'll bet."

"Might be."

"Speak of the devil." Hitting the cloud was like tearing into a deep feather pillow. The lights of the ship ahead did not dim gradually: they simply vanished. But the darkness suddenly brightened, for now mixed with the heavy driving raindrops were swirling water droplets that reflected the helicopter's own position lights, so that they moved in a faint aurora, green on the right, red on the left.

"Lead, we've lost contact," Bear called urgently. "Put on all your lights!" There was a chance that, if the cloud were not wide, the landing light and searchlight of the other ship would mark it well enough for them to follow while still keeping clear.

"Lights are on," Blood answered.

There was not a mark on the sky. Bear had instinctively slowed when he lost sight of the lights ahead. The gap between them had widened, and there was now no chance of closing it. His eyes went instantly to the attitude indicator. The ship was still flying straight ahead, but climbing slightly. He began a gentle turn to the right, feeling Covington's hands light on the controls. "Lead, are you still in cloud?"

"Affirmative. We're letting down. I think we can break out. Follow us down."

Bear ignored the order. "Making a one-eighty to the right."

"Negative one-eighty," Blood called. "It can't be far down through the ceiling."

"Not lower than the ground, anyway," Covington said over the intercom. "What's he trying to do, the crazy fool?"

"Watch the altitude," was all the Bear said. He continued the turn, descending slowly. After a hundred and sixty degrees of turn he rolled the aircraft out. He was allowing twenty degrees to compensate for the crosswind: he did not want to be blown west of their original course. The mountains were there, and the

47

clouds might be lower as well. Better to end up too far east, where at least the ground was flat.

Flying in the cloud was like being packed in gauze. Although there was no danger, so long as they could stay on the back course and not descend below the height of any obstacles, still they flew with racing pulses, and with a sense of being slowly stifled. "Don't let me go below three hundred feet," Bear said.

"Roger three hundred."

There was little chance of hitting anything down to about fifty feet above sea level. The plain was almost at sea level here, and the trees were low. But there was always the chance tall tree; or the altimeter could be wrong because of air pressure changes in the storm; or they might overlook a loss of altitude for an instant too long. A hundred things could kill you in a low cloud. But they had been flying clear of clouds at five hundred feet a moment before. Three hundred should be low enough to put them in the clear on a back course.

Blood came on the radio again: "Two, Lead is descending through three hundred, on heading three-one-five. Still in cloud. Do you have us in sight?"

"That's negative, Lead. We've made a one-eighty. We're now at three hundred fifty."

"Two, I said negative on the one-eighty! Do you copy?"

"I copy."

"Well, do we go back?" Covington asked.

"Wait a bit," Bear answered. "If the crazy bastard breaks out in the clear, we'll go back."

"There's a tree!" It was Atterburn's voice on the VHF, torn with panic. Then silence.

"Lead, are you all right?" Bear called quickly.

There was no answer.

"Wolf Lead, Wolf Lead, do you receive Two?"

Blood's voice replied, shaking at the beginning: "Ah, Two, this is Wolf Lead. We're making a one-eighty to the left. What's your present position?"

"Don't we wish we knew," Covington said on the intercom.

The halo suddenly faded from about their ship. "Get the searchlight on," Bear said. The beam, aimed down at a forty-five degree angle ahead, fired a myriad of water drops to silver shoot-

48

ing stars; but at the bottom of the shimmering column which they formed, a patch of red earth could be seen. "Lead, Two is in the clear at three hundred fifty. We have our searchlight on, and we'll be making a left circle."

"Roger."

They circled slowly at the same altitude. Once they brushed the flank of the cloud. It lurked in the rain, invisible until touched, and deadly to incautious pilots. They moved their circle farther south.

The voice from the ground came on the FM. He had been forgotten until now. "Wolf Lead, this is Cold Turkey. What's your position?"

Blood took a moment to answer. "Ah, Cold Turkey, say, we can't get through this little cloud south of you. We'll try to find a way in."

Blood's country drawl was a jarring change from his crisp radio procedure of moments before. "That must have really puckered his ass." Covington laughed. It was easier to laugh beyond the grip of the cloud.

Before the Bear had completed another three-sixty, Blood called out, "Two, we have you in sight at ten o'clock."

"Aircraft at eight o'clock, sir," Handy sang out at the same instant. "About a quarter mile." It was the first time since takeoff that Bear was aware of anyone but Covington with him in the aircraft. He and Covington communicated through the machine. Through it their actions were one. But Handy and Cripps were mere spectators, brooding on foreign thoughts. It was why all pilots hated to ride in back, as passengers.

He tightened the turn, and the blurred splash of light that was Blood's searchlight swung up across the windscreen.

"Two, join up, and we'll try to get around to the east."

Since they could not fly on instruments together, only two choices were left to them. They could probe along the edge of the cloud, as Blood was suggesting, hoping for an opening; or they could fight the cloud separately on instruments, hoping to home on the ground radio and let down overhead. If the overcast were high enough, they would be able to rejoin at that spot. If it were not, their weapons were useless in any case. Blood was proposing the safer course, Bear knew; but with their fuel burning away at nearly five hundred pounds an hour, time was of the essence. But when Bear suggested the second course, Blood's answer was chilly: "Negative. We'll get around to the east." Blood's voice had regained its procedural formality.

"He doesn't like that cloud so much as he did," Covington said.

"I'm not so fond of it myself, Cov."

They probed along the side of the cloud as low as two hundred feet for several miles to the east; but each time they swung north, the wall of mist closed around them, and they were forced to separate and turn back to rejoin outside. The pilots traded off flying every few minutes; but still the strain of searching through the rain for the lights of the other ship and of holding position in the turbulent air began to wear at them; and there was no true rest between stints of flying, for the one not actually controlling the aircraft still remained at the controls, his eyes on the instruments, ready to take over when the other ship disappeared.

"Wolf Lead, this is Cold Turkey. How you comin'?" Cold Turkey's voice had gone southern, too. Knowing what the man was facing, Bear admired his dispassion. From his tone he might have been merely solicitous of Wolf's health.

"We're still trying, Cold Turkey. There's a little bit of weather between us."

"Roger. Hope to see you soon. Charley's rippin' and snortin' out here." Machine guns punctuated this transmission.

The fuel gauge swung slowly toward the bottom of the dial, until less than four hundred pounds remained—less than an hour's flying time at most. They were fifteen minutes from home, and it was imperative to keep at least a half hour's reserve, for there was no knowing what weather might lie between them and home. Blood continued to poke at the listless cloud, but it refused to roll aside for them. If anything were to be done for Cold Turkey, it must be done at once. At last Bear called again, "Lead, suggest again we try to go in separately. We can home on his transmitter at different altitudes and hold on station while one of us tries to let down below the ceiling."

"Roger, Two. Do you know there *is* a ceiling?" Having tried once and failed, Blood was consumed with scorn that anyone should think that course was possible. He flittered along the cloud until the fuel gauge passed three hundred pounds, and there was no hope. "Cold Turkey," he called, "this is Wolf Lead. We can't get in. Wolf Lead turning for home."

When Cold Turkey eventually answered, his words were hard to make out. The continuous impacting of artillery rounds sent the microphone diaphragm into convulsions and broke up the transmission. The words they could make out were "Thanks for trying."

"How many did you kill?" Arp asked as they straggled back, wet and listless, to the alert hooch.

"Not any, unless we ran them down in a cloud without knowing it." Bear sat unhappily on one end of his cot, pondering his wringing-wet jungle fatigues and his merely damp sleeping bag, and wondering what Cold Turkey was doing.

"At least," Covington said, "we got back alive."

"That is a point in your favor," Arp agreed.

Atterburn came in shaking his poncho and cursing the rain. That done, he grinned at the Bear and said, with satisfaction only partly hidden, "The Blood would like to talk to you in Operations." As Bear rose from his cot with a sigh, he added, "I wouldn't make him wait. I may be wrong, but I'd say he has a case of the red ass."

Besides Blood standing at the counter completing the after-action report, the duty officer and sergeant, two off-duty slick drivers, and an Operations clerk were in Operations. All of them were silent—not merely silent, but inoperative, with the significant silence of an electrical machine whose power has suddenly failed as the storm closes around.

Blood slashed a signature on the report and pushed it across the counter. He motioned with a sideways turn of his head for the Bear to follow him to the far end of the hooch, saying as he went, "There seem to be a lot of people in here without any business in Operations." The clerk and the off-duty pilots began to gather their rain gear for the wet walk to their quarters. They were gone by the time Blood sat down on a desk at the opposite end of the hooch.

When he was angry, Blood's face became a pictogram of his name. The change of color in his face as he progressed was

51

matched by the climb in pitch and volume of his voice from the near whisper in which he began: "Mister, if you don't know this you had better learn it a lot faster than I think you can. When I am in command of a mission, I expect that what I say goes! I don't need any wise-ass warrant officers who think they know better to go off making their own flight plans and thinking they can laugh up their sleeves about it. If leading flights gave you such a big head that you can't take orders anymore, then it's way past time somebody dragged you out of command of that section. I thought it should have been done long ago, and what I saw tonight just convinced me I was right. If you haven't got the balls to fly in bad weather, then you're in the wrong line of work, let me tell you! I don't want to be on my way to a target again and find out I'm all alone. For two cents I'd ask the old man to ground you! But I'm not going to do it—not yet. Because I can't stand the thought of you sitting around on your rear, safe on the ground, while better men are risking theirs flying missions. But there had better be one whole hell of a lot of improvement, let me tell you! This is going into your efficiency report, believe me. And if you ever had any thought of making the Army a career, you'd better start learning to fix shoes or whatever the hell you're fit for!" Blood stalked back down the length of the hooch and erupted into the rain, leaving the Bear still suspended at the dark end of the building. After he was gone, the duty officer remarked to the sergeant, but loud enough for Bear to hear, "I'd think you lifers would learn sometime, Sarge, that the only one you can threaten with a bad efficiency report is another lifer."

"I ain't no lifer, sir." The sergeant laughed. "I got a little used-car business with my dad back in the world, and if you put me out on a bad conduct this minute, I wouldn't argue!"

Muffled voices, like the chirping of languorous birds, woke the Bear where he had fallen asleep in his fatigues on his own bunk after coming up from the alert hooch. The room was dark, although daylight picked idly at the corners of the plywood shutters. The air was clinging and sour. From the taste in his mouth he thought at first that the birds might be hidden there, but after a few deep breaths he realized that they were really only the hooch-maids sociably doing laundry on the porch. One came inside to hang a set of fatigues over a bunk rail, where they would remain slowly transpiring for days, until either the sun showed itself or they were put on still damp and dried by body heat. While the door was open, a shaft of light struggled down the center of the hooch, but without sufficient conviction to light the whole interior. The storm had passed over, leaving a residue of low cloud to darken the afternoon.

He struggled to his feet eventually, feeling too used up to be revived even by sleeping the day away. Staying ready to go out and kill was a stultifying business. He strapped on his pistol and started out to see what the day had left to him.

As he reached the door there was a little shriek out on the porch. The door burst open, and Yan thumped headlong into him. She caromed off into the darkness beside one of the bunks, to the accompaniment of a great deal of soprano laughter outside. Arp came to the door.

"You no let him in," Yan pleaded from the corner.

"Lieutenant, how come you're chasing my hooch-maid?" Bear demanded. "If anybody gets to chase her, it should be me."

"I was just taking a picture," Arp protested, holding up his camera to attest to his good faith.

"I haven't heard *that* one before."

"You no let him in!" Yan repeated.

"It's too dark in here anyway, Yan, if all he wants is a picture. Relax."

"You want picture, I bring you picture," Yan said to Arp. "You no take my picture now."

"I take your picture," Arp affirmed. "I take *beaucoup* picture, put them up all over my wall. Yan number-one girl: she *làm đẹp*." He said this laughing.

While Yan showed no objection to being called very pretty, she was not coming out of the corner, and finally Arp relented. He and Bear stood on the porch, feeling the sea wind, still northeast but warmer than before. "It's really strange how she won't let me take her picture," Arp said. "Do you suppose she's afraid the camera will take her spirit? The Montagnards are supposed to believe that."

"She offered to bring you a picture," Bear pointed out.

"But you don't know that she'll *do* it. You've seen Vietnamese

53

soldiers walking hand in hand. They say that's to keep them safe from spirits. Who knows what Yan believes about cameras?"

"I always thought the handholding was just friendliness."

"Atterburn would say it was just being queer. But it's not. Maybe it's not just friendliness, either. But there are lots of things I don't understand. For one thing I don't understand how you can snore away the whole of this sparkling day while others are out working."

"I thought I heard your flight go out this morning," Bear said. "So you got to fly in that little shower after all."

"It was all over when we got off the ground," Arp said. "The very clouds roll apart for me. You know that."

"Sure."

"While your lazy body was supine, we paid a visit to Cold Turkey. Just a recon. It's a pity you didn't get through. I understand he called in artillery on himself. Very few friendly casualties, surprisingly enough; but the American advisor was one. All we could get were Vietnamese voices on the radio. Dustoff came in for him while we were there."

"Was he alive?"

"No."

Bear studied the grey sea for the space of several seconds. "Well, I tried."

"Yes. I understand Blood had a different opinion. But it's not one that's widely believed." Arp said this as if it were an afterthought; but Bear saw that the whole exchange had been leading up to this reassurance. His business accomplished, Arp turned the subject aside by saying briskly, "If you're not going to help me lure Yan out into the light, I'm going to leave you to the company of these fair ladies." He made a motion as if to take the picture of the two old women squatting over their washbasins. The camera held no terrors for them: they cackled at the gesture.

After Arp had left, Bear hunkered down on the porch with the two. Suzie was Yan's mother. The other was an old crony of hers. Both were wrinkled old prunes, the remnant of too many years in the sun. Yan, twittering and fearful, hovered inside the door until she was sure that Arp was gone.

"*Chào, Bà,*" Bear addressed the two old women, using the reverential term "grandmother." They in turn called him *Dại-úy,*

54

which meant "captain," for they were very polite old women not much concerned with the *Người Mỹ* distinctions of rank.

The Bear spent a good deal of time chatting with the hoochmaids. Although he was fighting a Vietnamese war, and had seen from the air a large part of the Vietnamese landscape from Saigon to Hue, he had little contact with the people themselves. He wished sometimes he could land in a farmyard and simply talk to the people there. His Vietnamese was not good, but he would have liked to try. Instead he was confined to talking to those who came onto the American installation, those who swept his floors, made his bed, laundered his underwear—who in short were familiar with every detail of his personal life, although he had no conception of theirs. But they knew only his life in Vietnam, a monastic and harried existence that bore no relationship to life in America. What could they think of his own country, who saw only its weapons and its underwear?

"It seems your daughter fears the lieutenant," Bear turned his head slightly toward the door where Yan still lingered, listening.

"One who flees does not always fear," Suzie answered. Her friend cackled in glee. After a moment Suzie added, smiling, "The lieutenant tells Yan she is pretty, but she is more pretty in her finer clothes."

The simplicity of Yan's mother's statement caused Bear to pause. He looked up where Yan's mother was looking, at Yan in the doorway, and he understood. He had seen Yan always as she was now, in her black silk trousers and white blouse, with sometimes a light jacket or a conical straw hat. Today she had spent the afternoon scrubbing clothes in an aluminum washpan, and a few strands of long dark hair fell across her face. Even as he glanced up at her, she brushed them back with one hand. Yan in her work clothes *was* very pretty: but she was in her work clothes. And he had not even considered that she might have better.

He was ashamed, for he had thought of Yan as only a servant, in whom vanity was unthinkable.

He would have apologized to her mother, but he did not know how.

He was spared the need by a low warning from Suzie: "The captain with the loud voice comes."

Blood had been watching for some time from the back door of

his own hooch. "Don't that make a picture, though?" he re-marked to Lieutenant Rauch, the Operations officer, who shared the hooch. "A damn warrant officer squatting there on his heels with the Slopes, just like a turd on a plate. I've told him more'n once about keepin' up our dignity with the indigenous labor. But he don't amount to much where takin' orders is concerned. There he is, in there gabblin' like a turkey till you can't tell him from the rest of 'em."

"You goin' to chew him out *before* you get his signature on your recommendation, or *after?*" Lieutenant Rauch drawled. He grinned to see Blood squirm at the question.

"Neither one," Blood said at last. "I reckon it's good for rela-tions with the locals. Let him talk to 'em, if he wants to." The importance of the indigenous personnel had risen considerably in Blood's judgment that very day, since the battalion awards officer had called down with the news that the Vietnamese Army wished to give an award to the crews of the gunships that had made such a valiant attempt to reach the provincial headquarters during the storm the night before. The details of the mission were to be provided by the officers and men involved. The thrust of the awards officer's message had been "Send us some fancy language, and get the pilots to sign each other's recommenda-tions."

Leaving Rauch grinning, Blood went across to the Bear's porch, where he propped one foot up casually. "Winning the hearts and minds of the people again, eh? Well, Westy says that's the way to win the war: I reckon there must be *some*thing in it. If we get the mama-sans on our side, maybe they can pussy-whip their husbands into stayin' home at night, and we won't have to make any little trips like that last one." Blood laughed loudly at this, although he laughed alone. It had been drilled into Blood through a long course of officer training that a loud voice is the chief characteristic of a leader, and he prided himself on never forgetting a lesson learned. The nature of what he had to say next might have softened his voice, except that such a result would have made it appear that he hesitated to ask what was after all only a matter of right. He therefore spoke even more loudly as he launched onto his main topic: "Say, that reminds me, Battalion sent down a message that the Vietnamese unit we were looking for wants to put us in for some award. I guess Rauch's clerk is typing up the recommendations. ARVN awards don't count for a hell of a lot; but maybe it would be a good thing to get them for the crews. I told Rauch I'd get you to sign some of 'em. Whenever you get time. I don't want to interfere with your part of the war effort." He went away grinning, as if they shared some lewd secret. He was highly pleased with his diplomacy.

"So," Lieutenant Rauch said, "you're goin' to sign Blood's promotion ticket, are you? If he gets enough of these, he might make major yet. If he lives that long. I hear he tried to kill you all last night. That's all we need, is to lose two gunships. Division's already on our ass to get more ships in the air than we own, let alone have flyable."

"As I understood it," Bear answered, "this was to be for the benefit of our crewmen, who're feebleminded enough to pay attention to these trinkets."

"You haven't seen what Blood had me write about *him*. 'Course, if you want an award to get through channels, you got to make sure it sells." He took a form from the clerk and read at random: " 'Heedless of his own safety, led his flight into perilous weather which had stopped all other attempts to reach the ground position . . . showed outstanding leadership ability and skill as an aviator in locating the friendly position under impenetrable clouds . . . bravery above and beyond . . .' He forgot to say anything about dumb-ass attempts at suicide, but you can't remember everything. Here." Rauch tossed the papers across the counter. "Sign there."

Bear's face took on the features of Astonishment Cast in Bronze. "I thought I was signing for my crew."

"You'll get those, too. But you can't expect Blood to sign his own award, now, can you? And you're the commander of the number-two ship. Sign the mother."

"If I'd known we were going to get a medal, I'd have actually gone in and placed some fire for them, at least. I don't feel like they got their money's worth."

"One day one of them big fifty-caliber rounds is goin' to come right through where you're sittin', and they probably won't give you a medal for that at all, even if there's someplace left to pin one. Just figure it's all evened out ahead of time. If you're worried about tellin' lies for Blood, forget it. It's all arranged, right up through Division. They got to get rid of their quota of Vietnamese decorations, or some damn thing. This thing will go through like castor oil through a baby. Now sign the mother and let me get rid of it. So it was all a mistake, so what? You all risked your asses, and if Blood was along for the ride, he's only getting the same medal as the rest of you. Look, he signed yours. See there?"

"What do we do for the Medal of Honor?" Bear asked, signing.

4

The air being squeezed out at the edges of the cold mass over the continent of Asia swung in a long, right-hand spiral over the South China Sea until it collided with the Indochina coast, where crags and trees tore its lower layers to turbulent shreds. Flying at a few hundred feet became like driving a hilly road paved with cobblestones. Vertical gusts hammered at the three ships flying in a loose trail formation. They nodded up and down, and shuddered with the smaller gusts.

The aircraft seemed to be guided by no purpose. They wandered the mountain valleys as if their pilots were lost or witless. The leader was far ahead of the other two, which hung closer together but still a long quarter mile apart. A sharp eye, if any human eye existed in those remote valleys, would have seen that the first aircraft differed from the other two. The two in the rear were gunships, but the first was a slick. A knowledgeable eye would have noted that it was no ordinary slick. A narrow pipe extended in front of the nose and ended in a crossbar extending almost the width of the fuselage.

The slick was a flying bloodhound. In the crossbar were chemical sensors sensitive to the odor of human beings, a technological nose delicate enough to scent men below the jungle canopy three hundred feet below.

The slick flew a meandering course, drawing gradually toward the cup of a pass, still open below the clouds, that debouched into another wandering valley leading to the coastal plain and home. "It looks like Snoopy blew this one," Bear said. He parked the gunsight, put his feet up on the panel, yawned, and grinned in imitation of a Cheshire cat on its day off.

"I don't know what you've got against Snoopy," answered Martin, who was flying right seat. "I thought you liked animals."

"I wouldn't have Snoopy up my rear if I had room for a snow-plow," Bear answered flatly.

"Maybe Snoopy's got a cold," Sergeant Handy suggested.

"I'm s'prised if he don't have n-n-newmonia, if h-h-he's as much out in the w-w-wind as w-w-w-we are back here," Cripps's voice came over the intercom.

Bear's face crinkled with laughter. "Cripps, is that *you?* Your very first speech on the intercom! And all you can do is complain about the cold. You're farther south here than in Tennessee."

Cripps was seated at the back of the open side of the ship, with his machine gun cradled in his arms, shivering.

"I tol' you to wear your long johns this mornin', Cripps," Sergeant Handy said, "but what do I know?"

"I don't have n-n-none."

"Never knew you'd need 'em in Vietnam? Well, if you're good maybe Santy Claus will fetch you some."

"I tell you what, Cripps," Martin said. "I'll fly a little out of trim to put you out of the wind. Handy's dressed for the weather, so he won't mind." He increased the pressure on the left rudder pedal to swing the nose to the left until the ship was flying cocked twenty degrees to the left of the line of flight. Icy wind poured through the ship from the right side.

"God damn!" Sergeant Handy had no intention of suffering to save face. He shrank away from the open door to the end of his monkey-strap and huddled behind Bear's seat.

"Chilly, ain't it, Sarge?" Bear said.

"Feels just f-f-fine to me," Cripps said cheerily.

Blood, who was at that moment stretching his cramped legs while Atterburn flew, happened to glance back from the leading gunship. "Look at that!" he exclaimed, in the tone of one who expected to find a fly in his soup and has just been proved right. "Our glorious leader's been sitting behind a desk for a month, and he can't even fly straight anymore. If he can't do any better

than that, he ought to leave the missions to people who can."
Blood was in a sour mood because Martin had pushed himself in
to fly this mission. It was pure coincidence, of course, that Martin
chose to fly the one on which Snoopy was being tried out. Of
course. When there was a little free publicity to be had, the
Ringknockers would gather. The general himself would probably
want to see the results of this one. Martin knew how to get his
name in the right places.

A voice on the radio cut through Blood's gloom and Martin's
laughter: "Wolf Lead, this is Snoopy. I have a reading."

Blood came on the radio instantly: "What do you have,
Snoopy?"

"We just flew over some warm bodies, Lead. We'll make another pass and let you know."

Bear quickly refolded his pasted-up map of the operational
area to the segment that covered this valley. Martin had brought
the ship back into trim, and Handy was back in his seat, looking
eagerly out and to the front, where Snoopy was making a turn a
half mile distant. The slick ship, now very low, crossed at right
angles to their path.

"Bear, where are we?" Martin had been following Blood. He
knew the way home, but was uncertain of their exact location over
the ground. Below, everything was the uniform dark green of
jungle canopy, slippery with rain.

Bear looked up from the map. "Hill Four Seven Three, sir." He
pointed where the slick was crossing. A low mound, barely dis-
cernible from their altitude, bulged from the narrow valley bottom. "We're just inside the free-fire zone."

The slick was crossing the mound. "Wolf Lead, we have a
strong reading. He's right on top of this hill. Do you have us in
sight?"

"Affirmative. Two, do you copy Snoopy?"

Bear had the flex gunsight down in position and was lowering
his helmet visor with his left hand. "Affirm," Martin answered.

While Blood dived gently and loafed in over the hill a few
hundred feet above the trees, Martin made a fast diving swing to
the right to approach lower and from another direction. Snoopy
had gone on and now was taking up a left-hand circuit a mile
beyond the hill.

61

On the hill there was no sign of movement. The canopy of the forest was unbroken. Bear remembered the still columns of smoke rising from nowhere into the clear dry-season air. "If he's down there, he can't see us for the trees," Handy said. He added, "I still think Snoopy has a cold." They flew on until the whirling dark spot that was Blood's ship turned back. "Two, did you get anything?"

"That's negative," Martin answered.

"Let's try it again."

They came back in the opposite direction. The crew in back leaned from the doors out into the biting wind, searching for any chink in the canopy. Not even a patch of earth flashed between the trees.

"We ought to put a few rounds down to stir them up," Handy suggested.

"Maybe we're going to fly in circles till we run out of gas." Bear said the words casually, as though chatting over the intercom; but he pressed the mike switch in to the second detent, so that the words went out over the radio for Blood to hear. He knew he was skirting the edge of danger by saying it; but he could not resist the temptation to needle Blood with what the words would bring to mind.

Blood's face flamed. "Either the turd didn't learn anything the last time," he said to Atterburn, "or Martin put him up to that." On the whole he found it more satisfactory to blame Martin. "Golden Boy knows he's going to need a better body count than he's got so far, to impress the general. If you wonder why he didn't bump himself up to lead ship, I'll tell you: it's because that way his name's not on the report if we don't get anything; but if we come through with a big body count, you better stand aside, because he'll be coming right to the head of the line! The bastard thinks I'm too dumb to figure it out, because I'm not a Ring-knocker. Well, let him stew awhile."

They went around again, lower this time, and even slower. The wind whipped at the treetops; but what was below that, they could not tell.

"Where does the free-fire zone end?" Martin asked.

"About a mile up. Across the next stream." Beyond that was a second small stream, and then the pass and the valley leading home. "If anybody's down there, he shouldn't be."

"Well, there's no use carting all this junk home." Martin radioed, "Lead, how about dumping our ordnance here? We'll be lighter going home."

Blood's answer came quick and cold: "Two, you sure have my permission, if you need it. I was just going to call you and ask if you didn't want to."

Shy doubt fluttered for an instant toward the front of Bear's mind. But he could not really bring himself to believe that there was anyone at all on the ground. The hill was miles from the nearest village, more than a day's travel on foot over the precipitous terrain; and the whole area had been cleared by infantry and leafleted from the air as a free-fire zone. Anyone there should know he was subject to being shot on sight, or, apparently, on smell. And it had been a long dull day chasing Snoopy over wet jungle, through weather too bad to be pleasant but not bad enough to be exciting. His buttocks told him of every reticulation in the mesh seat. All small certainties joined to turn doubt aside. Then Blood's aircraft arrowed in, lacing the air with fire, and the sight of it sent doubt winging for cover.

Bear pushed the switches to "arm" and laid the glowing pip in the gunsight on the base of the hill as Martin followed the lead ship up in a tight climbing turn to five hundred feet. Martin leveled out toward the hill. "Anytime," he said.

To the Bear the flex guns had a sad voice. The six rotating barrels sent one bullet after another so quickly that the individual shots could not be heard, only a long bronchial rasp, or a groan. But the individual bullets could be distinguished. Seen from behind, a short burst was a bushel of glowing embers thrown to the wind. They fell in a long graceful arc and vanished among the trees. Hold the trigger down longer, and a long stream of red jetted forward, wavering, like water from a shaken hose. Shift the glowing dot of light in the gunsight, and the stream could be played onto the target on which the dot fell. It was a marvelous toy.

Against the tearing sound of the flex guns played the steady hammer of the slower-firing machine guns in the hands of the crew, who strained against their monkey-straps, leaning out to aim their fire under the very belly of the ship or even to the rear. And, finest of all, the Fourth-of-July *whish* and bright fall of the rockets as Martin touched his thumb to the red button on the cyclic stick. Their white stars dwindled and then flashed bright again as the warheads exploded on the heavy upper branches of the forest: a flash, and a lingering white blossom of smoke which quickly passed beneath the helicopter as it turned away to meet Blood coming back in.

Inbound again, and smoke was seeping up from below the treetops. Blood's rockets had pierced the crown and exploded somewhere below. "Going out in style," Martin announced. With his left hand he set the rocket selector switch to "all." He had fired only two pairs on the first pass: five pairs remained in their tubes below the flex guns. He corrected the rudder pedals to center the bubble of the rocket sight, put the glowing dot halfway up the hill, so that the rockets would not pass over and be wasted if he shot long, and gently thumbed the firing button. The aircraft shuddered, although no more than from the gentlest touch of air turbulence, as the ten rockets flashed free in a white ripple of fire. Bear held down the flex-gun trigger. The stream of fire sank without a trace into the unmarked hillside.

They passed over the top of the hill and followed Blood straight on toward home. Bear pushed the gunsight up against its latch. When he took the controls for a moment the ship, empty of ordnance, felt strangely light and free. His heart felt the same. The fruitless afternoon had burned up in the fires of the attack.

Snoopy, who belonged to a company at Da Nang, reported that he was breaking off to return home. He signed off their radio frequency and vanished up a side valley to the north.

"Do you s'pose there was anybody down there?" Sergeant Handy asked after a time. "I'd like to go back on the ground, just to see what happened." Handy took delight in his work. A field full of bodies was a fine sight to him. He was a true sportsman, who would if possible have put endless time into hunting down the last cripple rather than leave him to suffer. Target practice was better than carrying ammunition home, but it was second-rate business. "It's like shootin' through a curtain," he mused. "I sure wish I knew who was behind it."

"If it was anybody," Bear said, "I pity him."

"Well, sir, I'm *sure* glad it was him instead of me!"

Martin slid his seat back to stretch his legs and watched the wet jungle roll by below. Beyond the pass ahead, the light was already fading from the east. With the coming of evening the overcast would be lowering. He would not like to find the pass closed. But once over that, and it would be home again, home again, jiggety jig, as the Bear put it. The blade of Bear's ship, still chronically out of track despite the best efforts of the maintenance unit, gave the whole ship one vertical shake per revolution of the main blade, and an imbalance gave a two-per-revolution horizontal shake. The combination made the ship fly with the hop-shuffle, hop-shuffle of a little girl at hopscotch. The effect was soporific, at the end of a day's hunt.

Martin was snapped from his meditation by the radio, by an urgent voice calling: "Any helicopter in the vicinity of Bravo Tango two-six-zero zero-two-five, please come up on guard. This is Covey Two-three on guard. I say again, any helicopter in the vicinity of Bravo Tango two-six-zero zero-two-five, please come up." The transmission was loud; it came from close at hand. As Martin snatched up the area chart, Bear affirmed, "That's us." When there was no immediate radio response from Blood, he added, "Do you suppose His Leadership heard that?"

"If he didn't he's the only pilot in country not listening to guard," Martin said. The guard channel was the emergency radio frequency, automatically received on all military aircraft UHF receivers unless the pilot turned it off. There were no transmissions on guard except when immediate help was needed.

The coordinates were those of a river junction they had just crossed, not far from Hill 473. Martin switched his transmitter to the UHF guard frequency. "Covey Two-three, this is Wolf Two. Go ahead."

"Wolf Two, I'm Forward Air Control, standing by near An Lau. Arty just monitored an emergency call from a company somewhere in this area. They couldn't read the exact coordinates, but they're on Fox Mike frequency forty-six point twenty, call sign Battleax. They've taken heavy casualties and need an emergency medevac. Can you contact them?"

Before Martin could reply, Blood came on the radio: "Covey Two-three, this is Wolf Lead. That's affirmative. We're gunships:

I don't know if we can help on a medevac. But we'll try to raise them."

"Okay, thanks. I'll be monitoring guard, if you want to keep in touch."

"And we're out of ammo!" Martin lamented over the intercom. He was bitterly sorry now for the attack they had wasted. They might have been of some use as gunships, if not as medical evacuation helicopters. "How long will it take us to rearm and get back?" he asked Bear, switching hurriedly to the FM channel and turning back to the map at the same time.

Blood called on FM, and a young, shaken voice came up immediately, loud and almost shouting in panic. "Wolf Lead, Wolf Lead, we gotta have some help! The old man and the first sergeant are both dead, and two of the platoon leaders, and a whole lot of others hurt bad. . . ."

"Battleax, what's your location?" Blood demanded. "I don't have your coordinates."

"Uh, roger, I hope you can get in here; we're at, uh, just a minute, it's on top of this big hill. . . ."

"Never mind where they are, damn it!" Martin muttered. "Find out if they're still under attack!"

"We're just . . . we're on top of this big high hill right here. . . ."

"All right, Battleax," Blood radioed, "we'll find you. Just keep talking to me. We're not far away." Blood's ship swung into a gentle turn to the left. Bear followed him around. He had the FM homing indicator on, but Battleax stopped talking before the needle centered.

Impatiently, Martin called, "Battleax, this is Wolf Two. Are you still under fire?"

"Ah, Wolf . . . Lead, ah, this is Battleax. Negative, they've gone away. But we've got people in real bad shape here. . . ."

"All right, do you have a place where we can land there?"

"Get off the radio, Two." Blood's voice. "Battleax, what's the terrain like around you?"

"I don't know, there's just trees. . . ." Another voice came on. This one was young, too, but steady. "Medevac, this is Battleax. We're cutting an LZ. It'll be ready in ten minutes. Do you have our coordinates?"

"This is Wolf Lead, Battleax. Negative on the coordinates. Are you still taking fire?"

"No. No, it's all over. Coordinates of our location are Bravo Tango two-two-five zero-two-zero. Do you copy?"

"I copy. Look, we're not medevac. Did you get a call in for Dustoff on your net?"

"That's affirmative. We don't care who you are, Wolf Lead, if you can get some of our people out."

"We're on our way in."

"Roger. I think I hear you. There are helicopters off to the east of us."

During the exchange Bear had centered the needle on the FM homer. The two ships, bound directly toward Battleax, were retracing their course of a few minutes before.

Martin snatched up the map and searched frantically for the location of the coordinates Battleax had given. A low hill bulged up before them in the distance, beyond the metallic ribbon of river. "It can't be!" He stared at Bear, who was chewing the ends of his mustache as he flew. Bear said nothing, but his face told that he knew it already. There was but one hill ahead of them in the direction from which Battleax's radio transmissions had come. "A high hill," the voice on the radio had said. The one ahead was not much of a hill, but to a man on the ground, under the trees, unable to see the mountains towering around, it might seem high enough. It was Hill 473.

As the hill rose, Martin's heart sank, knowing where they were bound. "They're in the free-fire zone!" he said weakly. Battleax was on Hill 473. They had just attacked friendly troops.

It seemed impossible that anyone should be there. The smooth green canopy, still unbroken, sealed off the ground, covered whatever had happened there as though it had never been.

As they flew over, a tree fell. Its fall opened a hole in the canopy, removed a spot of green, replaced it with a spot of black without yet showing the ground. The edges of the hole moved back as other trees were dropped, but still no person was visible.

The second voice from the ground came on the radio: "Wolf Lead, this is Battleax, are you circling us?"

"Affirmative, Battleax." Blood's voice was strangely soft.

"Is that a big enough LZ, Wolf Lead?"

The hole in the treetops looked hardly big enough to spit in, let alone squeeze in a fifty-foot helicopter blade. "What do you think, Bear?" Martin asked.

Bear's voice, too, was broken. "We can try it," he said. "We have to." They had been flying longer than planned already. They would be burning their reserve fuel long before they could hope to reach Chu Lai, the nearest hospital. They could not wait. All of that was summed up in his few words, and was understood without discussion. And more: at their hands, men lay dying.

Martin did not press Blood for an answer, knowing he was thinking the same thoughts. The answer came: "Battleax, we'll try it. Give us a smoke."

The two ships circled the hill again before a puff of yellow showed at the bottom of the hole. It spread to fill the bottom without showing any drift: there was no wind there. A thin veil of yellow rose along the trees on one side, and at the top it was torn away to the west.

"I have a yellow smoke," Blood said.

"Affirm on yellow," Battleax replied.

"Two, I'm going in. Stand by."

Martin clicked the mike switch twice. As he swung the helicopter away from the hill, Martin asked, "How many packs will the ship carry, Bear?" It was the Bear's ship: he knew its performance better than Martin, who was only out for the day.

"Low on fuel, no ammunition"—at this the young officer seemed ready to weep, or to laugh: his face crinkled, and he turned away—"with the ship this light, maybe four. Maybe three. That's a deep hole."

"Battleax, how many casualties have you got?" Martin radioed, ignoring Blood's earlier demand for silence.

"Ah, you'll have to stand by one, Wolf. We're getting a count. Maybe thirty."

"Jesus!"

"We can get rid of the rocket pods," Bear said. "That would add one body at least." The rocket pods were not permanently fastened to their mounts. They could be jettisoned in flight in an emergency. But to release them over the jungle would mean the loss of weapons which might not be replaced for days. The ships would be crippled for missions. The guns, on quick release

68

latches, could be removed by hand on the ground. "We'll kick them off in the LZ," Martin said. "The guns, too. That should give us one other pack." He switched to his VHF transmitter and called, "Lead, this is Two. Suggest we jettison the weapons in the LZ to get as many casualties on as we can carry."

There was no reply from Blood, who was closing on the landing zone. The nose of his ship came up as it slowed. It hung for an instant, sank toward the trees. Then its nose went down, and it began to climb. Blood was going around. "Battleax, Wolf Lead. You'll have to take out more trees."

"Wolf . . . Wolf Lead, stand by." It was Battleax's first voice. In a moment the second came on: "Wolf Lead, we're out of C-four. We'll have to cut some trees by hand."

"How long will it take?"

"I don't know."

"We're low on fuel, Battleax. We can't wait long."

From a half mile out the hole in the treetops had not even been visible. They had closed within a quarter mile before Martin could see it again. He began slowing the aircraft. The jungle crawled underneath. Now it was not a blur of leaves, not a lumpy green carpet, but individual trees, reaching for the aircraft. The Bear was on the other set of controls now, but Martin could feel him there only at intervals, only the merest hint of resistance as the cyclic moved. The airspeed fell to forty knots, thirty, twenty. At twenty knots airspeed the ship was almost stopped over the trees. It inched into the strong headwind that whipped the leaves to a froth. Martin eased the ship forward over the hole. Through the chin bubble beneath his feet, faces stared up from a hundred feet below. Arms were waving. The aircraft hovered, almost at full power. "Is our tail rotor clear?"

"I think you're clear, sir." Sergeant Handy.

"Coming down."

He eased the collective-pitch stick downward. The ship seemed reluctant to descend into the dark hole, as if it had a mind of its own and dreaded what waited there. "Down, damn you!" Martin hissed under his breath, remembering flight school, ages ago: make a perfect approach and, at the critical instant, the ship would unaccountably refuse to land. But it was all, all, in the pilot's mind and hands. The ship would behave, if one had the

69

will to master it. He willed the aircraft to descend into the hole, with sweat trickling from under his helmet.

"Clear over here," Bear said. He was following on the controls and not turning his head, but looking to the side from the corner of his eye.

"How's the tail?"

"Still clear, sir."

At fifty feet above the ground, with a quick *whap-whap* the main blade struck off a protruding branch and cast it into the darkness among the trees; but the ship continued its steady descent.

The trees had been blasted off as low as possible, but the stumps a foot or more high studded the clearing. Their mangled ends stuttered white exclamations of shock against the mud. There was no place to land. Martin dared not look down to check his height, for fear of drifting from the center of the hole and slipping the blade into a solid tree. "How high are we, Handy?"

"Ten feet, sir."

"Tell me when we can't get any lower."

"Yes, sir."

"Just a couple more feet, sir." Handy was suddenly formal, under the strain of the descent: suddenly respectful to the man who held all their lives between the thumb and forefinger of his right hand. A movement of a quarter inch of those fingers could turn the delicately poised machine into a tangle of twisted, burning metal.

Martin could feel the Bear's touch on the controls now, although they did not move except when he himself moved them. It felt as though the ship were communicating to him the touch on the other stick, saying, "No, this way," when he tried to make a false motion.

Faces came into his line of vision at the edge of the trees. He could not see that there was solid earth there, nor bodies to stand upon it. There was nothing but faces, white among the white columns of the tree trunks. Jungle fatigues and helmets blended with the night which already lurked among the trees, but the faces stood forth like masks nailed on the darkness.

"Get 'em on."

Handy waved an arm, but they were already coming. Four men scrambled over a fallen tree, ducking to miss the blade, trying not

70

to drop the poncho on which a fifth man lay. They passed out of sight around the side of the ship. The aircraft lurched to that side. Martin fought the stick—with all his strength, it seemed, though it was but a fraction of an inch of movement to regain control, a pressure measured in ounces. "Tell 'em to keep off the skids!" he said through gritted teeth. "Tell 'em to get the men on and get back!"

More faces outside. Bear was talking to someone outside his window. "How many do you want, sir?" he asked.

"How's our power?" Martin did not dare glance down at the N_1 tachometer, which would tell what percentage of their maximum power they were using already. Whatever it read now, they would need more to climb out of the hole. It was a hundred feet to the treetops. If they tried to climb out with too great a load, the ship would only give up the ghost and settle back to kill itself on the stumps or in the trees. But there were men dying here, at his hands. He did not dare look down at the instrument, for fear of slipping into the solid trees. He flew and sweated, as the Bear checked the gauge.

"We can't take any more." Bear added, "We've only got three on."

"Cut the pods off." From the side of his eyes Martin saw Bear's hand leave the control stick and move to the yellow lever beside his own seat, to pull it up through the safety wire. The ship was suddenly buoyed up. Martin pressed it firmly back down. "Rocket pods away," Bear said.

Cripps's voice, so seldom heard, seemed strangely lost and out of place on the intercom when he spoke. "Sir, I could get off. You'd be able to carry more men." Bodies were still being carried out of the darkness, assembled along the edge of the clearing. They came out of that night draped in dark ponchos like black spirits, with faces white as death. "No, Cripps."

"But, sir, I can't do nothing for these guys. I'm just so much weight. You can get me later."

Martin knew Cripps was right. His own reaction was wrong. But it was like leaving one he knew among the dead to leave Cripps buried in this dark place. Yet Cripps was right. "All right. Handy too. And take off the guns. We'll be back for you. If Dustoff comes in sooner, come out with them."

"Yes, sir."

"Handy . . ." There was no answer on the intercom. Handy was gone.

A movement beside his head caught his eye, and he turned toward the movement for an instant. Beside the ship they were tearing the guns away. Another body came aboard. "We've got seven on," Bear said. "That's all."

Martin tested the collective stick, the lever in his left hand through which he must lift the whole weight of the ship. It seemed to him that he could feel every pound collecting in the palm of his hand. The ship did not want to come up. "Bear, take us out," he said.

"I've got it, sir." Martin remained on the controls, but the weight passed from his hand. The feeling of the life of the aircraft drained from his right forefinger and thumb. He was suddenly but a passenger. His eyes went to the N_1 tachometer. It stood fixed at 95.6%. MAXIMUM POWER, the placard next to it proclaimed, 95.8%. That was at sea level. They were fifteen hundred feet higher here: the engine was putting out all the power it had.

He felt the collective ease upward. The N_2 tachometer, whose twin needles told engine speed and rotor speed, crept back. The ship had hovered at normal engine output-shaft speed, sixty-six hundred rpm. As the pitch in the blade was increased to lift the ship, the drag increased, and with no more power available, the blade and engine slowed. The tachometer needle crept downward across the green arc. At six thousand rpm engine speed the tail rotor, geared to the main rotor, would no longer be turning fast enough to compensate for the torque of the main blade, and the tail would obey Newton's second law of motion by beginning an inexorable drift to the left, a drift which could be stopped only by reducing power or by striking some solid object. The needle crept below sixty-four hundred. The low-rotor-speed warning flicked on, driving its frantic pinging through their headphones. But the ship was rising along the tree trunks. "Strong-hearted ship," Martin said to it, to himself, "be strong." The tachometer stabilized at the bottom of the green. Martin watched each branch of the trees in front sink past. At fifty feet the blade clipped the same branch. The light increased as they climbed. At eighty feet he radioed, "Wolf Lead, Two is coming out."

"Roger, Two," Blood's voice answered. "We're inbound. How is it?"

"Tight. And the bottom's full of stumps. We've left our weapons and our crew there."

At the top of the hole the blade reached the wind above the trees. The Bear eased the stick forward as the skids cleared the treetops and in a flurry of blades they were released from the grip of the earth and climbed swiftly away.

"Lead, we're on the way to Chu Lai," Martin radioed.

"Roger, we'll catch you."

"I'll take it now," Martin said.

"You've got it." Bear had been surprised when Martin turned the controls over to him. He had flown with men who would sooner have crashed than do that. It was as much as to say, "I know you are the better pilot." Among pilots that meant the better man. The gesture impressed Bear. It made him admire Martin in a way he had not done before.

When Blood reported himself out of the LZ, Bear put on the position lights. Night was coming up from the valleys, and against the clouds they would now be almost invisible. Within a few minutes Blood's ship drew up alongside. Martin fell in behind.

It was then that Bear looked into the back of the ship for the first time. Four of the wounded were able to sit up. They had been perched on the bench seat which stretched across the back of the cabin, where they remained as motionless as statues, as medieval exemplars of the ills of the flesh. One's head was swathed in a turban of bandage which wound down over the left eye; another had one sleeve of his fatigues cut off, and the arm wrapped from wrist to shoulder; a third showed a splash of bandage under his half-open shirt. But it was those on the floor of the ship who caught Bear's eye. They were laid head to toe, but the floor was still too narrow for three, so one had been laid half on top of another. The feet of those sitting up had been worked between and around those on the floor as well as possible, but still they could be accommodated only by propping up an arm here, a leg there. The central man on the floor was conscious. He stared up at the cabin top with unmoving eyes and bit his lips, first the top one, then the bottom. Watching him, Bear was made acutely aware of the roughness of the ride. At every bump and jiggle the

73

soldier's body shook. His shirt was off; his chest had been bandaged all the way around, and blood had soaked through the bandage. One hand hovered always near his chest, but he seemed never to dare touch it. There was a catch in his breath, evident in the labored movement of his chest even though it could not be heard above the din of the machine. Bear supposed he must be moaning.

The third soldier, the one stacked closest to the front seats, was the first who had been carried out on his poncho. He was on it still. He lay with his eyes closed, his hair matted over his forehead, his arms limp at his sides. There was a band about his left thigh, over the trousers. It was a belt tourniquet, twisted with a stick which had been tied to a belt-loop at his waist to keep it from loosening. A ring of dark blood soaked the trousers from the knee to the ankle. It was some time before Bear noticed the strange way the leg rolled, like a log in a heavy sea. As the aircraft bounced, the leg and foot rolled, but the upper leg did not. The trouser leg had been severed at the ring of blood, and when he looked closely there was no knee there at all. What remained of the leg had come along with the soldier, still in the boot; but it was not part of him. As the ship moved, as the moaning soldier bit his alternate lips, the bodyless leg lay rocking, rocking, rocking. Bear turned away.

To Chu Lai from the hill was little more than twenty miles. The route could not be flown quite in a straight line, for the low cloud base made it necessary to wind down the river valley which debouched into Song Ben Van, the inland bay at the north perimeter of Chu Lai. But at a hundred and twenty knots, with the collective-pitch stick pulled as high as it would go, the distant grey of the sea soon came in sight, and the lights of Chu Lai just coming on against the evening. They whirled out onto the plain. Blood still had not called to alert the hospital that they were coming. They were near the control zone when Martin radioed to remind him. "He was just going to do it," Bear said grimly.

"Ah, Two," Blood replied, "I was just going to do it."

Chu Lai tower rogered Blood's call and in a moment called back to give them the medical evacuation frequency for the hospital. By the time Blood could call on that frequency, the tower had alerted the hospital. A black southern voice answered his call: "Wolf Lead, are you comin' from Battleax?"

"That's affirmative, and there's more casualties out there. Did you send Dustoff out?"

"Negative on that, Wolf Lead. We got three ships out on another mission. As soon as one comes back, he'll be on his way. It shouldn't be more'n twenty minutes."

While that was taking place, Martin had called company Operations. His hope was to find some of the slicks on the ground, either to send out in addition to their own ships, or to trade for them. The slicks would at least carry more bodies. But in that he was disappointed. Lieutenant Rauch answered in his unhurried buttery voice: "Man, we had a big CA come up, and *everything* has hit the fan. Everything we got is flyin' but the hangar queens. What's your problem, Wolf?"

"An emergency medevac's our problem! Haven't you even got the general's ship in?"

"You ain't goin' to get blood all over the general's ship?" Rauch did his best to sound shocked.

"I am if it's on the ramp."

"Nope—he's out, too, watchin' the big show. Medevac's a little out of your line, anyway, ain't it, Wolf?" Rauch had recognized Martin's voice, but not his seriousness.

"Then get us a fuel truck," Martin ordered. "We'll be on the ramp in five."

"Sure. You want to rearm?"

"That's negative."

"Roger the fuel truck."

They crossed beyond the main runway, low under the jet departure pattern, popped up over the ridge beside the officers' club, and together whirled to a fast stop on the pad outside the doors of the medical evacuation hospital at the end of their own parking ramp. In their months of flying from the same ramp, it was the first time any of them had been at the hospital pad. They had all of them a strange sense of dislocation, landing at the wrong end of the ramp, seeing the wrong end of the buildings and the canvas maintenance hangars swelling like deformed whales out of the darkness toward Ky Ha.

Before they were solidly on the ground, corpsmen in gowns or green T-shirts were running toward them, pushing litters on wheels. The men sitting up in back had first to have their feet disentangled before those on the floor could be moved. For a moment the two ships were the center of a milling mass, as if ants had converged on scraps of choice carrion. Then the bodies had suddenly vanished: the ships were empty. Bear did not see what had become of the soldier with the severed leg. He did not look back to see. When the last of the litters had vanished through the swinging doors, Martin pulled pitch and whirled down the ramp to the parking area, where a fuel truck had pulled out to await them.

They refueled with the engines running. The truck driver, who had never refueled before with the blade cutting overhead, handled the hose clumsily. He gaped about looking for Handy and Cripps. Martin pounded the cyclic impatiently as this went on. He waved off the driver when they had taken on only six hundred pounds of fuel. It would cut their reserve to the bone, if they should have to make a detour; but they could carry more casualties that way than with a full tank.

As Blood was being refueled, Lieutenant Rauch, who could see them from the Operations doorway, came on the company frequency: "Say, Wolf, what happened to your guns?"

"We'll talk about it later," Martin answered.

"God damn, you must of got into something big! I'll write you up for a medal!"

"Sure. You do that."

"Listen, where you bound for, Wolf?"

Martin gave him the coordinates and then switched off the frequency. He called to Blood that his ship was ready, and in a moment Blood picked up to depart. They climbed out over the ocean and turned quickly downwind toward what little remained of the day, west behind the mountains.

Darkness met them at the railroad beyond Route One, short of even the foothills fronting the big mountain. Rain began to spit against the windscreen. They crossed above the two villages named Thanh My Trung, but there were no lights. The Bear had put the panel lights on at their dimmest setting. The soft red glow of the gauges was no brighter than a remembered dawn. The only other mark on the universe was the lights of the lead ship. With-

76

out their guns they flew in uncomfortable awareness of what might be on the ground. The beacons were turned off, and Martin moved in close off the leader's port quarter.

As the cloud base lowered, the ground level rose beneath them, and the mountains were hidden giants on either hand. Into the narrowing funnel of earth and cloud they plunged on until they dared risk flying in darkness no longer. Blood switched on his searchlight.

Despite the open invitation to whoever had a weapon to try it on them, they all felt instantly more confident. Bear noticed it in Martin, who loosened his grip on the cyclic stick as he slid the ship farther back from Blood's. There was no danger now of losing sight of the other aircraft, and with the searchlight picking out the thread of river below, there was no danger of plunging into a mountain in the dark, at least until the time came to cross over the pass above Phu Tho, into the valley of the westward-running river beyond.

They found the pass still open. If the hill itself were not already buried in cloud, they would be able to reach Battleax. In answer to Blood's radio call Battleax spoke calmly from the darkness. It was the second voice that had replied that afternoon. Martin supposed it was that of the young lieutenant he had seen glance out once from the trees. The old man—the company commander —was dead, the other voice had said. And the first sergeant and the two platoon leaders. Their attack had killed nearly the whole command structure. He wondered whose the first voice had been. The radioman's? Or simply someone who had picked up the set, after the radioman was killed with the commanding officer? The lieutenant had been calm from the first. He must be a good officer. He had a future. Martin wondered if the lieutenant knew that he was speaking to his attackers.

"Battleax, how many wounded have you got left?" Blood asked.

"I've got eight. The Kilo India Alphas can wait." That was phonetic alphabet for KIA—killed in action.

"How many KIA?"

"Twelve."

It was some time before Blood spoke again. "We can't take

them all, Battleax." On the first trip they had got out twelve on the two ships. "Have you heard from Dustoff yet?"

"Negative, Wolf."

"He's supposed to be on his way by now."

"Roger."

How was it that a man could talk calmly to persons he did not know, about the death and anguish of those he did know, who lay in the wet dark around him, waiting for deliverance?

They homed again on Battleax's voice. The homing needle flicked over as the hill pushed up into the circle of light from Blood's searchlight. The landing zone was bigger now: Battleax had been busy cutting trees. Martin swung out into the darkness to let Blood land.

Outbound, he turned on his own light. As the beam stabbed into the night below them, a glowing aureole formed about the whole ship in the damp air. Their eyes ached suddenly as glare washed out everything beyond the windshield. Bear reached overhead to the rheostat that controlled the panel lights and turned it until the red gauges could be seen again through the glare. Waiting for Blood to call that he was coming out, they turned and flew slowly back toward the hill, brushing aside fingers of cloud which dangled from the overcast. At a half-mile range Blood's light popped suddenly into view. They tried to remember the spot but soon lost it. Bear manipulated the searchlight ahead as they descended, until the LZ was there, a black hole caught in the circle of light in which individual trees now cast hard shadows.

"Landing light," Martin said. The landing light was housed beside the searchlight in the belly of the ship. Stowed, it pointed straight down. When they were over the hole, they would need both lights, one to light the ground, the other to shine forward on the trees for a horizon reference, so that the ship could be kept level. Bear switched on the light.

The well of darkness slid under them and was suddenly filled with light.

The searchlight marked their inch-by-inch descent along the tree trunks. The tree whose outer branches they had struck before was no longer there. A light drizzle had slicked the clay between the stumps at the bottom. Poncho-draped forms, ghosts in mourning, slipped and stumbled toward them in crippled haste. In this scene from an everyday hell the spirits bore their sins on their shoulders in the forms of their tormented brothers. Among the bearers were Cripps and Handy. Handy grinned through the windscreen as he rounded the front of the ship. The thickness of Plexiglas which separated them seemed the breadth of eternity.

Bear watched the bearers hobble back beyond the reach of the lights, back to the night that pressed in all around. He pitied anyone driven into that night.

As Handy reached the edge of the trees, he turned to give them a thumbs-up sign. Martin pulled pitch and sank that hell behind them.

Blood had taken out all but three of the wounded. Those three were aboard, and to make up the load three bodies had been stacked on the floor. Martin saw the bodies when he turned the ship over to Bear to fly. They might have taken out Cripps and Handy instead, he thought. What was a night in the jungle to one already dead?

They had not gone far when they heard another aircraft calling, another lone wanderer in the void. It was Dustoff at last, calling Battleax. He was still east of the pass, where Battleax could not receive him. Blood answered.

"Hello, Wolf," Dustoff said in reply. "I hear you've been to Battleax. Can we still get through?"

"Affirmative, Dustoff. We've got the last of the wounded aboard. There's still some KIAs for you."

"Thanks a lot, Wolf. Glad you left some for us. I'd hate to come out here in this dark for nothing."

"Why doesn't the s.o.b. pass his chitchat on another channel?" Bear muttered on the intercom.

"If you've got room, Dustoff, we've got four crew in the LZ," Blood added. "Can you bring them in?"

"Ah, how many bodies still to go, Wolf?"

"Two, how many have you got aboard?" Blood asked.

"There should be nine more."

"Oh, that's dandy, Wolf. I'm a flight of two, so no problem on your crew. You can pick 'em up in the emergency room. You hear that, Ski?" The last remark was apparently meant for Dustoff's trail ship. The only answer was two clicks.

The flight back to Chu Lai was the longest in Martin's memory. After other missions there had been easy chatter on the intercom, winding down from the excitement of an attack, or staving off boredom after an empty patrol. Now there was no word spoken. Sunk in black private thoughts, they journeyed together, separated by a gulf of guilt and shame, hating where they were and yet wishing this flight might have no end, rather than face the inevitable ending. While the Bear flew, Martin sat, hands folded in his lap, watching the light from Blood's ship tumble down the valley toward a horizon that never arrived.

It meant his career: he saw that. He wished not to think of it, for it seemed to him ignoble, to think of his career when at his back lumps of battered flesh gasped for life itself. But he could not help it: he did think of it. Martin was not vain or self-deceiving. He had always seen himself as one marked out for eventual high rank, but only because others also saw that in him. He did not deceive himself now. He saw that it was over. There was no overlooking a mistake so great.

He leaned back and closed his eyes, and for an instant there came to him a vision, he did not know whether of hope or of despair, a waking dream that was to come over him many times in the weeks ahead, at moments when he was not guarding his thoughts—a vision so intensely real that when he returned from it he was startled to find himself still seated in the ship. He dreamed, for an instant, that he was indeed dreaming, in his quarters in his bunk, and that he was about to awake, relieved, from a shattering nightmare. Instead, he awoke and, twisting in his seat, found himself staring into the glittering eyes of one of the soldiers on the floor.

The soldier was dead. He lay on his back, facing half toward Martin. The poncho around him would not close because his right arm was raised, with the hand palm-out over his forehead as if to ward off a blow that would never fall. The eyes were half open and glittered back the light of a red map-light overhead. Martin reached back to push down the arm, but the soldier was already stiff. The arm was wet, not with blood, but with rain. One of the wounded men sitting above the body watched stonily, moving no more than the body on the floor. Martin turned away in confusion.

Entry into the emergency room was a frantic resurrection, a traumatic spillage from the dark, jolting metal womb of the helicopter into the chill uproar of the ER. Litters were manhandled onto trestles; hooked scissors ripped wet jungle fatigues from torn bodies; orderlies and medical corpsmen, nurses and doctors, milled for an instant in troubled eddies before falling into an orderly stream of procedure. There was no plan: each joined in at the point where he found himself. Yet, although the uproar did not diminish, their efforts suddenly coalesced, as the milling frenzy of a startled flock of geese swings, without direction, into a single V pointing north.

The soldier who had lost his leg came in through the swinging door and was installed beneath an overhead bar where bottles of clear fluid hung waiting like crystalline jellyfish dangling their plastic tentacles. There happened to be a doctor there. Nothing distinguished him from the corpsmen. Like many of them he wore a green sleeveless surgical shirt. Others, doctors and assistants alike, poured into the emergency room in fatigues or T-shirts and fell straight to work. Because he was at hand, the doctor turned first to the soldier with his leg off.

The bearers dropped the litter on the trestles and ran for the door, for another body. The litter rocked, and the leg rolled over the edge. It was not fully severed. A strand of skin and flesh still connected the calf to the upper leg. The boot and the bloody pulp above it dangled below the litter, swinging and slowly revolving, stretching slowly toward the floor. The soldier's eyes were closed. He was pale-faced, his skin clammy.

The doctor took the soldier's wrist. The pulse tapped weakly at his fingertips. "Give him two units of low-lite O straightaway," he said to the nearest corpsman. "He's shaky." The corpsman shouted to the rear of the room and put up his hands to catch a bag of blood which came through the air as if delivered from heaven. Another bag followed. The corpsman caught it between one hand and his stomach. While the doctor put a needle into the soldier's arm, the corpsman slipped a bag onto an overhead hook and attached the intravenous tube. "Get his pressure," the doc-

81

tor said. "I'll be back." Without a word the corpsman began taping the tube to the soldier's arm.

The census officer, a little man wearing fatigues with captain's bars, stopped beside the soldier's head. He did not look at the face. "His number's seven-five-five," he announced.

"Can't be," the corpsman grunted, inserting another needle. "I just gave that to the sucking chest."

"Now, don't tell me we're going to have the numbers game again!" The census officer detested the insubordination of medical people during a mass casualty.

"When did we have a mass cal that we didn't get into the numbers game?" the corpsman asked.

"We simply cannot go on this way!" the captain insisted. "The colonel's going to hear about this! All right, number seven-five-six?"

"Fine by me." The corpsman fished a blue felt-tip pen from a shirt pocket and wrote the number on the soldier's forehead. He emphasized it with a heavy underline which neatly connected the high arch of the eyebrows.

The doctor had gone to number seven-five-five, the sucking chest. A major whose name, according to his name tag, was Kant, was poring over the soldier's naked body while a nurse held the remains of a foil bandage below the soldier's left nipple. "Dan, my eyes are going bad," Major Kant said to the other doctor. "I can't tell the shrapnel holes from the mosquito bites." The soldier's torso bore several tiny red spots. A few continued to ooze thin streams of blood. They were all that showed where the bits of jagged metal had slashed into the body. "That's the zit that's sucking," Major Kant added, nodding toward the spot the nurse was covering. A tiny fragment piercing the right chest had allowed air to enter and collect around the outside of the lung when the soldier inhaled. When he exhaled the hole closed from the inside like a valve, sealing in the air, so that the lungs steadily increased the pressure that was collapsing them. Before he passed out, the soldier had felt the incubus Death enter with the air. It had set up quarters in his chest and was slowly elbowing his life aside.

Major Kant held a long hollow needle against the chest wall and with the heel of his hand thrust it forcibly between the ribs.

The air sighed out. The soldier no longer labored for breath. "That's better," the major said, "but there's a zit in the throat, too, below the larynx, and one that could have got the spleen. His pressure's only eighty over. I want him first for the OR, unless there are some more outside that I haven't seen."

"He's the only airway," the other doctor agreed. "We've got some bad bleeders—the amputee over there's fairly shocky, but he can wait once we get him stabilized. There's one for neurosurgery back there. He took a frag over the eye. We'll have to get films to see where it wound up. Were these the only choppers?"

"Apparently not. I don't know who's bringing them in, but they went back for more. They're not our choppers."

"Well, there are six for the OR, counting the one for neuro." A fragment in the brain had low priority for the operating room. A man could live long—until infection set in—with a fragment in his brain. It was the less spectacular wounds which demanded haste—any interference with the air supply first, then unchecked bleeding, and so down through the gamut of injuries, through fragments of steel in the brain, and ending with lowly fractures and other wounds which, although painful, never killed anyone quickly. Pain took a place in line when a mass cal poured through the door of the ER.

"This one's ready to go," Major Kant called out. "Chest and abdomen films first, then to the OR." Two orderlies appeared. They fastened tall rods like fishing poles to the litter, transferred the blood bags to the poles, and with the litter between them hurried out the door at the back of the emergency room.

A nurse hovered uncertainly in the vacancy where the litter had been. "You can take care of the one over here," the doctor said to her, "unless you've got something else pressing."

She had not. The rest of the medical people had by now fallen into task forces that had stabilized for better or worse. What needed doing instantly was being done. She followed the doctor.

The doctor glanced at two other wounded men on his way back to the soldier with the leg off, but he did not stop. From a shelf he took a clipboard, which he rested on the soldier's stomach. The nurse's eyes stayed on the leg which swung alongside the litter. "You can put it back up," he said. "What's he got, Dean?"

"Pulse one-forty. Blood pressure sixty over ten with a unit in. We just started the second unit."

"That's better. But you'd better put a pressure cuff on the bag and push it in faster." He began unbuttoning the man's jacket. "Get his trousers off," he said to the nurse, "and let's see what else he's got, before he gets to the OR." He handed her a pair of scissors from a pocket on his gown. "I'm Rawlinson," he said as he handed over the scissors. "Lieutenant Porter, I presume?" She was wearing fatigues with a new black-printed name tag.

"Alice Porter."

"I just got back from Hong Kong," he said, "but I know you weren't here when I left. When did you show up?"

"Yesterday . . . no, the day before."

"Mm. New in country?"

"Yes."

"Devil of a time to leave home, right before Christmas. Devil of a time to see your first mass cal, too. You have to see one sometime, but they don't always fall on you the first day." Dr. Rawlinson said all this quite absently as he studied the soldier's body for zits. He forestalled any answer by slipping his stethoscope into his ears.

She struggled to cut the soldier's trousers free without loosening the tourniquet on the thigh. She felt exasperatingly inept. She had not completely shaken off the effects of her flight halfway around the world two days before. Instead of the change to tropic heat she had expected, she had gone from a warm dry California winter to the chilly damp of the winter monsoon. The dry chill of the air-conditioned emergency room did not steady her hand. She had seen mangled bodies before, but so many at once was something new even if not unexpected. Twelve maimed young men together were, somehow, more than a cumulation of so many cases met on a ward. And another shipment was due to arrive within the hour!

She was determined to be a proper nurse, and so she was almost pleased to see something that did need attention. "We need more blood," she said, looking up at the bags hanging limp overhead.

"I'll get it, ma'am." The corpsman hurried toward the back of

84

the room, where one of his fellows was standing by with a cart of blood units.

The doctor unplugged his stethoscope and began scribbling on his clipboard. "You can clean up the stump a bit while he's waiting to go in," he said. He left without another word.

She began cleaning the debris and dead tissue from the soldier's leg. The outside was blackened and burned where the trousers had been torn away. There were ragged scraps of cloth glued on with dried blood, leaves, and bits of stick; and the splintered bone had somewhere gouged into red gritty earth that was packed up inside like petrified marrow. The trouser leg was stuck to the slender strip of flesh still holding the lower leg to the rest of the man. She knew the leg would be removed anyway, but she left it attached to him. Before she had finished, two corpsmen came to bear the litter away. She stood for a moment watching the empty blood bags swaying overhead after he was gone.

As the soldier with one leg began the trek up the corridor toward the operating room, his friend with the sucking chest wound lay under the hands of the surgeon. His chest wound had been probed, cleansed, and closed, with a tube inserted to reinflate the lung and keep pressure from rebuilding around it. The surgeon had only begun with the soldier, but already he felt good about him. The big problem, the immediate problem, was solved. There remained only the tedious job of sorting through yards of bloody gut, tracking down the perforations in the wake of the steel fragments. "Let me see those films again."

"There's one near the back, there," said Rawlinson, who had come in to assist. "Another one over here on the side."

The abdomen was hard under his fingers as the surgeon began to cut. It was distended with internal bleeding from the many perforations of the intestine. He finished pulling back the skin and muscle, cut into the abdominal cavity. Dark red blood welled instantly from the incision.

"Jesus, there must be three liters in there!" Rawlinson exclaimed. "Is it a spleen, do you think?"

"Doctor, he's going into shock," the anesthetist said.

"Now what?" The surgeon looked from the perforated gut to the soldier's face, which was going suddenly pale. He looked back at the incision, hooked a finger under the first loop of intestine, and stared. "Christ, it must be the vena cava!" He held out his hand for a scalpel which appeared with agonizing slowness because of this break in routine. When it came, he slashed the incision down nearly to the pubis and threw down the scalpel to paw frantically through the yards of slippery guts, trying to reach the bottom in time. Blood poured from the incision, slopping out bits of floating feces. It was chilly blood that had only now been forced into the soldier from a bag. As fast as they had forced it in, it had been running out the perforation in the vena cava, the major vein at the back of the abdominal cavity, until so much blood had collected there that it squeezed the vein closed and shut off the flow. Then the soldier's condition had appeared stable. But when the surgeon cut, the pressure was released and the flow resumed, draining the blood from the soldier faster than it could be replaced. Knowing that it was now the only hope, the surgeon plunged for the bottom, ignoring the perforated guts in the way, hoping to shut off the flow before the soldier died. He failed.

The soldier who had taken the zit through his head lay staring at the ceiling, and at the many obscene things dangling from it. Those bags, now, full of red goo like ketchup out of the refrigerator. They hung there sweating. They didn't have to do that. He could do his own sweating, even if the room was cold. Christ, was it ever cold! Why didn't they turn down the air-conditioning?

The bags sweated because, although the room was chilly, they were chillier, having just come from refrigeration. There was no time to warm the blood. The soldier was cold because the blood going into him was cold.

Mainly, the soldier thought about his wound. Not the one in his head—he did not even know that there was one there. The one he thought about was in his left calf. A machine gun bullet had gone through, taking a good piece of flesh along with it. He had begged Dunstable, the company corpsman, for morphine, but Dunstable, the son of a bitch, would not give him any. Zenakis, which was the soldier's name, did not think that was fair; but he put up with it, because he knew morphine was in short supply in the boonies, and there were plenty of other people who really did need it. Patulski, the poor bugger, was minus a leg. He got morphine. But in the hospital, now, there should be plenty of morphine or whatever else he needed, but no one would give him any. That really did not seem the way to treat a guy who had just given his leg—well, a piece of his leg—for his country. And it hurt. It hurt more the longer he lay there.

He tried biting his lips and then his tongue, but now his tongue was bleeding and the leg hurt anyway, so he quit.

"Can I do anything for you?" The nurse's face came into his view. It was a long time since he had seen blue eyes on a woman.

"Ma'am, please, can I have something for my leg?" It embarrassed him to have to ask. It was an admission that the pain was stronger than he was. But since she had asked . . .

She read the tag on his litter. "I'll get you something." She was a beautiful nurse, Lieutenant Porter.

She brought him a Darvon and a glass of water. Not knowing what it was, he took it gratefully. Another thing he didn't know was that, because of the head wound he did not know he had, he could not be given any morphine-based drug. The drug could mask the symptoms of brain damage. Zenakis swallowed his pill and lay back hopefully to wait for it to work.

She felt bad about giving him the Darvon. She knew the pain from the wound he had would not be teased away. She hoped the Darvon might help a little.

Zenakis thought the pain was only being stubborn, and for a while he gritted his teeth and told it to go away. But it did not. When the nurse came around again he asked, half embarrassed now and half anguished, "Please, do you suppose I could have a little more? I don't think it was enough." When she said no, he was mortified. But the pain did not care. The pain was stronger than he was. It drove out his scruples. The next time, he pleaded, "Ma'am, please! Please give me something!" He thought, when tears came to her eyes, that she would agree. But he was wrong.

Lieutenant Porter was too sympathetic to leave the soldier alone, and not hardened enough to be unaffected by his pleas. So she hovered around him, feeling guilty because she was unable to help. Zenakis and his head wound were far down the list for the operating room. He lay for another half hour. At the end he was pleading steadily, "Oh, please. You could give me something, couldn't you? It's just not fair! Please give me something!"

He was taken away just as the second flight came in from Battleax.

The helicopters landed with a pounding roar that shook the bare walls of the building and set loose bottles dancing on the shelves, until the aircraft were throttled down to a low flapping whistle. A second avalanche of bodies poured through the swinging doors.

Preparations had been under way for this moment for nearly an hour, so that the turmoil of the first arrival was not repeated in full. But uncertainty as to the condition of the men who would be arriving led to a moment of confused scrambling until the triage was well under way. Although she was near the doors, it was some time before Lieutenant Porter noticed that a soldier had wandered alone into the ER. She took him at first for one of the walking wounded. He was pale, and his large eyes glared strangely. He said nothing, but walked back and forth, pushing nervously with one hand at his bristling mustache. "Sit down," she said. "We'll have time for you in a minute." But instead he turned and rushed out.

On the helipad Martin turned in his seat to watch the last of the bodies unloaded. He turned back to find that the Bear had vanished. Only his helmet remained, perched on the left seat and still connected to the intercom cord. Martin knew where he had gone. To visit the wounded was at least an honorable gesture, however worthless to them. He waited for a short while, expecting Bear to return. Finally he picked up the ship to hover back to the company parking ramp.

He could see the lights of Blood's aircraft stationary in its revetment. As he hovered, Blood came on the company radio to report the flight down.

Rauch answered at once. "Hey, Wolf, glad to see you back! You better haul ass up here. Six has been waitin' for you." He meant that Major Hart was there: "six" was radio code for a unit commander.

After the main blade had run down at last, Martin caught it with the hook. He was tying the tapes to the tail stinger when Blood and Atterburn came down the ramp from their ship. They stood back a few feet until Martin finished. Then Blood cleared his throat.

"Well?"

"Well, Martin, what are we going to say?"

"Why don't you just turn in a body count of thirty, Blood, and we'll all go to bed with no more said?"

"How good a chance do you think that has?"

He had not expected even Blood to take the remark other than ironically. His tongue was thick with disgust. "About as much chance as Battleax had once we cut loose. There's only one reason the old man can be waiting for us."

"Well, God damn it, Martin, you don't have to put on that high-and-mighty act with me! You were the ranking officer on this expedition, you know! If you're going to butt in and tell me when to dump my ordnance and when not to, you could at least be man enough to stand up and admit whose fault it was!" This accusation was not founded on anything Martin had yet said; but it represented Blood's accumulated sense of the unfairness of everything; and it was near enough the analysis that had been lurking about the back of Martin's mind that he found himself unable to answer. Blood saw his advantage and pressed it: "We both know you only came on this flight to get your name in front of the general. I expect you'll be able to weasel out of it, since it didn't turn out the way you expected; but, by God, don't think I'm too dumb to know what you're up to! It's no accident that the first time you've had your sweet ass out of that swivel chair since you've been XO is a mission the general has his eye on!"

Blood's ambitions had always been apparent; but Martin was genuinely surprised at the depth of the bitterness now revealed. Blood failed to recognize that it was this rather than any accuracy in his charge which kept Martin silent now. So he began in a more conciliatory tone, hoping to press the advantage he thought he held. "There's no use our getting at each other's throats, Martin. It's not your goddamn fault that Battleax was in the free-fire zone, and it's not mine, either. For all we knew, they could have been Slopes down there. If they're going to blame it on anybody, let 'em blame it on Battleax Six, for getting his troops in there in the first place."

"He's dead; it won't hurt him," Atterburn said. He had moved farther and farther back, so that his voice seemed but a parenthesis to the whole matter.

"That's right. He's right, Martin."

Atterburn was, of course, "right" so far as any right was to be found in the tale of errors. But Martin knew that was not the end of the tale. With thirty men dead or wounded, there would be little enough credit handed round. Martin found the whole subject offensive—not least because he himself was not far short of casting blame on a dead man to keep his own record clear.

"If we keep together on this, Division doesn't even have to know," Blood said. "There's no way for Battleax to know who hit them. Snoopy's out of the division—word of this may never get back to them at Da Nang, or if it does, they may not remember where we fired off our ordnance. We chased all over hell today. Christ, it could have been anybody in the world who hit them!"

"If you believe that," Martin answered, desperate not to listen, "you're dumber than you think I think you are." He turned and strode off toward Operations.

If none of them knew quite what to expect in Operations, none of them expected quite what they found. In addition to Rauch and Major Hart there were two clerks and Lieutenant Harris. Major Hart, who had been seated beside Rauch at the desk, rose up open-armed. "The conquering heroes come!" he said. The three of them stopped, astonished. "Tidings of great joy from on high, gentlemen. The division commander called personally to say that awards recommendations for all of you will be on his desk tomorrow morning. So just tell us what you did, and I'll get these fellows"—a wave of his hand explained the presence of the clerks and Harris, who was company awards-and-decorations officer—"to work on them."

Despite his mock-heroic tone, it was obvious that Major Hart was pleased, and even excited. He was old, for a major, having joined the officer ranks late, after service as an enlisted man. He had been once passed over for promotion to lieutenant colonel. The major was not a greatly ambitious man. Left to himself he would have been pleased to finish out his twenty years' service in some quiet assignment and retire—or even continue in that quiet assignment, if that would have been permitted. The major liked

90

the Army. He liked flying. If he had been a warrant officer, expected only to fly or to perform low-level supervisory duties, he would have finished out his career in great happiness. He was not an incapable officer. As company commander he was liked by his men, who saw to it that the company's missions were performed well enough to reflect favorably on the old man. But he had no quality to catch the eye of his superiors, to make it appear that he must be promoted to positions of even greater responsibility. Worse yet, he had an inborn kindness that never failed to show through; and however pleasing a quality kindness might be in itself, it was not thought to have any great merit in one whose business was to order others to kill. It was not among the character traits evaluated on an officer efficiency report form. So, as an officer in an army which demanded that every officer go up or go out, Major Hart was well aware that his most likely course was out, and he was pleased at having come to the attention of the commanding general through the deeds of his men.

But Major Hart was not moved only, or even primarily, by thought of his own credit. He was pleased for his men, even for Captain Blood, whom he did not really like very much although he tried to hide that fact from himself. "If Major Hart doesn't like a man," the Bear had said once, "you know he's got to be an original-manufacture son of a bitch." Major Hart would have liked to see Captain Blood succeed simply because Blood ached so greatly for success.

The major brimmed with pleasure. "What kind of medals would you like? I guess it's carte blanche. DFC . . . Medal of Honor . . . The general didn't say, darn him. What's appropriate? How many Charlies did you get?"

"Not any," Martin said softly.

Blood flushed, and said, sounding as if he would choke on the words, "We . . . flew a medevac."

"Yes, I heard that. But too late for the action? That doesn't sound like my boys. Well, but you did the main thing—you got our men out. How many did you evacuate?"

Major Hart, so pleased at their accomplishment, took the ensuing silence merely as a pause to calculate. Blood said at last, "About twenty-five, sir."

"Twenty, sir. Plus three dead. Dustoff is bringing nine more

KIAs." It was the Bear, who had quietly entered the hooch unnoticed and was standing behind Blood. The number burned in his brain.

"My God!" Major Hart exclaimed. "Almost an entire platoon!"

"We flew two medevac flights," Blood said quickly. "Dropped our guns and our crews in the LZ. Dustoff's bringing them in. They had to cut an LZ for us. There was just room for one ship. . . ." Blood's voice showed more and more excitement as he went on. It took the puzzled Martin several seconds to realize that Blood really did believe that a medal should rightly come out of this. And, on the part of the tale which he told, he was right. The story was an awards-and-decorations officer's dream. Only the prologue killed it. But Blood had forgotten the prologue. It was of no consequence to him. Martin heard him out before he said quietly, "Blood, you are crazy!"

"Shoot, there ought to be a medal in that!" Rauch objected.

"If only we could go back and kill all the witnesses, there would be," Bear said. "But we blew our chance at that already."

"I don't follow you, Ben . . ." Major Hart ran his fingers nervously through his thinning silver hair. His forescalp glistened under the bare light bulbs.

"Sir, how did the general get into this?" Martin asked heavily, not having the heart to answer directly.

"I told the crew on his ship, when they called about more guns for the big do up north, that you were still out medevackin'," Rauch said, "and I reckon they told him. Hell, if you don't want the medals, I'll take 'em. I could use a DFC—I'm never goin' to get one flyin' this desk!"

"There won't be any medals, can't you get that through your thick head, Rauch?" Martin exploded. "There won't be any at all because we killed those men!"

Major Hart's smile was replaced by a quizzical incomprehension. He looked from Martin to Blood to Martin again, while Atterburn looked at the floor, and the Bear gnawed his mustache and pounded a fist steadily against the doorframe. Then there was absolute silence in the hooch.

Outside, the footsteps of mechanics on the way to the flight line rang in the damp air, and a voice sweet and thick as syrup:

"You see them gunnies come in? Lost they rocket pods some-wheres. I hear they was doin' a medevac. Thought they was s'posed to kill folks, not save 'em."

Major Hart smiled again, but now a reflective sad smile mark-ing the end of one more hope. One of the clerks quietly placed the cover over his typewriter.

Blood, when Martin first spoke, had turned to him fiercely, his face flaming with anger. But now he turned back to Major Hart and said with forced composure, "I wouldn't have sprung it on you like that, but it's true, sir."

"How? How did it happen?"

"When we were bound for home, Snoopy got a reading just inside the free-fire zone, and Martin ordered me to dump our ordnance." At this there was a snort from the Bear. Blood turned to Martin, his face flaming again: "Isn't that true, Martin? Are you going to deny it?"

"No. It's close enough." He had in fact been the ranking of-ficer. He could have ordered whatever action he chose, and he certainly had chosen as Blood said. He could not escape the blame. All he might do would be to drag Blood down with him. It hardly seemed worth the effort.

"We all should have known better," the Bear said. "All of us."

"It was my decision," Martin said, feeling as if he had stepped into a long hall whose end he could not see, and heard the door lock behind him.

Major Hart picked up the field telephone. "Give me Battalion —no, make that the battalion commander's quarters." To the clerks he said gently, "You boys can go on to bed. Thank you for coming."

Lieutenant Rauch sat behind his desk shaking his head. "We are into some deep shit," he said to no one in particular.

5

The investigating officer, an infantry lieutenant colonel, arrived promptly at nine hundred hours the next morning. He and his assistants had already been to the hospital. They interviewed the crew members one at a time in the back of the Operations hooch while the others waited in the alert hooch. The crews that would have been there on alert on other days had drifted away early, to the ships or to the steps of a nearby hooch—anywhere to avoid the chill silence. Except for Covington, only Arp had remained, having to be near at hand to Operations in case a mission came down. He was in charge of the platoon now, until the investigation was closed. When the Bear came back from his turn before the investigating board, Arp was lying on his bunk, reading *Catch-22* with a look of sour pleasure.

Atterburn paced the floor, while Handy meticulously cleaned and recleaned his machine gun to the accompaniment of a humming moan that flooded and ebbed about him with the endless surge of the ocean out on the reef. Covington and the Bear sat apart, sometimes talking and sometimes not. Cripps lay on his back on his bunk to one side of them. He lay with his hands folded on his belly and his eyes closed, as one laid out for his own funeral. His breathing was so shallow that he might have passed for dead, in the grey light; but he was listening to Covington and the Bear, when they spoke, and the rest of the time he daydreamed.

Sometimes Cripps wished he were an officer, so he could be friends with the two of them. They had never said anything that would keep him at a distance even though he was only their crew chief, but the constraint of military custom, however thin an overlay it might be, when added to Cripps's own shyness formed a wall he did not dare attempt to breach. Cripps would particularly have liked to say something comforting to the Bear, whose stricken look when he thought no one was watching was more than Cripps could bear. Cripps tried not to look at him, except when someone else was there to harden the Bear's face into one of his masks. Except with Covington. With him the Bear lapsed into a bemused sadness, his eyes like those of a hound that has finally lost a trail already long grown cold. Cripps envied them their friendship.

They were talking of the night before—or rather, the Bear was talking of it, trying to talk of it, in brief strangled phrases while Covington tut-tutted with helpless good intent. Once Covington turned to him, to Cripps, and asked, "What was it like down there, Cripps? You were there." That was after the Bear had attempted to convey the horror of the pit in the trees, but had tumbled to a halt. Cripps had only mumbled a reply that made no sense and then had turned away because the Bear had looked at him with fierce interest, awaiting his answer. Now, with them fallen silent, Cripps was rehearsing the answer he might have given.

When the helicopter rose away and its blade winked out beyond the edge of the hole in the trees, he had felt the forest edge closer around him. It was still daylight then, at least it was daylight above the trees. In the landing zone it was grey twilight while a few steps back from the clearing it was already night, a night echoing with the groans of men dying.

A fine mist settled gently in the clearing. Under the trees the water fell in great drops that had collected on the jungle canopy. When the helicopters came back, the turbulence in the treetops released a downpour along their flight path. Cripps had finally borrowed a dead man's poncho, but the smell of blood was still hot inside it, and he cast it away. Handy took it to cover the guns.

He and the other crewmen drifted around the clearing for a time, like swimmers testing the water, not wanting to plunge into

95

the darkness that lay beyond. He offered to help the corpsman who had collected the wounded near one side of the LZ; but the corpsman had long ago run out of medical supplies, and he only answered, "All there is left to do is fan 'em and give 'em ice water, buddy." At length the lieutenant who was now in charge of the company (the commander lay in the trees with a poncho snapped around him) became aware of them and sent them with their machine guns down to the perimeter in place of some of the wounded. The lieutenant himself wore a dressing on one arm, and his face trickled blood from many small cuts.

The men on the perimeter looked at them wide eyed once, as they stumbled past in their flight helmets, and then turned back to the more important matter of the darkness. He and Handy crouched in a shallow foxhole—it might have been a grave— while helicopters came and went ("Stay down there until I call you," the lieutenant had said. "I'll let you know when they're ready for you.") but the night stayed. They hoped the lieutenant's word was good. No one had asked them who they were, or how they came to be there. No one asked what part they played in this small tale of horror. But the first time the helicopters returned, Cripps heard a man in the next foxhole begin to breathe heavily—tremulous gasping breaths, half sobs, as if he were in the grip of some nightmare of anguish. "Take it easy, buddy," a voice said softly. "They can't hit us in the dark." Later the sweet burning-hay smell of marijuana drifted down through the night.

How the Bear imagined it Cripps did not know. Maybe it was better not to tell him. Knowing might only make it worse. Cripps wished he himself did not know.

But one thing that the Bear had said circled through his mind. "They asked me if I remembered anything else," the Bear had told Covington. "God yes, I remembered so much else—but how to say it? So I told them, I remembered Handy taking the guns off, carrying them away into the trees. And when they were gone, how the ship rose up, how light it felt—lighthearted. The colonel said he didn't catch what I meant."

Cripps understood. When the ship had risen away from him, he had thought for an instant how different it looked without the guns. How beautiful and clean. He wished he had said that much to the Bear.

One by one the other crew members came back to the hooch, Blood and Martin last of all. It became very quiet. At last Major Hart came in. He asked Arp and Covington to leave while he talked to the others. His message was brief: the investigating team had gone; the enlisted crews were to report for duty; the officers were grounded. "I wouldn't worry," he said. "It's only a formality until Division gets the report. The general will lift it after the investigation is complete." The words were kindly meant, but no one believed them.

After the major dismissed them, Blood caught up to Martin. "Well, Martin, it's all hit the fan now. That light colonel's going to try to make his eagle out of our hides. It looks like we'd better all pull together on whatever strings we can find." Martin walked on and left him standing.

Martin had told the investigators that he himself had insisted on attacking the hill contrary to the advice of all the others. ("Don't pride yourself on it," he told himself afterward. "It's only egotism again. If you're going down anyway, you know how to make it seem it was only because you tried to rescue others, don't you.")

The emergency room was the front entrance to the hospital. Its double swinging doors opened directly onto the helipad, and the long corridor giving access to the sprawling wards led back from the other side directly opposite the doors. It was a convenient layout, for all of the hospital's business came through the emergency room. Daily, helicopter loads of bodies arrived at the swinging doors, were disgorged into the chill pandemonium of the emergency room, were sorted, patched up, and held until it was safe to move them to a treating hospital. Then they were evacuated. The least injured went to the treating hospital on the cliffs of the next headland, a mile to the south. The more severely injured went to Qui Nhon or Da Nang. Those who needed closer care but might still return to combat before their year's tour of duty ended were flown to Japan, while those for whom the war was over went back to the Land of the Big PX, the United States. They were not always the lucky ones. Some made the trip in a body bag.

The emergency room was but an echoing cavity that afternoon, full of nothing but sunshine so wasted and consumptive that it seemed sustained only by the memory of summer. The Bear entered hesitantly, stood just inside the door gazing about in large-eyed distraction.

"What can I do for you, Chief?" He started at the voice. He had not noticed the orderly behind the counter at one side of the doors. The orderly was a lean black man with short curly hair going grey above the ears. He did not press for an answer to his question, but went on penciling check marks against a list on his clipboard. At his elbow the lights on a tiny plastic Christmas tree flashed on and off, on and off.

"You had some infantrymen brought in here last night. . . ."

"We got a pot full of 'em, Chief. You looking for any in particular? If you just want to look at an infantryman, take any ol' ward back there"—he waved down the corridor opposite them—"and you'll find all you can stand."

"They came in from Hill 473."

"I don't know where people come from, Chief, or even where they're going. You don't mebbe have an idea what unit they was in? Or mebbe some names? Did they have names? Friends of yours?"

"I don't know. Their unit was Battleax. They got shot up by some gunships."

"Oh, them! Yeah, we got some of them, if you really want to see 'em. We got some of them folks out already, last night or this mornin', though, the best of 'em, and the worst. Any of 'em particular you want to see?"

"I don't know," he lied, "don't know this guy's name; but I heard he was with them. . . ."

"You're not with this investigation, then? I thought you was one of them—they been comin' and goin' all day long. Well, it ain't visiting hours, but you can go on back if you want to. The ones that ain't in Intensive Care are in the second ward on the right. And you can look around. Bein' as you're a special friend of mine." He winked and grinned.

Bear paused at the second ward on the right before pushing through the doors. They swung closed like fate behind him.

It was absolutely still in the room. By the door was a desk with no one behind it. There were some two dozen beds ranged down

98

the ward, with crisp sheets laid over them. Blue pajama sleeves extended over some of the sheets, and on some of the pillows heads had been laid, sunburned or tanned or black. On one there was not what could be called a head at all, but a rag doll of bandages. Beside some beds, limbs were hung at odd angles—a bandaged arm cocked up on a wire frame, a leg in traction. The place had the air of a storeroom for spare human parts or a display of artificial limbs.

He walked slowly down the center of the room. His heels squeaked softly on the waxed floor. A few eyes were open, but none followed: most remained closed. He tried to appear to look for someone, and at the same time not to seem interested in anyone at all. He reached the end of the room, turned, and came softly back. He had almost expected to catch eyes covertly tracing his steps. A hate-filled glance would have been deserved. He thought, comfortlessly, that he would even have welcomed it, if it meant someone to whom he could explain, apologize. He turned back to face the room. A few faces were turned toward him now, faces with unoccupied eyes, faces slack-jawed as though they had been dropped on the beds and by chance rolled to a stop facing toward him. He wondered uneasily if they were all dying, these empty faces whose spirits perhaps wandered in witless dreams while the bodies waited glassy-eyed. These were not the men, the reeking, burned, and battered but indeniably human flesh he had torn from the jungle the night before, but something more horrible still, mere vessels waiting for the breath of life to be poured back, or to fail utterly.

"What do you want?" a voice demanded behind him. He had not heard or felt the door swing open, and he started again, as he had in the ER. It was a woman's voice, low but positive, stating and not questioning. Yet it had the liquid hoarseness of a gravel-bedded stream. "What do you want? You aren't supposed to be here."

"I . . . I was looking for someone." She was not, as he had expected from the voice, a middle-aged field-grade career nurse. She was a lieutenant. Her name tag said her name was Porter. He did not know he had seen her before.

She could not place him at first. She felt she had seen his face, but the only scene that came half to mind was a zoo somewhere:

the round face, the great sad eyes, seemed for an odd moment to stare at her from behind a wire screen. "It's not visiting hours," she said. "You can't talk to anyone now."

Although nothing about his face changed describably, the eyes seemed to become limpid with pain. She remembered then—the wild eyes racing over the carnage of the emergency room under the cold sputter of the fluorescent lamps. She had thought for a moment he must be another investigating officer come to badger her charges for statements. She was instantly sorry for the harshness of her tone. She asked, more gently, "Do you know someone here?"

"No." He could not face the admission. He started to go past her to the door. On an impulse he stopped and asked, "There was a soldier with one leg. Is he . . . here?" *Dead*, he might have said.

"Private Patulski? He's still in Intensive Care."

"Then he didn't die." As he pushed quickly out the door, she was going to add, "You can't visit there." But she checked herself, thinking that perhaps she had said enough already. She did not know quite why she thought that. In part she believed he had saved the soldier with one leg. She had seen the wings on Bear's jacket, and she knew that many of the casualties the previous night had been brought in by pilots of other helicopters before the medical evacuation ships came in carrying the dead.

She sat down behind the desk to face the pain- and drug-glazed eyes and wished for a moment she had not sent him away. Dreams of good to be done were easy; but the flesh was harder to face.

The Bear went on back along the corridor, pausing outside doors but not going through them. He was unable to face the empty eyes behind the doors; but he could not bring himself to leave the place. He wandered the empty corridors until he had completely lost himself.

There were voices behind some of the doors he passed. At times he paused to listen, but he did not open the doors. While they were closed the illusion remained that life, and not death, was in progress here.

The hospital was a rambling aggregation of one-room wood frame buildings connected by enclosed walkways that crossed and recrossed in an immense checkerboard. Once he saw a nurse cross on an intersecting corridor far ahead; but when he reached the spot, the cross-hall was also empty. At last he worked his way completely to the back of the complex. The sea, fitful grey and blue as sunlight fell or vanished, was to be seen beyond the windows of the rear corridor, in the intervals between the separate buildings of the wards.

Turning again toward the front of the hospital, Bear was brought up short by a glimpse of a familiar figure coming toward him. It was Captain Martin.

Although he could have given no logical reason, Bear did not want to be seen there by anyone he knew—as if kindness might need to be explained away. He turned quickly down a side corridor. He waited at the next turning to be certain that Martin had gone past. Then he escaped quickly toward the hospital entrance.

Martin was moving slowly. His walk, normally rapid and purposeful, was now the meander of a stream run out onto a delta, its force suddenly gone. In a way it pleased him to wander about these halls, occupied as they were only by echoes of his own movements. They struck him as near kin of his own present condition, a life empty save for the echoes of his acts. For the present the lives of his friends went on behind doors closed to him.

Bear had been sitting by himself at dinner until Covington came in. He had not been the first to the mess hall, nor the last. He had not sat with anyone who was there ahead of him; and, before Covington, no one had come to sit with him. Blood and Atterburn were seated together, a little apart from the other officers then in the mess hall. Bear, for his part, was happy enough with the arrangement. He knew there was no order or plan to separate the four of them from the company: their ill was not contagious. But he was not of a mind, either, to join the conventional round of scatology and carnality that passed for dinner conversation, nor to burden the others with sympathetic silence. Covington, not understanding these grounds for the Bear's own reluctance to join the others, began a loudly incensed harangue about those who were afraid to be seen with people in trouble. Bear shushed him and steered the conversation to the safe subject of Pinky.

101

"She's fine," Covington said. "And speaking of her, let me just look at this letter a sec, okay?" He plunged into his letter, leaving the Bear to watch the top of his head with some amusement at having been rescued from his solitude in this way. Occasionally Covington's face bobbed up to relay a fragment of information.

"Your home life sounds delightful, Cov." Bear smiled. Covington had made him feel better after all.

"Yeah, you ought to get married, Bear. It's really great." This he said without raising his head.

"I believe that's contrary to my nature as a free-ranging creature of the wild."

"We'll see. When we get back to the world I'm going to fix up your free-ranging frame with a nice girl—" He came to a full stop. His face bobbed up and down twice, but he said nothing.

"Well?" Covington was so totally astonished that Bear could not help laughing. "What's your wife up to now?"

"I'm going to have a son!"

This was proclaimed loudly enough that every face in the officers' section of the mess hall turned toward them. Among shouted congratulations, someone called, "How do you know it's going to be a boy?" Under his breath Blood muttered, "If *he* got it, it's likely to be nothing but a squirt of curdled milk!"

"When is he due, Cov?"

Covington counted on his fingers. "June. He'll be three months old before I get to see him! Wow! I wonder who I can get to take standby for me tonight, so I can get up to the MARS station and call her?" When he looked at Bear, his happiness burst instantly, for the Bear's face had gone grey with sorrow: now that he and the others were grounded, there were no gun pilots not on standby. The platoon was already short three officers before the grounding. "I wish I could," Bear said.

"Don't worry about it, Bear. I can call another night. Hey, I tell you what. I want you to be the godfather. Would you do that for us? Pinky would love it, too—I know she would. Here, she asks what kind of cookies you like. She's sending us some." Covington was too overwhelmed by it all to be distracted for long by anyone's sorrow, and his excitement carried the Bear along with it. Covington reached across the table and gripped his friend's arm: "You'll make a classic godfather, Bear. The mustache bristling in all its prickly glory, like porcupines copulating! What the devil are we going to call the little nipper, now? Give me some suggestions: I want to get a letter off to Pinky tonight."

The pierced steel plank of the parking ramp could not completely contain the red Vietnamese clay which crept upward through every hole and joint, covering the steel with a fine dust which now had turned greasy in the evening drizzle. The Bear skated arms-out over the rough surface. He had started out for no place that he could name, but he saw that his skating steps were tending toward the hospital. Perhaps, he reflected, that was only because it was downwind, as cattle stray downwind before a storm. But he could not decide whether this was really the path of least resistance for him. The hospital repelled him, and yet something drove him toward it—the same thing, perhaps, which drove men to kill others they had never met, because to do so was their duty. Duty was a porcupine: it stuck you from whatever side you took it. The one-legged soldier came to his mind. Patulski. It was an easy enough name, for being Polish; but "one-legged soldier" told all the facts of military importance. If the soldier had been Viet Cong, as he should have been, then duty would have been to put him in the condition he now was in, or worse, and it would have been proper to shoot through the trees without stopping to ask his name. But since he was not Viet Cong, duty was to visit him and pray for his recovery. In all this the name somehow became lost, and not only the name, but everything that made him Patulski and not someone else. Duty did not care that it was Patulski who lay on a starched bed with dangling tubes spitting life into his veins and phantom fires roaring through a leg that had become purely imaginary but ached nevertheless. Yet the fact that he now knew the name made the memory of the soldier the more painful for Bear. Even though he knew nothing else of the man, the name invested him with the trappings of humanity, made him more than duty's anonymous object.

The Bear stopped at the end of the ramp and looked up for a long time at the hospital buildings sprawling under the floodlights. Even the outside repelled him.

As he stood there, a helicopter appeared out of the darkness over the ridge, descended like a whirlwind to the pad near the emergency room doors, swung its tail downwind, and settled to rest. On its doors stood the white square enclosing a red cross. Bear hung back, breathless, but no one issued from the swinging doors to carry away wounded men. He saw then that there was no one in the back of the ship. There was not even a crew chief aboard. The blade plopped steadily for a minute as the pilot let the engine cool down at idle, and then there came the dying whistle as the fuel was shut off and the turbine ran down. As the blade slowed, Bear walked down to the ship. He caught the end of the blade as it teetered to a stop.

The pilot, a short, dark-haired, and quick-moving warrant officer, stepped down from the cockpit to assert his authority over the blade; but seeing the wings on Bear's shirt he handed over the hook and watched as Bear dragged the blade back and tied it to the tail skid.

The aircraft commander was coming down the other side of the ship. "Primo, what say we—" He broke off when he saw the Bear. "God damn, Primo, you changed shape on me again! You're getting slick at that." He extended a hand and a quick grin. "Thanks, even if you're not Primo. You're not joining this unit, by any chance?"

Bear shook his head. "I fly with a company down there." He waved toward the far end of the ramp.

"Too bad. As short as we are on crews, I was hoping you were an FNG."

"I haven't been a friendly new guy for a long time."

"Too bad. Too bad. Well, this *is* Primo." The other warrant officer had come back to join them. His name tag said he was Guiterrez. "I thought we had a new pilot, Primo; but it's just a refugee from down the ramp."

"We don't see many of you guys," Guiterrez said. "You ought to come visit."

"Well, he's visiting now, Primo. Just in time for a root beer."

"A what beer?"

"Root beer. We may have places to go yet tonight."

"Couldn't be any worse than last night," Guiterrez answered. "C'mon . . . what's your name?"

"Bear." He was so rarely called anything else, except by Major

104

Hart or sometimes Captain Martin, that he gave it without thinking. "That is, Don."

"Bear, that is Don? What kind of name is that?"

"We can eliminate Polish and Spanish," said the aircraft commander, whose name was Wolcheski. "Scandahoovian, maybe? Leave it to the Swedes to call someone 'Bear.' Well, we're about to have a beer, Bear. Come join us. Do bears drink beers?"

"In fabulous quantities."

"Then it's a good thing I'm not buying. Guiterrez is buying. Thanks, Primo."

"I distinctly didn't hear that part before, *Trung-úy.*"

"Must have been the radio, then, because right when we were on short final I heard a little voice say, 'Primo is buying, Lieutenant.' The voice specified fabulous quantities."

"I'm much obliged to the voice," Bear said.

"Don't mention it," said Lieutenant Wolcheski.

Guiterrez mumbled under his breath.

The Bear turned with relief to an offer of company who would not feel obliged to sympathize. He was normally gregarious as a seal, but among those who knew of his trouble he felt like an iceberg, chilling everyone around him even if he only lurked in his bunk. Talking to Covington would mean sitting in the alert hooch with the rest of the platoon. The movie at the officers' club he had seen years before, and he did not want to sit in the bar, where Blood and Atterburn would be putting a brave face on the situation. But being alone only forced his thoughts back over the same rutted path again and again. He pretended to be lighthearted and followed the two medevac pilots up the hill.

The hospital officers' club was only a room on the end of a two-story officers' quarters. They hung their weapons on pegs beside the door.

"I thought medevac people went unarmed," Bear said.

"The ships do," Guiterrez told him, "and some of the corpsmen do; but the crews don't."

"This one sure as hell don't," Wolcheski said. "A couple months ago one of our ships went down in a PZ, and the crew had to shoot their way through to the friendlies. In the air we are all tender mercy; but on the ground we are some mean sumbitches." He grinned at Bear: "Another illusion crushed?"

"Yes," Bear said. "You should be ashamed."

"I am. No Ba Muoi Ba. American beer is all we've got. But, as my Polish grandmother used to say, 'Bread is better than cake anyway, when you don't have cake.' " Wolcheski helped himself from the untended bar. He handed Bear a beer, but Bear saw that Wolcheski was in fact drinking root beer himself. "Eight hours from bottle to throttle." Wolcheski shrugged apologetically.

"Better take two, Bear," Guiterrez suggested. "Fabulous amounts may take a while, a can at a time."

"Maybe fabulous amounts are better lingered over," Wolcheski said. "Be sociable, Primo, or I won't let you buy next time."

"You couldn't be so cruel."

Wolcheski picked his way around a table full of arguing doctors to where two nurses were sitting in the shadows along the wall. He presented the Bear with the air of a diplomat presenting the President to a girls' school: "Ladies—and I use the term loosely —may I present Mr. Bear. Mr. Bear, Lieutenant Swensen, Lieutenant Porter."

Lieutenant Porter's half-smile might have had recognition in it, or only disinterest. She did not speak. But Lieutenant Swensen asked him, "What kind of name is that . . . Bear?"

"Scandahoovian," Guiterrez said. When Swensen punched him in the arm, he complained, "That's what *he* said," pointing at Wolcheski. "You know these Anglo names all sound alike to me."

"It doesn't say Bear on your shirt," Lieutenant Swensen said. "Why not?"

"I believe 'Bear' is only a temporary appellation," Wolcheski told her. "A *nom de guerre.*"

"A *cri de coeur?*" Coming from Lieutenant Porter, the words stung Bear. He was sure she remembered him then; but what she knew he could not tell. Everyone laughed at her words, except himself. But when Lieutenant Porter saw that he did not, she stopped, too, with a look of sudden confusion. No one else appeared to notice. "I won't listen to any more horrid words in Polish," Swensen said firmly.

"It ain't Polish, dear," Wolcheski told her.

"Hebrew, then. Those Eastern languages all sound the same to me anyway. But if your name is Bear, Mr. Bear, then you are wearing someone else's shirt. Why is that?"

"It keeps his back from the cold," Wolcheski said.

"But doesn't the real owner care?"

"Of course he cares!" Wolcheski sighed. "He doesn't want our friend Bear to have a cold back. That's why he lets him wear the shirt."

"Then he's a very obliging person. Cheers to the owner of the shirt!" Swensen raised her beer can in a toast, and drained it.

"That's not so great," Guiterrez insisted. "There are plenty of spare shirts around."

"Oh, really! Where?" Swensen demanded.

"They throw away hundreds in the ER every day. How about those guys that got medevacked in last night? One of the companies up the ramp brought 'em in. Plenty of spare shirts there. He could have picked up a dozen! I bet you were on one of those flights, eh, Bear?"

Bear saw then that, wherever he turned, there was going to be no escape from that piece of the past. It traveled with him, and he felt as if he somehow radiated news of it to everyone around him. Guiterrez, meaning no more than a jest, had found the tender point at once. Bear turned his head and chewed at his mustache. Swensen, misreading the turn of his head, giggled at his expression. "He's modest. Look, he's blushing! Why, you should be proud, Mr. Bear! You saved some of those boys. Not like our 'professional rescuers' here"—she tapped Wolcheski on the arm —"who only got there in time to bring in the leftovers for graves registration like so many sides of beef!"

"For God's sake, Janet!" Lieutenant Porter murmured, lowering her eyes.

"Oh, you can't get involved with a dead soldier, Alice."

"How about with a live pilot?" Guiterrez suggested, gazing speculatively at the ceiling. Lieutenant Porter's eyes remained lowered.

Wolcheski, sensing the discomfort spreading around him and thinking to change the subject, said quickly, "Our other ship brought in some crewmen and weapons last night. Were those yours, Bear?"

The Bear nodded slowly.

"Then it was quick thinking on your part, if you were flying a

107

gunship. You couldn't get many casualties out on a C-model, with a full crew and guns aboard."

"Oh," Swensen said brightly, "do you fly a gunship? I think it's wonderful, then, that you rescued those boys. Maybe you don't know that some of them were wounded by gunships? All those investigating people were coming and going all day! And Alice was very cross about gunship pilots when she heard it. Now, see there, Alice? They're not all so bad." She flung a friendly arm about the Bear's neck.

"They were hit by guns?" Wolcheski said. His voice trailed like smoke vanishing, and he stared thoughtfully at the root beer can as he rolled it between his palms.

"Boy," Guiterrez said, "wouldn't that make you feel like day-old shit?"

"Yes," Bear agreed, "that's just about it." He thought Lieutenant Porter looked at him more closely as he said it.

"Those things happen," Wolcheski said, now with the tone of one who is positively changing the subject.

"Not if you're careful," Bear said. He felt principle should be defended by someone, even if it had to be himself.

"There's a war on." Wolcheski shrugged. Wolcheski had a fondness for old Army sayings, though he only said them ironically.

"It ain't much," Bear answered, "but it's the only war we got." Wolcheski was surprised that Bear understood the irony—few officers did. "You can't make an omelet without breaking some eggs," Wolcheski tried, with just a touch of a grin.

"There's three ways to do things," Bear responded. "The right way, the wrong way, and the Army way. But," he added, "I don't know that any of them include shooting up your own troops."

"You do your best, and hope it works out," Wolcheski said—not ironically. He found himself liking this strange warrant officer, and he had a feeling that a certain amount of kindness—although he was uncertain what might be looked on as kindness—would be well bestowed at the moment. "You cut corners when you have to, and hope it works out. We had a ship try to get out of a pickup zone with one KIA too many and end up killing eight live guys, besides two dead ones."

"At least he was trying to save someone," Bear said.

"I guess the gunnies are, too."

"I guess that's the theory," Bear said. "I guess."

Bear had been crumpling his beer can. He now pushed it slowly endwise between his hands until they almost met.

"That's great," Guiterrez said. "You could do that with Victor Charley, and save the cost of ammo."

Wolcheski laid a hand on Guiterrez's shoulder.

"Primo, buddy, nobody has called us yet, but we'd better stroll back to the ready room and be ready, for a change."

"Maybe tonight you can bring in some live ones, instead of leaving your work to poor Bear here," Swensen said.

"Swensen, you're sweet but you sure don't know when to keep your mouth shut. Why don't you just walk down with us, huh, and stay out of trouble? But you have to say 'May I?'"

"May I?"

"You bet your sweet—"

"Your sweet censored," she said, putting a hand over his mouth as they all rose. "Bye, Bear. Come again." -

"How come Bear gets left with the new nurse?" Primo asked.

"I don't know, buddy," Wolcheski said, "but there it is."

"How come," Bear asked after they had gone, "Bear does get left with the new nurse?"

"I don't know, but there it is." It might have been only shyness that caused the hesitance now, as it might have been what caused the harsh words of the afternoon. Her voice, though still rough-edged, was gentle. A part of a smile came and went from her lips, as if undecided where to break out next. She had a kindly look about her—not maiden-aunt kindly, but kind-to-all-small-harm-less-things kindly. He suddenly wanted her to like him; but he was afraid to allow it. She would be too easy to like in return. He felt his face about to put on a small-animal expression, and suppressed it ruthlessly.

His face was treacherous: he could not always tell what it was doing. From the fading of her unborn smile he feared the worst. "All right," she said, "I apologize. So now there's that, too."

"Apologize? For what?"

"You know for what."

"If it's for saying bad things about gun pilots, they all deserve worse than anything I've ever heard on a lady's lips." He put all the gun pilots of the world into his remark as a screen between them.

"I'm not apologizing to them," she said. "Only to you. You know it's not for that, so don't ask me to play the fool, please."

He did not feel worth the contrition in her voice, and now wanted only to make her smile again. "Yes, sir!" he answered quickly. "Uh, yes, *ma'am!*" His eyes, when he said it, grew large as saucers, and his mustache bristled. She laughed. He had not willed it, but the walrus had come to his rescue.

He had started doing the walrus to amuse his hooch-mates, but it had taken on a being of its own and sometimes came out when he was not even aware it was in the neighborhood. It seemed to thrive on a woman's laughter.

As for the Bear, if a woman's laughter sent bells ringing through him, well, bells were fine. However, he said sternly as he stroked his mustache back into place, "You shouldn't laugh. I gave myself hemorrhoids, straining to grow this thing. At least have a little respect."

"I am sorry," she said, still laughing.

"You should be. If a woman won't respect a man's mustache, what will she respect?"

"I really am very sorry." Her words were for more than the mustache. Softly, touching his arm, she sounded as if she did mean it. How strange to find her voice, her touch, so soft after all. He sank helplessly in her words, words he did not merit from anyone, and struggled not to forget what had led to his hearing them.

They talked for an hour without ever mentioning the night before, or the afternoon, but those were always at the back of his mind. He did not have to avoid the subjects. They were avoided for him. But when at length she told him that it was nearly time for her to report for duty, she added, as if it were a joke on herself, "I turn back into the wicked stepmother now. You can walk me there, if you're not afraid."

"I am afraid. Not of that," he added.

"I hope not. I wouldn't like to think I was so terrible—so terrible as I was to you this afternoon."

"I've deserved worse."

"Like all gun pilots?"

110

"No—just like me."

"You don't seem to be such a bad person," she said, with a gentle smile that had found where it belonged.

The drizzle had ended for the moment, although the air still tasted of rain. A moon glanced through breaks in clouds fleeting southwestward. It silvered the sea in spreading patterns of moon dapple. They had twenty minutes to spend before she must report to her ward. It was a night for walking on the beach; but the beach was not theirs for walking. At night it spread under the glare of the floodlights above on the cliffs. Within the dark ring behind the floodlights squatted cubical bunkers, great sandbag piles with slits for machine gun barrels. They walked along the cliff behind the line of the bunkers. "At home," he said, "we stacked hay bales that way. And we used to drag out bales to make blockhouses, just like those, to play war. I remember once when a bale broke and buried my brother. We dug him out, but we made him be dead for the rest of the day because his bunker had been bombed. Or we tried to. He thought it was too long to be dead."

"You were wicked even in those days."

She felt him shiver. "Don't tease."

She faced him, and with two fingertips wiped a stray pearl of rain from his cheek. "No, I shouldn't have. You're really not a bad person."

"Good or bad—do they apply in this country? Or can you be a good man when you've killed . . . more than enough men?"

"Does it depend on why you did it?"

"I've been told that."

"It couldn't have been all wickedness," she said, smiling again at the word. "I didn't see that in your eyes."

"A bear's eyes are notoriously deceiving." He took shelter in light words.

"Yours weren't last night, in the emergency room."

He stopped. They had come to the end of the headland, to where the earth fell away at their feet. "Were you there?"

"Yes."

"You understand what it meant—what Wolcheski said, about bringing in my crew, and our guns?"

"It means that you cared enough about . . . what happened

111

. . . to go back." Her soft voice had the rasping catch of a wave dragging down the beach, seaward.

"To go back. And before I went *back*—can you know what happened then, without hating me?"

"I can hate what happened, without hating you. Last night I thought, how terrible it is, that these beautiful young men should . . . But there's nothing in you that could have caused it."

"Something in me agreed to it."

They stood above the cold rolling sea whose waves died on the reef below. A gust whistling in from the sea cut like cold steel across their cheeks. Lieutenant Porter shivered inside her rain jacket. "I hate to be a spoilsport, but I have to go to work," she said. Her breast brushed him as she turned. His hands hovered indecisively about her shoulders, then fell to his sides. "Curse you," he said to his hands.

From the nearest bunker between gusts of wind floated a summery murmur of voices, the words lost on the wind, but the drawl there, thick as molasses on grits. A laugh, and the murmur renewed. Bees in the magnolias, and kudzu vine spilling over the ditch banks; hot sticky afternoons at Fort Rucker, waiting for a helicopter, for his turn to fly. Flying, flying. The blue humidity haze blotted the horizon, while low forested hills rolled below on all sides. They slipped in and out of one-ship clearings, with grass belly-deep to the ship. Flying at night, forty miles out to locate three tiny flare-pots lost in wilderness, land, take off again, and fly home. Flying with the air full of ships all around, snuggling closer, two blade-widths, one and a half, until the IP said, "Let me show you how we did it in Nam," and moved the ship within a half blade-width of the ship bouncing through the turbulent afternoon out the port windscreen. "Now hold it there." Sweating with the strain of holding the other ship so close and yet *away*, right hand in an aching death-grip on a cyclic stick that a finger's touch could move. And blasting home to the tactical base after the mission, skimming the treetops in trail formation like ducks on a string, bursting out suddenly over the open field, lowering the collective pitch, pulling up the nose, and floating, floating out to a soft, satisfying landing. Waiting for Vietnam.

None of them had known what to expect, or what they were expected to expect, of Vietnam, the big field exercise. The tactics instructors, those for the final stage of flight school, were all just back. They were there to tell the new pilots what to expect. Each one told something different. Mr. Jackson, round-faced and balding. He had flown a Piper Cub for a gas-line company, before joining the Army. Every day he made a three-hundred-mile patrol, checking the pipeline. For a change of scenery he went to Vietnam. "What was it like? Glad to have seen it. You boys go have a look now." A ground-school instructor in gunship tactics was going back. "That's where the medals and the combat pay are, and that good flyin'." His voice caressed the words—"goood flyin'"—as his handsome black face glistened under the lights of the classroom. His sports car had the cyclic-stick grip from a gunship mounted on the gearshift lever, with its switches wired to the lights and the horn. The rocket trigger flashed the lights.

The voices in the bunker brought it all back. And gone again before it could be grasped. What had been in their hearts then?

"A penny for your thoughts." She was half sorry she had said it; a startled small creature flashed across his features.

"They're worth less than that," he said. "I was recalling Alabama. Flight school. All those Suthun voices."

"They must have been worth more than a penny. You sound nostalgic."

"I loved flying."

"Loved?"

"I'm grounded."

There seemed to be nothing to say to that.

The two of them stopped beside the emergency room entrance. "I must go . . . Bear." She used the name shyly. "Isn't there another name I can call you?"

"I have been called Don."

"I must go, Don." She added after a moment, "If you come again, I promise to be friendlier."

"A promise like that could seal your fate forever."

She squeezed his hand and vanished through the swinging doors.

6

Major Hart hunched over the table on his elbows with his shoulders up against his ears like the wings of a grounded vulture. He watched his executive officer swirl the dregs of beer around and around the bottom of a glass before putting it aside with a disgusted snort. "Well, Ben?" The major was wishing to find some opening for a kind word, for whatever a kind word might be worth to Martin.

"Thank God Arp isn't here, to tell us about man's plight, tossed like the foam in the beer glass of life."

"I know it looks like a tough spot now," Major Hart said, "but that will change. The disciplinary letter isn't in your file yet; and you know you're going to get a good efficiency report as my XO. In fact, I've been thinking of putting in a special OER on you anyway, because quite frankly you are one of the best young officers I've seen."

Martin shook his head. "Aside from what it would do to *your* career, you know it can't work. You submit a special report on me at the same time the CG gives me a reprimand? The battalion commander would have to endorse that report of yours. Whose line is he going to follow?"

"Ben, by God, something is going to work! You're too good a man to . . ." What Martin was too good a man to do the major did not say, perhaps from that intuitive feeling, which in him never quite became a superstition, that to say the thing might tend to bring it about. Although Major Hart believed in the abstract rightness of everything he had said, he felt less hope than he professed. He had tried to take the issue directly to the general, but had been shunted to the chief of staff, who talked wary circles around the incident. "Wait until the investigation report comes in. We have to have the facts to go on, Major. The general is very concerned about this matter: very concerned." So Major Hart avoided any concrete reference to possible outcomes. But Martin's grim determination to stand up to whatever came, and damn it all, did not hide his inner turmoil from the major, who had all day to watch him across the width of their tiny office.

"You take it too much to heart, Ben," the major said. "You need to be a little more like Captain Blood." Before the objection in Martin's face could be formed into words, Major Hart raised a hand and went on, "Sometimes if you act as if there's only one thing in your head, people assume it's there because there's no other possibility. If Captain Blood insists often enough that he's being treated unjustly, well, someone's going to believe that he is. I'm not saying you have to go as far as he does," he added, seeing the slow shake of Martin's head.

"The only thing is, whatever happens to me is my own fault."

"Ah, if everybody suffered the results of all his own choices, Ben . . ."

"Yes?"

Major Hart this time shook his head sadly, as if the result would not bear contemplation.

"If you don't want to suffer the result of your own choice," Martin advised, "you'll take the chief of staff's hint and get rid of me yourself."

"Nonsense! You may think I'm keeping you out of some sense of loyalty, but that's sentimental humbug. I'm only doing it because it *looks* like that's the reason. The real reason is that the general admires loyalty to subordinates, even if he doesn't admire the subordinates. It's not costing me anything."

"You almost made that sound reasonable," Martin said dryly.

"Thank you, Ben. But somehow I have the feeling this is all going to turn out for the best."

Martin went back to swishing the remains of his beer. "The

115

question is, for whom?" He thought of broken soldiers being dropped like fallen logs into the back of his helicopter.

The struggle the major sometimes surprised in Martin's eyes upon looking up quickly from the papers on his desk was fiercer than the old man knew. Martin had always wanted to be a soldier. He could have been anything, and knew it, but he did not want to be anything. He wanted to be a soldier. Soldiering was a hard life, when it was real soldiering. He knew that. His father was a brigadier, dead in Korea, not of wounds but pneumonia. Some who knew Martin would have said that was the reason he wanted to be a soldier—to meet the worst head-on, and not flinch. In some part they were right. But Martin did not have a Marine mentality. Up the hill into the teeth of the guns was not for him if there was a better way. God gave man brains as well as guts, and gave them both for use. There were softer reasons that weighed more heavily with Martin, although he did not speak of them. If his reasons for being a soldier were all boiled down into one image, it would have been West Point on a clear autumn evening as the flag was struck and the bugle played "To the Colors." God gave man heart, too. It was not that Martin loved ceremony. Forms long empty were less than nothing to him. He had incurred the deep suspicion of at least one colonel by suggesting that the Red Chinese army had done a good thing if it had really abolished all badges of rank. But there were traditions, too, that grew brighter with use. And there was comradeship. It was a word he never used, for many in his society had thrown it away. But the thing itself hung on here and there. Wherever men banded together in the face of duress and danger (even self-imposed, as duress and danger often are) there it existed still, although unmentioned because the word was in disrepute; but except for such odd sorts as these, it was hardly to be found in that part of the population which had passed the age of majority. In the military it still flourished unnoticed.

Martin wanted to be a soldier for those reasons, and others like them that he was equally unwilling to name. His inability to think yet of any other life led him back again and again over Blood's suggestions: there were ways out of this, if he would look for them. During this time Martin lived among haunting dreams, for it was still possible to believe that Blood might be right. Yet

116

Martin was determined to face the wrong he had done, for that was the only way to preserve what he valued. To be what an officer and a gentleman should be was more important than to be an officer and a gentleman. But it was a hard position to hold against the assaults of rationalization. It was to cut off his own escape that Martin had admitted full responsibility for the accident. But he still caught something within himself wondering at times if there was not reason to hope. He was forced to struggle against hope, for if there was hope, there was reason to help hope along; and that was the harder struggle. And sometimes, as he sat at his desk nodding over reports or as he lay in bed listening to the ships with predawn missions running up on the ramp, there came to him like a glimpse of salvation that always faded before his eyes could take it in, the dream: it has not happened—soon I will wake.

Martin considered himself lucky in one way: he still had duties to perform. The others had not even that consolation and were reduced to fluttering about the edges of the company either hoping to be unseen or like the ancient mariner demanding the ear of all who could be stopped to listen.

Blood was still platoon commander for ground purposes, but his ground duties were few. Nevertheless, he adopted the pretense that it was a good thing that he had some time on the ground for once, to catch up on the many things that demanded his attention. He elaborated this thesis at great length for the major, the first sergeant, Lieutenant Rauch and the Operations sergeant, Mr. Rowland the supply officer, and his own platoon sergeant. Sergeant Magruder had successfully managed the enlisted men and the equipment of the platoon without the help of the platoon commander under both Captain Blood and Captain Martin, and under Captain Stoddard before them. Blood's eye over his shoulder now had him so bedeviled that he swore to the first sergeant he would pitch Blood over the cliff into the sea the next time he came down to the pits to tell the crews how to rearm a gunship. "We got only so much time in a day, Top; and there ain't much of it put aside for listenin' to pep talks on how to cut down our turnaround time. We spend more time listenin' to that these days than we do gettin' the rounds in the ships! And maintenance! My God! Let a ship be on the ground ten minutes, and here he comes with his clipboard, wantin' the windscreens waxed, wantin' a light bulb changed, not because it's out but because it's too dim, wantin' the wolf heads touched up, for Chrissake, in case the general happens to see one of our ships on the ground somewhere! As if nobody had any more to do than he does himself. Christ, if the general don't get him off the ground, and off my back, I'm goin' to shoot myself in the foot like that gunner over at the Mustangs last month! Only I'd be afraid he'd end up at the hospital, tellin' the docs how to cut my turnaround time there, too!"

If, in this estimate of how Captain Blood spent his days, Sergeant Magruder failed to give credit for the time Blood put into convincing the world that grounding him was a foul injustice, the sergeant was right in his complaint that Blood stalked the ramp making work where none had been before. On the third afternoon they were grounded, Blood hailed the Bear crossing the ramp. "Now, how come it is that you're leaving the company area so much? Every time I see you, you're off down the ramp. What is it down there that attracts you? I wish I was a young officer with nothing to do but run off somewhere and diddle myself. If nothing else I can get you a detail of men to refill our revetments; some of these barrels are leaking sand."

Sergeant Magruder, whom Blood had been dragging along to inspect the ships on the line, quickly put a stop to that with "I don't know what you'll do for men, sir. We ain't got an enlisted man that's not flyin'. And you know Major Hart wants all details sent through the first sergeant."

"Yes, of course I know it. Well, where is it that you're going, Mr. Bear?" This combination of the Bear's nickname and the proper military form of address to a warrant officer was ridiculous, and was meant to be.

"I was going up to the hospital, sir."

"The hospital! What in hell for?"

"Well . . . there are some people up there we know."

"There's nobody from the company there. . . . You don't mean the troops from Battleax? Oh no you don't! You're not to leave the company area, and that's an order!"

The order was short-lived. Blood broke into Major Hart's of-

118

fice with the haste of one who has just uncovered quicksand beneath the foundations of his house. "It's that damn fool of a bug-eyed warrant officer, Major! He's been running off to visit the troops we medevacked to the hospital!"

The major did not immediately see what harm that might cause.

"Why, damn it, sir! There's an investigation on! If that infantry lieutenant colonel finds out that one of our pilots is hanging around there to see those troops, what can he think but that someone has a guilty conscience? How will that reflect on the rest of us? I told him not to leave the area. But God knows how much trouble he's caused already!"

"You know, of course, that I went to visit them myself two days ago?" Major Hart said quietly.

Martin, listening in a quiet rage from his side of the office, was as surprised to hear this as was Blood himself.

"That's a different thing," Blood said at last. "As company commander you've got a duty, of course, when an incident happens. . . ."

"I think, Captain Blood," the major said, as close to openly angry as Martin had ever seen him, "that if one of your officers wants to visit those men, we should just let him do it. I don't think that's doing any harm."

After Blood had left, Martin said, "I didn't know you had gone to see the men, sir."

"Now, that's strange, Ben. I knew *you* had. Who'd think an old codger like me would know more than you sharp young officers?" He put on his best paternal smile and seemed unusually pleased with himself the rest of the afternoon.

Finding the ward silent, the Bear turned to step back out into the hall, but a voice from the far end of the ward turned him back. Its rattling hollowness was in the silence so like a voice from a graveyard that it made his mustache bristle although it had only wished him a Merry Christmas.

"There's nobody here to greet visitors," the soldier rasped. He spoke with broken pauses, as if the words tore at his throat. "In fact, it seems sometimes like . . . there's nobody here but me." Walking to the back, Bear saw that the one who had spoken was a

119

red-haired boyish soldier he had seen here before, but always asleep. His open pajama top showed a dressing about the chest. "Well," the soldier said in some surprise, "I didn't expect to . . . see you again, sir."

"You remember me?"

"Oh, yes, sir. I couldn't hardly forget."

"No, I don't guess you could."

"Not after the way Lieutenant Porter . . . run you out of here . . . the other day. Was it yesterday? I lose track."

He did not remember the attack, then.

"Longer than that."

"Longer than that. It's not like . . . being out in the boonies. There, you forget what day it is . . . but at least you know . . . when it's day or night. I guess they had me out for a while . . . when I came in here. I won't forget . . . seeing Lieutenant Porter run you out, though. *Chieu hoi!* I'm glad it was you instead of me. But she's really pretty nice. I wish they hadn't . . . sent her away."

"Did they?"

"To another ward. You never came back . . . when she was on . . . did you?"

"No." Not because he had not wanted to see her. Perhaps because he *had* wanted to.

"She talked to me for a while . . . that night . . . when she came back on . . . 'cause I didn't feel like sleeping. You ought to talk to her again."

"I guess I should."

"She's number one." The effort of so much talk seemed to exhaust him. He shrank back on the pillow gasping, but his eyes remained on the Bear's face. "Didn't I see you someplace before . . . before that? I know! You were flying the medevac!" He gasped for air again. "Damn! I'd buy you a beer, sir . . . if there was one to be had . . . in this place."

"I'd buy *you* one. It's the least I could do."

"Oh, Jesus, no! You saved my rear! After the gunships came over . . ." He stopped there, rasping air into his lungs.

"What?" Bear asked, found himself asking without volition. "When the guns came over . . . ?"

The soldier shuddered visibly. "I dreamed about it. That's kind

120

of how it was . . . like a dream. Not even a real dream . . . like
a dream you see . . . in a horror movie. Where they run and run
. . . and never get anywhere . . . and they don't know what
they're running from. I never had that kind of dream before.
That's . . . kind of how it was. I was supposed to be diggin' in
. . . for the night. With Lewis—that was my buddy. We had a
two-man foxhole. But I was up the hill . . . taking a whiz. When
the choppers went over—passed on by us—I heard Lewis cuss
. . . 'cause there wouldn't be any chopper . . . with hot chow
and beer . . . 'cause we were so far out in the boonies. And then
they come back. You know how they sound . . . when you can
feel them coming . . . all the way through your guts? I felt them,
way off someplace . . . but coming closer. And then all of a
sudden . . . a big round went off . . . right up at the top of the
hill . . . and somebody yells, *'Incoming'* . . . and I hauled ass
for the foxhole . . . but I tripped over something. I got up to
run again . . . and when I come up . . . I saw Lewis sitting
there looking dumb . . . so I shoved him in the hole. I didn't
know where the fire was from. I thought it was just Charley . . .
potting a few mortar rounds at us again . . . until I heard the
guns. You ever heard one of them . . . the kind they have on
gunships?''

Bear nodded, biting at his mustache.

"That's what I dreamed. The guys shouting for medics . . .
and Lewis lying there looking silly . . . in the mud. I didn't even
know he was hit . . . until they come around collecting casualties. And that sound coming down on us . . . coming right overhead . . . and you couldn't see anything but treetops. It was like
. . . something up there hated us. And then the tracers came
down . . . through the canopy . . . streams of them, bushels
of them. I jumped for the foxhole . . . I guess I had been standing there . . . kind of dumb, like I'd never seen incoming . . .
when the tracers walked all around me . . . and I got hit. I
remember lying there . . . with Lewis . . . wondering what the
hell. I still didn't know what it was . . . until I heard somebody
up the hill . . . holler that it was gunships . . . for somebody
to get on the horn . . . and report we were being hit by gunships. Then I heard them coming back . . . and I just shriveled

up and prayed. I dreamed that—the waiting and the sound. I hope to God . . . I never do again!"

Bear nodded again, remembering the evil voice of the guns. The soldier closed his eyes and gasped.

"How are you now?" Bear asked. It was a helpless silly question, of no use to anyone, but the soldier answered, sounding pleased: "Every day I'm getting better. That's what this hospital . . . is here for. Pretty soon . . . I'm going to take up my bed and walk. It doesn't hurt now . . . just a little hard to breathe. It must be this bandage . . . they've got me in. Right at first . . . it was like a hot poker . . . had been laid across my ribs. That sucker almost missed me . . . just one bullet . . . took a piece out of a rib. Half an inch over . . . and he'd have missed me clean."

"And how's Lewis?"

"He died." He said after a moment, "No reason for you . . . to trouble over it, sir. It's not your fault. It wouldn't have done any good . . . to get him here sooner. He was dead . . . before the medic got to us. I said to him . . . 'Lewis, buddy, I'm hit. . . . How you doin'?' . . . but he didn't answer. We carried him up . . . in his poncho. He was the third buddy . . . I've had killed out of my foxhole . . . in seven months. Probably a good thing I got it too . . . this time . . . or I'd have been going it alone anyway. People already were kidding Lewis . . . you know?—'bad luck to be with McWade.' Ah! Bad luck! There's not one of them . . . wouldn't trade with me today. A few days ago I had five months to do . . . and now I'm short."

"But they wouldn't trade places with Lewis."

"Well . . . at least they'll wait their turns . . . for *that*, sir. No rush." His arms relaxed over the blanket, and he lay dozing. "Merry Christmas, McWade," Bear said under his breath. He tiptoed out.

"Merry Christmas, Bear!" It was Carter. He went bursting through the hooches like a monsoon wind, sweeping officers before him. "You coming to the Christmas Eve party up at the club?"

The Bear was lying on his bunk studying the curve of his mosquito net overhead. "I don't think so, Carter. Not right now."

"Not right now? Does that mean, 'I'll be there for sure later'?"

"Maybe I'll come later."

"Maybe! Look, Bear, you don't have to be a hermit, just because you're grounded. We still love you! Come on!" When the Bear didn't move, he added coaxingly, "Tonight we're all equals anyway, because with the truce tomorrow we're *all* grounded. You can be a hermit again the day after. Starting tomorrow night."

"The guns are on standby tonight," Bear said. "Cov won't be at the party."

"Okay, you're right. And not everybody will be sitting around to open presents tomorrow. I'm flying myself. But why take that out on your poor tired bod? Flying or no, it's the season for mellowness and good cheer and good will to men."

"And peace on earth."

"And absolutely peace on earth! Listen!" He cupped a hand behind one ear and struck a pose of absurd expectancy.

"I don't hear anything," Bear said.

"That's it! Peace on earth! Divarty shut down at sunset. That's peace you hear out there, Bear, or don't hear. All over the land, nobody dying. Not a single poor soul for you to worry about. Now, come on, Bear—come help us be happy."

"After a while, Carter. I'll come up later."

"Ah, Bear, you're a hard man! Promise you'll come?"

"Maybe."

"Wonderful! Now I've got to go before I catch your enthusiasm." Carter bounded out the other door. Bear heard him calling to the other slick pilots as he hurried to catch up.

When he could no longer hear their voices, Bear went out the opposite door. He really did not want to join their party. Or perhaps more accurately, he did not think he should want to, and did not think his company would be of much cheer to them. He wandered along the edge of the cliff staring off into the emptiness where the ocean rolled listlessly.

There *was* a great silence, all around. Now that he listened for it, it astonished him. Nowhere was there a roll of artillery. No jets rumbled, over the ridge of the main airfield. No helicopter beat the night sky. Against that great silence smaller sounds could be heard, sounds that ordinarily would have been lost—the sounds of human voices. Across the ramp in the enlisted men's area there was laughter. A snatch of song floated down from somewhere up on the ridge. Far down the ramp from the direction of the club there was a single distant burst of happy noise, as if a door had opened and closed on a room where a party was in progress. Only the sea kept on in its old pattern.

Suddenly he was more lonely than he could stand.

"I wasn't going to come."

"That's certainly a complimentary thing to say."

"Not because I didn't want to see you. More because I did."

"I understand perfectly." She said this ironically, as if to show that she didn't understand at all; but he had the feeling that she did understand perfectly.

They stood in the darkness outside her hooch above the cliffs. The only sound was the slack surf washing at the reef below.

"There's a Christmas party up at the officers' club. Would you like to go?"

"I'd like to be with you. But I go on duty in an hour. And I don't feel very Christmasy, somehow."

"Christmas does need snow."

"Not for a California girl. Christmas needs family and friends. I'm glad you came along."

"Are you from a big family?"

"Four sisters."

"That'll be tough for me to do." He tried putting on a sisterly face, but he couldn't make it work. "Nope, that isn't it. Can you make do with one friendly soldier?"

"A friendly soldier is what I was most hoping for."

"You came to the right country."

A faint glow spread about them. He barely noticed it at first; but her fine face, lean and beautiful, came slowly out of the darkness, seemed itself to glow, to stand out from the surrounding night. She was wearing jungle fatigues, as he was, and he could hardly see her in the darkness, except for her face and her short pale hair. For an instant there came to his mind the faces in the darkness of Hill 473. Then they were gone.

Some sound caught his attention. Turning, he saw that the light was a distant flare, so far off that the battery that fired it had been almost unheard. Its single star hung alone in the sky, flickering slowly for uncounted time.

"A star in the east," she said. "We could follow it."

"If He's come back, He's got a big job ahead of Him." The light went out. "There, it's gone."

"Let's go see."

She took his hand, led him along the rocky cliff edge.

Near the end of the cliffs, beyond the bunkers and the floodlit beach, the darkened shape of the graves registration hooch squatted at the very top of the rock.

"No business for them tonight."

She seemed to know whom he meant, although he did not look up at the building. "No business for any of us," she said.

"I could probably stir some up for you, if I was flying."

"Stop it."

"You're right. I'm just trying to get you to feel sorry for me."

"No, you're trying to feel sorry for yourself. I *do* feel sorry for you. But that's different."

"I don't want you to feel sorry for me."

"Why not? Something bad happened to you that you don't deserve."

"Something bad didn't happen to me. Something bad happened to McWade, and the rest of them. I'm okay."

"I hope you are." She took his arm. Her grip was firm.

"I was in to see some of them, this afternoon. When you weren't there. I talked to McWade."

"How was he?"

"I don't know. How can *I* tell? I wanted to ask you."

"Is that why you came to see me?"

"No."

"McWade will be all right."

"He sounded terrible. Like he was drowning."

"He has some fluid in one lung. He'll be all right."

"Is it okay if I feel sorry for him?"

"I hope you do. *I* do."

"I don't see how you can feel sorry for both of us. It isn't fair to McWade."

"Stop it."

"You were a lot easier to talk to the other night."

125

"So were you."

"I never was good at talking to girls."

"You were the other night."

"Was I? I must have been in shock."

"It affects some people that way—makes them suave and debonair. That's one of the first things they teach in nurses' training."

"Don't tease the troops, Lieutenant."

"Teasing is the conversative course of treatment for absurd self-pity."

"And if it doesn't work?"

"Ve haff means." As she said this she stroked her upper lip with the thumb and forefinger of one hand, as if stroking a mustache. "Ve haff means."

He could not help smiling. "I won't make you resort to heroic measures."

"Darn! Just when we were getting to the fun part!" Her eyes were laughing at him.

"In that case," he said, "maybe heroic measures are called for. How do they work?"

Her lips grazed his cheek.

"That's it?"

"Moderate dosages, to begin with."

"I think they could be addictive."

"Trust me."

He turned to face her, took her arms in his hands. "Alice," he said seriously, "this conversation has got to stop. You're getting all the good lines."

Then they were both laughing.

A moment later he was kissing her earnestly. She returned the kiss, but only for a moment. She stepped back, and her eyes searched his.

"It's all right," he said. "I understand that you're only acting in a professional capacity."

"Am I?" she whispered. "That *could* be addictive."

They stood looking at one another for a long time. He broke first. "Merry Christmas, Lieutenant Porter."

"Alice. I won't be kissed by anyone who calls me Lieutenant Porter."

"Merry Christmas, Alice. I wish I had a gift to give you."

"It's a gift just to have you here, on Christmas Eve with no guns firing."

"You don't even know me."

"I know your heart."

"Nurses' training?"

"Intuition."

"If you do, I'm definitely in trouble."

"Pretending to be wicked won't save you." She kissed him lightly, but dodged anything more serious. She took his hand and started along the cliffs again. "Now let's stop talking about sad things. There are enough good things in the world."

"All right. What do you want to talk about?"

"Tell me about flying. Flight school. You were nostalgic for Alabama. That must have been a good thing."

"Flying." He pondered. "Yes, that's a good thing: good flying is. Old Tate would never forgive me if I denied it."

"Old Tate?"

"He was my first instructor. In Texas, not Alabama. I never had another one like him; but he was enough. More than any pilot deserves."

"*Was* he old? I thought all pilots were young and bold."

"As they say in the Army, 'There are old pilots, and there are bold pilots; but there are no old, bold pilots.' I don't know how old he was. He was old for what he was doing. Or maybe he only looked old. Old Tate was a cowboy who happened to be one of the great helicopter pilots of the world. He looked like a fence post with a couple of knots for eyes, and was about that lean and weathered and hard. He was a civilian instructor, not a soldier. Always wore a cowboy hat, indoors and out, except when he was flying—he hated the Army for making him wear a helmet even then. He looked seventy, but I don't guess they'd have hired him if he was. Or maybe he never had a birth certificate and didn't even know his age. Or maybe his first name really was 'Old'—I don't know. That's what everyone called him—not 'Tate,' but 'Old Tate.' Even to his face: 'Hello, Old Tate, how you doin' today?'

"Old Tate had been a fixed-wing pilot before he took up helicopters, and he'd flown every aircraft known to humankind. Show him a picture of a Fokker trimotor, and he'd say, 'Hell, I flew one of them in Bolivia back in thirty-two.' And he wasn't just blowing smoke. He remembered the numbers. 'That ship was the meanest cuss to fly that ever was put together in sheer spite!' he'd say. 'Stalled at sixty-three knots, and wouldn't fly more than sixty-four.' And you'd look it up in some book nobody had opened for thirty years, and the old coot would be right!

"Mostly, old fixed-wing pilots don't take well to rotary wing. They can't think in three dimensions, and slow speeds scare them. But Old Tate could think in every dimension at once, and nothing scared him as long as he could reach the controls."

"You sound like you loved flying with him."

"The first two weeks, he had me scared to death."

"How could that be?"

"You have to understand what it's like to fly a helicopter. I suppose it was helicopters that had me going, and not just Old Tate.

"The way you start out learning to fly a helicopter is one control at a time. There are three—four, counting the throttle, which pretty much takes care of itself on a Huey, but didn't on the trainers. Four controls: collective pitch, for up and down, in your left hand; cyclic pitch, for forward, backward, and sideways, in your right hand; two pedals for turning the nose left or right; and by then the average pilot has run out of appendages and still has the throttle left over. So they put a twist grip on the collective, and you twist that with your left hand to control the power. There are a few other things, of course, like microphone switches and trim buttons, and, on a gunship, triggers for the guns and the rockets. But not so many you can't work them with one finger or another. The things you might need in a hurry have to be on the cyclic or the collective, where you can reach them without letting go of the controls, because a helicopter isn't like an airplane. An airplane will fly itself, if you just let it alone. A helicopter you have to actually hold right side up.

"The hard part is that all the flight controls are interconnected. The ship is just dangling under the disc of this whirling blade, and it drags along in whatever direction the disc is tipped. The cyclic stick controls the tilt of the disc. But when you tilt the disc, some of the lift that was holding you up goes into dragging you along, so you have to add more power unless you're willing to lose altitude. So you pull in more collective pitch—the collective stick is the up and down control. But adding more lift with the collective requires you to have more power, or the blade will slow down, so you have to roll on some throttle at the same time. But rolling on throttle increases the torque being applied to the blade —that's what keeps the blade from slowing down—and so up pops Isaac Newton and informs you that the blade is going to twist the engine just as hard as the engine is twisting the blade— see Newton's second law—and since the engine is attached to the fuselage, if you don't do something quick the ship will be spinning just as fast as the blade is. So to keep the nose pointing straight ahead you add a little left pedal, which increases the pitch of the tail rotor that pushes the tail to the right and keeps the blade from spinning the whole ship. But having the tail rotor push the tail around takes power, too—there's no free lunch— and takes power from the main blade unless you add still more throttle . . ." Bear halted, panting as if out of breath. "And so on. Getting it all together is complicated."

"How do you ever do it?"

"You don't think about it. It's like riding a bicycle. You just do it. Of course, right at first you *don't* just do it. In fact, you'd swear it can't be done by any single human being. That's where Old Tate comes in.

"You learn to fly a helicopter by trying one control at a time. Pedals first. Old Tate gets you out in a big open field with plenty of room all around and sets up at a three-foot hover with the nose pointing at a tree over yonder. Then he says, 'Okay, I'm going to hover this thing, but you have to keep the nose pointed at the tree. That's all. Feet on the pedals, and keep off the other controls so we don't die in this thing.' Well, that sounds easy. So you get on the pedals, and Old Tate gets off them, and for about three seconds everything is dandy. And then the nose starts to turn to the right, for no reason at all. You push in a little left pedal—what seems like a little—and the nose shoots to the left, and Old Tate's trying to bring in enough throttle to keep the ship from sinking through the surface of the earth, and about that time you poke the right pedal, and the ship jumps fifteen feet in the air, spinning at the same time, and Old Tate hollers, 'I've got it, dang it, before you kill us!' "

"It sounds like as much his fault as yours."

"It's just that two guys can't fly a helicopter. But it'd be even worse if he gave you all the controls at once, right off the start. You'd die in fifteen seconds. Actually, it's *not* as much his fault, because after about, say, three hours, you *can* actually keep the nose pointed more or less in one direction, with Old Tate on the other controls. You can do it quicker with Old Tate than with most instructors, because Old Tate is as smooth as a spanked baby's behind.

"After those three hours he gives you the collective, and you go through the same thing, in the vertical instead of the horizontal, for a few hours more.

"Eventually, you get to the place where you can almost control the whole ship, most of the time, as long as you don't need any major power changes. For taking off or landing, though, you do need major power changes. As the Marines say, 'The difficult we do at once; the impossible takes a little longer.' I remember learning to land the ship. Along about the time I should be ready to solo, I got blocked. I would set up a beautiful approach—fly level until the landing pad comes down to the right spot on the windscreen, adjust power, nose up to slow the ship, just hold it and let it fly down the path to the landing pad—and at about forty feet, the ship would start to slide off to the right. Bring it back, and it would slide off to the left. But it wouldn't go down. Push down the collective, and it would bounce right back up. You've seen the ads on TV with the 'invisible shield'? That's how it was: no human force on earth could make that damn ship fly through the invisible shield protecting that landing pad!

"Old Tate would get real impatient. He didn't use profanity; but he did express impatience rather well. He would say, 'Dang it! Why don't you get on down there? You see a snake there, or sumthin'?' But he wouldn't help. Because there is no help. Sometimes you'd swear there was someone else on the controls, blocking every move you tried to make. You look over there, and there's Old Tate, leaning back with his arms folded, grinning like a possum. He must have seen this a thousand times. And you'd know that there was nothing keeping that ship in the air but you, yourself; and you still couldn't get it on the ground."

"How did you get over that?"

"Grace."

"Grace?"

"One day, there you are fighting that damn ship, trying to poke it through that invisible dome over your landing pad, and all of a sudden the dome isn't there. She just flies on down, sweet as can be.

" 'And that,' says Old Tate, 'is when you're a helicopter pilot. Not by works; by the grace of God.'

"Old Tate knew how far I still had to go then. I didn't. But he had me convinced I was going to make it."

"He sounds like a character."

"He was a lovely man. He convinced me I could fly. 'By God, boy, you are sumthin'!' he'd say. 'All the equipment to make a first-rate pilot, packed in this silly-lookin' carton! It's like findin' a damn movie star in a box labeled *dwarf*.' "

"Whatever he was, he wasn't very kind!"

"He was a grand gentleman. He'd never say anything he thought would hurt you—not hurt you when you'd thought about it. He didn't mind letting you know how screwed up he thought you were at any given moment, but he was gentle of what counted. And by God he convinced me I could fly! I'd never been especially good at anything before that. Raised a little hell, took what came. I've got a brother—"

"The one who didn't want to play dead in the hay bales?"

"That one. He's a genius. Everybody loves him. He went off to Stanford. Haven't heard from him for months—he's against the war now. Well, who isn't? I'd sure as hell quit if Charley would! But when he went to Stanford, I decided to go into the Army. They gave me some tests to see what I was good for. When I qualified for flight school, I think everybody really figured they got the wrong scores under my name, and I'd be out again soon enough.

"Instead, Old Tate made me a pilot. He had me at the head of my flight class in no time. When we moved on to Alabama for the advanced stages, it sort of stuck with me. I guess everybody had got used to me as the ace pilot by then. I don't think I ever flew as well as I did for Old Tate, though.

" 'Good flyin' is important,' Old Tate would say. 'Flyin' right is like livin' right. You don't do it because it's fun—though it is—

and you don't do it because it's healthful—though it surely is that, or a lot more so than bad flyin'. You do it 'cause anything less would be a cheat on your Creator, who gave you the gift to do it right. You got that?"

"That was Old Tate's sermon: the only one he had." Bear shook his head in sad admiration. "I loved the old coot. I hope he's got students worth his while."

"It sounds as if he had one, at least."

Bear blushed. "I didn't mean to brag quite so much."

"I don't think it was bragging, except on your teacher. And everyone who's good at something should brag on his teacher."

"Old Tate was one to brag on." He sighed. "I wonder what he'd think of it all."

"Of what?"

"The killing; the dying. I don't think he was much in favor of either of those; though we never talked about it."

"No one's in favor of those."

"Not of dying."

"Surely no one likes killing."

"Some do. Handy, my door gunner. If Handy gets a VC in the open, he'll chase him across the paddy with a trail of bullets, and get him right at the end."

She shook her head. "I can't imagine it."

"Don't try."

They had come eastward to the end of the cliff, and then north where it skirted the parking ramp of Bear's company. The blades of the helicopters angled up from the revetments in stiff Roman salute. A guard, passing among the revetments, did not see the two of them.

Below the ramp, out of sight of the hooches, a road had been graded down the low cliffs to the beach. A roll of concertina wire followed the edge of the cliffs, connecting to the bunkers farther up; but the road was left open. At its foot there was only a short strip of beach between two coral reefs, where crew members could swim when not on duty. Alice turned down the road.

Bear poked at the concertina with one foot as they passed, curious at its misshapen bulk. A vine had climbed into it. The vine wound comfortably through the coils, issuing leaves among the thorns of steel.

132

"There's your truce," Bear said. "Peace is having friends with weapons."

"You're a wicked cynic."

"It's an occupational hazard: it comes from killing people." He wished he had not said so much. He had forgotten himself, talking about flight school. Now he was back.

They stood at the shoreline in the darkness. The waves were low and slack. There was no star.

"If you waded out," he said, "you'd find nothing but water from here to San Francisco—nothing but that and the horizon. And that's nothing at all." What change could it work, a mere curve of the sea, a mere nothing at all? How could it make a difference in good and bad? "What's to keep the war from just walking down the beach some night, and walking up again in California?"

"War isn't carried by water," she said. "The only carrier is the human heart." She laughed, embarrassed. "They teach that in nurses' training, too."

"I wonder if it's in mine," he said.

Some piece of wavedrift bobbed in the broken water, alternately surging landward and being dragged back. Happiness was like that, he thought; washing in and out, but never quite making shore.

"We've got to do something about the Bear," Carter said. "He's not even going to show for the Christmas Eve party."

"Why not shoot him and put him out of his misery?" Atterburn suggested.

"Shut up, Atterburn. It's just not like old times without the Bear," Carter said to the rest of those at the table. He pointedly turned his chair away from Atterburn. "We need to think of some way to cheer him up."

Atterburn didn't notice Carter's hint. "If he's sorry, it's his own fault," he insisted crossly. Atterburn was just on the edge of being drunk, and it made him feel like a man. He was not old enough to drink back in the world.

"He needs to fly," Carlisle said. "He'll rust away, sitting on the ground."

"We'd *all* still be flying, if it wasn't for him," Atterburn said.

133

"Atterburn," Carter suggested, "why don't you go have Griggs teach you how to do a carrier landing?"

"What's that?"

"If you weren't so new in country, you'd know. Go ask Griggs."

Those of them who had been there in the early days—back when the Marines still inhabited part of Ky Ha—had all been initiated into carrier landings. Carrier landings were a party game in which a body in a state of drunkenness sufficient to convince it that it could fly was coaxed into taking a belly-slide down a series of beer-slicked table tops. Griggs, who was much like a Marine himself, had taken it on himself to pass on the art to the next generation of helicopter pilots.

"Maybe he'll overshoot and break his neck," someone suggested hopefully.

"You can never count on Atterburn to do the right thing," Carlisle muttered. He returned to Carter's subject: "The Bear is about to go nuts doing nothing. But I don't see what's to be done about it. He can't fly until that investigation board clears him for it."

"Maybe," Carter said thoughtfully.

"What do you mean, maybe?"

"Maybe he could if he was somebody else."

"If I was the general, I could let him fly. But I'm not. You're too deep for me, Carter."

"Think about it, T. H. You and I are flying the goody run tomorrow with Christmas dinner for our starving troops in the field. Right?"

"Sure."

"Well, then it's easy. You've always wanted the day off anyway."

Carlisle frowned. "I see what you mean. But what if you go down? If it's me that's killed on the ship, then the me back here will have to be the Bear for the rest of my life."

"It'd be a big step up, I admit, but . . ."

"I don't think I could hack it." Carlisle tried rolling his eyes, but they were too small to have much effect, and his mustache would not bristle.

"It's a beginning," Carter said sympathetically.

"Well," Carlisle agreed, "if it might save a dumb animal's life. . . ."

134

"Wake up, Bear."

It was dark in the hooch. Bear grumbled and blinked at the darkness. He had gone to bed early, but he felt as if sleep had come only that instant. Some sounds would wake him instantly—an incoming round or the scramble horn—but Carter's voice was not one of those.

"You didn't come to the party," Carter said.

"Oh, Carter, I'd just spoil it. Don't drag me over there now."

"I'll drag you out, all right, but the party's long over. It's time for Santa's little helpers to be on their way, if the troops are going to have their Christmas turkey and mail. Get your helmet."

Bear sat up and shook his head energetically, as if to rid his ears of water. "My helmet? You're going to feed the troops out of my helmet?"

"No, dummy, we're going flying."

"You're crazy." He lay back down and pulled the blanket around his neck.

"I thought you'd like to do a good deed for your fellow man."

"I would. But I don't know how, except by not getting out of bed."

"I'm telling you how. I'm flying resupply this fine Christmas morning, and you can come with me."

"Unless you know something I don't, Carter, it'd be everybody's rear if I do that. The general doesn't approve of my flying."

"What the general doesn't know won't hurt him."

"But if the general does know, it could hurt you and me both."

"Well, Bear, I'm old enough to decide for myself what will hurt me, and I don't know why you should worry about your position."

Bear sat up again. The sleep was gone from inside his head. He had decided Carter was serious. "Who's your copilot supposed to be?"

"Carlisle."

"It's not just to cover for a drunken wojug, then," Bear said.

"Drunken wojug! How you talk about poor Hitch when he's only trying to do you a favor!" Carter exclaimed in delight.

135

"Drunken CW. Two, maybe. Now, if you're coming, let's haul ass. We've got a six-thirty takeoff."

"I'll beat you to the ship if you don't get moving." Bear was on his feet before the words were out of his mouth, and his fatigues were going on his body. "What are we flying?" he called to Carter, who had started for the door.

"Number ten thou."

"I'll see you there."

When Bear reached the flight line, Carter was atop his helicopter with a flashlight, inspecting the rotor head. Theirs was the only early mission. Bear tried out the right seat. It felt strange to him, after so many months in a gunship. The D-model sat on the ground at the wrong angle. "This is crazy," he said to Carter as Carter climbed into the left seat.

"What is?"

"Letting me fly this mission."

"We'll pray for light loads and good weather; and I'll keep a hand on the stick." Carter was pretending to misunderstand.

"I didn't say letting me fly this *ship*. I was driving D-models around Nam while you were still chasing clouds at Rucker. But isn't it going to look funny for Carlisle to be sitting around the company area while his mission is taking care of itself?"

"I don't know what you mean, Carlisle. Do *you* understand what Mr. Carlisle is driving at?" Carter asked, turning to the crew chief, who was mounting his machine gun at the back of the cargo door.

"No, sir. Not me," the crew chief said. "Merry Christmas, Mr. Carlisle," he added, grinning at the Bear.

"I can tell you that the Bear will be mighty scarce around the company area today," Carter said, "but that's not unusual these days, I understand. Last night he said something about going off to visit one of the Marine officers' clubs for the day. Now, then, Carlisle, are you ready to crank this thing for me? No sense in the aircraft commander doing all the work."

"Yes, sir," Bear said.

The day passed in a series of twenty-minute jumps. In twenty minutes a helicopter could reach nearly any point in the division area of operations from the main post. They shuttled back and

136

forth from the Division Artillery supply point to all the lonely hilltop outposts where little groups of tents and bunkers clung like barnacles to the rock. On the broader hilltops howitzers stared silently skyward from sandbagged shallow pits. On the narrow ridges—some so narrow that the helicopter's skids overhung both edges as it perched on the top, and the engine could not be rolled back to idle as the cargo was unloaded—mortars leaned idly on splayed legs. Everywhere, soldiers in wet, mud-caked fatigues scrambled toward the helicopter. The cargo of insulated containers, with dinner hot from rear-area kitchens, vanished within seconds. The helicopter would dive over the side of the mountain, with Carter's hearty "Ho, ho, ho!" ringing in the headphones, and be off for Chu Lai and another installment of Christmas dinner.

And the ship—the ship felt alive in his hands. Picking it up from a pinnacle, Bear could feel the weight of it in his left hand—not heavy, but somehow there, all of it cupped in his palm and rising at his will. And through the cyclic stick the fingers of his right hand felt the whole being of the ship to the very tips of the blades, and at the touch of his fingers it bowed and went where he willed. With swift and untouched grace the ship passed over the miles of warring land.

Between the mountains stretched winding stream-laced valleys. On the seaward side the valleys stair-stepped down in long flights of terraced paddies until they opened on the plain. The white circles of peasants' hats winked up at the helicopter from the steely luster of paddies that glittered back the grey of the sky. On the landward side the valleys were choked with jungle. Nothing was seen to move there; but the guns brooded over those dark valleys. Their keepers turned with relief toward the glimpse of sunshine down over the plain toward the sea, or turned inward in the silence, and tried to forget the dark forests where the rain, the artillery rounds, the light itself, seemed to be swallowed as they fell. Bear flew uneasily over these valleys, knowing they were less empty than they seemed.

But even there over those black lands he felt lighter at heart than he had for many days. Toward noon the clouds began to break above Chu Lai, although they still hung low and heavy over the ridges to the west, and by early afternoon each trip back to the supply point was a plunge into haze-silvered sunshine. When there were no more supplies to be carried, Bear said to Carter, "You've made a new man of me."

"You're not done yet," Carter said.

"No? What now?"

"You'll see." He took the controls and headed the ship around the south end of the main airfield to the division headquarters pad.

"You're going to show the general that you've rehabilitated me," Bear suggested.

"Close, but no cigar."

At the headquarters pad a mixed group of Air Force officers and airman came aboard. One signaled to Carter that there were no more, and Carter took the ship away over the headquarters buildings scattered among the low evergreens at the edge of the sea. He continued south at five hundred feet until they had passed beyond the jet traffic pattern and then turned directly across the bay toward the peninsula that curved into the sea beyond the mouth of Song Tra Bong. The ship climbed rapidly, and the rocky peninsula dwindled in the haze below them.

"You're taking me to California?" Bear asked.

"You're getting closer." Carter put the peninsula behind them without changing heading, and then Bear knew where they must be going. Short of California, there was only a handful of islands. The nearest was Cu Lao Re.

As they flew out to sea, the haze thinned but did not disappear. The coast vanished behind them, but no land came in sight. There was blue above and blue below, and silver all around. Only a narrow circle of wrinkling waves directly beneath them marked down from up. To the Bear, who had seen the island only as if it had been a mirage, it seemed almost an act of faith to leap off from the earth in this way. The island might be only a mark on the charts, and not really exist at all. Carter flew by the instruments, unconcerned, and the slap of the blade carried them across the silver chasm.

The island materialized from the mist.

It glowed in the sunlight. From afar it had seemed but a single peak; but now he saw that there were three crescents—the shells of old volcanic craters whose sides the sea had broken—joined by

138

a low shelf. The whole island except the tallest crescent—that on the east—was quilted with hedged-in fields and pastures. Some were plowed, and burned a rich reddish brown, while others glowed golden or emerald green. These fields climbed even the sheer sides of the two smaller crescents. Rooftops were scattered among them. On the south shore of the island the roofs condensed into a series of towns spread under fluttering palms. The eastern crescent towered over it all. It formed nearly a complete circle. Its outer slopes were grassed, but within the shell was cupped a dense unmarked jungle.

There was a grassy shelf on the northwest side of the tallest crescent, not far below the rim. A few tin roofs glistened at its edge, beside the dish of a parabolic antenna. The Air Force maintained a radio relay station there. Carter made a low pass over the buildings. By the time he turned the ship back, a smoke grenade had blossomed from the grassy shelf. Carter circled and landed into the light northeast wind.

Several airmen strolled down from the buildings as Carter shut down the ship. One came to his door. "Can you wait, sir? Some of the guys going back with you haven't come up from the beach yet."

"Are we likely to get attacked sitting here?" Carter grinned.

"Not hardly." The airman laughed. "Not hardly at all. There's no war here, sir."

As if to prove his point, a jeep came bouncing up the narrow track around the side of the crater. There was no road—only a set of tire tracks through the deep grass. At some places the jeep was almost awash in the grass; at others it clung to bare rock and seemed in danger of rolling down the outside of the crater. In the jeep were four men in swimming suits. The air was cold, but it would be warmer on a sunny beach out of the wind. The men were shouting and laughing. None of them carried weapons.

"They wanted to get in one last swim," the airman explained. "They won't get much swimming back in the States, this time of year." He didn't say "back in the world," as everyone did on the mainland. "I'll go get them moving for you." The airman walked back toward the buildings where the jeep had gone. Like the men in it he carried no weapon. Bear saw that there was a barbed-wire fence below the buildings; but the gate was open, apparently permanently.

"They say the island is a VC rest camp," Carter told Bear. "I flew a doctor out here once. There's a medical station of some kind down in the town for the Vietnamese. He told me they see a lot of wounds, one kind and another. No use asking what kind. They always pretend not to understand. It's always *'Come bic! Come bic!'* He said he thought they were Charlies, come over from the mainland to get fixed up. But the police say no. They don't want to push it as long as it's quiet here."

"That's a funny attitude," Bear said. "Haven't they ever heard of duty?" He got down from the ship and walked out across the meadow. They had landed in a shallow saddle between the main crater and a projecting knob somewhat below the rim. Bear walked out toward the knob. The grass clung about his knees. It was green and shining, and it whispered back at the gentle wind. At intervals spikes of yucca-like cactus thrust out of the grass. He wound among them toward the top of the knob.

Beyond the knob the hillside fell away, too steep even for walking, in a great cascade of green all the way to the blue sea hundreds of feet below. But at the very edge of the drop there stood a small bare tree. Its dense gnarled branches formed a globe perhaps ten feet across, perched atop a twisted trunk. There was not a leaf on it. It had the look of immense age, of an old man gnarled and lined; and yet it seemed extraordinarily alive. Against the bright silver haze it glowed even more brightly, as if it were wholly carved out of light, and each branch a stroke of lightning. The grass flashed about its feet. Behind it the sea wrinkled and glittered. But the tree, as the spirit of the place, gathered all elements into itself, contained them all, as if in its dry age it contained the secret of renascence. Bear sat down in the grass, enchanted. "What *do* you know, Tree?" he asked. He knew the tree had a message, if only he could hear it.

He heard the jeep coming down the track behind him once more. Turning his head, he could see it beside the helicopter. Carter was waving to him. He went back down the knoll feeling he had all but touched the Happy Isles.

"What did you see?" Carter asked him.

"Grass, and haze, and the ocean, and a tree."

"It *is* empty up here," Carter said. He was a little disappointed. He had expected the Bear to like the island. That was why he had held it back as a surprise. "But it's a nice setup they have. You could sleep at night without one hand on your weapon and the other on your boots." He said this with a hopeful eye on the Bear, but he saw no reaction. He shouted, "Clear!" out the side and pulled the starter trigger. The engine whistled, the blade pounded, and the deep grass slid away behind them.

The Bear said little until the helicopter was on the ground at Ky Ha. Clouds had closed back over the coast in their absence, and on the ramp it was almost dark. Carter parked well down the ramp to be out of sight of Operations. They sat on the ship waiting for the blade to stop. Carter was filling out the log book. "Do you want to sign it?" he asked the Bear. "That'd shake up maintenance, if they ever read these things."

"Only as Carlisle," Bear said. "You risked your rear for me, Carter, but let's not leave any record of it."

"Maybe we should—a memorial of our Christmas in Nam. The Bear Memorial Ash and Trash Run. It'll become a company tradition."

"If they're all as good as the first, I'll come back annually," Bear said. "You saved my life, Carter; or at least my mind."

"Ah, it's all right, Bear. If I ever need anyone killed, I'll call on you."

"I wouldn't do that for just anybody, Carter. But I would for you."

The blade had stopped. Bear got out to help the crew chief tie it down. What remained of the day was fading. A thread of smoke still issued from the tailpipe. It vanished against the heavy sky. He hoped the memory of the island would not vanish in the heaviness of his mind.

The crew chief's eyes followed his to the tailpipe. "She's sure a smoker, sir, old ten thou," the crew chief said. "And gettin' worse."

"Your engine's going to go, then," Bear said. It was easy to slip back into professional matters. They relieved him of remembering for a little longer.

"That's what maintenance said," Carter told him. "But she's still a strong ship. I'm going to fly her until she quits."

"Thanks for telling me before we got over the water," Bear joked. *Number ten thou*—a bad sign, slang for *the worst possible*, infinitely worse than *number ten*. Today the number had been no omen. Even if Carter had said the engine was about to fall out, Bear knew he would have gone anyway. They left the ship to the darkness and went up the hill. Somewhere far to the northwest a series of explosions rumbled down the hills. It was past sunset. The truce had ended.

7

The nurse on duty was a friendly weathered old captain whose jungle fatigues hung like Spanish moss from her limbs. She peered up at him with a slow puzzled gaze, but at last she remembered him from some earlier day. "We only have one of your friends here today," she told him. "One came down from Intensive Care; but one we had here was sent there last night. McWade was his name. Oh, I think he's in no danger," she added quickly.

The one who had come down from Intensive Care was Patulski, the soldier with one leg. He lay with the blanket drawn up around his shoulders against the air-conditioned chill of the ward. His eyes were closed, but when the Bear stopped at the end of his bed, he asked without opening his eyes if there was anything he could do for his visitor. He did not sound as if he intended to comply with whatever it might be.

"I just came to see how you were."

The eyes opened. "You're not one of them investigation jerks? They keep coming around and around, nothing better to do than bug a wounded man with stupid questions. I haven't seem 'em for a day or two, and I hope I'm rid of 'em. What do *you* care how I am?"

"I brought you in from the field," Bear said. But his answer, sliding over the initial fact as it did, made him think of Blood in the Operations hooch that night, and he fought down a spreading blush.

143

The soldier seemed to take that for a sign of modesty, and he became less unfriendly. "A pilot, huh? Well, if you medevacked me, you're the only one that did me any good. Those investigation people keep asking me what happened. I don't know why they didn't listen the first time. You know what happened to me? Some dumb-ass pilot came along and shot my leg off. This chaplain was in to see me. 'Could be worse,' he says. Well, it could be better, too. I didn't ask to have my leg shot off. That dumb s.o.b. Carpenter, I heard he only took a few frags through the legs. Shipped him off the next day, and now he's in Conus. Talk about a million-dollar wound! And then that chaplain tries to tell me it could be worse. He'd think it was worse, if it was his leg."

"Well," Bear said, "it could be worse." He did not intend to laugh at poor Patulski, who was lying there one-legged and rightly angry. But from somewhere inside him a bubble of the humor which would have laughed at self-pity in himself escaped without warning. Patulski unaccountably took the remark as a friendly gesture, a sign of common contempt for the chaplain. He broke into a grin which had no pleasure in it, other than that of shared ill-will. "He was a damn poor excuse for a chaplain," he said.

Talking to Patulski was for Bear like being dragged over the rocks of his past. Yet he did not tear himself free. He listened as the soldier crisscrossed the injustices of his present condition. "Excuse my not knowing you—you being my medevac pilot, I mean—but I was flat out cold when you brought me in here. It's not really so keen, being short a leg. Last thing I knew, I was leaning up against this tree, supposed to be digging a foxhole, listening to the choppers buzzing around—I was thinking how nice it would be to go home every night and sleep in a clean bed with no mosquitoes, and here we were, out four nights with not even a chopper to bring us hot chow or a beer—when I heard this noise, *whish!* just like that, and I was laying on my back and there was this little fountain coming out of my knee. And then I was in the other room up there, all that stuff dangling around me like spaghetti, and Charley grinning at me."

"Charley?"

"Yeah, there was this little Slope in the next bed, just grinning like a loony, or at least I thought he was grinning. I thought, what the hell, Charley's got me and put me in a hospital. We blew up one of those places a few weeks back. It was all underground—must of been forty foot deep. Well, that's where I thought I was, until I saw this round-eye nurse. And then I thought, Patulski, you're short. Jesus I was happy! And then my foot hurt like a son of a bitch, and I looked down, and there wasn't any foot there at all! But it hurt anyway. Is that fair, that the damned thing should hurt when I haven't even got it anymore?" As he spoke, Patulski alternated between great animation and deep sullen brooding. He ended in a slow angry voice, "That's what Charley was grinning at. And when I looked him over better, *he* had *both* legs gone."

"I guess they get some Arvins in here," Bear said, to fill the silence left as Patulski's voice trailed off coldly. His words reignited Patulski's scorn: "Naw, he wasn't no Arvin! He was Victor Charley. They come in with an armed guard after a while and took him out. I heard one of 'em say he was off to the security ward. And I laid there all that time with him watching me. He could of got up and stuck a knife in me when I was out cold—except he didn't have his legs. No telling how many of my buddies he's killed, even if he didn't look like much. They're little shits, but they're tough. But then I thought, shit, no telling how many of his buddies I might of killed, either. And who was it got me in the end—me and more of my buddies than Charley ever got? Some dumb-ass officer in a gunship!"

"Lord, forgive him," Bear said, but only to himself.

"If you want to know what a dumb shit he was," Patulski continued, "you ought to talk to McWade. He didn't get hit right off, and he was awake through it all. Not only did the gunships shoot us up once, they turned around and came back to make *sure* they got us! Talk to McWade; he'll tell you. He was in here last night when I come in here. We talked some, and he told me. But he didn't feel too good, and they took him out."

"I saw him one day," Bear said.

"Yeah, McWade didn't get it near as bad as I did. He never was in Intensive Care. I don't know where he is now—they took him out while I was asleep, I guess. Maybe they shipped him out. I don't know."

"I'll try to locate him."

"Yeah, we're the last ones here, he said. Everybody else has gone on. Carpenter went out the first day—right straight to Japan, McWade said. I suppose he'll be going next, and then it'll be just me. Son of a bitch, that leg hurts!" He was slamming his hand on the bedcovers as Bear left him.

He had not thought to check who were the nurses on duty in the Intensive Care unit. When he stepped through the door, Alice was there.

The ward had filled with new bodies. They stretched behind her desk, two neat rows of beds festooned with tubes and hoses and straps and frames. A few balloons, and they would be ready for a party. One near the front had an oxygen tent erected over it. He recognized McWade's red hair inside it.

The rows of beds took his eyes beyond her; but she rose to meet him. "I didn't expect to see you here."

"I came to see one of your customers."

She knew the one he meant: she led him to McWade's tent. He was asleep, and breathing heavily with the short gasping breaths of a swimmer surfacing after long submersion. "He has shock lung," she said, before he could ask.

"What is it?"

"The bullet that struck his ribs bruised the lung, and fluid is collecting in it. He's on Demerol. That's partly why he's sleeping." The rippled Plexiglas tent made McWade look like an aquarium specimen, on underwater display.

"Is he dying?" He could not manage a more positive question. Though it had been only two days since she had told him McWade was all right, McWade did not look all right.

"No. This condition comes on a few days after the wound. The other lung will get him through. He'll stay here until he stabilizes; but he won't die."

"How many have?"

If she heard the question, she pretended that she had not.

She stepped out into the hall behind him. Through the windows the sea could be seen. It stretched and wrinkled in the pale sunshine.

"I didn't know you were on this ward," he said.

"I'm not. I only stopped by to see Private McWade, too. The poor guy. He's so sweet and brave." When she saw Bear flinch,

146

she added quickly, "He'll be leaving so soon, I'll almost be sorry to see him go."

"I don't see why I couldn't have met a harder-hearted nurse," he said.

"I'm sure you couldn't find another nurse who would throw a kindhearted officer out of her ward for trying to visit her patients. But I'll make it up to you." She held out her hand to him. "You can come visit the ward I'm on now. There's no one you need to worry about there."

She led him along the corridor toward a back corner of the hospital. A soldier with a rifle was leaning back in a chair opposite the doors to a ward. He smiled and waved them inside. Another guard was posted inside the door. He stuffed a magazine quickly behind himself as they entered. "Caught you again, Johnson," she said. It smoothed away his sheepish grin.

"This is my ward, for this week at least."

The patient closest to the door turned to watch them. Haunted eyes gleamed out from deep hollows above the cheekbones, while the mouth at one side was pulled back into a perpetual grin by an old scar that meandered up the cheek toward the ear. He propped himself half upright, his forearms lifted clear of the bed, leaning on his elbows rather than his hands because there were no hands. He was protecting stumps that ended above the wrists. He wore pajamas with the legs pinned over, for his own legs ended above where the knees had been. But the eyes—the eyes were screens behind which nothing moved. Bear recognized with a shock the true figure of Patulski's drugged perception. "Charley," he said softly.

"Yes, he's VC. This is a prisoner ward."

The ward was half full. All the patients—prisoners—were Vietnamese. They lounged on their beds empty-eyed, as though they, like the American patients, had resigned their bodies to this place but sent their spirits elsewhere for the duration. None of the others paid any attention to Alice and the Bear—except for one. At the far end of the room was an old woman sitting on her bed. Her eyes were fixed on them as if she sought to penetrate to their very hearts while guarding her own thoughts. She had sparse white hair floating about her head like wisps of cirrus. She had no eyebrows. Leprosy had mined her bones until the wrinkled flesh collapsed into the subsurface channels, leaving a flattened nose below the heavy bare brows that stretched up to a forehead arched in the taut curve of a drawn bow. It was a stern, almost fierce face, a leonine face, majestic even in ruin.

"All VC?" Bear asked. "Even her?"

"Yes. She was here before I was, but I was told she was found stalking through the jungle with her AK-47, half starved and eaten by mosquitoes, but not ready to give up until she ran out of bullets. There's nothing we can do for her, but the prisoner compound won't have her. So she stays here. Her name is Phuong."

She did not move even her eyes when they spoke her name. But, though the body she occupied seemed but the relic of a human frame, the fire in those eyes had survived the disease that had consumed her. "She looks like Mother Courage herself," he said.

"Mother Courage! It's exactly the name for her! If she's as indomitable as she looks, she'll endure forever."

"If anyone can, in this land." He looked back at Charley, who had fallen back now on his pillows, exhausted by the effort of propping himself up. He was shivering. Alice went to draw his blanket over him. The terrible grin etched across his face masked whatever emotion might burn behind those eyes. Was there any less courage to be found there than in the old woman, because her trials had left her outwardly fierce, while his had made him only terribly, foolishly grotesque? The lips moved, but no words emerged. Bear saw then that the scar down the cheek extended all the way into the throat and out of sight inside the pajama top. Whatever had struck him had taken his voice as it furrowed his face and jaw. "Lord," most would have asked, "what could have done it?" But Bear could name a dozen things that could have done it. He had seem them in use: most of them he had used himself.

To kill or be killed was not so hard a choice. But daily to face the true product of the choice seemed to him now to require a different order of courage. "I don't envy you your job," he said to her. Charley was the ideal product of the art of war—not a dead man, but a casualty, useless in battle yet eating up resources that could go to keep his fellow soldiers alive. But he had by some

148

twist of his fate fallen into the hands of his maker, and there he remained, little more now than a trophy.

The kindness Alice showed made him admire her the more even as it made him more acutely aware of how limited was his own compassion. His own desire, he recognized with shame, was to turn away. To face this daily, without tears and without callousness, surely required a strong rein on one's soul. He forced himself to watch her trying to make the broken body comfortable. "Were you good with pets when you were a little girl?" he asked. "You have kind hands." He did not mean the question to belittle her patients, nor did she understand it that way.

"My father says I was. Puppies and kittens at least, and a pony." She added, "I never had a chance to be kind to a Bear." She touched him lightly on the arm, smiling.

It was then that his will capitulated. His heart had done so days before. "This one would take it kindly if you had time to see him tonight," he said.

She considered for a moment. "I'd be pleased."

The hazy afternoon ended in a cool humid evening which lingered beyond the Grandfather Mountain, Nui Ong. In the side door of one of the gunships on the line, Bear and Covington sat talking. Covington had got onto his favorite topic, his son-to-be. Bear was pleased enough with the subject, since it relieved him of any need to speak. His own life seemed to him to be a subject best left alone.

"I don't know what to do about Pinky," Covington said. "She says she's still smoking. I told her two weeks ago that I thought she should quit. That can't be good for a kid, can it? To have the mother smoke while she's pregnant, I mean. Do you think she didn't get my letter?"

"Maybe not by the time she wrote. What was the postmark?"

"It was a week ago. She should have had my letter. Maybe it got caught in that attack on Da Nang. Wasn't that about two weeks ago? I'll bet it was on one of those C-130s that was hit on the runway."

"Why don't you tell her again?"

"Ah, you don't know how women are, Bear. Little things set 'em off. Especially when they're pregnant."

"Of course, you've impregnated thousands."

"Well . . . I *was* quite a performer in my bachelor days." Covington lay back on the floor of the ship, grinning with what Bear thought might pass for wickedness in Iowa. The claim, however, was greater than Covington's slender nineteen years could carry. And Bear had heard from him more than once that he had never considered, never even dated, any girl other than Pinky. Their parents had been against the marriage, which came so shortly before he left for Vietnam. But he had great stubbornness for so small a frame—he was a mere apostrophe of a man—and he had had his way. Only he was sorry he would not be home in time to see his son born. "I don't think she should smoke anyway," he said, "but she only does it when she's nervous. Now she claims the whole thing makes her nervous, with me here and her there. You know how women are."

"You just told me I don't."

"Well, you don't, except when they're nervous."

"Why don't you suggest she wait up until you get home?"

"Thanks a whole lot, Bear." Then he sat up again. "Hey, you know what would be neat?"

"No, Cov, what would be neat?"

"Your DEROS date is in April."

"I'm not going around hollering 'short' yet, but you're right again."

"Well, my son is due around the end of April; and what would be neat is if you were around—you're going to be on leave then anyway, and you can't go anywhere in the States without going through Iowa, believe me—you could just stop in and see my son and my wife for me, and tell them both how lucky they are to have me for a husband and father, and how much I miss them. . . ."

"Come on, Cov, let's not make yourself all lonesome again tonight."

"I won't. Cross my heart. I had enough of being lonesome on Christmas while you were off pretending to be Carlisle. But Pinky would just love to see you. And you could write and let me know how they both are. I wouldn't mind an unbiased opinion on how handsome my son is."

"Pinky might have better things to do than entertain soldiers, being a new mother and all."

" 'Entertain soldiers' sounds like something illicit. But no, she'd really like to meet you. And she's thinking about beautiful girls to introduce you to. I told you about this friend of hers who's going to a modeling school?"

"Cov," Bear said impulsively, "I'll be glad to visit your bride for you. But it's too late for the girls."

Covington stared. "Too late for girls? What the devil does that mean? I don't recall that you took a round between the legs while *I* was flying with you. What have you been getting into on the ground these last few days? Listen, you haven't really got something going with Yan, have you? The major won't go for that." Although he admired the Bear's ability to chatter with the hooch-maids, Covington half-shared Atterburn's opinion that there could be only one purpose in it.

"No, Cov, I don't mean Yan. She's just a little girl."

"Well, you could fool me, but I've only seen the wrapping, not the package. But I wouldn't have thought Suzie or any of the other grandmothers were to your taste. And there's nobody else around. Carter said they flew some doughnut dollies out to Colt the other day, but they live way up at the headquarters compound, and you said you've only been between here and the hospital. Unless you found something out in the boonies . . . Oh." He squinted one eye at the Bear. "You haven't been going to see someone besides wounded grunts at the hospital, have you?"

"I haven't," Bear said, "not really, but I thought I might. Shoot, I don't know, Cov. I met this nurse down there. . . ." He stopped. He wanted to tell Cov about Alice Porter; and yet he did not know what he could say about Alice Porter, did not know what he felt about her, knew only that whenever he thought of her he felt that she was squeezing out of him some element of compassion that ought to be there instead of her. But he could not help thinking of her.

"You met this nurse down there," Covington prompted him.

"That's all. I met this nurse."

"That's all? 'No more girls,' he says, but that's all. He met a nurse, just a friendly handshake, but it's too late for the beautiful model. Jesus, Bear, tell old Daddy Covington about it!"

"Don't make a big deal out of it. She's a nice girl, and I like her.

151

I'm going to go up and see her for a while this evening. That's all."

"Ah, the Bear strikes again! While the rest of us swelter in the ready room, the Bear is out romping with a friendly nurse!" Covington seemed transported by the thought. He lay back in the ship with his eyes closed and a wide smile on his face.

"What have we here but two leisured gentlemen?" It was Lieutenant Arp checking the ships that were on standby. Washington, the crew chief on this ship, was with him. "They're holding down my ship so it won't blow away," Washington said.

"No insults now," Covington insisted. "Don't forget who's flying this thrashing machine tonight, Washington. Your life is in my hands. That's one leisured gentleman," he said to Arp, "and one working man."

"Mr. Covington's working, sir." Washington grinned. "He's straining to grow a mustache." Washington stroked his own Mexican-bandit growth.

"It appears to me that he's given up on it," Arp said. "Or else it's dying of loneliness."

"Maybe you could give him lessons, Washington," Bear suggested.

"He couldn't use my method, sir. It's not fit for a married man."

"You'd better teach it to the Bear, then," Arp said. "He needs something to pass the time. Now if I were you, Bear"—Arp paused to cross himself—"I wouldn't be spending my time down here on the ramp sitting in a gunship. You're going to be doing enough of that when you come back on flight status. You'll pull duty for two weeks straight just to make up the time Covington and I have put in for you. Here we are on our sixth day of twenty-four-hour standby, and you add insult to injury by hanging around showing off your freedom. Why don't you go get drunk with the animals?" He meant Blood and Atterburn.

"Little does he know," Covington said with satisfaction. Bear shoved his heel into Covington's ribs.

"Know what? That the Bear's drunk already? You know, Bear, if I thought I'd get away with it, I'd sneak you into my bunk and just run on up to the club to watch the horror movie."

"Just give him your cap, *Trung úy*, and nobody will know the difference."

"He couldn't pass for me," Arp said with a grin. "I'm not as ugly as Carlisle."

"I've heard that debated," Covington answered. "But the insult I meant was that, with a different bar on his hat, Bear would run this outfit to beat all hell. But I will say the flying end of the platoon has been running one heck of a lot better since you've been doing it than when Blood was. Maybe the trade we should make is Blood's hat for yours."

"Don't be heretical," Arp said. "I'll have to report you up the chain of command."

"So what can they do—ship me to Vietnam? They couldn't even bust me or ground me, because either way they'd lose a pilot, and then there wouldn't even be enough people for standby."

"Rationality will get you nowhere," Arp said. "Not in this army." He went on up the ramp.

"Everybody in the company seems to know about me and Hitch and the Christmas run," Bear said.

"Only people who are safe. Don't fret."

"If everybody knows about Alice, I'll know how the news got out."

"Anybody but you would be shouting the news from the rooftops, Bear. But *I'm* not going to tell. No, never. Wild horses couldn't drag it from me."

"If it matters *that* much to anybody, Cov, you can tell them. But nothing less."

"Tame horses?"

"No."

"You're a hard man, Bear."

He had arranged to meet Alice at the hospital officers' club, but he found her there with Janet Swensen and Wolcheski. Wolcheski was off for the evening and had borrowed a jeep. The four of them drove down to one of the huge officers' clubs built by the Marine Air Groups on the main airfield.

The club was a towering hall of lashed bamboo, walled with plaited mats and thatched with palm fronds. The columns were

153

single poles of bamboo as thick as a man's thigh, and the rafters disappeared into a smoky darkness. The seaward side opened directly onto a broad white beach where the sea flapped idly beyond the reach of the lights. It had been built by Seabees as a dream of tropic architecture, the dream of the tropic isle transposed to an American scale.

A band led by an off-duty sergeant in civilian clothes hammered out hard rock while Vietnamese serving girls in *áo-dàis* threaded among the tables. On a semicircle of open floor, fighter-bomber pilots were dancing. They danced alone. There were no women in the club.

Alice and Janet's entry provoked a barrage of stares, but no one, at first, approached to ask them to dance. Those who were already on the floor went on as they had begun; and when a song began that seemed to be a favorite of the house, the floor was instantly crowded with men shaking in stylized abandon, while those sitting around them shouted out the chorus: "We gotta get out of this place,/If it's the last thing we ever do. . . ."

"I thought only Greek men danced alone," Janet sniffed. "It's disgusting."

"She hates to see anything in trousers going to waste," Wolcheski said to the Bear. Janet pounded his arm. When one of the Marines did come to ask her to dance, she went off with only a sidelong look of triumph at Wolcheski. He shrugged. "Why not share the wealth? I'm the one who's taking her home." When she returned, she held his hand and worried about the edges of his serenity like a puppy trying by being a nuisance to draw attention to the fact that it is now prepared to behave.

It was the strangest evening Bear had spent in Vietnam. While Marines danced alone to a rock band, jets boomed off the runway just across the main post road, drowning all conversation until they turned out over the sea to begin their long swing to the north. Between jet departures they sat over drinks and talked quietly of nothing to do with the war. That was the strangest part of all—when it was like an evening in real life.

He danced with Alice eventually. Within the slow music her body touched his lightly. And in the jeep going home she had no objection to being kissed.

154

Outside her door she reached up and touched his mustache with one finger. "Share with me," he said, when she laughed.

"You bristle."

"You've discovered me. Most people don't know that I'm the walrus." He had taken hold of her finger, and he kissed it before letting go.

"As far as I can recall," she said, "I've never been kissed by a walrus before."

"Many strange experiences lie before you," he murmured. "You will live a rich full life—" He broke off abruptly.

Sensing the reason, she said nothing.

After a long time he said, "You know, I could just as well have met you under some other circumstances."

"I wish you had, if that helps." She turned and looked out over the cold dark sea into the depth of emptiness. He looked off in the same direction, as if somewhere their eyebeams might intermingle, in some neutral space far removed from this where they were caught within the wrong lives.

"I don't know why you wish that," he said. "I'm just the ugly Bear, and you're a fair princess of a lieutenant."

She touched his hand. "Poor Bear."

"It's not fair," he said. "Why should I have met you because of . . . because of my damned stupidity? While they . . ." Gone into the earth. And he could not mourn them with his whole heart, as he should, because his heart was sliding into love.

He walked up the still ramp in the sea mist, hearing the distant boom of the jets regular as clockwork, seeing the damp blades of the silent glistening gunships angling up into darkness, troubled by how easily he might forget.

A poker game was still going forward in the little empty hooch that was the company officers' lounge. A half-dozen pilots from the lift platoons were slumped about the battered card table. The game had started early and now only inertia kept it going. They greeted him with slow bored turns of the head: "Hey, Bear."

"Get some of that fresh money in here and liven things up," Warrant Officer Griggs muttered. Griggs had not been losing, but he was never pleased with less than elimination of the other

155

players, and he was frustrated by a long evening in which he had gained no edge.

"The Bear won't play poker," Carter said. "He's saving his pay to buy a pink Cadillac when he gets back to the world. With a stove and refrigerator in it." Griggs had once informed Carter that a pink Cadillac was the pinnacle of motorcardom, and Carter would not forget.

"Up yours," Griggs snarled.

"Originality will get you nowhere," Carter said happily. He was never so pleased as when he was ragging Griggs, whom he detested.

"Deal those mothers!" Griggs demanded. He shook his head as if to dislodge Carter from his ear.

As the cards flicked out around the table, Lieutenant Harris, one of the slick platoon commanders, came in the door at the back of the hooch. "Missions." He tossed a sheaf of mission assignment sheets onto the table as the cards went around the far side.

"What kind of shit did you stick me with this time?" Griggs asked him. He folded his cards and leaned back as if daring the lieutenant to give him the wrong answer.

"How would you like artillery resupply?"

"What?" The blow of Griggs's hand on the table bounced off the bare walls. "God damn it, Lieutenant, I haven't had a day off in thirty days now! Do you know how many hours I've flown this month? When the hell do I get a day off, I'd like to know?" The strength of Griggs's sense of injury was matched only by the loudness of his voice.

The lieutenant only smiled. His lean freckled hatchet face had wrinkles about the eyes when he smiled. "I thought if I let you fly ten hours tomorrow, you'd be over the limit and I'd have to let you rest for a few days," he said seriously; but he winked at the dealer.

"You know, Lieutenant," Griggs said, as if explaining to a child, "I'll get over there at oh-six-thirty tomorrow, and I'll wait an hour for some supply sergeant to haul his ass out of the sack, and then I'll spend half the day screwing around while they try to find out where this next load of C-rats is supposed to go, and there's no way in hell I'm going to get ten hours tomorrow. I'm on alternate flare ship tonight besides. What if I have to go up? I can't see dragging my own rear out of the sack at four thirty after being up all night."

"Charley won't be out tonight," Jones observed. "There's not enough weather to keep the gunships down. If he didn't come in all that weather last week, he won't be out tonight."

"Leave it to a New Guy to tell you how the war goes," Griggs snapped. "What I want to know, Lieutenant, is why the hell you pick me for all the shitty missions?"

"It's because he knows you were in this Army when he was still a gleam in his daddy's eye," Carter put in, echoing one of Griggs's favorite Army sayings.

Griggs, although not that old, was an ex-sergeant who knew his rights and stood on them. He had no use for lieutenants. "Why?" he demanded.

"I always try to suit the mission to the personality of the pilot," Harris answered with a shrug, to the laughter of everyone except Griggs. He handed the mission sheets around. "You're on a standby tomorrow," he said to Griggs, who smirked in triumph.

"Damn it, sir, I need some hours," Carter said. "Why don't you let me fly artillery resupply tomorrow."

"Can't. I have to take this young stud up"—he pointed a thumb toward Jones—"and give him a workout. He'll never make aircraft commander, if somebody doesn't take him in hand."

"Give him to me," Griggs said. "I'll make an AC out of him."

"Or see that he dies trying," Carter said.

"Speaking of dying," Griggs said, grinning about the room before he looked at the lieutenant, "did you hear about the Dink I got today?"

"I saw the report," Harris said.

"We got that son of a bitch just bigger than shit. He thought he had it knocked when he got two fields between him and the infantry. But I wasn't about to let him get away. And then he thought he'd get out of it by dropping his weapon and putting his hands up. That Rogers is a sweet gunner! He holed him on the first burst. I'm having him paint a Chinaman on the ship."

"Why didn't you capture him?" Harris asked. "He might have known something that infantry company wanted to know."

"Christ, he had a weapon! If we tried to land, all he had to do was pick it up and blast the crap out of us!"

"You couldn't keep him pinned down until the infantry got there, I don't suppose," Harris said, with the tiredness of one who had been through the routine before.

"Low on fuel, sir," Griggs answered pleasantly. "Anyway, one more dead Slope makes the war that much shorter."

"It could be true," Harris said. He turned and walked out abruptly.

"You in this game, Bear?" Griggs demanded.

"No." He went out into the damp night air. "Deal me out, too," Jones said behind him. "I've got to fly tomorrow."

"You going to let the lieutenant scare you off to bed, are you?"

"Well, Griggs, we don't all have a late standby tomorrow morning."

"I handled him all right on that, didn't I?" Griggs sneered. "The bastard might make a decent officer, if he wasn't so rubbery. He wanted to stick me with that resupply, but he didn't have the guts to stand by it."

"I notice he had your name on the standby mission sheet already," Carter pointed out.

"Sure, and probably on the resupply, too. You notice he didn't let anybody else see that one."

"Why should he? He's flying it himself, as usual."

"Suck-ass trick," Griggs answered scornfully. "He thinks Major Hart will notice. The old man's been around. He knows who's worth a shit and who's not."

"Too bad we can't say that for everybody," Carter said.

The Bear lay on his bed, dressed only in his OD undershorts, feeling the mosquito net breathe gently as the night land breeze sliding down from the mountain passed through the hooch. Someone came down the walk behind the hooches. The walk was made of a mixture of pallets, steel and wooden, left from some company move so long past that almost no one was left in the company who could recall it personally. The unit had moved up the coast from near Qui Nhon more than a year before. A year was forever here, where men arrived, grew to maturity in their jobs, and departed, all within a year, leaving only a name to be

158

remembered for six months more by those to whom he had been an old hand when they arrived and now were old hands themselves. Then they, too, departed, leaving their own names to linger for a little while on the lips of other soldiers. A few stayed on for an extra six months as volunteers in exchange for thirty days' extra leave in some other part of the world. Only a very few, like Sergeant Handy or some generals, stayed on and on unable to give it up.

The pallets of the walk rang under the steps of one more set of feet soon to become a faded name. They stopped behind the hooch. The officer, whoever he was, had stopped to feel the air, to judge the dampness against the chance of rain by morning. Another came down the walk. "Why are you still up, Jones?" he asked. Lieutenant Harris's voice.

"Just looking at the weather, sir. It should be good flying tomorrow."

"You'll be too tired to enjoy it. Young officers need their beauty sleep."

"Don't worry, I'll be down on the ship before you are, sir."

"I sure hope so. These six o'clock takeoffs will be the death of me yet. I don't like 'em any more than Griggs does."

"Griggs! I don't know how you can put up with that ass, sir."

"Well, he's a body in an airplane. You have to have enough ACs to fly the ships."

"What you need is more ACs, then. How long do you think I'll have to fly right seat before I get my own ship?"

Harris laughed softly. "I don't know. Not more than a year, at the outside. We'll see how it goes tomorrow. You've got plenty of time to fly."

"Never enough time for that, sir."

"Remember that when you're short, Jones." Lieutenant Harris had a soft pleasing laugh, Bear thought.

When Jones came into the hooch he turned on his small lamp inside his mosquito net and moved softly about, prolonging the last moments before sleep as much as possible. He pulled off his boots slowly and placed them loosely laced beside the head of his bed, ready for quick use. His pistol belt he hung on the back of a chair next to the boots. He stretched and scratched and grinned

159

to himself. Bear remembered the night before his own check ride for aircraft commander. For a combat pilot that was graduation.

Jones became aware that he was being watched. "Hell, Bear, I'm sorry." He blushed. "I was trying to be quiet so I wouldn't wake you."

"I wasn't asleep."

"I don't feel like sleeping, either. Isn't this a great night?" He tactfully said no more, supposing that his grounded hooch-mate might not wish to be reminded of his own misfortune by chatter about check rides. They slipped into private thoughts, not speaking, listening to the sea worry the beach below the cliffs. Bear thought of the sound of the surf below the Marine club, and of Alice.

Out of the still depths of the night, not loud, yet close at hand, as if they could reach out and touch the sound itself, came a low hollow thump like a wood mallet striking an iron pipe. It was a small drop of sound falling into a sea of sounds—the rustle of surf, muffled voices from the poker game, the groan of a truck on the main post road, the distant boom of Phantom engines testing. It was a sound no civilian in real life would have noticed. It brought them both bolt upright in an instant.

"Did you hear that?" Jones asked. But Bear had already snatched up his boots and pistol belt and was off for the door, with Jones at his heels, both bawling like demented cattle: "Incoming! Incoming!" They fled across the slippery clay and into the mouth of the sandbag bunker between the hooches.

There was a sudden dead silence. The voices from the poker game had stopped; even the jet had shut off. Griggs's voice cracked the mirror-surfaced stillness: "Who the fuck's that?"

Jones hesitated at the mouth of the bunker, suddenly uncertain what he had really heard. He knew if he were wrong, it would be long before the subject would be put to rest.

The mortar round they had heard coming out of the tube impacted on the ridge of their hooch with the flat spreading crash of a chest of drawers being toppled on an upstairs floor. Instantly there was the thunder of boots over plywood floors and the sticky slap of bare feet on clay. "Who's blocking the door?" Bodies scrambled urgently over the Bear's legs inside the low, ninety-degree angled entrance to the bunker. "Get the hell inside!"

160

The bunker was low, only high enough to sit in—hardly higher than a coffin, someone had remarked as it was being built—as wide as a man lying down, and twice as long. The walls were a double row of sandbags, cross-laid and braced by steel fence posts. The all-important roof was a layer of steel plank over heavy timbers, topped by two layers of sandbags. It had been built in the heat of summer, by men whose backs ached, and other men now prayed that they had not thrown down their tools before the job was truly done. None of those inside had ever seen a bunker hit directly by a mortar shell. They did not know what it might do, and so they expected the worst.

Someone switched on a flashlight. There were seven faces. Their eyes were mere walls of blackness as the flashlight shone obliquely down the length of the bunker. Outside, the alert siren began to wail slowly up from the bottom of its throat, sounding far away.

"Did everybody get out of the hooches?" Lieutenant Harris's voice was calm.

"I think so." "There was nobody inside ours but Jones and me." "The lounge cleared out, but some guys must have gone to the other bunker." "Where did that mother land, anyway?" "Close, man! Close!"

After that rapid burst of words a long silence set in. They listened.

A vehicle started up nearby and roared away to the north on the road around the ramp. "Some crazy bastard," Griggs muttered.

"It's Captain Martin going over to the perimeter."

The vehicle was gone, and still nothing.

"What the fuck?" Carter said. "Is that all?"

"A one-shot Charley," Griggs snorted, as if disgusted at having been bothered.

Three rounds fell almost together—*ka-bom . . . pom*—far off, like flour bags falling onto a hollow board floor.

"Four-shot," Carter said.

Bear tried to guess how far they were, but he could not judge the sound from inside the bunker. They could have been as far off as the hospital. But surely she would have a bunker there. As for McWade, and Patulski, and the rest . . .

161

Another round dropped, closer.

"Oh, Christ."

"They're going for the ramp."

"I hope to shit they don't come after me!"

The siren wailed alone, its high steady scream desperate in the darkness.

Harris had switched off his light. The darkness within the bunker was absolute: a narrow right-angled tunnel of sandbags meant to stop shell fragments closed off all view of the outside. Waiting was a three-dimensional Chinese water torture, waiting for the drop to fall and wondering where it would be, as well as when. The plodding giant steps of the incoming rounds crashed back up the ramp toward the area they had first leaped over—*pom!* at the gunship ramp—*pam!* the Operations hooch—WHAM! Shrapnel rattled through the tin roofs on either side of the bunker.

The inside of the bunker was suddenly like a tomb. It had even the smell of death about it. It etched on Bear's mind suddenly the dark prison of the LZ on Hill 473. He ached to be outside, even if only to die under the open sky rather than be buried before life ended.

"Come on," Griggs muttered. "God damn it, fall!"

Pam! It was beyond the major's hooch. The rounds had walked on by.

"I forgot my damn weapon," Lieutenant Harris said.

"At least you brought a flashlight. You can blind the little dears if we get a ground attack."

"Hell," Carter said, "Bear doesn't even have any clothes on. You're obscene, Bear. And who the hell was in the door? I damn near broke my neck on him in the dark."

"Jones was right behind me," Bear said.

"Was that you, Jones? Jones? Hey, Lieutenant, switch your light on."

Jones was seated just inside the door, where Carter had pushed him. His knees, encircled by his arms, were drawn up to his chest, and his head bent forward to rest on them. Carter put out a hand to shake the young officer gently by the shoulder. He drew it back covered with blood. The sweet cloying smell filled the bunker. "Jones!"

The note of the siren broke to a rising and falling wail, the signal to report to Operations. "Carter, stay here with him," Lieutenant Harris said. "I'll get a medic up here. Everybody else get your flight gear and get moving."

Outside, all the lights were out. Every hooch was black; the ramp lights were extinguished; the hospital floodlights beyond the ramp were not to be seen. Bear rushed into the hooch—the door did not hang straight—and struggled into his clothes. With his helmet bag in one hand he ran for the Operations hooch, joining a current of dark shapes moving in the same direction. Up from the ramp floated the whistle of the gunships cranking. Lieutenant Rauch was shouting from the Operations room door: "Spread out, damn it! Spread out, but stay in the area. We're not goin' to evacuate the ships yet, so spread out!" The pilots wandered about with the curious nonchalant bravery of men in the open air and not yet under fire, each believing that the first round will not land at his own feet.

The four gunships, as each came up to operating rpm, whirled in a rapid arc past the takeoff point and climbed out beyond the cliffs. One slick fell in behind them; but when they broke off and swung low toward the north, it climbed on. It was the flare ship. "Griggs! Where's Griggs?" Rauch was shouting.

"Right here!"

"Griggs, get the number-two flare ship loaded! And be sure the damn thing is fit to fly before you take off!"

Bear worked his way back to a point near the corner of the Operations hooch, where he could hear the radios in the bunker. The voices from the gunships crackled out of the dark cave of the bunker, metallic and emotionless, as did that of Carlisle in the flare ship clearing his flight path with the artillery control center.

From high up beyond the naval yards at the end of the peninsula came the chest-thumping beat of the flare ship's blade as it turned inbound. "He's close!" a voice said from behind Bear. The voice meant Charley.

"He wasn't shooting from far off," Bear said. "How far up did rounds land?"

"I don't know."

He asked the anonymous voice from the shadows, "They didn't hit the hospital, did they?"

"I don't know."

A soft white glow spread over the sky above the island opposite the naval yards. A few seconds later came the gentle pop of the flare igniting. The guns were hunting up and down the island but not firing.

The island was a sickle-shaped flat spit of land built up in the mouth of the broad Song Ben Van. Its brilliant white crescent beach faced the sea in a curve from the high rock at the end of the island two miles away. The whole island covered an area of nearly a square mile; but beneath a dense cover of palm fronds, villages sprawled over most of its surface. The mortars were somewhere among them, where the gunships could not fire.

A second flare popped toward the far end of the island. The flares drifted down on their parachutes, leaving long fluffy columns of smoke that slowly dissolved into the damp air. The two pairs of guns cast about the island, plaiting their patterns from side to side, watching for the flash of a weapon. The sound of their rotors broke like waves over the compound as they turned outbound on each pass. The flare ship passed back and forth above them, steadily ejecting the magnesium flares which carried downwind to hiss out at last in the sea. One fell onto the small sandy speck of land beyond the main island, where it lay for a long time like a distant bonfire.

A field ambulance, driving with only blackout lights, rumbled down the rutted clay road to the ramp and accelerated away toward the hospital.

As the minutes wore on, men began climbing up onto the Operations vehicles and the hooches for a better view of the gunships. The Bear worked closer to the bunker. He had heard Covington's voice on the radio, but he could not make out the words. He was about to join the men on the top of the bunker when Covington's voice again startled the silence: "Lead, we're taking fire." It was a dry impassive announcement. But it was instantly followed by an exclamation which might have been meant only for Boroff, who was flying right seat with him, transmitted by mistake in the excitement of the moment: "There he is! There's a muzzle flash at nine o'clock!"

At Covington's words the crowd atop the bunker stretched and craned for a better view. Almost at once there was a low concerted gasp. "Oh, Jesus, will you look at that! He's on fire!"

Bear scrambled for the top of the bunker. He stood up in time to see a fireball swinging rapidly seaward. The pilot might have been trying to land in the shallow water just offshore, or even to turn back to the beach, to land facing upwind. Instead, Covington's voice came again over the radio, steady but faintly disgusted: "Shit, we're out of control."

"Cov, get your nose up! Get your nose up!" Arp's warning cry on the radio had no effect on the path of the fireball. It arrowed earthward until suddenly, irrevocably, it winked out.

Three brilliant stars—the gunship searchlights—blossomed above the sea, now fading as the ships searched in another direction, now bright as the star of the Magi.

Bear was alone atop the bunker when the ships turned homeward at last. Lieutenant Rauch and the major had shut off the bunker radios and moved back into the Operations hooch. Lights were back on in the company area and around the ramp. Captain Blood, who had been in the officers' club at the other side of the ramp, had come puffing across and installed himself inside Operations to wait for the flight crews. Only when the landing lights stabbed out of the night, burning their dazzling streak through the white haze, did the Bear climb stiffly down. He slung his helmet bag over one shoulder, hooking a finger through the straps, and walked slowly down to the revetments where the ships were shutting down. He stopped at a little distance and waited as the crews tied down. Arp left the ships first, walking slowly and alone. He stopped and did not speak for a moment. Then he hooked both thumbs in his pistol belt at the front in a characteristic gesture of anger. But his voice was soft, almost apologetic. "He's gone, Bear," he said. "They're all gone."

"I saw it happening."

"I don't know where the weapon was. I turned back and there he was, burning."

"Were there any bodies?"

"Nothing. Not a trace. Not even any wreckage."

To stand on the shores of a strange land quietly discussing the death of friends would have seemed to him a year before to be an act of despair or callousness. Now he found it was neither, but perhaps only a substitute for both.

"Oh, God, I'm sorry, Bear!" Arp put out a hand and touched him on the sleeve. Then he went on up the ramp to Operations to complete his duty by turning in his report.

Bear turned aside from the rest of the crews who were beginning to leave the ships. Down the ramp he stumbled on a torn patch in the steel plank. One of the rounds had landed there. It had left a jagged hole not more than six inches wide, with the metal edges curled up. The round had barely penetrated the surface.

At the end of the ramp a guard challenged him. When he gave the password, the guard stepped forward nervously from the shadow of the revetment, beaming a flashlight. "Oh! I'm sorry I didn't know you, sir. I should of known." It was Cripps. Bear had seen him only rarely since he had been grounded. He had supposed Cripps was flying.

"Weren't you up tonight, Cripps?"

"Oh, no, sir. The ship's down for inspection, and I drew guard duty besides."

"Did you hear . . . ?"

"About the crash? I seen it, sir. But I didn't hear anything. Do they know who it was?"

"It was Covington."

"Oh, Jesus, sir! Oh, Jesus God!" Cripps shouldered his rifle and turned away. After a long pause he asked, with an effort to control his voice, "Was there anybody . . . ?"

"They're all dead."

"Oh, why him, sir? His poor wife!"

"I thought you went in, too, Cripps," Bear said. "I forgot . . . forgot he had a different ship tonight. Let's give thanks you're still with us." He in his turn gripped the soldier by the arm, as Arp had done with him. The touch of a friend was little enough, but it was more than nothing.

"If not me, then somebody else," Cripps said. "There's no thanks in that. It just changes who suffers."

There were lights in some of the nurses' quarters at the hospital, and voices eddied out through the screens, talking of the

166

attack. Alice's room was dark, but she answered immediately when he knocked, and in a moment she came to the door. Seeing him there, she gasped and hugged him. "You're all right!"

"I'm all right," he said. "I was worried about you."

"*I* was worried about *you!* Nothing happened here. But all those explosions . . ."

"We took a few mortar rounds."

"But you're all right!" She hugged him again, as if to be sure. "Was anyone hurt?"

"They brought at least one of our pilots up here."

"You want to find him. Let me come with you."

"If it's all right?"

She was already dressed. They went around by the wooden sidewalk to the emergency room. The sound of their feet was the sound of hard earth falling on a coffin. "What happened to him?"

"He took some fragments from the first round. I think it was bad. I don't know." He added, as if by afterthought, but his voice gave away his feeling, "We lost a ship, too."

"Oh, no!"

"Covington—my friend I told you about . . . you'll never get to meet him."

"Oh, Don!"

"He went into the ocean with his whole crew."

She stopped him and held him close to her for a long time. She could hear his heart pounding in his chest. Then they went on.

Dawson, the orderly who had directed Bear to Alice's ward, was on duty in the ER. It was empty except for him. "Casualties, ma'am? I ain't heard of any casualties, praise the Lord"—Dawson crossed himself, and grinned as he made the gesture—"and I sure would of known if they'd come through the swingin' doors." He added, "You might try graves registration."

Graves registration was where they found Jones. Inside the small white building the walls were lined with square doors like lockers in a bus depot. Each was the end of a drawer. The drawers slid into refrigerated cabinets. Bodies were laid in them for keeping until they were shipped back to the world. "Jones," a sleepy spec-four repeated. "Oh, yes, he's here. The one who came in after the attack. Wasn't that something? I'm too short for that crap. I'm going to be out of here by New Year's. My bags are already packed. You aren't here to identify Jones already?"

"No. Only to find out what happened to him. Thank you."

"Any time, sir." He put his head back down on the desk.

Outside her door she asked, "Do you want to come in?"

"Yes," he answered. "Yes, but . . ."

"You can. The head nurse isn't watching."

"Don't you have to work in the morning? I forget about things like that, since I'm out of a job myself."

"I'm not asking you to spend the night." She smiled, squeezing his hand to show that the remark was meant kindly.

"I'd better not."

"All right. I hope I see you tomorrow."

"You will."

As he went back up the ramp, Blood was out with the platoon sergeant inspecting the ships for damage. They had a portable generator with a spotlight and were going over the aircraft inch by inch. A tiny fragment in the wrong place could sever a control cable or pierce a hydraulic line, leaving the ship nearly uncontrollable. "Well! Mr. Bear," Blood said. "Where have you been?"

"Out on the ramp. I wanted to be outside."

"Be careful Charley doesn't catch your rear end out on the ramp. He may not be through for the night. We ought to put up another ship, if we had a crew. We would have, except for this half-assed investigation. I had to make a heavy fire team out of the three we've got left. Might not be a bad thing for *us*, though—you and me. Division wants two fire teams from us, and we don't have the bodies to do it, they've let us go so far under strength. If they need the ships bad enough, they just may let some people fly who can't now, eh, my friend?" Blood chuckled at his own cleverness.

When Bear walked away, Blood's friendly manner vanished. It had risen only from his hopes for a quick change in his own status, and it collapsed when Bear appeared to doubt his dreams. "Don't wander out of the area!" Blood called heatedly. He fell back into recalling that the whole business was at least half the Bear's fault for insisting that they all deserved some blame for Hill 473. It was hard enough to keep ahead of the Ringknockers on fair terms, without having pansies in your own platoon drag you down.

The Bear's hooch was still empty. Except for Jones, only gun platoon officers had lived there, and they were still in the alert hooch. He did not look into the bunker; but the building itself smelled of death. The door opened under protest. His flashlight showed a ragged yard-wide hole in the roof at the ridgeline. The galvanized iron was blackened around the edges of the hole, and there was the sour smell of burnt gunpowder. The mosquito nets over the beds near the door had been ripped by the shower of metal. The floor and the walls were pierced with dust-shot holes which seemed too small to have been made by anything more dangerous than termites. But what had made them had killed Jones.

His own bed at the far end of the building was untouched. He tossed the mosquito net aside and lay down fully clothed.

8

He awoke to the sound of the dawn patrol taking off. A soft fog-diluted daylight poured through the roof and the plastic-covered screen door. As the two ships hovered up the takeoff lane he could feel each revolution of the blades go trembling through his bed frame, and through the pit in his stomach. The ships beat their way into the rising offshore wind and swirled away along the cliffs toward the island. The hissing whine of the engines lingered far down the wind after the sound of the blades was gone. He rose sour-mouthed and weary and stepped out into the dawn.

The late-night fog was already giving way to the sun and the wind. Shreds of it passed through the low evergreen trees among the hooches.

Other ships were cranking in the revetments now or hovering up for takeoff. They trickled out by ones and twos as he walked slowly along the clifftop. The grey waters were far down the beach and the reef was uncovered.

The patrol soon returned. The two gunships beat low over Ky Ha and swung beyond the ridge before turning upwind for landing. Bear walked down to Operations and sat on the steps until Arp came up from his ship.

"Nothing," Arp said.

Bear walked back to his hooch.

The deuce-and-a-half truck that brought the hooch-maids to work from the main gate shuddered to a halt in the soft dirt

170

alongside the road below his door. The women's voices flowed among the hooches, broke like water into a dozen eddies that subsided into whispering pools.

He was lying on his bed when Yan came in. She gave out a soft *Trời ơi!* when she saw the hole in the roof. She set about rearranging Jones's bed as well as she could, clucking softly over the torn blanket. When she became aware of the Bear in his far corner, she caught her breath, startled, and then laughed in embarrassment: "Oh. You sleep."

"Yes, I sleep," he answered, wishing he did.

"You number-ten GI, you sleep so late. Boss no like." She twittered like a bird about its nest as she went about the beds. When she came closer to him, she said tentatively, "You no hurt?"

"No."

"VC number ten," she said firmly, looking at the hole in the roof.

"You might say that again."

"*Khong biết,*" she said, not understanding him. She added, "Sergeant at gate, he number-ten GI. He touch me here, and here." She demonstrated gravely how she had been searched. "We come late."

"Better late than never," Bear said.

"*Khong biết.*"

Near midmorning Martin came to the hooch. Bear was in a chair on the low open plywood deck at the back. Martin sat down on the edge of the deck at his feet. The island, all but the near shore, could be seen from there. The beach was clean and bare. Beyond it the white sails of fishing boats dotted the sea.

"He was a hard one to lose," Martin said after a time. "They all were; but Cov especially."

"Do you think they'll be recovered—the bodies?" Bear asked it hesitantly, as though words could somehow still make a difference.

"A Swift boat went out this morning. There was nothing. But maybe they'll come up on the beach: I don't know how the currents run." He sighed. "I just finished writing the next of kin. I hate this business."

171

"When do they find out?"

"They should know already—at least that they're missing. That was reported to Saigon last night. Division will hold the letters of condolence until they're confirmed dead."

"Confirmed! Is there any question?" Bear got up and stared at the empty sea. There was the confirmation.

"Not to us. But until the bodies are identified, they'll be carried as missing."

In Iowa it was evening, and Pinky would know her husband was missing, but not that he was dead. It would be, by the calendar, the evening of the day before, there on the other side of the International Date Line, and she might have learned of her husband's misfortune even before the calendar would show that it had occurred. But no one would say he was dead. "And if the bodies never come up?"

"I don't know, Bear. I suppose the Army will be satisfied some other way." Martin stood up. "I have to pack their gear. Do you want to do Covington's?" He did hate this business.

"All right."

"You don't have to."

Bear did not want to do it. It was like sealing his friend's tomb. He knew it was time even if his heart was not ready. So he agreed: "It's all right."

They stripped the beds Yan had just tightened. The blankets and sheets were to be returned to Supply. Bear sat on the mattress of Cov's bed sorting his possessions into two piles: one for Pinky, one for the Army. In the Army's pile went the jungle boots, fatigues, blanket, helmet liner, and steel pot. In Pinky's, one set of civilian clothes (shirt and wash pants, shoes and socks, no coat and tie), razor, toothbrush, soap, three paperback novels, a thick sheaf of letters, and a picture of Pinky, dark-eyed and short-haired and pretty in the mist-edged dream an Iowa photographer had created. "What about the letters?"

"The rule says to read all papers. They'll go to his wife. Anything you think she shouldn't see, destroy."

"I doubt that Cov had much to hide."

"No. You don't have to look at letters from Pinky. Take a look at the rest."

There were only a few others, but Covington had mixed them

172

up. Bear came on one of Pinky's in an envelope from Covington's mother. It began, "My dearest darling, When I feel our child just beginning to make itself known . . ." He put it away hurriedly, feeling as though he had stumbled clumsily into some secret place. He did not read any others. He tied the letters into a single packet, put them into the waterproof bag with Covington's clothes, tied that at the neck, and locked it inside one of the duffel bags. All that remained of Covington's life in Vietnam went into the bag, to be locked away like a genie in a bottle.

Covington had lived like a monk—sent his money home—but Jones in his short time in country had assembled a more respectable variety of goods. His tape recorder, stereo, camera, and guitar were scattered along his wall of the hooch, mixed with those of some of the other officers. Martin gestured with his head toward the records and tapes. "Can you tell me how much of this stuff belonged to Jones?" Bear moved down to help.

"Is this his?" Martin held up a shortwave portable radio he had found on the window ledge midway between Jones's bunk and the next one.

"Yes. Two hundred bucks. I don't think he ever used it."

"He didn't have much time," Martin said. He pulled out the telescoping antenna of the radio and switched slowly through the bands. Snatches of Oriental music, ethereal whistles, code transmissions, and foreign words burst forth and were abruptly silenced. Emanations of Malaysia, Indonesia, Japan, Red China revealed their presences. Bear was startled by a voice like Covington's, but it was clipped off. The dead were packed away, and if the room was haunted, it was by the voices of men still living.

Yet, if those speaking were alive, they were no more than ghosts to the Bear, no more alive than Covington who lay silent in deep water. Their lives could not touch him.

There was an English voice—deep, deliberate, sonorous; "This is the Australian Broadcasting Commission. The time is . . . twelve noon." Martin left the radio on that station. The anonymous Australian voice read the news: Parliament, cricket, the weather in Sydney (fair, eighty-six degrees), the prime minister said, the price of wool on the international market, forthcoming season at the Sydney opera house.

173

It had no meaning to the Bear. The voice told echoes of lives uncomprehended, things too far removed to catch at his heart.

Yan and Suzie, scrubbing laundry in flimsy aluminum pans on the next porch, tittered and called out to their neighbors. They, too, haunted the room. This was all of life to Yan and Suzie: by day, a job with the *Nguoi My*, the Americans; and by night—what? Suzie's husband was dead, Bear knew, dead years ago of some disease. They lived in one of the villages, but he did not know where. Not on the island, but somewhere around the shores of Song Ben Van. He saw them daily, but knew no more of their lives than of those whose echo filled the room from a six-inch radio speaker. The only thing more than an echo was war, and that overwhelmed everything.

Listening to the same civilized voice from the radio, Martin was struck with surprise that ordinary life was going on all about him. He could almost reach out and touch it. Only an eyeblink away barmaids and stockbrokers were at the very instant passing back and forth under a fair sky, taking their lunches, reading their newspapers, laughing.

The hooch-maids on the next porch tittered and called out. For them, too, this was everyday life. Yan, at least, had grown up with war, known nothing else; but she survived. She laughed. War had not defeated her.

Through the screen in the window Martin could see the fishing fleet from the island scattered like snow across the grey plain of the sea. In any but bad weather the sampans were out by day and sometimes by night. Fishermen's lives were regulated by wind and tide, by the sun and by the clock. Boats at sea after the curfew might be sunk on sight by the National Police, by the Swift boats, by prowling gunships. War regulated their lives, or cut them short without warning. But that was only one more regulation, no harsher than wind and tide.

Martin felt his grip on life tighten, at the same time that the Bear's was slipping. The Bear had always taken strength from outside himself, from people and things around him. Grounded, he had already lost the place he thought he had found for himself as a man. Now that had led to the first great personal loss he had known, and he was shaken. Martin's case was different. He had never been one to look at life rather than touch it, any more than

174

the Bear was: but ultimately even his belief in comradeship came from within himself; it appealed to him as an idea, and he could take as much strength from what he saw or imagined in others as from what he experienced himself. Whatever happened—and he knew no more than Bear what it might be—he would endure it.

"Jesus Christ, ain't that a purty picture!" Rauch was standing in the door of the hooch. "Our high-culture hour for sure. Captain Martin, sir, you're goin' to seduce that poor boy yet."

"Hello, Rauch." Martin was sensitive enough to the pain lurking in the Bear that Rauch's voice annoyed him. Loud voices did not belong in the house of dead men.

Rauch, who saw none of that, went on loudly, "Bear, you're goin' to get a flat ass sittin' on the floor like that. Why don't you get up off it and I'll give you a little somethin' to do?" He said this with a broad grin.

Bear looked slowly from Martin to Rauch. "Whenever Captain Martin's done with me," he said without interest.

"I'll bet Captain Martin will even let you go for this," Rauch said. He was almost hidden now by his own grin, like the Cheshire cat.

"What's happening, Rauch?" Martin asked.

"Oh, nothin' much. Major Hart just called over, is all, and told me to get the Bear down to the ready hooch. The chief of staff just cleared him for flight status."

Bear climbed to his feet slowly, to the obvious puzzlement of Rauch, who had expected more of a reaction. His grin faded.

"The investigation report came out?" Martin asked.

"I don't know about that," Rauch answered. "The major just said to tell Bear and Blood and Atterburn they're back on flight status. So get your gear and haul ass down to the flight line, kid. We got a ship nobody's preflighted because we didn't have bodies to man it."

"What about Captain Martin?" Bear asked.

"I don't know. I reckon the major will tell you himself," Rauch said to Martin. "Come on, Bear. I'll see you down there."

After Rauch was gone, Bear walked up and down the aisle of the hooch. Martin congratulated him, but he only said quietly, "I don't want to fly until you do, sir."

"You may have a long wait if you wait for me."

"I don't care. I don't know if I want to fly at all."

Martin looked at him, startled. No man flew the way the Bear did unless he loved to fly.

"I don't know if I can," Bear blurted, in answer to the look. "Maybe it seems like I'm letting down Cov, and the others, if I don't get back at Charley. Maybe I am. I hadn't even thought about it until just now. I don't know. But I thought about this— you didn't do anything the rest of us didn't do. To go back on flight status is like saying it wasn't my fault, it was yours."

"It wasn't your fault, Bear. I was the flight commander, or could have been. I was responsible."

"Whatever that means. I killed as many men as you did."

"But I made the decision."

"Was there a 'decision'? Snoopy made as much of a decision as anybody, and Snoopy's nothing but a trunkful of fuses and wires."

"For all we know," Martin said, "the investigation has cleared us all. I wouldn't be flying anyway. We're hard up for pilots, but the paper-pushers stay with their paper forever." He knew it was not so. Blood was right about that infantry light colonel: he hadn't come down from the hills for nothing. But he said, "We've got men who've been on standby for a week straight, and it will be worse now that we're shorter on pilots. Get your helmet and get on down to the flight line."

At this Bear stopped in the middle of the aisle and stared up at the hole in the roof. "I guess one man dead flying my mission *is* enough," he said.

"I didn't mean that, Bear."

"I know you didn't, but it doesn't matter. I know truth when I see it." He picked up his helmet bag and pistol belt from his bunk, pulled on his cap, and plunged out the door.

The radio was uttering something about the Vietnam war. Martin snapped it off, turned it upside down, and copied its serial number onto the list of Jones's property.

Bear felt odd and out of place stepping into the alert hooch where he had been a regular inhabitant little more than a week before. It was like stepping back into a life left far behind. The hooch was crowded with the rest of the gun platoon and a handful of slick pilots. When he came in they stood and clapped and cheered.

Bear was ashamed how grateful he felt at that moment.

Blood stood at the back of the hooch wrapping himself in a benign smile. "Speech by Bear!" someone shouted. "Speech by Bear!" They were all so raucously pleased that he did not have the heart not to pretend it was not just like old times. He raised both arms in the manner of the pope pronouncing a benediction, and when they were quiet, he said solemnly, "Screw you all and the horse you rode in on." It was just the speech they expected from him. They roared and stamped and applauded.

But after others had crowded around and fallen back, and he had sat alone for a moment, he was aware that he was still being watched. Cripps was seated on the bunk in the back corner of the building. He came forward—indirectly—as if he were really bound out the door and stopped only as an afterthought. Cripps's shyness disarmed the Bear's comic defenses.

"Ah, I'm glad you're back, sir," Cripps said.

"Thanks, Cripps."

"Not that I mind flying with anyone else so much, but everything's been so serious."

"It doesn't do to be serious when you're out killing," Bear said. He wished he hadn't said it, for Cripps's eyes switched away from him. Bear saw that Cripps had prepared a compliment and now felt foolish. He tried to smooth it over with a soft word of thanks, which he meant seriously.

Bear did not see Alice that day, as he had promised, nor for many days after. Duty left him no time for anything other than flying or waiting to fly.

And when he did go flying at last, he could not stop his heart from racing. Arp was flying with him for the afternoon. Arp was delicate about the protocol. Although he was, as senior officer, the aircraft commander, he insisted that Bear take the right-hand seat; and when they cranked for takeoff, he said, "You fly. I've been doing this too much lately." They had the Bear's own ship, with Handy and Cripps as crew. Lifting the ship to back out of the revetment was for a moment like coming home, in a way moving back into the alert hooch had not been.

It was an easy mission. They led a light fire team as escort for a flying crane delivering guard towers to Special Forces camps along the Song Tien, west of the first range of mountains. The interstorm monsoon weather was at its best—hazy, cool, with a weak sun silvering the edges of the sky. They flew out and back four thousand feet above the highway west from Tam Ky. They saw nothing but mountain, tree, and haze, except at one point a few tanks pulled off in a paddy beside the highway. While the crane shuttled towers in and out, they circled overhead, studying the roofs of the distant town of Hoi Lam or watching buffalo souse themselves in the marsh at the edge of the rain-swollen river.

They parted from the crane at Tam Ky and returned toward home over the sand dunes on the seaward side of Song Tam Ky, the broad, slow-flowing, many-channeled river which partly emptied into the sea north of the crescent island and partly turned into the Son Ben Van behind it. The plain on the landward side of the Song was paddy and marsh mixed with sandy waste, split by dikes and hedges and pathways; but on the seaward side there was only a broad belt of bare dunes, with a few evergreens tucked into the hollows. Outside that belt was the narrower channel of the Truong Giang, a tidal river lying parallel to the sea, marsh-bordered and separated from the sea by a bare quarter mile of blowing dunes. Fishing villages huddled at wide intervals along this shore. They sheltered among the evergreens behind the first row of dunes from the sea, for during the monsoon the wind blew fiercely, and the boats were pulled far up on the sloping beach that ran straight and unbroken for fifty kilometers from Chu Lai to Hoi An. The villagers' homes were thatched roof and wall, so that they had the appearance of haystacks among the scrubby trees. They were chimneyless and stained black by the smoke which filtered through the thatch. Bear led the flight low down the strip of dunes between these two worlds of farmer and fisherman, over the regular V's of the fishing weirs pointing upstream in the Song, the nets on gin-poles stretched above the surface to dry, and the sampans with painted eyes plodding patiently upcurrent with the wind behind them.

The helicopters broke out over the palm forest of the crescent island. Bear started to swing back inland in a climb which would take them above the ridge behind Ky Ha for an upwind landing, when Handy called out, "Sir, what's all them people down on the beach?"

Arp, who was on the seaward side, stared out the window for a moment. Although the islanders lived by fishing, there was rarely anyone to be seen on the beach on the seaward side. Their landings were in the quiet waters of Song Ben Van, on the far side of the island. "Let's go have a look," Arp said.

As the two helicopters broke out over the edge of the beach, the crowd there dissolved and flowed toward the shelter of the trees, leaving only a piece of seadrift at the high tide line.

"Put it down," Arp said.

They made a low turn over the water and swept rapidly up the beach. Bear feathered the ship to a quick stop.

The thing the sea had cast up was a body.

It was pale, and shriveled from the water. Sand whipped over it as he put the ship down on the beach beside it. Except for one black sock, it was naked. Some of the clothing had been dropped farther up the beach by the villagers who had been stripping the body. "Put the gun down, Handy," Arp said. Bear saw that Handy had raised his machine gun and had trained it in the direction of some conical straw hats which were still visible along the edge of the trees.

"Let me kill the bastards, sir," Handy pleaded. "They did it to him, and now they're stealin' his clothes. The sons of bitches! Stealin' a dead man's clothes!"

"I said put down the gun. Now get him on board." Handy got down and rolled the sea-whitened body clumsily onto the cabin floor. Arp waved him back to collect the articles which had been dropped along the beach by the crowd. The straw hats vanished when Handy started toward them from the ship. He returned with a pair of trousers and a holster with no weapon in it. "Let's go," Arp said.

An ambulance took the body from the aircraft. It was not Covington, as Bear had expected, but Washington. His body was unmarked. The arms were rigid, spread slightly from the sides, and the head was pulled forward toward the chest. The skin of the body was wrinkled and bleached white as flour, but the face looked quite like Washington. He looked peaceful and unconcerned about the sea-foam in his fine mustache.

The dusk patrol picked up the body of the pilot, Boroff, who came ashore at almost the same spot as Washington. The patrol also brought in part of an engine cover panel. The paint was blistered, and there were two bullet holes.

Every aircraft that went out made a pass over the island, but there was no sign of another body. Part of the fiberglass nose cone was tossed up on the third day. That was all.

On the fourth day Martin checked with the Navy. A strong tidal current flowed parallel to the shore twice a day, he was told. A body might come ashore miles away, if it came ashore at all. When Martin told the Bear that, Bear asked, "How long does the Army wait before it decides they're dead enough to tell the next of kin?"

Martin could only say that he didn't know.

That day was New Year's Eve. The Bear spent it in the alert hooch next to Covington's empty cot. He was awake when the New Year came, but he did not mark it. The rejoicing in the clubs around the ramp was lost in the rumble of artillery up and down the plain, where the New Year's truce was going up in fire and smoke.

On New Year's Day the weather held fair, with a light southeast wind and a calm sea. The gun pilots sat on the Operations officer's jeep letting the sun ease out the stiffness of a night of interrupted sleep. Inside Operations, Blood was explaining the tactical situation in detail to Lieutenant Rauch, who cared only about getting his quota of helicopters into the air by the proper hour each morning. When the telephone rattled, Rauch snatched it up at once, but Blood's voice went on, addressed now to the Operations sergeant, who could not take cover behind a telephone.

"Captain Blood says Charley's licked," Atterburn said. "It's just mopping up now." He was half-listening to Blood inside the hooch, although he had heard this analysis a dozen time before.

"Considering what mileage Charley got out of his New Year's truce," Arp said, "I can hardly wait for the Buddha's birthday."

180

Blood came to the door. "That was graves registration on the line," he said. "They need two officers to identify a body." He looked straight at the Bear. "Why don't you go on up and tell them who it is, Mr. Bear?" He added, "I'd do it myself. After all, it might have been my mission he was flying. But I have to be here in case a fire mission comes in. You and Arp go."

"You're remembering we're on standby, too?" Arp asked.

"Ah, don't worry. It's just up the ramp. Rauch can telephone if anything comes in. You can get to a ship about as quick from there as from here. Take the jeep."

Atterburn climbed down, and Arp and the Bear drove down onto the ramp and past the tails of the parked ships. "That didn't make the most sense I've ever heard," Arp said.

"He wanted me to see the body," Bear answered.

"Even Blood isn't that much of a bastard." They both knew it was Covington.

The graves registration clerk said, "There's nobody here by that name."

"Somebody just called and said there was," Arp told him.

"From here? Not from here, sir." He flipped through the papers on his desk again. "What unit are you from?" When Arp told him, he threw up his hands: "Oh, sure! You've got a body here! But his name isn't Covington. At least not as far as *we* know."

"Not Covington?"

"No, sir. It's Laforgue. That's what his name tag said. He didn't have any dog tags. There were some papers in his wallet that you could still read. They say LaForgue, too."

"Yes, we had a LaForgue." LaForgue had been the gunner on Covington's ship that night.

"Well, we're pretty sure that's him, sir. Unless he changed clothes with this Covington before whatever happened, happened."

"I doubt he did," Arp said dryly. "All right, let's see him."

"Sure. He's outside, sir." The clerk hesitated. "You don't have to view the remains if you don't want to, sir. If you don't have any question about the identity, I mean. You can, but . . . he's been in the water a long time, you know, and . . . the fish have been at his face."

"Who brought him in?"

"The Navy sent him up. A Swift boat picked him up offshore."

"Let's make sure," Bear said.

"All right," Arp agreed. "But you don't have to come. There's no need for both of us."

"Not looking won't change things."

Outside behind the building there was a brown Conex container, a seven-foot-high steel cube used as a shipping container by Army units moving overseas. "This gives us a little spare capacity," the clerk explained as he opened the container, "and it saves handling, on people like LaForgue."

The container was refrigerated. On either side within there were racks built against the walls. On one of these there was a black rubberized bag. The clerk slid it forward and unzipped the end. An evil odor spread from the open end.

The body could have been anyone. There was no face, only a ragged mass of pulp which looked as if it belonged in the sea, as if it should be growing on a coral reef. The bloated carcass strained at the bag. Arp motioned for the clerk to shut the Conex.

"Let's look at the papers," he said.

"Anything you want, sir. We're sure they're LaForgue's papers, even if we ain't sure it's LaForgue."

The wallet contained a few dollars in scrip, a washed-out letter no longer legible, and a plasticized driver's license which was unquestionably LaForgue's. The clerk was right: the body could not have been Covington unless they had changed clothing on the way down. Bear remembered the swift plunge of the fireball. He signed the identification form after Arp.

They drove back in silence. As they crossed past the end of the hospital, Bear looked up toward the nurses' quarters, but no one was to be seen. He had been on standby since the morning after the mortar attack. It was only a few hundred meters from the company to the hospital; but he had not seen her.

Arp went into Operations. Bear remained outside on the jeep. Arp was back outside in a minute. He sat on the jeep and pounded his fist on the hood.

"What did he say?" Bear knew that Arp had reported to Blood.

"Nothing."

"Don't shit the troops."

182

"Well, the first thing he said was 'How did Covington look?' in his best egg-sucking voice. So I said, 'He looked a lot like LaForgue.' Blood said to Rauch, 'LaForgue? I thought you told me it was Covington' and Rauch said, 'Naw, sir, I said graves registration wanted a couple of officers to identify a body.' 'What the hell did they ask for officers for,' Blood asks, 'if they had an EM to identify? They could get the first sergeant for that.' As if LaForgue wasn't worth the waste of an officer's time."

" 'Even Blood isn't that much of a bastard,' " Bear said.

"I was wrong."

Tired of endless standby in the alert hooches, some of the pilots had wandered down to the ships, where they sat restless and bored, watching the sunny patches slide and shift over distant ridges. Warrant Officer Ruth pulled down the gunsight and stared around the area through it. "I wonder if vis fing works," he grumbled. He had come into the company two days before, and there had been no action in all that time.

"It works, Rufe," Arp assured him. "Have faith."

Ruth's nickname came from his speech defect. When Blood had first asked him his name he had made a special effort and came out with a clear, "Ruth, sir." "Okay, Ruth," Blood had said, "what's your last name?" Arp thought it a shame that Blood had been serious. "I'd like to hear Captain Blood make a joke before I die," he said.

After that Ruth gave up on his name. He had a slow crooked smile, the beginnings of a Vietnam mustache, and no objection to being called anything at all that showed he was liked.

"It took me a week and a half to get here from Saigon," he complained. "I don't want to spend anuvver week waiting for Charley."

A Chinook delivering water flapped overhead dangling a five-hundred-gallon rubber bladder from its cargo hook. Ruth watched it with interest, but Arp frowned and said, "I wish he'd fly somewhere besides over the ramp. I saw one of the buggers drop a ton of lobster into Tam Ky one day." Lobster was the radio name for ammunition for the 105-mm howitzer.

"Did it go off?" Ruth asked.

"No. But what if it had? Or even what if it hadn't, if it landed on

183

somebody. How would you like to get a five-hundred-gallon bladder on your skull?"

"I'd like to get the Hook pilot that dropped my ship," Griggs muttered from his seat in the door. Griggs was standing by with a command and control ship for one of the infantry battalions and had come over to Arp's ship while waiting for a call to fly. "Did I ever tell you about that, Rufe?"

"Not more than three times, Griggs," Arp said. "But Rufe's only been here a couple of days."

"I was on this rat fuck down south," Griggs began, "and on short final the whole world went up."

"That means someone took a shot at him," Arp said to Ruth.

"Look, Lieutenant, you tell your stories, and I'll tell mine," Griggs said. "Okay? Anyway, there we were on short final when the Christmas tree lit up and the engine quit. Well, I put 'er down and we unassed the ship. AK-47's everywhere. We got the guns off and snuggled down in this little gully to wait it out. Finally things quieted down enough that the next lift came in, and we could have gone out then but I wanted to save the ship. That was a good ship, number zero eight five. So we spent the day there after the infantry moved out. We took some sniper fire, but along about dark we got the ship rigged and a Hook came in after it. Carlsen came in and got us out at the same time. Damn good pilot, he was. I hated to see him go. Well, we took off after the Hook, and we caught up with him at about three thousand feet—just in time to see the bastard drop my ship! The thing wasn't even rigged wrong—they just hit the cargo release by mistake, and off she went."

This story was Griggs's set piece, but he embellished it less than usual because Arp was leaning back in his seat with a bemused look. Griggs did not like being around Arp. "I wish the Gunfighter would get his ass in gear so we could go get some Dinks," he grumbled.

"Who's ve Gunfighter?" Ruth asked.

"Who's the Gunfighter!" Griggs said this with pity for anyone who didn't know the Gunfighter. "He's the commander of the Fighting Forty-ninth infantry battalion, that's who."

"So called," Arp told Ruth, "because his chief delight in life is to take his C-and-C ship down into any firefight he happens across."

"The man's got a pair." Griggs shrugged.

"Maybe a little less than the issue amount of brains," Arp said, "but balls, yes."

"He just wants to get his share of Slopes before we run out, sir." Griggs grinned, pleased to see that he had annoyed Arp. "Though we ain't likely to run out soon enough to suit me. You made any live Slopes into good Slopes lately, Bear?" The Bear had just come up to the side of the ship.

"Don't worry about it, Griggs," Bear said. "We'll keep your tail safe."

"I'm like the Gunfighter," Griggs said. "I never worry about dead Slopes. I just worry about the live ones."

"I didn't know you were so tenderhearted."

"That's what I am. I'll tell you how tenderhearted I am. I think we ought to give this fucking country back to the Slopes. I figure if we gave every one of 'em about six feet of it, the war would be over in no time."

"Why don't you take yourself back to your own ship, Griggs?" Bear said. "I'm tired of hearing your jaw flap faster than your brain works."

Griggs tried to outstare Bear; but after a moment he gave it up, climbed out of the ship, and sauntered away.

"Don't mind that asshole, B.," Arp said.

" 'Mind' is the wrong word to use in a sentence referring to Griggs," Bear said. " 'Asshole' comes pretty close, though."

"For sure." Arp sighed. "Between the assholes and the hearts and minds of the people, this is one complicated war. Well, what's up, Bear?"

"My ship. Handy has the new rocket tubes boresighted. If you can find me a pilot, I'll take it down to the range to test them."

"Hey, have I got a pilot for you!" Arp clapped Ruth on the knee. "Rufe has just been panting for some exercise. You take him, and I'll go ask Rauch for someone else to stand by with me until you get back."

"You think it's a good idea," Rauch said to Arp, "to send Rufe up with Bear, his first mission in country?"

"If I didn't, I wouldn't have sent him," Arp said, a little coldly. "I wish *I*'d had a chance to fly with the Bear my first mission in country." He expected backbiting from Griggs, but not from Rauch.

"Nothin' against Bear," Rauch said. "But it's the first time he's flown with anybody but you, since Cov went down. I don't know how he'll feel about it."

"There's nothing special about me." This was said with considerably more warmth: Arp was grateful that his suspicion had been so wrong.

"I'd be the last to admit there was, for sure," Rauch remarked, grinning at Arp. "But you and Bear go back a long ways. Farther even than Bear and Cov. You know how close he was to Cov; flyin' with you wouldn't be so different. But takin' up a Fuckin' New Guy . . ."

"Bear will take care of him," Arp said. "Anyway, they're only testing weapons. It'll give them a chance to get used to each other *before* the shit hits the fan."

At the south end of the five-mile-long Chu Lai beach, beyond the fishing villages clustered at the mouth of the river Tra Bong, the shore hooked back northward in a rocky peninsula that cradled in its arm the bay Dung Quat. The steep flanks of the coastal range to the south trailed off there into a low tumbling ridge that stretched for a half mile into the shallow waters of the bay. From anywhere along the Chu Lai shore fighter-bombers could be seen daily working along the mountains south of the peninsula. On sunny days their wings flashed as they rolled into inverted dives and then upright again before releasing their bombs. Tiny golden flashes would twinkle against the mountainsides, and, when the wind was in the south, a quarter of a minute later the sound would pass by, a weak mutter of distant trouble. The peninsula was said to be a VC stronghold, but that belief apparently arose from the high visibility of the jet strikes, which might, for all anyone in the helicopter company knew, have been training missions, like their own weapons testing.

The ruin of a large house stood at the tip of the peninsula. Once a rich Frenchman's seaside villa, now its yellowing walls were a convenient mark for testing weapons. A low pass could be made from seaward with no danger that a wild shot would do any harm.

Bear was fond of the building. It stood firm to its daily fate. Although pocked and splintered by machine gun, rocket, and grenade, its walls and even part of its red tile roof still stood. Its bare back was turned on the sands of Chu Lai five miles away: the empty sockets of the windows were turned to the sea, where of old, on the clearest of days, Cu Lao Re might have been seen floating above the horizon.

The gunship came in low over the bay, out of the silver haze that hung between sea and sky. A cluster of fishing sampans lay slack-sailed far offshore in the haze, at the limits of existence. One, bound homeward under power, plowed a silver trail through the blue sea below, its painted eyes fixed on the mouth of the Song Tra Bong.

Ruth drank in these sights. He was still dazzled by the Orient.

A half mile out Bear took the controls and turned in toward the house. "Ready to arm?" he asked.

"Ready."

"Okay. Let's go hot."

Ruth flipped the switches to the armed position.

Bear called out the range to the house. "There's a thousand meters." How the Bear knew, Ruth could not say, for the house on the rock seemed to float at the same untouchable distance in the same endless blue. But he took down the gunsight and twisted the bright dot onto the house.

Bear touched the red button of the rocket trigger with his thumb. The ship was enveloped in light. Through the gunsight Ruth watched the twin flares of the rocket motors slide down the hill of air. They looped above the distant red speck of the roof, then against it, then below it, and vanished in a single smoke blossom against the side wall of the house. The smoke drifted away beyond the end of the rock to join with the bright sea-haze. The building still stood.

"Were they short?" Ruth asked.

"Not hardly, sir!" Handy said. He was watching over Bear's shoulder. Handy was pleased. He had just boresighted the weapons. He loved to see the first cold shot be on target.

"Your turn," Bear said. Ruth squeezed the trigger switch on

the gunsight. The steady spray of tracers played about the walls of the house. As they closed within a hundred meters, he released the trigger. Not until he had released it was he aware that the Bear was watching him with an amused smile.

"You never get enough of that in flight school," Bear said after Ruth had let the guns fall silent. "Maybe you'll find satisfaction here."

Ruth had the uncomfortable feeling that he should have broken off sooner. But the Bear was right: he liked seeing the tracers flash on the target.

As the ship broke away short of the house, Ruth saw that the rockets had indeed been dead on, as Handy had known: a fresh scar had appeared on the back wall of the house. One rocket had broken through, and now the sun shone in. "I'm afraid she's not long for this world now," Bear said, to no one in particular.

"She's been standing a long time," Cripps said. It was the first thing Ruth had heard Cripps say.

"All things come to an end, Cripps," Bear answered. "The bad with the good."

Ruth felt as though he were overhearing a part of a private conversation, the key to which he had somehow missed.

Bear turned to Ruth. "Do you need another pass?"

"I'm satisfied." Ruth could not tell whether Bear was asking if he needed to fire again to check his sight, or just for the sheer pleasure. Ruth wanted to make another pass and watch the tracers' slow burning fall, but he did not, somehow, care to have Bear know that.

Bear turned the ship toward home, climbing out rapidly over the open bay.

As the gunship turned away, a scout helicopter bored in below. The two fixed machine guns on its skids left a stuttering stream of smoke as the pilot tested his weapons. The gunner and crew chief, who rode one on either side of the pilot in the three-seat cockpit, were leaning from the doors to fire their hand-held machine guns. Handy leaned out to watch them close on the ruined house. "Would you lookit them work out!" he called in delight. To Handy there was nothing so beautiful as well-aimed fire pouring onto a target—the more the better.

Bear held the ship steady on course for home.

Suddenly there was a voice on the radio: "Mayday, Mayday! Skeeter Six-eight is hit and going down on the target range!"

Bear thought at first it was a joke. The point was worked over daily by weapons of all descriptions, and no one had ever taken a round of return fire. The broken rocks offered hiding places in plenty; but a squad of infantry could seal off the peninsula, trapping anyone hiding there. To fire on a gunship from there was suicidal. Yet there was something in the voice on the radio that demanded belief. There was no panic in the voice, but there was that adrenal tension that could not be hidden under orderly radio procedure.

Bear wrenched his ship around in time to see the tiny scout ship flare to a teetering stop at the very tip of the peninsula. "Switch 'em back on!" he said to Ruth, who sat stunned as the crew of the other helicopter piled out and raced for the shelter of the rocks below the ledge where they had suddenly come to earth.

Ruth later remembered only the lazy way the small helicopter's blade ran down as unseen bullets smashed its windscreen, while the three crewmen scuttled like crabs among the rocks. He could not find the enemy weapon. He threw the switches to "arm" and reached for his gunsight, but by then the Bear had dived the ship to sea level. When Ruth looked out, he thought for an instant they could not pull up before hitting the water. Then they were racing for the shore below the scout helicopter. "Any tracers in sight?" Bear was asking. Both Handy and Cripps answered with quick negatives. "Without tracers that guy could eat our lunch before we find him, alone up here," Bear said. "I wish the hell we had a trail ship to keep his head down when we break off. But maybe if we sneak in low enough, that ledge the other ship is on will block his fire."

The shelf the scout helicopter had landed on was a few yards above the water. The crew had dropped over the edge of the shelf and were firing their sidearms from among the seaweed-strewn boulders the sea had piled there. Bear drove his ship for those rocks with its skids almost cutting the water, slowed in a rattle of incoming gunfire, swung the tail to one side, and came to a hover with the main blade overlapping the rock shelf but with the body of the ship below the shelf's edge, partly sheltered from the

189

gunfire. He parked one skid atop a boulder, and two of the crew of the scout helicopter stepped aboard dry-footed. Bear started the aircraft hovering toward the third crewman, who had become separated from the others and was now behind a boulder on the far side of a low break in the shelf. As Bear hovered his ship down the shoreline past this break, bullets suddenly snapped all around them. A machine gun was firing down through the break in the shelf. There was a ringing clang from the rear as one bullet struck metal. They could not cross the break.

Bear peeled the ship away and dashed low over the sea until they were beyond small-arms range. A few bullets skipped around them, but none struck the ship.

"Ask the pilot where the weapon is," Bear said to Ruth.

Ruth leaned back and asked, but the pilot did not know. He stared unhappily down toward the shore, where his gunner was huddling behind his rock. "He won't last long there!" the pilot shouted. "If we leave him . . ."

"We won't leave him," Bear said. He turned back inbound for the point. "The fuel is low. We have to find that weapon quick." Bear appeared to be holding a conversation with himself. It took Ruth a moment to understand that Bear was doing more than deciding the best way to proceed. He was pointing out the things Ruth would need to remember if a bullet suddenly left him as the pilot in command.

They came in higher up this time, where they made a clear crisp target against the silvered sky. There was no difference from the approach they had made while sighting in, Ruth reflected, except that now they knew a weapon was waiting. Charley could have potted them on the first run, if he had been ready. Perhaps he had been caught asleep, and they had wakened him in time for him to hit the other ship. Whatever Charley's reasons, Ruth knew that it felt different now, flying down to the muzzle of a hidden weapon. He saw things now on the peninsula that he hadn't suspected were there on the first pass—the folds in the black-veined rocks near the ruined house, the glint of sun from a thousand facets of broken stone, the dry dead bush whose branches might have been the barrels of a dozen weapons. The ship bored relentlessly in.

"If he's smart, he'll wait for us to break off," Bear said. "So I'll start a break and then turn back in. Be ready." He broke off farther out than he might have otherwise, at five hundred meters, barely within machine gun range, unless it was a fifty. "Let's hope he bites."

"There he is!" Handy called out. At the same instant the air came alive with the crackling of bullets. Handy fired off a burst of tracers that fell toward a fold in the rock three hundred meters from the house.

"Put it on him," Bear said to Ruth. In the violent turn back toward the weapon, the main blade now blanked out Handy's fire, and Cripps was facing the opposite direction. Bear's rocket tubes pointed straight ahead, not yet on the target. Only Ruth's flex guns were able to fire. He alone held the defense of the ship in his hands.

He could not keep the sight on the spot. His tracers spewed all around it. He could see the weapon now—a point of sputtering light that stood out from the reflected flashes of sunlight on the rock. He watched it sputter at him. It was such a small thing, hardly larger than the glowing dot in the gunsight. It seemed to have no connection with the snapping fingers of death all around him.

The ship had rolled off target in an instant: it seemed an eternity coming back. Ruth held the trigger down. The guns growled. The stream of tracers swept up the rock, beside the muzzle flashes, above them, back on the other side. They would not settle down.

A hole appeared in the windshield before Ruth's eyes. He did not hear the bullet strike, nor feel the ship rock: but he saw the hole, a neat thing the size of his finger. Nor did he hear the rockets go, but he saw them. Two pairs rippled away, four bright points of light, much brighter than the muzzle flashes toward which they fell. They did not fan out, as rockets would do if fired across the wind of an uncoordinated turn. The ship had come steady for that instant when the tubes were first on target, and the four rockets sped in a tight cluster toward the cleft rock.

For perhaps two seconds the bullets continued to crack about the ship: they had been already on their way when the rockets were launched. Any one of them could have been enough to bring an end to the flight of the ship, and the lives of those on it,

191

even if, when it struck, he who had sent it was himself already dead. For the space of two seconds the living on either end could watch their fates cross, and know that all was now beyond their control. It had been determined already who would live and who would die. There remained but to wait and see.

A pair of rockets blossomed where Handy's tracers had fallen. The second pair exploded within a second of the first, on the same spot.

The rattle of bullets went on, went on . . . and ceased. There was sudden silence, if the pounding, whistling interior of a helicopter could be called silent. It seemed silent to Ruth, who had been hearing only the incoming rounds and the tearing growl of his own guns. Now there was nothing.

"You got the motherfucker!" Handy exulted. "He is *gone!*"

"Keep an eye out," Bear said. "There may be another baddie."

They prowled the edges of the peninsula, first well out, then closer in, and finally flew directly over the spot where the weapon had been. What could have been a body lay at the bottom of a split in the rock. Handy showered it with bullets as they passed over. "Don' never hurt to make sure," he said complacently as he brought the gun back inside.

"All right, let's go pick up that crewman," Bear said to Ruth as they made a wide circle beyond the tip of the peninsula. "One more thing you should know: the hydraulics are out." For the first time Ruth noticed the stick bucking in Bear's hand. The bullet that had come through the windshield had gone on through the back of the cabin and cut a hydraulic line. With no hydraulic boost the ship could be flown only with the full strength of the arm, and not by the pressure of two fingers. It turned from an obedient thoroughbred to a kicking rebellious mule as every revolution of the main blade fed an amplified blow back through the control rods to the pilot's hand on the cyclic stick. How Bear could have rolled it out exactly on target, Ruth could not imagine.

The approach to the shore this time was slow, careful, and effortful. Ruth, merely following on the controls, felt the sweat crawling down his ribs. The cyclic struggled in his hand like a wild live thing; but the Bear had the other cyclic locked in his fist, and leaned forward to get the strength of his shoulder behind the

192

strength of his arm. The controls kicked; but the ship was steady as rock. It eased among the rocks; the gunner scrambled aboard; and they were climbing safely away.

The pilot of the other ship pounded Bear on the shoulder. "Some flying, by God!" he shouted with a happy grin. Over the noise of the ship his voice was but a weak echo of what Ruth was thinking himself.

When Ruth flew on the way home, to give the Bear a rest, the cyclic slammed at his right hand, and the collective was a leaden bar in the palm of his left. The ship flew angrily, as if grudging every second it was forced to remain in the air.

Blood was enraged to learn that the company that owned the scout helicopter had recommended Bear for a Distinguished Flying Cross. "What do those bastards know about it?" he demanded.

Lieutenant Rauch, who was the only person to hear this performance, went on reading after-action reports. He was unsympathetic but not up to pissing off a senior officer. He could not resist observing, however, "I expect they've seen a little flyin' in their time."

"So all right, the son of a bitch can handle a ship! He doesn't have the first fucking idea how to follow an order, and he needs a special delivery telegram from God before he'll shoot. If he gets another DFC, he'll just be that much worse. Why didn't the bastards ask his own company, before they start sending off papers to Battalion? The son of a bitch doesn't need a medal: he needs to be busted to buck private!"

When Bear heard about the citation, he wasn't as pleased as Ruth had expected him to be. He looked mostly tired, like some faded zoo animal that had long since given up hope of escape.

"You deserve it, B.," Ruth urged. "I fought . . . I fought that was the best flying I've ever seen."

"Good flying is important, Rufe," Bear agreed. Old Tate would have liked it. But Ruth did not know quite what to make of the answer, accompanied as it was by an enormous fart, and a sigh which might have been profound physical satisfaction or grief, Ruth could not say which. He tried again: "You deserve a medal for it."

"Yes, I guess I do." Bear's face took on the pensive look of a shorn sheep pondering the winter sun. "I was brave, resourceful, cool in the face of withering enemy fire. . . . It does make a great citation, doesn't it?" Though Ruth did not know it, Bear was quoting from one of his own earlier citations. "Also, I killed an enemy. Not many, but one can be enough, in the right place. Kill 'em dead'll win a medal. There wasn't any way not to kill him, was there, Rufe?"

The morning the letters came down from Division, Martin was endorsing efficiency reports on the company officers. Every officer was rated at least twice during his year in Vietnam, or whenever he changed duties or changed units, or when his rating officer changed. To a career soldier his rating was everything; but to most of the pilots, who were in the Army for three years of flying, it meant nothing. Still, there was no telling what a man would want to do in another year, and so Martin weighed each one with equal care. He resisted equally the desire to be creative and the desire to tell the truth. There was no place in an officer efficiency report for either imagination or truth.

Each report had two parts. The Army believed that one part was subjective, the other objective. On the former the rater or endorser wrote a paragraph describing the subject's performance of his duties. On the latter he gave a numerical rating to the officer with respect to certain specified qualities (tact, forcefulness, decisiveness), and also gave him a numerical rating between zero and one hundred. The number represented the percentile of all officers into which this officer would fall, rated from worst to best. An officer scoring one hundred was to be more effective than ninety-nine others out of every one hundred. There was a nice graph provided, showing rows of angular men at attention, to indicate what proportion of rated officers should fall into each ten-percentile block.

A rating below ninety could destroy a man's career. As a result there were no scores below ninety, unless the rater was bent on the destruction. An unimaginative rater intending to end a man's career scored the problem underling at seventy. One more subtle might award an eighty-six. Since every officer at every level was aware of the inflation of the numbers, eighty-six could be taken as a mark of true incompetence, while seventy was a warning of personal bias. Every man was rated by his immediate superior and endorsed in the same manner by the next higher person in the chain of command, so it was expected that bias would come to light through an inconsistency of scores. Sometimes, in fact, that did happen.

The subjective part of the report was as stylized as the objective. Since all officers were, by the numbers, outstanding or better, the density of superlatives in the description became the only distinguishing characteristic. There was a vast difference between "the best officer I have known" and "absolutely the best officer with whom it has been my pleasure to serve."

When Martin had left the gun platoon, he had rated the Bear at ninety-nine. Now he had in his hands Blood's report rating him at eighty-eight. He was struggling to find a way to make Blood's bias evident without going beyond that point at which it would seem that he was raising the rating only because he himself was biased against Blood. He suspected that the Bear would have found the whole business merely comical; but he nevertheless had spent a half hour poking at the problem. It gave him a grudging admiration for Blood's calculation. Blood certainly knew that a really low rating would fare badly with Major Hart; but the major was not blackhearted enough to believe that an eighty-eight was anything worse than misguided. The major would not pressure one of his officers to change an honest rating, however much he might disagree with it himself.

Major Hart came back from the morning battalion staff meeting with an envelope in his hand.

"We have high-class messenger service this morning," Martin remarked. The major stopped at the side of Martin's desk and stood there studying the envelope. Then he threw it down before Martin. "That came down for you."

It was from the chief of staff of the division. "So it got here at last," Martin said. He picked up the envelope, tapped one end on the desk, and tore off the other end. "Here's looking at you."

There were two letters in the envelope. One was the report of the investigation of Hill 473. He read it as carefully as he could. It was hard to read it seriously after endorsing four efficiency reports, because they and this report all sounded as if they had been wrung from the same damp dishtowel, wet with the thin scrapings of real language. The report concluded: "Command of the flight was taken from the flight leader by a higher ranking officer in another aircraft. This officer, in ordering fire on an unknown target, failed to utilize approved procedures of identification and fire clearance which were adopted to minimize the chance of occurrences of this nature. The recommendation of this investigating board is that appropriate disciplinary procedures be instigated."

Martin handed it over to Major Hart while he read the accompanying letter from the chief of staff. "In accordance with the recommendation of the official investigation, I feel that your most unmilitary conduct on this occasion cannot pass unnoticed. However, because of the excellence of your past record, it is my decision that no disciplinary action will be undertaken in connection with this matter. A copy of this letter and the investigation report will be inserted in your records."

"A brief enough end to a glorious career," Martin said as the major took the letter from his hand. The major read it, put it back down on the desk, and then walked around and sat down behind his own desk. He sat there leafing back and forth through his mail without reading it.

"I think I'll go out for a little walk, if you don't mind, sir," Martin said.

"Surely, Ben."

He did not go far. He left because he did not want Major Hart to have to go on struggling for kind words. He knew that the major expected him to be stricken. He had expected it himself. He could not yet decide why he was not. But he was not.

He went down the hill past the tech supply building and the communications platoon, across the main post road and down onto the ramp. The ramp was nearly empty. The slicks were all out, except for three that were down for repairs and two that were torn down for periodic inspections. The ships were torn down every hundred hours. The slicks sometimes picked up that much time in two weeks, so there were always two or three torn apart.

He went down to the gunship row above the cliff and sat in the door of one of the ships.

A thin watery sunlight poured over the revetments. The early haze was beginning to retreat offshore for the day. It was going to be a beautiful day. At the mouth of Song Ben Van, fishing boats were standing out for the open sea.

For the first time since he had taken his ship down into the LZ on Hill 473, he suddenly felt fully awake. This was no longer a dream from which he might waken. It was real. But now that it was real, he could accommodate it. He could endure it.

As he sat there the beat of a flight of Hueys had been growing around him. He stood up now to see them swinging low over the island. It was Blood and the Bear coming in. Their blades flashed in the sun. Martin wondered, for a moment, why Blood, who despised the Bear, had assigned Bear to fly in his own fire team. Martin could imagine no reason.

The gunships swung wide over the sea and made a low, slow approach to the clifftop landing lane. The heavy thump of their blades ran through his whole body, waking his heart.

The first thing to do, he decided, was to get back on flight status. He set off back across the ramp to the orderly room.

When he came in, Major Hart was behind his desk with his head in his hands. "Well, Ben, how's your constitution?" he asked without looking up.

"Fine. Don't worry about me, sir."

"Ah! There are so many people to worry about, Ben." He turned over a letter on his desk. "This came this morning, too." He handed Martin the letter.

It was addressed to Major Hart. The return address said "Covington." Martin read it quickly. Mrs. Covington had been informed that her husband was missing, but not that he was dead. What, she asked, could Major Hart tell her about him? Martin laid the letter back on the major's desk.

War spoiled soldiering.

"Do you want me to answer it?" he asked.

"You know we can't, Ben."

"I know we're not supposed to. But he's been dead for two weeks. She should be told."

197

"You know how the Army is when there's no body," Major Hart said. "You can't chance a mistake."

"There wouldn't be a mistake. We know he's dead." Martin had the unpleasant feeling that he was rerunning his conversation with the Bear, from the wrong end. Or perhaps from the right end this time.

"We know it, Ben, but the Army doesn't."

"Well, I know it. What if I just happened to write? In my position nothing can hurt anyway." This remark earned him a quick glance from Major Hart. "I don't think that's so, Ben," he said.

Martin supposed it wasn't, but he didn't care.

"I wish you wouldn't," the major said. "She may have heard by now."

"The body hasn't been found."

"No."

"It never will be, now."

"No, it won't." The major sat back in his chair, rubbing at his forehead with his hands. "But the Army has had more experience handling these things than we have. It's for the best. I hope it's for the best."

"I hope it is." If it were left to him, he would have written to Pinky. He knew the risks. When she learned that her husband was dead, and that the Army knew it but hadn't told her, the next letter would be to her congressman. The Army would be displeased. Martin felt sudden absolute freedom from the tyranny of "proper channels"; but Major Hart could still suffer for what his XO did. Martin did not feel so free to jostle the old man's delicately balanced career.

9

A week of sun had faded behind a high thin overcast that lowered slowly during the night. It was a grey Sunday morning. They knew it was Sunday because, about midmorning, the bell beside the chapel rang. Lying on their cots or sitting on the ready-room steps they heard its slow toll fall among the empty hooches, and reecho from the walls of the hangars mixed with the clatter of tools and the ring of voices.

"Sunday mornin'," Handy said. "Used to go out for a drive of a Sunday afternoon, back in the worl'."

"Maybe we'll get a chance today," Ruth said.

"You'll get all the chances you can stand before you leave Nam, Rufe," Arp told him.

"Don't pine away waiting, Rufe," Bear advised. "Just remember, the pilots that fly together, die together." He added gloomily, "When you go over six months your thoughts will begin to turn to new things, like how the devil you can survive long enough to get home. The shorter you are, the easier it is to sit on the ground."

"Is that an Oriental saying?" Arp asked.

"That's a short-timer's saying."

But Ruth walked down to the ship to check the switches just one more time, in case they had to fly in a hurry.

Sunday morning was filled with cold northeast wind and long

hours of waiting, waiting. Bear drowsed on his cot, dreaming of Alice Porter, unseen for so many days.

The other way they knew it was Sunday was that dinner was special. The cook at least had a list of menus to separate one day from the next. They were midway through ham with raisin sauce when the field phone clattered. Operations needed a fire team. Aboard the platoon three-quarter-ton truck Blood's crew and Bear's lurched desperately from the mess hall to the flight line.

Within three minutes they were pounding southward under the sheet-lead sky, dodging wisps of rain along Route One. By the time they reached the Song Tra Bong, Blood was calling ahead for the ground unit, seeking directions. But even before he received an answer, it became obvious where they were bound. The sky ahead was slashed with distant streaks of red. "Somebody working over vere," Ruth said, elaborately casual in his remarks for his first real mission. A puff of smoke issued from the exhaust of Blood's ship ahead as it nosed over and accelerated toward the firefight.

There were two other fire teams ahead, working in long frenzied passes. "It's the Sharks," Handy said. The grinning bloody maws painted on the ships could already be seen from a mile away. "Damn, they must have somethin' good!"

As the Wolfpack fire team flashed out over the open field the Sharks were working, the ground suddenly came alive with running men. A Shark gunship plowed its way through the mass of men, who parted or fell to the earth before it. They were Vietnamese; but they were in uniform. For an instant Bear could see only the bloody uniforms coming out of the dark on Hill 473. Were these government troops? *"Give 'em all six feet of their ground,"* Griggs had said.

"Shit!" Handy exclaimed, "those are NVA!"

Handy was right: they were enemy, caught between the government troops on the west in the trees, the river Song Pra Khuc on the south, and gunships and open land on the north and east. Blood was on the FM calling for smoke to mark the friendlies, and colored smoke quickly blossomed from the tree line a mile distant, while the Shark leader came on the ground frequency to confirm their location. "Help yourself, Wolfpack," he offered. "There's plenty for all."

What organized movement there was among the men below was westward, but ten miles of open country lay between them and the mountains, even if they broke through the ARVN lines. They could not even scatter and run—there was nowhere for them to go. The evidence of that lay all around, in fields on every side, where some had already tried. The gunships had ended the escape.

Down along the river a steady slow rain of artillery was falling. The few trees that had stood there were already cut to stumps and shreds. Now air bursts flashed in steady rhythm all along the riverbank.

Charley, trapped, went down before the guns like grain before a reaper.

The Sharks, their weapons dry, left for home to reload. Blood was not being prodigal with their own ammunition. There were too many targets for the ordnance they had on board. He had already called for another fire team, but it would be twenty minutes or more before they could come on station. The Sharks, flying to Duc Pho to reload, could not return for nearly an hour. Meanwhile, to keep the trap closed there was only one Wolfpack fire team. After the first full-firepower sweep up the center, they stood off and worked the edges of the killing ground.

Reluctance to fire was the soundest strategy; but with each pass Bear felt a wrenching sensation inside. There was no way to avoid hitting something. A rocket launched blindly would fall on living flesh. At each pass, a touch of the thumb against the little red button, and a thousand meters away, men died. He could see them dying, see their death reaching for them in its whole long slow arc to the ground. For all his reluctance to kill, men died.

The other fire team arrived. Blood led a last pass to drain the dregs of the ammunition, and his ship and Bear's turned for home. "Leave us some," Blood called. "We're coming back."

The Sharks were back on station when Blood's fire team returned. They had moved in and were working closer to the river now. On each pass they overflew fields scattered with corpses. The living had dwindled.

As the Sharks again departed, a last remnant of the enemy unit, hopeless whether they stood or fled, pressed a determined attack on the ARVN troops in the tree line and broke through near the

201

river. With all the weapons again empty, Blood broke off and pounded for home. They made the turnaround this time in forty minutes flat. A man running for his life can travel far in forty minutes; but no farther than a gunship can follow in three. The team hunted up and down the tree lines and paddy dikes, flushing a covey here, a single there, and killed them. The other fire teams had done the same before them. The trails of dead and dying men dotted the plain from the breakout point.

It was late afternoon when the ships finally turned for home. There were still a few rounds in the ammunition boxes under the back seats, but there had been no one to kill for twenty minutes past. They cruised slowly back over the battlefield, where the ARVNs were out collecting weapons and counting the dead. They turned for home through spitting rain. "Wasn't it somefing!" Ruth bubbled. "Wasn't it great, Bear?"

At home Blood pounded the Operations table as he dashed off the after-action report. "We must of set some kind of record for one-day kills! Dammit, I'll bet any man here that we get credit for two hundred KIAs! Lord! Wasn't that something? They went down like turkeys on Thanksgiving!"

"You never seen so many dinged Slopes in your life," Handy told the first sergeant over a beer at the NCO club. "That was a battalion at least."

Cripps, lying in his hooch, in his own bed for the first time in three days, said to his buddies, "Today I killed more people than there are in my hometown."

"Is that three, Cripps, or four?" someone asked.

"I wish you'd save some for me, Cripps."

"I'm surprised you got any at all," another said, "flying with the Bear. I heard he swore off killing."

"I don't know about that," Cripps said. "I don't know how you do that."

Dawson greeted him at the emergency room entrance to the hospital. "Well, Chief, we haven't seen you for a few days. More'n a few."

"I went back to work," Bear said. "I haven't been able to get here."

"Well, your frien's are all gone anyways. We shipped the last of

202

'em out days ago. We don't stockpile bodies aroun' here." He added, raising an eyebrow, "Lieutenant Porter, she's aroun'. She ought to be goin' off duty about now. I'll show you how to find her ward—that is, *if* you want to see Lieutenant Porter?" He added with a grin, "She ast me once if you'd been aroun'. I wouldn't tell you that, Chief, if I didn't like you. You ought to come around more."

"You'll have to tell that to the Army," Bear said.

They went around the covered walkways to the prisoner ward. "Lieutenant Porter? She just left," the guard outside the door said. "If you want the nurse, Captain Newton just went up the hall a minute, but she'll be back."

"Can I go inside?" Bear asked.

"I don't reckon you're goin' to disturb anybody's recovery much," Dawson said, "or bother anybody if you *do*, except maybe Lieutenant Porter. She is the kindes'-hearted person! Me, I wish they'd ship 'em up to the POW camp where they belong. I figure everybody's forgotten they're here. Except you, Chief. Checking up on your handiwork, I guess." He winked at the Bear.

When they entered the ward, Mother Courage was sitting on her bed, as if she had not moved since he was there last. She studied them impassively.

But the face that drew Bear's eye was that of the man still lying in the bed nearest the door—the one he thought of as Charley. His handiwork. His handiwork made slow vegetable stirrings on the bed.

"That one might just as well be dead," Dawson said. "What can they do with *him*? I don't know why we keep him aroun'."

Charley tried to move his body to face the door more fully. His helpless embryonic movements, so painstaking and laborious, hardly served to shift the trunk at all. Armless, legless, even voiceless, the mere remnant of a person, he was alive enough to be killed, if found outside the wire. Life was guarded behind the eyes. If man had a soul, one was there. As clay, the weight of him would not have borne down on Bear's heart.

But beyond the wire even that spark would be extinguished. He thought of the bodies he had left strewn in his wake over the fields by Song Pra Khuc.

He went out the side door which Dawson showed him and

along the board walkway to the nurses' quarters. When she did not answer his knock at her door, he went down to the hospital officers' club. She was not there, either. He went around the end of the buildings to the cliffs. She was sitting against the rocks down at the edge of the sand, watching the waves come in a curve around the end of the point and break at a gentle angle down the length of the narrow beach. He picked his way down the cliff. When he threw a few grains of sand on her leg she looked around and saw him. Her face hardly changed, but her eyes went large, and then she smiled. "I was worried about you," she said.

"I've had to fly."

She turned quickly to him and took his hand. "That's wonderful! I wish you'd told me. I wouldn't have worried about you then."

"There's something wrong there," he said, sitting down where she had made room for him on the narrow shelf of stone. "It's when I'm flying that I get shot at."

"Oh. Yes, of course I know it. It's hard for me to think of 'shot at' as happening *now* to anyone I know, though. It's what happened to someone before I see him. And you wanted so badly to fly."

"Yes, I did, didn't I."

"Is something wrong?"

"What could be wrong?"

"Don't be sarcastic," she said. "You'll spoil having you back. I did miss you." She made it sound impersonal, as if the words were just the thing to help the attitude of a difficult patient. He scowled toward the waves.

"Your people are all gone now," she said brightly after a moment. "McWade was the last one. We sent him home, and he's going to be all right. I was almost sorry to lose him, he was such a nice person. He had just a golden outlook." She stopped talking then and looked at him for a long time. "Don?" she said gently. "Don, I'm so happy to see you again."

"I wish you wouldn't sound as if you mean it," he said.

"I do mean it. And I wish you wanted me to."

"Your wish is granted, Alice." He touched her on the head and put on the face of a fairy godmother.

"I just don't think I understand you all of the time," she said.

204

"It's just that I feel like two people at once. Like now. I don't know whether to feel like Christmas or the first day of school. I feel like both. If you weren't around I could just feel rotten all the way through, instead of half rotten and half wonderful; and then I wouldn't feel guilty about feeling so great when I should be feeling guilty."

"You're really a terrible person," she observed, amused.

"Don't wrinkle your nose at me, lady. You're likely to get kissed for it."

"That would be nice."

She left her hand on the back of his neck. He started to tell her how he felt, but what he meant for winged words of love were clumsy as the remembered flight of a penguin, and he quickly tumbled to a halt. She kissed him again gently. "Do you want to tell me the other, too?" she asked.

"What other?"

"Whatever it is that's on your mind."

"No . . . I don't think I do. It's just that I killed a lot of men today."

"Oh."

"Not Americans this time," he added. She said nothing, and he was glad for it. After a time he said, "Mostly, you don't see them, the ones you kill—the *people* you kill. It's just a tactical exercise. The good guys have taken fire and they call for support. You locate them, you locate the enemy, or the place they say he is, you consider the surrounding terrain, you calculate the most effective direction of attack, and you suppress the enemy. 'Suppress the enemy.' That's a nice way of saying you kill people. If you can. And most of the time you don't even see them. You shoot the hell out of a tree line, a paddy dike. . . . The grunts go in afterward and count the bodies."

They sat again in silence.

"It's harder to kill a man in the open. For the other you're a pilot; but for that . . . I think you'd have to like that, to do it well.

"The hard part," he said, "is not being what they want me to be. The complete gun pilot. You can see it in their eyes, the people who like me: 'There's the Bear—he's killed a hundred men, two hundred.' "

"Have you?"

She was instantly sorry she had asked, for she saw the serpent fascination that troubled him most.

"I don't know," he said. "Some pilots claim a number. I don't. I don't count them. I *won't* count them. But I could tell you how many I've seen die under my guns—I remember them all. Until today. There were too many to remember today."

They walked up the hill to the Artillery Battalion club in the remnant of the day. Rain was curling up over Nui Ong and threatening around the fences of Chu Lai. The wind smelled of it. At sea darkness had already come. They stopped to look back seaward from the quiet yard of the chapel on the hill. The sea wind rattled the broad leaves of the banana tree there. They stood, not quite touching one another, yet each feeling the other's presence as if their hands had met. "It's so dark there," she said. The blue lights of the helicopter ramp spread at their feet, bounded on one side by the hospital floodlights and on the other by the yellow slashes of light seeping around the storm shutters in his company area. But those ended abruptly, and beyond was nothing. On a calm night the sea would have been strewn as thick with lights as stars in the sky, where the villagers were fishing far at sea. Tonight the boats were safe ashore, and beyond the cliffs raged the empty black sea. Yet there was peace at sea, while no men were there. Was there peace only in the void? Nothing to hope for but blackness? He turned her away and led her quickly to the club, out of sight of the cliffs and whatever lay beyond.

Inside the door someone called to them. "It's Janet," Alice said. "Over on the balcony." Wolcheski and Guiterrez were with her. "Do you want to be sociable? We can pretend we were only looking in."

"Sociability is better than thought," he said. She took his hand as they crossed to the balcony.

"Say," Guiterrez said, "it's that shaggy critter, out guzzling beer again."

"I thought you were among the missing," Janet said to Bear. "We haven't seen you for such a time."

"Pull up a chair and tell us some war stories," Guiterrez offered. "How's gunning?"

"Busy," Bear answered. "Very busy."

"You should have been down toward Quang Ngai today," Guiterrez continued. "Somebody got a potful of them down there today."

"Don't talk shop," Alice told him.

The balcony was on the landward side of the club, out of the sea wind. Mortar flares were dropping to the west. First there came the light, yellow and weak and wavering, too weak even to cast a shadow at this distance. Sometimes the faint plop of the flare igniting reached them, many seconds after the light. Sometimes there was a distant rumble of artillery like the stirring of an uneasy sleeper.

"I hate artillery in the night," Wolcheski said, speaking for the first time. He had been slouched back in his chair, watching the Bear when he looked at anything at all.

Wolcheski had watched the Bear carefully, although Bear did not know it. Wolcheski was a born watcher. As a small boy, he had been told, he would spend hours watching anything that crossed his path—a snail, a cat, a thunderstorm. He would try to outwait a dead bird, until dragged off to supper. He also loved all moving machinery, not only trains and fire engines, but electric fans, toasters, and jackhammers. Later he had turned scientific. His schoolwork won prizes in physics and biology. Somewhere in his late teens, however, he discovered people, and thereafter he concentrated on watching them—natural enough, since in the absence of angels people showed the most complex behavior of any objects available. He did not outgrow machinery, however; and so after he was drafted and made his way to Officer Candidate School, flight training was his first stop.

Wolcheski considered himself a failure as a scientist: he tried to be a detached observer, but never could retain his detachment intact. But, while he knew that this was a shortcoming, it was not one that bothered him. Real people were more fun than was theoretically possible, so who needed theory? Real people were also more heartbreaking than was theoretically possible. Wolcheski tried to do what he could about that, but had long since found that he usually could not do much. Bear's sorrow saddened him. He liked Bear, and did not see what he could do about him. He suspected that if anything was to be done, Alice was it.

"I hate artillery in the night." As he said the words, Wolcheski looked away toward the mountain. Or toward where the mountain stood. It could not be seen in the darkness beyond the pale distant flares. "When I hear artillery I always expect a call in twenty minutes. I hate to fly at night."

"Any particular reason," Guiterrez asked, "other than that it ain't safe? At least we don't have to fly tonight, *Trung-úy*, knock on wood."

As if in warning to guard his words, a prolonged heavy burst rolled in from the northwest. "I wonder where that one is," Guiterrez went on. "Probably Tam Ky. They're always after the province headquarters. Anyway I'd rather it was out there than as close as those rounds that came in a couple weeks back. Did they wake you up, Bear?" Guiterrez had a quick grin that came and went when he had said something he thought was ironic. It flicked across his face and was gone. "I hope you went up and shot their asses off. I take that personally, when Charley starts pegging at me in my own quarters. You ought to be like the Bear, *Trung-úy*," he said to Wolcheski. "Carry a gun and when you crank you don't worry about flying at night. If Charley knows you're the meanest mother out there, he leaves you alone. With us, he sees that red cross and cuts loose right now!"

"But when *you* crank," Bear said, "you don't have to wonder who you're going to kill."

"It wouldn't worry me *too* much," Guiterrez said, "not so much as who's going to kill *me*."

"You two should trade places," Swensen said brightly. Bear stared at the table.

"*Trung-úy* Wolcheski couldn't get along without me," Guiterrez said. "Who'd drag him home when he gets lost out there in the dark?"

"Never happen, Primo," Wolcheski said, sitting up with sudden decisiveness. He added quietly, as if for Bear alone to hear, "You know we're short a warrant officer in our unit. If you were to put in a ten-forty-nine, you might end up with us."

Bear shook his head. "My company's still so low on pilots, they'll never let go of a warm body."

"Deep down the Bear's attached to his guns," Guiterrez said. The quick grin came and went.

"Would you check out that shit!" Atterburn exclaimed, coming to a stop inside the door of the club. "His Bearness himself, sitting with a couple of round-eyes!"

"I never heard of a mirage appearing at night," Arp said. "Where's that?"

"Over there!" Atterburn kneaded his cap in his hands. "The Bear out with a round-eye! How'd he ever get himself into that position?"

"We could ask," Arp said. He was already on his way. He stopped behind the Bear. "It didn't take *you* long to get the war off your mind, Bear," he said. "I like to see the troops enjoying themselves; but I didn't know you were so widely acquainted." He pulled up a chair between the Bear and Janet Swensen. "May we join you? This," he said to Lieutenant Swensen, pointing to Atterburn, who was hanging a yard away, "is Mr. Atterburn. You can forget about him. He's easily forgettable."

Swensen smiled at him. "I seem to have forgotten you, too, Lieutenant. Have we met?"

"We would have, if Bear were doing his duty by his leader. Come on, Bear. These nice people will think I haven't taught you any manners."

"My glorious leader," Bear presented him. "And his faithful sidekick Atterburn." He made an effort to sound lighthearted; but Arp gave him a puzzled glance, hearing something strange in his voice, and Alice squeezed Bear's hand under the table. The others were pleased enough, though. Not to spoil their pleasure, Bear began seriously to try to be happy. He drank, he told jokes, and eventually at Atterburn's urging he even ordered drinks from the waitress in polite Vietnamese. But happiness fled with its tail unsalted.

"You're a man of rare talent," Wolcheski said. "I wish I could speak Vietnamese."

"It's easy," Bear said. "You just have to give up your inhibitions."

"*He* doesn't have any," Swensen said.

"Few," Wolcheski corrected her. "Few, but firm."

"From your Polish grandmother, no doubt."

"Absolutely. But from her also, my aesthetic sense."

"Polish?" Arp raised an eyebrow.

"Absolutely. The heritage of Chopin and Paderewski. All that sort of thing. But Vietnamese, now—a lovely language."

"At least if you spoke the language, you could get laid," Atterburn said. "Not that it helps Bear any."

Alice blushed; but in the dark, who was to know, except Bear?

"A lovely language," Wolcheski went on, ignoring Atterburn, as did everyone else. "Even if you don't understand it. *Chu Lai*—a beautiful name. Who cares what it means? Or *Ky Ha?*"

"Bear was always pointing out names to me, when we first flew together. It's been a long time, huh, B.?"

"A long time."

"He used to chant Vietnamese names as we flew," Arp said to Alice. "What were some of them, B.?"

Bear closed his eyes. He chanted slowly—slowly, and a little sadly: "Chu Lai, Dong Xoai, Quang Ngai; Phuong Tan, Vinh Giang, Hoi An; Tam Ky, Khanh My, Que Son."

"It's beautiful," said Alice. "Is it a poem?"

"The list of villages," Arp said. "I remember when you composed that. It was longer, though. And there was one for rivers. How did it go?"

"Rivers I can't do on a night like this," Bear said. "The names of rivers are sad names."

"How about 'Song Tra Bong'? That's not sad. Any people who call a river a 'song' can't be all bad, can they?"

"Song Be," Wolcheski said. "There's another. Or Song Ben Van. The whole country sings."

"How many ways are there to say 'river' in Vietnamese, Bear?" Arp asked.

Bear was reluctant. "A lot. If you count creeks, and watercourses, and tidal streams and the rest."

"For instance?" Wolcheski asked. Wolcheski saw that Arp was trying to draw Bear out. For the first time Bear seemed ready to forget whatever was on his mind.

"*Sông*," Bear said. "And dialect, *tong*. And some others: *ea, ia, ya, O, hô, houei, Bao, Ngoc,* or *nu'ó'c*—that's 'water.' *Tam, nam, ràò, Khê.* That's one we all know—*An Khê,* where the First Horse is camped: 'river village.' *An* means 'village.' "

"How do you learn all this shit?" Atterburn asked.

210

"Mostly, I read charts. And think about what's down there. Try it sometime, Burn. Don't think about *who*'s down there, though."

"All good pilots read their charts," Wolcheski said, addressing Arp. "Now Bear mentioned Vinh . . . what was that village, Bear?"

"Vinh Giang," Arp told him.

"Vinh Giang. How about Vinh Qui Nhon, Lieutenant? Have you ever seen that one on your chart?"

"Qui Nhon we all know is a coastal city. Vinh Qui Nhon, you no doubt expect me to guess, is a village in the area. But it isn't. Vinh Qui Nhon is the bay on which Qui Nhon is located. Very tricky."

"The two *'vinhs'* aren't the same word, of course," Bear pointed out. "Vinh Giang—*vinh* or *viñh* or *vîñh*. Vinh Qui Nhon—*viņh*. They look the same on the map if you can't see the tone markings; or they sound the same if you can't hear the tones."

"Don't confuse us with knowledge, Bear," Arp said. "It's my turn to ask the lieutenant one. How about this: if Nui Ong is out there"—he nodded out the open door across the western balcony, into the night—"where is Nui Ba, and why do I ask?"

Wolcheski pondered. As he did so, he seemed to sink inside himself. His eyes closed. His lips curled down, to match the curve of his dark brows. He shook himself, surfacing. "Don't know," he admitted. "They're both mountains; but that's trivial."

"Nui Ba is on the coast south of Bong Son," Arp said. "And I ask because . . ." He pointed to Bear, to cue him.

"*Ông* means 'man,'" said Bear, "or politely, 'mister.' Or 'grandfather.' The Grandfather Mountain. And *bà* means 'woman,' or 'Mrs.' or 'grandmother.'"

"You only knew that from flying with Mr. Bear, though, didn't you," Wolcheski challenged Arp.

"Sure. But he was my wojug, in those days."

"What's a wojug?" Swensen asked.

"Warrant Officer, junior grade. Boy, was he ever new."

"About as new as a certain lieutenant," Bear said. "But how about this one, then? Now that you've got Nui Ong, where is Hon Ong, and why do I ask?"

Wolcheski and Arp both pondered. They glared at one another. Each started to point an accusing finger at the other. "Well, I'll give up if you will," Arp said. "But not before."

Wolcheski thought a while longer. "Okay. On three."

Janet counted: "One. Two. Three." They both turned to Bear.

"*Hòn* is another word for mountain," Bear said. "And Hon Ong is a mountain not far from the coast, between Qui Nhon and Ninh Hoa. Boy, was I ever new last time we flew by there, Lieutenant. New enough to read the chart."

"That's a cheat, Bear," Arp said. "And if *hòn* is a mountain, how about Hon Tre, that island off Nha Trang? Or is it a different word, in disguise?"

"Same word," Bear said. "A mountainous island."

"Then how about Cu Lao Re, off the coast here? Why don't they call that a mountain island? It is one."

"I don't know," Bear said. "I didn't invent this language. I didn't invent this country or this war."

Three of those at the table heard the sudden darkness in Bear's voice; but none knew why it was there.

Alice thought it was the memory of the ocean, dark as endless night, and never a star to see.

Arp, too, thought of the sea, and the fiery fall of a dying ship, a dying friend.

"Is there an island out there?" Wolcheski asked. "I've never seen it."

"It's on the charts," Arp said.

"Have *you* seen it?" Wolcheski challenged.

"No."

"Some days it's there," Bear said. "Some days it isn't."

"That sounds mysterious," said Janet. "If it's there, why haven't you two seen it?"

"Maybe if a guy just had faith," Bear said. "To fly off into the blue . . ." The memory of the island, of his vision of it, overwhelmed him.

The Bear was dancing with Alice. They circled slowly off in the darkness toward the other end of the bar. Martin and Major Hart, sitting there far back in the shadows talking quietly, seriously, glanced up more than once at the couple.

Those at the other table also watched Alice and the Bear. "Who'd of thought the Bear was such a lover, Lieutenant?" Atterburn said to Arp. "He's hardly met a dollie, and he's off into the night with her."

"And not the first time, either," Guiterrez said. "He did the same thing the first time I introduced him to her."

"To her? You mean the Bear's been seeing her before?"

"Sure. Weeks ago. But he hasn't been around lately. You kept him out of my way. And it didn't do me a bit of good."

"The Bear's been pining for a round-eye!" Atterburn exclaimed. "And I thought he was doping around like he had a turd hung up in his tubes just because he'd lost his nerve after Hill Four Seven Three!"

"The state of his soul is more complex than you apprehended," Arp told him dryly.

"All that time on the ground he had everybody feeling sorry for him, and all the while he was off getting some squeezies from a warm round-eye! It definitely ain't fair, Lieutenant!"

"Fair is what you make it," Arp said.

"Well, I thought he'd missed *his* chance, too, when he was gone so long," Guiterrez said. "She's been around Dr. Rawlinson pretty much lately."

"Be quiet, Primo," Janet said. Bear was coming back leading Alice by the hand. Because the others were watching, he capered at the edge of the floor.

"Is that a blimp coming in for a landing?" Atterburn greeted him.

"It's the walrus bellying up to the ice floe," Arp suggested. "Cold! Very cold. You can tell by the way the tummy shivers. Listen, do the walrus for us, Bear. Have you seen the walrus, Lieutenant Swensen?"

"I think the walrus has gone on," Bear said.

"Gone south for the monsoon?" Atterburn asked. "What is he, a fair-weather walrus?"

"I guess he is," Bear said softly. "A sunshine walrus."

"A sunshine walrus," Wolcheski repeated in the direction of the mountain. He smiled. He liked the Bear's turn of phrase.

The sound of shots rang out from the side room off the bar. It was only the cowboy movie reaching its denouement. From somewhere out toward the mountain where the flares were falling, the sliding thump of artillery rolled in around them. "Cannon to the left of them, cannon to the right of them," Wolcheski suddenly declaimed loudly. He drew the attention of no one but Arp. Atterburn and Guiterrez were watching Bear talk privately to Alice. Arp had been zeroing his attention in on Janet; but now he turned to Wolcheski: "I didn't know anyone here spoke Tennyson."

"Don't pay any attention to him," Janet said. "He's always quoting some dead poet."

"Her main objection to them," Wolcheski said to Arp, "is that they're dead."

"Well, who was that poet who said there's no poem like a real live woman?" Janet asked. "You told me about him yourself. Doesn't that go for men too?"

"Keats," Arp said. " 'Let the mad poets say what e'er they please/Of the sweets of Fairies, Peris, Goddesses,/There is not such a treat among them all,/Haunters of cavern, lake and waterfall,/As a real woman.' "

Bear and Alice had drifted off again to dance. Guiterrez and Atterburn stared after them, and then Atterburn asked Janet to dance. Guiterrez wandered sadly away to the bar. "You don't like poetry?" Wolcheski called after them, but no one answered.

"You aren't afraid he'll snake your date?" Arp asked, indicating in the direction of Atterburn and Janet.

"If *you* can't do it, *he* sure as hell can't," Wolcheski said. "And you can't."

"I could," Arp insisted—but laughing—"but I'd rather swap lines with you. Keats to the contrary, women abound; but how often do you meet a man who knows Tennyson? I couldn't steal a woman from a man I've exchanged quotations with."

"Very gentlemanly of you."

"You know how Thucydides told of the Greek generals spending the night before a battle exchanging lines of poetry? That always seemed to me the proper way to run a war. But I never thought I'd have the chance. Do you suppose that's the way the CG spends his evenings?"

"Considering that your Greeks were writing of the blush of color on a boy's cheek," Wolcheski said, "I think I won't answer

214

that. You never know who's listening." He looked around and then said quietly, "I'll give you a quotation for the Bear, though:

There *is* confusion worse than death
Trouble on trouble, pain on pain,
Long labor unto aged breath,
Sore task to hearts worn out by many wars
And eyes grown dim with gazing on the pilot-stars."

"Meaning?"

"If you're flying guns with him, you should already have seen it," Wolcheski said.

"The Bear is the best gun pilot in the company," Arp said firmly. "He has two DFCs and a third in the oven, and he earned them all. In fact, he's earned a couple he didn't get."

Wolcheski shook his head. "I didn't say he was afraid. I'd like to have him fly with me, anytime. But . . . 'Men may come to worse than dust.'"

Arp looked toward the Bear and Alice, who swung about one another in an orbit inclined toward the far end of the bar where it was dark, as though together they made up a planetary system that had slipped the bonds of its star and was drawn inescapably toward the darkness from which there was no return.

When he woke, Bear saw the letter on the mosquito netting over his bunk. He had not looked for his mail after the mission of the day before. He had gone first to see Alice. He supposed Ruth had got it for him. He had not turned on the lights when he came home.

There was no return address on the envelope. It had an Iowa postmark. He put the letter aside to dress, wondering who he knew in Iowa now that Covington was dead.

Without buttoning his shirt he snatched the letter up again and tore open the envelope.

Dear Bear [Pinky had written], Dear Bear, I don't feel right calling you anything but that, because Wes always wrote of you as the Bear. I hope you won't take it badly that I think of you by that name. As you can see by the address on the

215

envelope, I know you have another, but Wes's letters made me like you so much by this one that I want to use it.

I suppose you don't think I wrote just to chat about names, though; and you're right. I'm writing to you now because it seems you're the last hope I have of finding out about Wes. You see, the Army told me—so long ago, it seems!—that he is missing in action. But I haven't been able to find out anything more. Wes told me in one of his first letters what "missing in action" means. If any pilot is reported missing in action, he said, it means he's dead, but they haven't found the body. I believed him. Now I don't want to believe it anymore. Surely the Army, or someone, somewhere, in the Army, must know more than that he is just "missing in action"? I've tried every way I know how to find out. I even wrote to your company commander. But there has been no answer. Now I am turning to you as my last hope. I still want to hope, but I hardly know how. You see, I still believe what Wes told me, because he never lied to me. I want you to write and tell me there is still some reason to believe that he is alive. But even if there is none, I want to know that. Anything is better than not knowing. Please, write and tell me.

Pinky

Bear raged up and down the aisle of the hooch, cursing silently. He threw on his clothes and his pistol and set off for the Operations hooch.

Lieutenant Rauch was behind the desk, his feet up and his arms behind his head, apparently speculating on the height of the ceiling. He turned his eyes, but not his head, to see who had come in. "What's up, Bear?"

"I have to go see the old man. And I'm due on standby. So give me a call if we get a mission." Bear was too much in a hurry to frame a polite request.

"Well, Jesus, yes sir, *Chief!* Anytime. Just let me know. Do you want to take my jeep?"

"Yes," Bear said. He ignored the sarcasm in Rauch's voice. Rauch did not try to stop him when he climbed into the jeep.

Before Bear could drive onto the ramp, he was flagged down by Lieutenant Arp. Yan was with him. She was crying. "Well, what are you doing to my hooch-maid now, Lieutenant?" Bear asked. He was annoyed at being stopped. He thought it was only Arp teasing Yan again, until he saw how serious Arp was.

"Bear, can you make sense of what this girl is saying? She came running up to me saying somebody's caught her mama-san, but *I* don't know what she means! Talk to her, will you?" But Yan was not easy to talk to. She was near hysteria. Her Vietnamese rattled past too quickly for Bear to understand, and her English had shrunk to "He take my mama-san away! She no bad! You tell him bring mama-san back!" To Bear's attempts at Vietnamese questions she only answered wildly, *"Không biết! Không biết!"* Several minutes had dragged past before they calmed her enough to learn that Suzie had been picked up on the ramp by Captain Blood as she was returning from the other side. He had forced her into the gun platoon truck and driven back in that direction with her. One of the other hooch-maids had seen that much and had told Yan, for none of them liked Captain Blood. "I run quick look for *Trung-úy* Arp," Yan said.

"Ask her what the devil Suzie was doing on the ramp," Arp said. The hooch-maids were not allowed among the aircraft.

"She come back from other side," Yan said. She took questions from the Bear but she put her answers directly to Arp as best she could.

"Then what the devil was she doing over there? She works here, not there!"

"Không biết!" Yan wailed.

"Oh, Christ! Ask her, Bear."

"Bà đã làm gì đây?" It took two tries with this question before Yan understood, because Bear used the wrong tone on the word *đây* the first time, so that it meant "here" instead of "there." The second time through, Yan understood that he was asking what her mother was doing *there.*

"She lose ID card," she said to Arp. "She think friend catch it."

"If that's all, it's much ado about nothing. Are you going that way, Bear? Check on Suzie, will you? And tell this girl her mother's all right. Yan, mama-san number one okay. All right? Trust me."

When Bear reached the orderly room, Suzie was there. She was in a chair, quiet and frightened. Blood was pacing up and down.

"There's your Slope expert," Blood said as the Bear came in the door. "Let *him* find out what she's up to." This was a sneer directed toward Martin, who was leaning against the screen that closed off his desk and the major's.

"Intelligence will have somebody down here soon enough," Martin said. "Just let her alone, Blood."

"Sure, we'd send her on home to blow us all to Kingdom Come if you had your way."

"I'm glad she's alive," Bear said. "Yan was all gone to pieces. She thought her mama-san had been kidnapped. What happened?"

"Never mind what happened," Blood snapped. "Aren't you on standby? What are you doing here?"

"I want to see Major Hart. But I told Lieutenant Arp I'd find out what happened to Suzie."

"Well, go back and tell Lieutenant Arp that I'm taking care of Suzie. And since when does he give people permission to leave their duty area?"

"Captain Blood thinks Suzie was pacing off the ramp," Martin explained.

"Thinks? Why the devil else would she be stopping at every row of revetments? She didn't have any business down there anyway."

Martin ignored Blood's outburst. "Someone will come down from Division to interview her," he said to the Bear.

"Yan said she lost her ID and wanted to see if her friend over here had it." Without her ID Suzie could not enter or leave the post.

"Then we'd better talk to her friend, too," Blood said. "What if she does have it? It's easy enough to rig something like that. If Charley gets the ramp measured off, his mortars will do a lot worse next time than they did the last."

"It could be true, Bear," Martin said. "We have to check on it."

Since Suzie was apparently in no danger of anything worse than a talking-to, Bear let the matter pass. "When can I see Major Hart?" he asked Martin. He could see that the major was not in his office.

"He's gone up to Division with the battalion commander. Is there anything I can do?"

"I think I'd better see him, sir."

"All right. I'll call Rauch when he comes back. You'd better go back across if you're on standby."

Blood muttered something about disciplining his own troops, but he said nothing else to the Bear.

Lieutenant Arp was waiting for Bear at Operations. He went up to the hooch to tell Yan about her mother, while Bear went down to his ship. Rauch put his head out the door and called after him, "You're welcome, Bear!"

"Thanks for the jeep, sir."

"Anytime."

Ruth was on the ship. "I've preflighted it," he said. "And I set the radios. Everyfing's okay."

"You're a good boy, Rufe," Bear said. He began to preflight the ship again. Whatever he felt, the preflight was something he always did for himself. Normally he did without the checklist, but today he got it out and forced himself to read off every item. He knew he would miss something if he didn't read it. His mind was everywhere but on flying. Ruth followed him around, anxiously watching over his shoulder.

"You got a letter yesterday," Ruth said. "I left it on your bunk. I hope you found it."

"Yes," Bear said. "Thank you." He finished the preflight at his door to the cockpit, where he adjusted the seat and his harness and plugged in his helmet. He got down and closed the door. "You're right, it's ready to go, Rufe," he said. "You done good." They walked together back to the alert hooch. Blood's truck was outside the door.

"There he is," Atterburn said, "the sunshine walrus. Where'd you go off to last night, Bear, that took you so long to get home? Captain," he said to Blood, "did you hear that the Bear has been getting his squeezies from a round-eye nurse all the time we were on the ground?"

Blood had not seen Alice, but he had his own idea of what kind of American girl would keep company with a specimen like the Bear. He ignored the question, but muttered irritably, "What's the sunshine walrus business?"

"The Bear's animal imitations," Atterburn said. "They've migrated for the rainy season. He's only a sunshine walrus."

"The hell," Blood said. "About time, Bear. Everybody grows up someday, eh?"

He expected Blood to say something about his being at the orderly room; but Blood seemed willing to let it go. In turn Bear asked nothing about Suzie. He supposed Martin had sent Blood away. He knew that Blood would not have left otherwise. Bear sat down on his cot with his clipboard. He was going to write to Pinky. But before he could begin, the scramble horn sounded.

Coming out of the hamlet, the infantry platoon had taken fire from the tree line across a deep paddy. It was light fire, and they returned it and maneuvered toward it. Before the platoon leader realized how deep the paddy was, his men were bogged down or swimming, and automatic weapons fire was coming in on them. They struggled back with heavy losses. From behind the paddy dike they called for gunships.

Bear listened to Blood talking to the company commander on the Fox Mike. Smoke coming out now. A smoke grenade popped near the trees. Green. Damn them—green was hard to see in a planted paddy. But Blood had seen it; he began to acknowledge, when a second grenade popped, far down along the trees. Yellow. "Well, Panther, I have a yellow and a green. Which one are you?" Blood asked.

Panther said his was the yellow.

Charley had a receiver on their frequency; but he had outsmarted himself.

Or else, Bear thought as they turned inbound, it was some dumb grunt who got his signals mixed up.

Ahead, Blood's ship enveloped itself in a shroud of smoke as a brace of rockets streaked earthward. In the seat next to Bear, Ruth had the gunsight down, and the crew in back were leaning out the doors in anticipation. "Hold your fire," Bear said.

"We're in range?" Ruth said hesitantly.

Bear did not answer. The ship flashed down the length of the tree line. There was no fire from the ground. There was no one to be seen. But someone had thrown smoke.

"What's the matter, sir?" Handy asked.

"Did you see anything?"

"No, sir. But Charley's in there. I can all but smell him."

220

"Hold on."

Outbound, they passed the lead ship turning in. As they passed, the other ship lit up with rockets and tracers.

"They sure as hell got something," Handy said.

Bear was on the radio: "Lead, any Victor Charlies in sight?"

"Negative, but he's in these trees. Work out."

Inbound again, there was no one. It was like a hundred other missions. You never saw whom you were killing. Yesterday, seeing men fall, had been exceptional. For standard operations you shot up a target area and let the ordnance kill whoever was there. A rocket had a killing radius of thirty meters. No need to hit a man dead on. And there was someone in the tree line. But who was it?

Out the other end of the tree line again. "What's the matter, Bear?" Ruth looked at him with concern.

He couldn't say it. Ruth had seen men die in the open, but he hadn't been there at Hill 473. He hadn't been at the hospital.

Over by the place the yellow smoke had been, heads began to pop up behind the dike, American heads watching the show. "Go get 'em, Wolf," the radio said. It was the ground commander's voice. So the friendlies were accounted for.

"All right," Bear said. There was no longer a way to hold back.

With a fierce whoop Handy strained at the end of his monkey-strap as he directed his weapon under the belly of the ship. Ruth squeezed the trigger switch. A-a-a-a-ahh, said the flex-guns. A-a-a-a-a-hhh.

In the tree line no one moved. But one could die without moving.

As the guns departed, a medevac helicopter called in on the ground frequency, coming for the wounded. It was not Wolcheski's voice; but others flew for Dustoff, too.

Before the blade had stopped, Blood was at the side of Bear's ship. He waited until Cripps and Handy had gone to bring up more rockets before he spoke. He made a point of waiting. One officer did not point out the shortcomings of another with enlisted men present. It was a rule Blood often forgot when impassioned but it pleased him to remember it now. A leader should do the correct thing. After they were gone, Blood asked, "What was wrong with your weapons?"

"Nothing," Bear said.

"They didn't work very well, right there at first."

"I wasn't sure who I was shooting at."

"I'll decide when to fire and when not to," Blood said. "All you've got to do is follow me around, mister. That shouldn't be so hard. You don't need to decide who you're shooting at."

"I made that mistake at Hill Four Seven Three," Bear answered.

Blood's face slowly became livid, and his jaw muscles worked; but in the end he said nothing. His nostrils flared wide, and he snorted in disgust and walked away.

Ruth, still in the left-hand seat, was pale and wide-eyed. "See that we get rearmed," Bear told him. "I'm going to the orderly room."

Major Hart had come back, and the battalion commander with him. Bear sat in the orderly room listening to the low voices from behind the plywood screen. He wondered if the battalion commander was always so friendly with Major Hart. Congratulations were in progress for something; but what it was, the Bear could not tell. The first sergeant was grinning to himself as he played at fitting names onto a duty roster. "There's something big coming, sir," he said, nodding toward the back offices. "Tell Handy to keep his guns cleaned." When he saw that Bear was not going to answer, he tried a different subject: "Did you come to check on your hooch-maid?"

Bear shook his head. He had forgotten all about Suzie.

"I thought maybe you wondered what happened when she never came back," the first sergeant said.

"Never came back? I've been gone. What happened to her?"

"That interrogation team that come down took her away with them. I thought you come to check up on her, sir."

"Where did they take her?"

"I don't know. Back to Division, I guess. They talked to her for a while, and then they went off with her in their jeep."

"Christ, what is going on around here, First Sergeant?" Bear's anger would have boiled over then and there, but there was a scraping of chairs from the back office, and Major Hart and the colonel came out followed by Martin. The first sergeant jumped to his feet, shushing the Bear with a quick hidden gesture.

"Let's see that this one goes like clockwork," the colonel was saying. "We don't know when the general will be looking in, but we'll be there sometime." Seeing the Bear there, the colonel stopped. "Glad to see you're still with us," he said. The colonel had cultivated a bluff way of speaking that sometimes left it a mystery whether he was pleased or angry, until a slow smile followed, accompanied by an unconscious gesture of rubbing a hand over his bald forehead. "I lost a lot of sleep over you," he continued to the Bear. "I'll be damned if I'm going to let you out of my sight now. You're doing some decent flying, judging by the DFC recommendation that crossed my desk lately. And Hart says you're a good man. I don't know whether Hart knows shit from applebutter; but I can't find anybody to take his job, so I'll have to take his word." Before his slow crooked smile had faded, he was out the door.

The first sergeant lapsed back into his proprietary slouch behind his desk. "This young warrant officer came to see you, sir," he said to Major Hart.

"In case you missed it," Major Hart told the Bear, "that was a compliment from the colonel. Well, come on in, Don. Captain Martin said you wanted to see me about something."

"I wanted to see you about this, sir." Bear took Pinky's letter from his pocket and handed it to the major. "But," he said to Martin, "sir, what happened to Suzie?"

Martin shook his head tiredly. "I don't know, Bear. Somebody and his interpreter came down from G-2, and they thought they had to talk to her back there. It just got out of my hands." Bear could see that Martin was embarrassed by the way things had turned out; but he also seemed annoyed that the Bear should question his judgment. "Whatever we think of Blood," Martin added, "sometimes he's right. She could have been stepping off the ramp, and we can't take a chance. Some things just have to be done. She'll be back to catch the truck home: just look at it as a day off for her."

Bear saw that there was nothing more to be said.

The major had stood behind his desk during this exchange. Now he sat down and smoothed the letter out carefully. He read slowly, turning the page at the end to see that there was nothing on the back. "Well, Ben," he said, "here we go again." He handed the letter to Martin and thoughtfully rubbed his nose with one forefinger. While Martin was reading the letter, the major asked Bear, "Have you answered it?"

"Not yet, sir."

"Are you planning to?"

"Yes."

"Of course. You know it's against regulations, don't you?"

"Not officially. Is it?"

"Yes. Now that you know 'officially,' are you going to answer it anyway?"

"Yes, sir."

"Yes, sir. You know, Ben, if we had many officers this honest the Army would have to be disbanded. If you're going to answer it," he asked the Bear, "why did you bring it to me, for God's sake. Never mind, I know that one. It's because you wanted to take me to task for not answering the letter Mrs. Covington says she wrote to me."

"Not exactly, sir, but I—"

"Oh, hell, if not exactly, then close enough. Well, Ben, what are we going to do with this one?"

"With Bear, sir? Nothing, I hope."

"No, no, of course not with Bear. What kind of animal do you take me for? They'll be calling all of us by the names of beasts before it's all over anyway," he said aside to the Bear. "No, with the letter."

"I think he should answer it," Martin said.

"So you said about the last one. It's still against regulations."

"I know."

"Is that all you can say? I thought you were going to try to tell me that people are more important than regulations. Who's going to set me straight if my own XO won't?"

"Maybe one of your warrant officers," Martin suggested with a smile.

Major Hart sighed and removed his reading glasses, "Insubordination is spreading in the ranks. What's the Army coming to? Well, Don, here is an old man's apology, on behalf of his Army, to you and to Mrs. Covington. I thought she would be properly informed in due time. But, as my XO has so persuasively argued, people are more important than regulations, and something has

224

gone amiss. You'd better get your letter off to Pinky. And for his fluency, the XO gets to draft a letter for me, apologizing for my tardiness in answering her. What else can I do for you?"

Bear hesitated. "Well . . . one more thing, sir."

Major Hart sighed. "Name it."

"I want to transfer out of the unit, sir." Major Hart stiffened behind his desk, and Bear heard Martin move suddenly at his back. "It's nothing to do with the letter," Bear said. "Or with Suzie." He was not sure why he had added either of those—or even, now that he had said them, that they were true. Everything had suddenly fallen together.

"Are you having trouble with Blood?" Martin asked.

"No. Well, no more than usual," Bear said with a shake of his head. "It's nothing about the company. I want to go to Dustoff."

"Any particular unit?" the major asked, leaning back in his chair and studying the ceiling.

"The detachment at the hospital"—he gestured down the ramp—"is short a pilot, sir."

A long silence followed. Major Hart continued to study the ceiling. Martin sat turning Pinky's letter on his desk, while the Bear looked uneasily from one to the other until the major looked back at him. Then, remembering the bar and the night before, a blush spread slowly over the Bear's face. "It has nothing to do with . . . her," he said quickly. He had not even considered, until that moment, that the move would put him in daily contact with Alice.

"But it would be convenient," Major Hart said. He hated to say it. It was unkind, and, left to his own feelings, he would not have said it even if he believed it was the reason behind this request. But he thought it was his duty to the Army to say it, to examine the Bear, whom he liked, as any pilot requesting transfer from a shorthanded command should be examined. And there was another reason: he did not want to lose a first-rate pilot because every pilot would be needed for the combat assault that was coming in a week, the combat assault that the colonel had come to discuss.

"I hadn't thought about it, sir," Bear said. He was tempted at first to take back the request, rather than be thought to have asked for that reason. In merely asking he was setting himself

225

apart from his fellows, saying that he should not be asked to do what they would do. But having gone so far, he found himself looking back on the request as a bridge crossed even though he had not known he was approaching it. Finding himself somehow across, he was reluctant to go back.

"You know how short we are on pilots," the major said, with the tone of one who thinks he should be closing the issue.

"Yes, sir."

"People will be back on continuous standby."

"I know that, sir." He could have offered to wait for a replacement. He thought that was what the major was waiting for, as a way gracefully to allow the major to do what he wanted. But to offer that would be to deny the reason for the transfer, would be to recross the bridge. He was determined not to do that.

"And if you leave now, Don," the major said, leaning forward across his desk, "some people may think it's because of . . . the incident. I don't know if you're planning to stay in the Army, but these things can follow you, even when they're not your fault at all." Major Hart flashed an apologetic glance at Martin as he said this.

"That's not important to me," Bear told him.

"Maybe it isn't, now. But you never know what tomorrow will bring. You think about it, will you? I'll tell you now, in confidence, that we're going to need every man we can get during the next week. I can't let anyone go before then. After that . . ." He shrugged. "We'll see."

Bear's sudden determination had been a spring blizzard. It melted before his sense of obligation to his friends, and his desire to please a man he admired. He was half ashamed of his request, for he felt still that it was selfish. When he was gone, others would be left to do his job. But the determination melted, leaving him only the feeling that he had lost his way and was alone.

Bear set out to tell Arp what had become of Suzie, but he found that the lieutenant already knew and had told Yan. They both believed that Suzie would be back before the end of the afternoon. But when the truck came to take the hooch-maids to the gate, Suzie was still missing. Yan looked about pale and frightened from the back of the truck.

"Maybe they'll pick her up on the other side," Arp said to the Bear. They watched the truck roll away. Yan was still staring from the tailgate.

Suzie was not on the other side of the ramp, either. She was returned the next morning, before the rest of the maids arrived, by a sergeant from Intelligence who, according to the company clerk who was the only person in the orderly room at the time, would not say what she had or had not told. She would not walk across the ramp to her place of work, and so she remained in the orderly room until the major and Captain Martin arrived. Martin took her across the ramp in the major's jeep.

She was squatting alone on the back deck when the Bear came up to his hooch for a change of fatigues. She was soaking clothes in a washpan. Her own clothes were rumpled. Bear supposed she had slept in them. She answered him when he spoke to her, but she did not smile. She had a bandage low on one leg.

"We were worried about you, Grandmother," Bear said. He felt awkward with her. Because he did not know where she had been nor what had passed, he did not know what to say.

She thanked him politely for his concern and asked him whether Yan had gone safely home.

"She went. She was also worried."

Suzie studiously massaged the laundry in her pan and did not look up again. At length Bear left her there.

During the day Martin tried to learn what had been done with her, but he had no more success. "They've got a one-way telephone line at G-2," he said to Arp and the Bear. "You can ask questions, but you can't get any answers." He added, "I should never have let her go." But, like the Bear, he could not think quite how to apologize to Suzie herself when he did not know what had occurred.

Yan, too, was subdued that day. She did talk to Arp, but she knew little, or claimed to. She did know about the bandage. "She says the Vietnamese interrogator tried to scare Suzie with a dog," Arp said to the Bear, "and the dog got too close."

227

10

Nervousness ran through the company. Although nothing was said openly, everyone down to the cooks and supply clerks felt it. The company was not one, as some were, that led assaults two and three days of the week. Instead, it supplied aircraft for other units' assaults, two or three slicks to fill out a formation, and a fire team for suppression when others' gunships were down for maintenance. The individual pilots were veterans; but the company's joints were tight through disuse. And whatever was coming was not an ordinary company assault. Before the first briefing, while the detailed plans still simmered above in the chain of command, before it had even been said that there was to be an assault at all, that much was commonly understood. The pressure of it could be felt already, like a monsoon storm offshore speaking to arthritic limbs before any cloud could be seen.

Lieutenant Rauch stewed around the Operations room, going often to the large-scale chart of the division area of operations. "It's gotta be up the Que Son Valley," he said. He spoke to no one in particular, but both fire teams on standby were there for an audience.

"Captain Blood says it's going to go out of Duc Pho," Atterburn said.

"Duc Pho! Nobody works out of Duc Pho but outfits just in country, trainin' for the real war! What makes the Blood think it's going out of Duc Pho?"

228

Atterburn shrugged. "I don't know. But he has a way of knowing what he's talking about."

"Is that the Blood we all know and love?" Arp asked.

Ruth put in shyly, "The night I was off standby—"

"You had a night off already, Ruth?" Rauch demanded. "You ain't been in country two weeks. What is this?"

"The night I was off standby," Ruth began again, "I heard Captain Blood talking to some uver officers in ve club, and he said it looked like Major Hart was going to be leading ve mission, and if vat was so, it was sure to go from Duc Pho because he hasn't had enough experience to lead a battalion operation anywhere else. I fink he said ve major hasn't led a CA since he's had ve company."

An uneasy silence fell in the room. "Leave it to fucking Blood to talk out of school," Rauch muttered, to one side so that Atterburn would not hear.

"He said vat a mission around Duc Pho is all ve major needs to get his promotion anyway," Ruth went on in all innocence, "so vey might as well save ve big ones for someone who needs ven worse. But I fink it is going to be a big one: Captain Blood said ve major was going to have every body in reach in ve air vat day, if he had to turn down R and R's to do it."

"We *know* it's going to be a big one," Atterburn said. "The only question is if it's going to be hot."

"Pray for rain, Bear," someone said. Everyone laughed, except Arp and the Bear. Arp would have laughed, if the Bear had. But he had been watching the Bear since the night he talked with Wolcheski. He did not think the Bear had laughed since then.

"Captain Martin, sir?" Someone stepped out of the shadow beside the first gunship revetment. Martin thought at first that it was a guard; but the man was not wearing a helmet. "Who is it?"

"Arp, sir. Do you have a minute?"

"In abundance. They come in bundles of sixty, and every day I accumulate a surplus. I was just trying to burn up some extras by working late."

"Better store them up for your old age, sir. You'll be glad of them then. All I need is a few from one bunch."

"When you're looking at it from behind a desk," Martin said

229

with a shrug, "a year in Nam contains more hours than will fit into the average lifetime."

"You should fly more," Arp said. "It passes the time." He knew Martin was back on flight status, for as company IP he had given him a check ride. But he did not think Martin had flown since then.

"You're assuming I've been offered a choice," Martin said. "Napoleon thought an army marched on its stomach, but he was wrong. It's paper that keeps it moving. And it takes more paper to make it fly than to make it march. But—we do what we have to do."

"Or what we're told to do. But there ought to be a way out sometimes."

"I haven't found it."

"I don't suppose you've looked, sir," Arp said, without meaning any flattery.

"There isn't any." Martin could not see where the conversation was leading; but he supposed Arp had met him out on the ramp for a reason; and he was less impatient than he might once have been. He lingered there.

"I was hoping you could find one for the Bear," Arp said.

Martin considered for some time before he answered: "He's already asked."

"I suppose that shouldn't surprise me," Arp said shortly, "but it does."

"It surprised *me*," Martin said.

Without a suggestion by either one they began to walk down the gunship row. The empty ships, their doorless sides cavernous in the night, loomed in the revetments, their guns pointing out over the cliffs. Martin and Arp climbed into the back of the farthest ship and sat on the creaking canvas seats. It was a ship Martin had flown often. Number zero-seven-four. He remembered it well, trying to bounce its swollen toadlike bulk off an asphalt ramp on a hot afternoon with its belly dragging too many pounds of fuel and rockets and cartridges. But he remembered it fondly. It smelled of kerosene and cold steel.

"I don't think the Bear wants to quit flying," Martin said. "I used to think he lived to fly. If he quit flying, he wouldn't exist anymore. Flying was what defined him. Maybe that's not so anymore." He remembered Bear and the nurse.

"He wants to fly," Arp said, "he just doesn't want to fly guns. But I don't know if what he wants is what matters."

"Then why are you here?"

"It's not so important that he get what he wants, even though I'd like to see that happen. We've got to get him out of the guns, sir, or it's going to mean his life, or worse."

"It's meant a lot of men's lives. But how do you mean, worse?"

" 'Men may come to worse than dust.' Something's gone wrong with the Bear, sir. I don't know if it was Hill Four Seven Three, or Covington, or what. But he's not a gunnie anymore."

"The Bear always hated to kill people. Is that all that's wrong?" Martin laughed.

The laugh held an irony that Arp did not hear. "It's serious, sir," he protested. "Cripps told me—"

"Ah. If Cripps said something, it is serious. What was it?"

"Cripps is worried the Bear is going to get himself killed. He won't let his crew shoot anymore. Cripps came to me himself to tell me."

"Is Cripps afraid?"

"Probably. But the only thing he asked me was if I couldn't do something for the Bear. He loves the old Bear, sir."

"He should."

"Sir, the Bear's ship has been coming in with three fourths of its ordnance still on board. Handy's been complaining to the platoon sergeant. You know Handy doesn't care about anything but his body count. The platoon sergeant reported it to me, and I didn't say anything; but I know he's been reporting to Captain Blood, too."

"Well? It's Blood's platoon."

"Why hasn't Blood sent Bear to the flight surgeon, or to the major, or something?"

"I don't know. Why not?"

"I think, sir, it's because he's storing up things to make a case for charges against the Bear. Blood doesn't want him out of the gun platoon, because that's what the Bear wants. Blood wants to get him court-martialed." After a time Arp added, "Even that isn't the most important thing."

"What is, then?"

"Having to go out every day and sooner or later squeeze the trigger. It's killing him. He's not the same Bear. I've been watching him, sir; and it's like seeing him shrink before your eyes. The crews laugh about it, when Cripps isn't listening. But it's not funny, sir. The Bear is still the best pilot in the platoon. There are so many things he could be doing: why does he have to go on at the one thing he can't do? It's worse than killing him or court-martialing him! You know the Bear, sir: he wouldn't have asked, if it wasn't serious."

"Then we'd better try to get him out," Martin said. He knew that Arp was right. The Bear would not have asked if it were not serious. Neither would Arp. He thought of Suzie, sitting in the orderly room awaiting the result of his misjudgment. "I'll talk to Major Hart."

Bear was still in his seat filling out the aircraft log book after the mission when Captain Blood came around the tail of the ship. "Has your crew rearmed your ship already?" he asked, in elaborately feigned surprise.

"No," Bear said.

"No what."

"No, sir." The Bear went on writing.

"Don't you have a lot of rockets left?" The tubes were still all loaded. Bear did not answer.

"If that switch isn't working, you'd better get Cripps to check it out."

"I'll do that, sir," Bear said.

Blood stayed no longer. He walked away at his plunging gait like a man charging an obstacle. He was smiling.

Blood was talking to Major Hart when Martin came in.

It annoyed Blood to have Martin listening. He was not worried about anything Martin might have to say: he had prepared his ground too carefully for that. But he did not like being around Martin. Since Hill 473 he liked it even less than before. Martin's Ringknocker smugness was unbearable in a man who had nothing to be smug about. Hill 473 had showed that he was no better than Blood was himself, but still he went around with a superior air, as if he was above being hurt by a reprimand. He had kept the letter of reprimand quiet, but Blood knew about it—there were ways to find out that kind of thing, and any fool knew it had to come. A man with that on his record had no place being smug.

"Ben," the major said, "Captain Blood was just showing me some interesting figures." He handed to Martin the sheet which Blood had given him. There was penciled on it a neat column of dates, and opposite each, two sets of numbers.

"What is it?"

Major Hart looked to Blood. "Rockets," Blood said. "Rockets left on board the ships in my fire team after the last dozen fire missions."

"Is that significant?" Martin recognized the meaning at once, but at least Blood was going to have to say it.

"The first number is for my own ship," Blood said. "As you can see, I've come in with from zero to two pair. And I try not to waste any ordnance, as you may remember. The second number is the number of rockets left on board the other ship. In case you haven't been keeping up with details, Martin, our friend the Bear is AC on that ship. As you can see, he's come in with an average of ten pair unexpended. He hasn't fired a round in the last four missions."

"Very economical," Martin said.

"Economical! If the point is to save money, we could all go home and save the whole bundle!"

"Well, what is the point?" Martin asked.

"The point," Blood said, "is to kill Charlies. And that AC won't do it."

"Really? How do you explain that?"

"How do *I* explain it? The question is how does *he* explain it!"

"Isn't he in your platoon, Captain Blood?"

"In my platoon? Of course he's in my platoon! Am I supposed to hold his hand on every mission because he's in my platoon?"

"Well, have you tried ordering him to kill Charlies?"

"Christ, Martin, what is this? Of course I haven't, not in so many words. You don't have to do that. Did *you* order him to when you were leading that platoon? I've told him when to open fire. He knows the SOP."

"Then why isn't he firing?"

"Well, I'll tell *you* what he tells *me*," Blood said, "if you really want to know how he explains it. He can't see the targets. Or he doesn't know who they are—just like he needs a personal introduction to every man he fires on. Today he told me his selector switch was inop. That was a lie. I had the switch checked before and after the mission and a member of his crew states that the aircraft commander never even armed the system!" Blood played this last statement triumphantly and sat back to watch Martin react. Martin shrugged and looked at the major.

"Well, Ben, I think that just about seals it," Major Hart said. "I suppose there's nothing else we can do." He turned to Captain Blood. "I appreciate your bringing this out, Del," he said. "Captain Martin has been telling me that the Bear was having a hard time; but he's been such an excellent pilot that I was sure he'd bounce back. I can see now that he hasn't. He asked some time ago for a transfer, but I refused him. He wanted to fly Dustoff. I think now it would be best for all to let him go."

Blood's face reddened. He started several times to speak, but he found no words. His effort was such that the eyes bulged from his head.

Major Hart was musing and studying the ceiling. "It will take some time for the papers to go through," he said. "And I was studying the hours-flown figures today. You've got some aircraft commanders near the limit for this month. We're going to need every ship we have within a few days. You know, I suppose, about the operation coming up?"

"I . . . heard something about it," Blood managed to answer. "Nothing definite, sir."

"Well, it'll be definite tomorrow. Lieutenant Rauch went out to recon the area today, and I'm going up with the colonel in the morning. You're not to let any of this out, of course."

"Of course, sir."

"Well, to make it short, if I ground him now, we'll have to import an aircraft commander to make up our complement of gunships, and since it's a battalion operation, I suspect there won't be any aircraft commanders available anywhere else, either. That could be hard to explain—why we're not using a flyable pilot. There's no sense getting the colonel in on this. Is the Bear's ship of any use at all to you, as things are now?"

"The rest of the crew is fine, sir!" Blood said. "They do their best. It's hard for them to press an attack home, when the AC . . . when the AC won't fire. But at least there's another ship up there for Charley to have to keep an eye on."

"All right," Major Hart said. "Let him fly, then. Ben," he said to Martin, "get the papers started. You can tell the Bear before tomorrow's briefing. And Del," he said, turning back to Blood, "thank you. You've made me see what needs to be done. We need more officers who keep an eye out for their men."

Blood, seeing no better way, took the thanks and bowed out hastily.

As he sought through the file for a form, Martin stole several glances at the major, trying to decide what he really thought of Blood's visit. The major was sucking at his empty pipe. Whenever his eyes met Martin's he smiled benignly.

The helicopters began to gather at the pickup zone before dawn. Companies thundered down out of the darkness and crossed the grey foredawn in tight formations. Gunships ranging the flanks of the formations circled lazily out over the paddies and returned to settle at the edge of the PZ as the slicks dragged in alongside the troops spread across the middle of the field. Arab Six, the battalion commander's ship, came in alone and parked to one side near the head of the column of slicks. Blood left his ship at the head of the five Wolfpack gunships and plunged off across the rutted field toward the command ship in order to arrive before the other element leaders. He slowed when he saw Baker already there. Baker had been promoted to major, and he was XO of the Mustang company now. Blood did not want to have to talk to Baker. He had not seen Baker since Martin became XO, and he did not want to see him now.

In the open ships it was chilly. Cripps huddled in his flight jacket, but Handy sat on the cabin floor running a cleaning rod through the barrel of his weapon.

Arp came back from the ship ahead of Bear's. Bear's was the last in the Wolfpack element. He was flying behind Arp because Blood had sent him out of his own fire team once he saw there was no longer a point in counting leftover rockets. A special maintenance effort to get everything flying for Major Hart's mis-

235

sion had got five Wolfpack gunships up, and Blood was leading a three-ship heavy fire team.

Arp stamped his feet against the chill and studied the eastern horizon. The cloudless sky promised warmth once the sun was up. "It looks like you get a good sendoff for your last day," Arp said. He spoke in a low voice. Bear, who had not told anyone of this coming departure, gave him a sidelong glance but said nothing.

"Or," Arp went on, "maybe we can call it your first day." He punched Bear's arm gently.

Captain Martin, coming up from his aircraft at the trail position in the company formation, turned from his path toward Arab Six to pass by the Bear's ship. "Well," he said, "here it is at last. End of the line. Starting this evening you'll be a ground-pounder, until your transfer goes through." That he spoke in Arp's presence told the Bear how Arp knew.

Now that the time had come, a sense of loss filled the Bear, for the shame of leaving his friends behind to do what he would not was still with him. "I wish there was another way to do it," he said.

"If you find one, let me know," Martin said. He went on toward the leaders' briefing.

The field began to brighten. The briefing was not yet over when Blood came steaming back across the dew-whitened grass. "I'd better see what that is," Arp said. He went up to meet Blood beside his own ship. Bear could see Blood's breath condense around him as he huffed violently at Arp, shook his head, puffed again, and finally waved a hand palm-out in disgust and marched off once more. Arp came back to the Bear's ship.

"It all looked exciting," Bear said.

"Very. The Mustangs are short a gunship this morning. We have to send them one."

The Bear sighed and pulled on his gloves. He did not want to fly with strangers today. It would be hard enough with men he knew. But he had no doubt that Blood had sent him to the other company and given Arp their own extra ship. "Where are they parked?" he asked.

"Never mind that," Arp said. "I'm going myself. Blood is sending Ward back here to fly with you. You'll be in charge of the fire team."

"Me?" Bear cried. "Why?"

"You sound just like Blood," Arp grinned. He tapped Bear on the shoulder again and stepped down from the door. "It'll be a milk run. And you deserve your place back as fire-team leader for your last day."

Bear knew that he could have argued and got out of it. But Arp had argued with Blood for his sake, simply as a kind gesture. He did not have the heart to argue in turn. He gave Arp a thumbs-up sign through the windscreen. Arp waved and walked on away. In a moment Arp's ship began to crank, and Ward's hovered out and moved in behind Bear.

The meeting broke up. The first lift of troops was aboard the slicks. Arab Six had turned on his beacon, and the whole formation began to crank. As the blades spun up in slow drunken swings that gradually vanished into stable transparent discs above the fuselages of the helicopters, the sun leaped from the sea, and the whole field trembled with lightning as the blades caught the sun. Gunships slid away low over the fields and peeled off in their loose teams of two or three. Behind them Arab Six climbed steeply out, and the whole formation took to the air and turned west toward the mountains.

Bear's unease passed as the slicks discharged their loads into the first landing zone. There was no enemy fire. Troops strolled across the open field toward a tree line as the slicks thundered away. It was a cold LZ, and it was the only dangerous one on the list. Two other infantry companies were to be inserted, but they would go into the pacified fields nearer the coast. Bear turned the controls over to Ruth.

With his ship empty Martin gave it to his copilot to fly on the return to the PZ. The copilot was a new warrant officer. Martin knew the face and the name, but he had hardly spoken to the man. That was the worst thing about not flying, for him: his comrades, the men on whom his life might depend, were nothing but names on a list. Martin studied the man as he flew. The ship was in the slot behind a V of three others, and the pilot was nervous. His neck was rigid; his right hand engulfed the cyclic stick. "Don't strangle it," Martin said dryly. Then he laughed.

237

The man gave him a sidelong sheepish grin and relaxed his hand. The fingers soon crept back around the stick; but Martin knew that the man would work out his tension now, if left alone. He turned to watch the show outside the ship.

Martin wished he could be with Arab Six high overhead, or in a gunship—not to be able to fire on the enemy, but only to see better. Even from the inside, from the trail ship in the first of three elements, the formation was a beautiful thing, a dense phalanx of aircraft pressing forward as war swirled around it. Gunships crossed and recrossed at different levels, like goldfish swirling in a bowl. Chinooks with artillery pieces dangling from their umbilical connections barged past, while air strikes flashed and rumbled along the ridgelines. Nothing could match it.

The ships refueled after the second sortie. The guns had no need to rearm—no ship had fired a round. They had time to spare, and they shut down in the PZ for a short time. "Damn dull, this," Atterburn said. "I see Arab Six got tired of it and *di-di*'d for home. Let's hope for more action, eh, Bear?"

"If it keeps up like this," Bear answered, "we'll all live long happy lives."

"Not you, damn you. You'll screw yourself to death with your nurse."

"Thank God it's not contagious," Bear said. He was too happy to be offended by Atterburn.

"You certainly haven't caught it, anyway, Burn," Arp said. "How's it going, Bear?" The Mustangs had shut down at the same time, and he had come back to check on his fire team.

"Quiet," Atterburn answered for Bear. "Just the way he likes it."

"Would we all had as much sense," Arp said.

"Shoot, Lieutenant, it ain't much, but it's the only war we got," Atterburn said.

The third sortie had been changed from the original objective. It was to go into the river valley west of Quang Ngai. Bear checked the coordinates on his chart during the wait; but he did not recognize the place until the formation turned the corner of the mountain. Then he knew it at once. The houses were still there, clustered beneath the tattered palm trees like chicks under the ragged wings of a long-legged jungle fowl. It was a village he had seen evacuated, its people moved to "pacified" territory. The village was to have been burned: there should have been nothing but ashes; but roofs and walls winked at him in the sun. Far ahead a buffalo was browsing along the edge of the paddy.

"Ah, Wolf Lead, do you have that fuck-ox in sight?" a voice asked on the VHF radio, the gunship frequency. It was Block, the pilot of the second ship in Blood's fire team.

"That's affirm." Blood had on his professional voice.

"Ain't he in a free-fire zone?"

"That's affirmative."

"Permission to fire?"

"Let's go." Blood's fire team was on the opposite flank from the Bear, out along the river. A puff of black smoke issued from the tailpipe of Blood's ship as it nosed over and accelerated across the front of the formation of slicks a mile behind the gunships.

"Sir, what've they got?" Handy asked in sudden excitement. He could hear only the intercom on his headset, not the radios; but he had seen the other ships dash forward.

"Vey have a fierce buffalo," Ruth said, laughing. Blood's ship spat a pair of rockets which arced ahead as two glowing dots that touched the earth and sent two muddy fountains into the air behind the startled buffalo. The buffalo did not stay to chat but broke into a frenzied run in the direction in which his nose was pointed. The second ship was armed with a grenade launcher. It came in low behind Blood, sending out a stream of forty-millimeter grenades whose flashes rippled under the buffalo and threw it rump upward onto the paddy dike beside the village. The two gunships swung away over the paddy and back toward the first element of slicks now beginning a long final approach to the paddy.

"Good shootin'," Handy said enviously on the intercom. "Good shooting, Two," Blood's voice echoed over the VHF.

Across Blood's voice Major Hart's said on the company FM frequency, "Wolf, we're taking fire." His voice was unmistakable, ancient and craggy but somehow restful despite the urgency of the words.

All the radios were talking at once. The Bear had switched his transmitter to FM: "Coyote Six, where's your fire?"

"Uncertain, Wolf," Major Hart said. "No tracers."

"They're taking fire," Bear said on the intercom. Handy and Cripps came to their feet instantly. They hung one-handed in the doors searching the ground ahead as Bear rolled the ship toward the village.

"Ready to go hot?" Ruth asked. Bear affirmed with two clicks of the mike switch, knowing that he should have given the command before that. Ruth flipped the switches to the armed position.

As the ship flashed over the buffalo, they could hear the rattle of a machine gun.

"Where is it?" Bear asked.

"Can't see anything," Handy answered. Ruth was hanging half out his window. Both of the crew in back strained against their safety straps.

"Wolf, we have fire from ten o'clock," Major Hart's voice said.

"There! There's somebody down there!" Handy exclaimed. He was pointing his machine gun down into the village.

Bear had seen the figure, too. It was a young boy, unarmed. "Hold your fire!" he said desperately. Had all the villagers really been evacuated? "Do you see a weapon?"

"No weapon," Handy said.

"Wait until we come around then." He said over the radio, "Coyote Six, do you have the weapon located?"

"Negative, Wolf," was Major Hart's answer. Even now his voice had a soothing, fatherly sound, as if to minimize the importance of his problems.

"That's Charley, sir!" Handy protested.

Bear switched back to the gunship frequency. "Ward, do you have the weapon?"

"Negative," Ward answered him.

"Dammit, work over the village!" Blood called. His return from the pass at the buffalo had taken him out of range for the thirty seconds in which the Bear's team had been inbound. During that time the slicks had come from a mile distant onto a long straight final approach toward the village. If a weapon were there, the relative motion of the slicks would be almost zero. They would be fat sitting ducks that grew in size with every passing second.

Bear made a short run out and wrenched the ship back inbound. Suddenly gunfire rattled like popcorn around the ship. "Where is he?" Bear called. "Where is he?"

"We got to get some fire on the village!" Handy insisted.

"Wait." Sweat ran down his nose from beneath his helmet. The trap had closed about him. He must fire, somewhere; but he could not fire blindly today, of all days.

Suddenly voices were calling out on the FM: "Two's hit!" "Four is hit!" But the formation drove steadily earthward, and landed. Troops scrambled for the cover of the dike. All of the ships were off the ground as Blood's rockets began to fall into the village.

"There!" Ruth shouted on the intercom: "There!" A burst of tracers had streaked from beyond the edge of the village, from the perpendicular dike at the far end. Ruth had his gunsight trained on the spot without waiting for an order to fire. The flex guns muttered their fierce hate. Bear lined up the rocket sight, leveled the bubble, and touched the red button with his thumb. The range was so short the rockets exploded almost under the ship.

The slicks had nowhere to go except over the machine gun. As they scrambled for speed and altitude, the lead ship dropped suddenly from the formation. "Mayday, Mayday. Coyote Six going down." Major Hart's voice did not rise even to the level of excitement. It was his only communication. His ship nosed up and slid to a mud-spewing halt in the next paddy, a quarter mile beyond the village.

"Six, stay close," someone called. "We're coming in after you." The trail ship in the formation had broken away and turned back, racing in low and downwind. But there was now no one on the lead ship to hear. The crew were out and scrambling for the shelter of the nearest dike. Out in the paddy the ship was the center of a storm of bullets.

The Bear heard, and recognized the voice. It was Captain Martin.

The men on the ground had strung out in a line. Major Hart was the last. It was a long run to the dike. Martin's ship jinked twice like a broken-field runner, made a last hard turn, and dropped ahead of the first of them. As it touched the ground, the men began to fall—first Major Hart, then the two ahead of him. None rose again. The fourth, although he was far ahead, turned back. He took the arm of one fallen man over his shoulder and started again for the waiting ship.

Martin saw the tracers streak across the paddy ahead of him. He put them out of his mind. He took his eyes from the men on the ground, too. The only thing that mattered was the one spot on the ground where the ship would touch down. He was running downwind and much too fast. If he overshot the spot, the machine gun might be on them before he could turn and hover back. He pulled the cyclic back against the stop and pushed down the collective pitch. The nose of the ship came up. With the big blade acting as a brake the airspeed indicator unwound: fifty knots, forty, thirty. The ship floated, floated. The tail skid touched the mud. He felt it, as if a guiding hand had brought the tail up for him. He pulled the power back in as the skids touched. The ship slid to a halt.

He did not see the men fall. He did not need to. "One . . . no, three of them are down!" the crew chief called out. When he had time to look, Griggs was staggering toward the ship with Major Hart's crew chief over his shoulder.

Griggs tumbled the crew chief onto the cabin floor and fell in behind him. "I think they've had it!" he shouted to Martin.

Martin picked the ship up from the ground, turned toward the two bodies collapsed in the mud. Neither one was moving. He hovered the ship toward them. Something in the air caught his eye. White flakes were fluttering all around him. They came flashing down through the blade and were spread through the air over the paddy. Snow? No, they were butterflies! They dodged and drifted across the paddy, fearless in their innocence. "Look at that!" he said. Then the butterflies were joined by other white flashes that twinkled across the windscreen.

The pilot flying with Martin did not see the butterflies. He was looking at the bodies on the ground. But he saw the tracers. They snapped around the ship and dug little spurts of mud alongside the bodies. Then they slammed against the ship.

The life went out of the controls. The pilot looked over at Martin. Martin was slumped forward against his harness, and his hand had fallen from the cyclic stick. The stick kicked against the pilot's hand. The hydraulic boost was gone. He pulled at the collective to bring the ship higher off the ground. It took all his strength to move the collective at all. Another bullet hammered through the ship.

"Take 'er out!" Griggs was shouting. "We can't do anything here!"

The pilot forced the nose over and accelerated away.

Bear saw Martin's ship climbing away, and the two bodies still sprawled on the red mud of the paddy. For one instant he started down after them. Before he was close to the ground, bullets pounded against his ship. A Christmas tree of warning lights lit up the console. He would have gone in anyway, but as he turned toward the paddy he glanced across at Ruth in the left seat. Ruth was on the controls, following him through. His dark visor was down so that the Bear could not see his eyes, but his tongue was licking his tight lips. Ruth did not want to go in, but it was not his place to say that. He was on the controls, as he should be, ready to try to complete whatever mission his aircraft commander chose.

Bear pulled in full power and broke away.

Bear's ship sat alone in the fuel pits as a maintenance team out from Duc Pho for the day poked at its guts, while the ships still able to fly continued the lift. Before the last of the warning lights was extinguished, other gunships and an air strike had pounded the village. The troops had worked their way up on foot from paddy to paddy, and the machine gun had been silenced. Bear and his crew rejoined the company for the last sortie. The sky was clear. Sunlight sparkled from the paddy. The bodies of Major Hart and Durand, his door gunner, lay there, biding their time, ripening in the sun along with the dead buffalo so sportively upended on the paddy dike. A pall of smoke rolled from the village. It had burned at last.

Dustoff had finished their work with the living wounded farther back down the village perimeter and reached the final paddy during this last sortie. The medevac aircraft commander checked in with the gunships during his approach. Bear knew Wolcheski's voice. As the gunships blazed along the tree line, the red-crossed helicopter flashed in low over the treetops, flared to a quick stop, snatched the bodies aboard, and was gone.

The slain buffalo remained, to the delight of its growing coterie of flies.

There was no overhead break when the formation came back from the mission that day. On other days the ships that had flown in a combat assault would fly the length of the landing lane in tight formation at five hundred feet, and on reaching the end would break sharply away one at a time in a diving turn to slide easily over the landing pad at four-second intervals. After a good mission there would be smoke grenades tied to the skids, to be set off by the crew members pulling a wire tied to the pin.

The grenades had been put on the skids that morning, but they were not used. The ships came directly over the ridge and hovered to their revetments. Lieutenant Rauch did not come out of his Operations hooch to watch them land. Aircraft commanders turned in their reports in silence and walked away. Only Griggs and Captain Blood showed any animation. Griggs, who was back from the dead, was licensed to show his relief in ways that would not have been tolerated that day in others. Also, Griggs was a hero, for he had risked his life in turning back to pick up Murchison, the crew chief. Special tolerance was extended to heroes, at least for the first day. Griggs exercised his license by becoming rapidly—almost instantly—drunk and roaming from hooch to hooch recounting the great events in exhaustive detail.

As for Blood, he left the platoon after-action report with Rauch and was off at once "to get things squared away over at the orderly room."

"What's to square away over there?" the Operations sergeant wondered.

"He means," Rauch said, "that he's goin' to get his rear behind the major's desk and hope the colonel lets him stay there."

"God help us!" the sergeant responded.

244

Although he didn't mean to do it, it was Ward who started the speculation that this time the Bear would be grounded forever. "Why wouldn't Bear let us fire?" he asked Ruth. Ward was no enemy of the Bear. Although he had heard rumors, he ordinarily flew in a different fire team. He remembered the old Bear, and he assumed that there were good reasons for not firing.

Ruth said nothing. But Griggs had heard the question. At the time it happened, Griggs was too busy with other matters to wonder what the guns were doing. Now, safe on the ground, he became alarmed over the value of the skin he had so nearly lost. "Not fi'? Wh'cha mean, not fi'? What the hell're gunships for if they don't fi'?" he demanded. Griggs, who had no great opinion of anyone's ability but his own, had heard the rumors, too, and had always thought that a reputation as great as the Bear's had been must be overblown enough to leak somewhere. "Was that bastard not shootin' 'gen? I'll be damn' 'f I'm goin' fly with a asshole who won' be with me when the bullets fly!"

"Don't worry, Captain Blood will take care of that," Atterburn said. Atterburn flew with Blood day in and day out. He had seen the list of rockets not fired grow day by day. He knew what its purpose must be. But he did not know that the list had already been expended. He assumed that Blood was preparing to use it.

Atterburn was wrong. The Bear was not then in Blood's mind at all. He had thought it all through already, and dismissed it from his mind. There was the perfect case against the man, of course. But Blood knew, without really bringing that part of the matter to his consciousness at all, that if the company had been without gunship support because the Bear's fire team had not fired, someone was sure to ask where the other fire team had been at the critical instant. Out of range chasing a buffalo? What?

Blood sat at the major's desk leafing through the day's papers. The morning report was unsigned: the major had gone out before it was prepared. Blood signed it as ranking officer in the company. But the morning report was not enough. He needed to get the attention of the battalion commander somehow. Time was everything. The colonel was not really high enough, either. The CG would be better; but he was out of reach. If Blood had been a Ringknocker like Martin, he supposed, he could have done it. They had their ways. But if you weren't one of them, what you wanted you had to get on your own.

Blood pounded the desk in frustration. The company was here, leaderless. It needed him. He could take it over and remake it into what it should be, a superb fighting machine. But first he had to get it in his hands. He *would* find a way to get the attention of the chain of command. He squared the major's papers neatly in the center of the desk, pulled himself into a perfectly rigid military seated posture, and proceeded to think the problem through in a military manner.

"First Sergeant!"

From the time Captain Blood disappeared into the major's office, the first sergeant had been sitting at his desk staring furiously at one sheet of paper. Now he banged it down on his desk, looked at his morning report clerk with a look that, if the clerk had been combustible, would have set him aflame, and forced himself to march to the opening in the plywood screen. "Sir?"

"First Sergeant," Captain Blood said, "have you started arrangements for the memorial service?"

"No, sir. Memorial service, sir?"

"Yes. For the men we lost today. For Major Hart, and . . . the executive officer. And a crew chief."

"Door gunner, sir."

"Yes, door gunner. I think a memorial service is in order, for men who made that sacrifice. I want it tomorrow."

"Tomorrow. Yes, sir. Any particular thing you had in mind, sir?"

"Yes." Blood knew just the thing he had in mind. He had attended one at another company while he was still flying in the slick platoon. It needed some sprucing up, but he would see to that. It would be a memorial service he would be proud to have for himself, if he were to fall in battle. A company should honor its fallen. That was one of the things this company lacked. It had no traditions. No decent honor for the fallen.

On the wide hover lane of the parking ramp, between the ranks of revetments on the seaward side and the landward, the company was drawn up in platoons abreast. The revetments were nearly all occupied by helicopters: the sun was almost down, and all but the long resupply missions had returned. A forest of blades slanted upward all around the men. A single helicopter was parked across the center of the hover lane at the front of the formation. In its open cargo door three helmets lay on wreaths of evergreen branches.

The men were ill at ease in their long straight lines on the ramp. There had not been a company formation with men and officers together within the memory of any of those present. Although they stood at parade rest, there was shuffling of feet and a low murmur of voices from within the ranks. Parade drills seemed years distant to all of them.

Captain Blood had positioned himself the regulation twelve steps in front of the center of the company, where he was braced at a rigid parade rest as he waited for the battalion commander. Although he did not turn his head, he was aware of the fidgeting in the ranks. The men—and the officers, too—could fight a war, but they had forgotten how to be an army. They needed more discipline and a leader to hold them together and make them a fighting unit and not a mob. Blood pleased himself with the thought until the colonel came down the edge of the hover lane on foot.

With the colonel were the battalion sergeant major, the chaplain, and a major whom Blood did not recognize at first. When they came closer, Blood saw that it was Baker. He did not have time to wonder why Baker was there. He brought the company to attention and greeted the colonel: "Sir, the company is formed!" His salute had snap to it; his hand vibrated as though the arm contained more energy than could be dissipated by a salute alone.

The colonel tossed off a salute in return. "All right, Captain Blood. Begin when you're ready, then. The CG sends his regrets."

"Yes, sir." The colonel's remark hollowed Blood's reply; but it was not a soldier's place to show disappointment at the actions of his commanding general. Blood executed a smart about-face, commanded "Puh-raid, *rest!*," faced about, stepped into line with the colonel's party, faced about again, and nodded to the chaplain to begin their rehearsed ceremony. The company had slid to thankful ease, feet apart and hands somewhere behind the back.

247

At the chaplain's suggestion a microphone had been set up between the company commander's position and the formation. The chaplain stepped to the microphone and suggested, "Let us pray."

The chaplain was wily in the ways of men standing in formation. A merciful God would not hold his men long at parade rest. Nor did the God of Battles care for cajolery. The prayer was short and unobsequious.

When the chaplain had stepped back, Captain Blood marched forward again, but not all the way to the microphone. A leader with a command voice could dispense with artificial aids. He read at the top of his voice from the note cards he had been carrying in the palm of his left hand: "Major Howard Hart, born 1928, entered the United States Army in 1949. He was commissioned second lieutenant, Infantry, United States Army Reserve, in 1951, upon completion of Officer Candidate School, Fort Benning, Georgia. He served his country with distinction in war and in peace. In the Korean War he was wounded twice and decorated twice for bravery. His awards and decorations are the Purple Heart, three awards, the Bronze Star for valor, two awards, the Bronze Star for service, the Air Medal with ten oak leaf clusters, the Korean Service Medal, and the Vietnam Service Medal, two awards. He died in battle, in the service of his country, fifteen January, nineteen sixty-eight."

The Bear, buried within the ranks of the warrant officers drawn up in front of the enlisted men, heard out this capsule life of a man whose death weighed on him. Hart was born, he was commissioned, he was awarded, he died. Was it all the Army knew of him? Or only all that mattered to Blood? The records were a sieve too gross to catch the man himself. He had dropped through without a trace. Where were the kindness, the concern for his men, the love of the country in whose service he *had* died? Where was even the concern that he might remain in that service, the concern, Bear thought ruefully, which led him to cling too long to the rotten thread, the man who failed him and so caused his death? He had passed away from all that. That it even had existed, no one now could tell. He was a pile of paper, which told what was of no importance to anyone.

And Captain Martin. Blood marked his milestones, too. It was a shorter life, but brighter as the Army saw such things. Born 1940. Educated United States Military Academy at West Point. First Captain of Cadets. Honor graduate, Ranger School, Fort Benning, Georgia; Outstanding Officer award, Airborne School, Fort Benning, Georgia. Awards and decorations: Distinguished Flying Cross, the Bronze Star for service, the Air Medal with two oak leaf clusters, the Vietnam Service Medal, the Purple Heart. Died in battle, January 15, 1968.

The record said more, that Blood did not say: letter of reprimand, ending his useful career as an officer of the United States Army. And what the record did not comprehend: an intelligent man who felt what some would say no intelligent man could feel —love for the military and its traditions of honor and service, while despising the insensitivity and brutishness that passed, with some, for dedication to duty; an ambitious man who knew what his merits deserved, but did not brag, and who rose by his merits, and not (as Blood's envy told him) by influence (or if by influence, only by the influence his merits earned among those who knew him); a man believing in himself, determined to endure and conquer what would finish lesser men; a man conquered by that which conquers all men.

And the gunner Durand. He was born, he went for a soldier, he died January 15, 1968, having been awarded the Vietnam Service Medal and the Purple Heart.

Blood called the company to attention and present arms. Behind the formation, from behind one of the revetments where a helicopter stood, taps sounded. But as the bugle call rang across the air between the ridge and the sea, a helicopter was running up at the company down the ramp. The sound of the bugle was lost in the crescendo of the blade coming to operating speed. As the men saluted, the helicopter hovered out of its revetment to the takeoff lane and turned to face the sea. Blood cursed to himself and made a mental note to coordinate the next ceremony with the neighboring company; but to the Bear there was nothing about the ceremony so moving as the appearance of this unplanned visitor. It hovered easily in the last sunlight, hanging delicately, impossibly, suspended, like a soul about to depart. As the bugle call died it dipped its nose and moved away to mount the hill of air, leaving behind a long sigh.

249

"Order, arms!" Blood's voice rang down the ramp. He ordered the platoon commanders, "Dismiss your platoons!," took their salutes on one of his own, and turned toward the colonel full of self-congratulation as the company was dissolved behind him. Blood saluted the colonel again. The salute was not required by the field manual on drill and ceremonies. It was merely an expression of good feeling. In spite of the wayward helicopter Blood was happy. The ceremony had made him sentimental himself. He thanked the colonel for coming.

"It's the least I could do," the colonel said. "But I'd have been coming anyway. I think you know Major Baker?" He turned to include Baker in the conversation. "Major Baker is your new commanding officer."

Blood's happiness dissolved and flowed away like the men streaming off among the revetments.

"I tried to talk Division into giving me two field grades," the colonel added. "Or at least a senior captain. We must be the only battalion in country that's underranked. But the buggers wouldn't do it. They said they'd try to get us a first lieutenant next month. Or squeeze the pipeline for a couple of junior captains. So, it looks like you two are it." He grinned at them at the end. "It's your company. Try not to wreck it." The colonel had liked Martin and Hart. He did not like Baker or Blood, either one; but they were the senior officers available, and Division, for reasons that escaped him, would not pry loose an outside officer. The colonel hid his distaste under apparent irony. A reputation for ironic humor could be useful at times: no one knew when you were serious.

"Sir, we're gonna do you proud," Baker said. Blood saluted again and said nothing.

When he saw his name on the duty roster, Bear set straight out for company headquarters. He walked past the company clerk and straight to the back, behind the plywood partitions where Baker and Blood's desks were.

Blood was alone, staring gloomily across to Baker's side of the room. "Who the hell invited you in here?" he demanded.

"I saw my name on the duty roster," Bear said.

250

"Bingo. You can read. Learn to shoot, and maybe you'll be worth a shit after all."

"Major Hart approved a transfer to Dustoff for me," Bear said.

"Don't look like you're gone to me," Blood said. "How'd that happen?"

"That's what I came to ask."

"I don't know anything about a transfer," Blood said. "You got your ten-forty-nine?"

"No. But Captain Martin told me it was approved."

"Oh? It's convenient that Captain Martin is dead, isn't it?"

"For some people it is," Bear said.

Blood was not to be baited into anything. "So you want to go to Dustoff, eh?" he asked.

"Yes, sir."

"Tired of being shot at, are you? Ready to crawl off where it's safe? That's right, Bear, let a *soldier* die."

He dismissed the Bear with a wave of his hand. But as Bear turned to go, Blood called him back. "This came down from Battalion," Blood said. "Your name's on it." He tossed Bear a box. It contained Bear's third Distinguished Flying Cross.

"Bear, what are you still doing here?" Arp asked. The Bear was lying on his side on a bunk in the alert hooch, resting one cheek on the backs of his hands like the reclining Buddha carved on a mountainside east of Saigon.

"I keep asking myself that," the Bear answered without moving. He fetched up a long sigh, then rolled up to a sitting position. "The answer I keep getting," he said, "is that I'm on standby."

Arp had just landed from escorting a pickup assault with the Mustangs, and he was tired of war for the day. "I thought you were done with this business," he said.

"I guess that makes two of us who were wrong," Bear answered.

It increased Arp's irritation that Bear showed no concern at still being on standby. "Aren't you supposed to be on ground duty?"

"That's a matter of opinion. The opinion of the Operations officer is that I'm supposed to be on standby. My day off isn't until tomorrow."

251

"What do you mean, your 'day off'? You're done. *Fini. Hết rồi.*"
Heads up and down the hooch turned toward them as Arp said this. What they thought, Arp did not care. He supposed they thought he meant that the Bear was being grounded for failure to fire the day before. "I'm going to see Rauch about this."

"Rauch's opinion comes from the CO," Bear said, "so you can save that step. And," he added, "the CO's comes from the XO."

"Blood? What kind of horse manure is it now? He knew about your ten-forty-nine! I'll go see him, then."

"I already did that," Bear said quietly. He had pulled his legs up under himself on the bed so that he looked more the Buddha than ever, and he had folded his hands in his lap. He was meditating on the space between the balls of his thumbs held a quarter-inch apart. The thumbs had a barely visible tremor. "The Blood doesn't know anything about any ten-forty-nine," he said.

Arp turned without a word and went out of the hooch. To Rauch in the Operations hooch he said, "Give me the keys to your jeep. I'm going to the orderly room."

"If it's about the Bear, I'll tell you for a fact you're wastin' your time, Stud."

"Probably. Now, are you going to give me your damn keys?"

"Sure." Rauch tossed them across the counter.

Blood was alone behind the screen in the orderly room. He was sitting with his arms folded, leaning back in Martin's chair, studying the empty chair behind the commander's desk opposite him. Arp's sudden appearance brought Blood quickly down to a more military posture. "What do you want, Lieutenant?" he demanded, as if in his translation from platoon commander to executive officer Arp's name had been lost from his mind.

"I want to talk about the Bear, sir."

"Well?"

"He's still on standby in the gun platoon."

"You *are* his acting platoon commander, Lieutenant," Blood said. "If you want him to have the day off, give it to him. Just so somebody flies the missions."

"You know it isn't the *day* off, sir," Arp said. "He has papers in for a transfer to Dustoff. Major Hart had arranged for him to be on ground duty until that came through. He was not to fly guns again. That ought to be honored."

252

"As his platoon commander," Blood said, "you ought to know how short of pilots we are. As for the transfer, your warrant officer came to see me about that. According to the first sergeant and the clerks, nobody ever gave them one to send up. I know he did request a transfer to medevac. As I hear it, Major Hart turned it down. I think there was a nurse down at the hospital, if I'm not mistaken?"

"You're mistaken," Arp said. "Captain Martin told me that the transfer had been approved, and that you know about it."

"I can't say what Captain Martin might of approved," Captain Blood said, his drawl deepening as he spoke. "But I'll tell you this: the only thing that matters is what Major Hart put his John Henry on and sent up through channels; and there ain't been a ten-forty-nine out of this office. Now if Martin said I knew about any other deals, he was just plain wrong."

"Then I want to see the CO," Arp said. He knew already how hopeless that would be. But whatever he had to lose had been cast away already, by coming to Blood, and he was determined now to press the issue to the end.

"Does that mean you're calling me a liar, Lieutenant?" Blood asked.

"Yes, sir," Arp said.

Blood's next words astonished Arp, who thought he knew his captain through and through. Blood said in a low voice, calm but intense, "Lieutenant Arp, I'm goin' to forget you ever said that. Okay?"

Arp could think only that somewhere there existed paperwork on the Bear's transfer that had escaped Blood's hands. Arp had no hopes and no illusions of aid from Baker; but a signed ten-forty-nine in Major Hart's hand might embarrass Blood enough to make him give in. So Blood's words only encouraged Arp. "Forget it if you want, sir," he said, "but I'm going to take it to the CO."

"Then you're a damn fool!" Blood snapped. In fact his reason for the sudden uncharacteristic offer was not fear, or not fear of unknown paperwork. He had already put beyond reach the draft that had been in Martin's desk. Nor was it any concern for Arp, whom he considered an overeducated wise-ass whose rich father protected him from his smart tongue. But he would have traded the chance to court-martial Arp for the chance to separate him from the Bear. Blood could understand why Martin would stick out his neck to get the Bear out of the company alive. Martin and the Bear were both mush-hearted; and Martin owed him something for the mess at Hill 473. But Arp owed the Bear nothing. Having him spurn what Blood meant to look like friendship was like seeing Martin, not even in his grave, come back to life. "Major Baker will be back from Battalion right shortly," Blood said. "You can see him anytime he's got the time to waste on you, Lieutenant, as far as I'm concerned. But don't expect too much."

The sound of Baker's jeep pulling down over the dirt bank behind the orderly room stopped any reply Arp might have made. Baker came in the back door, talking excitedly before the door was open: "Blood, there's big times comin'. Big times. It's goin' to be . . . Well. Lieutenant Arp. I didn't know you had the day off. Have you killed all the Chinamen in country so quick?"

"The lieutenant wants to talk to you about one of his officers," Blood said. "A bug-eyed one."

"Oh, yeah? Are you ready to cashier that turd so quick, Arp? It's about time somebody did."

"I'm ready to get him out of the company," Arp said.

"A dandy idea. What have you got on him?"

"Major Hart approved a transfer for him before . . . before he was killed. I want to see it go through."

"What kind of transfer?" Baker asked, putting aside his offhand manner.

"He was supposed to go to Dustoff."

Baker pursed his lips. "You know anything about this, Blood?"

"No. No, sir." Blood had difficulty remembering that Baker now outranked him; but when he did remember, he added the proper tag. "I know that he asked Major Hart for a transfer and got turned down. He has a girl friend up at the hospital, I hear."

"That right, Arp?"

"No."

Baker raised his eyebrows in an exaggerated query. "No girl friend? I've seen him with a nurse, Arp, with my own two little eyeballs. What kind of dummkopf do you think I am?"

"That part is true," Arp admitted, "but Major Hart approved the transfer."

254

"Well, show me the paper."

"I don't have it, sir," Arp said. He looked closely at Blood as he said this; but Blood showed no sign of knowing more than he was telling.

"Hart sure as hell didn't transfer anyone out without paperwork," Baker suggested, raising his open hands palm up and shrugging his shoulders. "God himself couldn't do that."

"No. But maybe he hadn't forwarded it yet."

"Come off it, Arp! My XO just said that Hart turned down the transfer. Have you seen any paperwork, Blood?"

"No." Blood left off the "sir" this time. He did not care for having Baker call him "his" XO. "Neither has the first sergeant," he added sullenly.

"Well, Arp?"

Arp said stubbornly, "Captain Blood knows it was approved, sir."

"He just said he didn't."

"I know."

Baker, who had been pacing between his own desk and Blood's, threw himself impatiently into his chair. "Jesus H. Christ, Arp, what are you after? If I wasn't so damn short of officers, I'd have you court-martialed for insulting my XO! And I'll tell you one thing—even if I had the paperwork in my hand, I wouldn't forward it. I have to run this company now, Arp, and I am not goin' to give up any warm bodies until out replacements improve. As I was starting out to tell Blood, there are some big missions coming. G-2 has the word out that Charley is going to be all over this area for Tet. I don't plan to give up anyone who can fly a helicopter; not even as poor an excuse for a gun driver as that one in your platoon. Now, is that clear enough for you?"

"He's no good where he is now, sir!" Arp pleaded. "For God's sake, let him go where he can do some good! What can you gain by holding him on? If nothing else, put him in a slick platoon!"

"Isn't he the great gun driver?" Baker asked rhetorically. "I remember him telling me how it was done. Months ago. Let him show me, now."

When Arp returned, the Bear was still lying on his bunk. Arp almost knocked down Cripps at the door. Cripps had been lurking there watching for his return. He muttered an apology and stepped aside guiltily, but stayed in the vicinity of Bear's bunk.

At the back of the room Atterburn was watching Handy fit together the newly cleaned pieces of a Thompson submachine gun. Handy had got it in a trade, for a Chinese rifle and an NVA straw cap. From time to time he lifted it in his left hand and shook his head admiringly, feeling its weight. It was too heavy for a grunt to carry. That was why the previous owner had parted with it so cheaply. But for a helicopter gunner, that was no objection. Handy loved it as the Bear had loved helicopters. He had no thoughts of sculpture, but he loved each piece of the weapon, loved their fine finish and their shapes and their weight in his hand and the exact way they slid together, because he loved the thing they became. "Lookit that, sir!" he exclaimed to Atterburn as the bolt slid into place. "Ain't she a beauty?"

Bear raised his head to look at Arp. "I see how much satisfaction the great man gave you," he said. "I wish you hadn't bothered him. I have enough men's lives on my conscience already, without yours. Even if you would be the first lieutenant in my bag." A self-deprecating smile sneaked out under his mustache as he said this, as if to show he knew that it was silly to worry about other men's lives. One hand came up to poke at the mustache, driving the smile back into refuge. "But thanks," he said. "Thanks."

When he smiled, the Bear's face had a mock-angelic look—a cherub with a mustache. Arp was not sorry for having tried to help him. He deserved better luck than he had got from this war. "There's still a way out," Arp said.

"I don't believe in suicide." The smile came back briefly, giving his face the fugitive light of summer lightning reflected on far clouds.

"It doesn't have to be that serious," Arp said.

"Don't wanna shoot myself in the foot, neither," Bear said, picking up for a moment the drawl of a southern grunt they had once brought into a field hospital when he and Arp had both been flying slicks, so many months ago. The soldier had displayed a neat bullet hole in his left foot. (He had been left-handed.)

"If you can stand to be serious at all at a time like this," Arp told him, "you should consider having the flight surgeon ground you."

The Bear's face instantly did become serious, more serious than Arp wanted. The hands went back to the meditating position. Bear said after a moment, "There's nothing wrong with me, sir."

"I didn't say there was anything wrong with you."

"Then why would the flight surgeon ground me?"

"There are a potful of reasons for grounding people, Bear. You know that. You're nervous, for one thing—that's reason enough."

"Oh, no. Nervous is one thing I'm not." He held up his hands, with the thumbs still spaced a fraction of an inch. "See there? No tremors." The hands were steady. "I can fly like an angel, sir. Check me out with any IP. They'll tell you."

"Bear, you're no damn good as a gunnie! I hate to say it, but you know it's true. If you keep on, someone's likely to get killed!" His voice was low, but intense.

Bear laughed at that. It was a short, low laugh unlike his old cackle that shook his cheeks and belly. "Oh, yes, I *am* a good gunnie! I can prove it!" He took out the box Blood had tossed to him, opened it, and held up a medal by its ribbon. "See there? Certified. USDA Choice. My third Distinguished Flying Cross. Besides, how would anybody get killed the way I've been flying? My body count hasn't amounted to much lately. Ask Captain Blood!" He waved a hand to forestall Arp's objection. "I know. You mean one of us. I'm sorry, sir, but I've thought it through. Lord, have I ever! When you shoot too soon, you get Hill Four Seven Three. How many men died to teach me that? And when you don't shoot soon enough, your friends die. Captain Martin and Major Hart died to teach me that."

"That wasn't your fault, Bear," Arp said. "No one knew where the weapon was. If you'd done what Blood said and shot up the village, you'd just have been wasting ordnance, and you'd have been out of position to do any good at all. We might have lost *more* men."

"Nice try, sir, but that doesn't help much. Whenever you shoot, no matter if it's soon or late, someone dies. I don't know if you ever wonder who's down there, sir, where your rounds are falling. I hope not. But I keep seeing bodies—how they trailed away at Song Pra Khuc." His voice trailed off. A deep silence had fallen in the hooch. "Well," he began again, "you say, a man can quit. If he's had enough, he can have the balls to say, 'Screw it. I've done what you said, and I won't anymore. So take your guns and stick 'em.' But it's not . . . I can't get just myself out, sir. If I don't fly, somebody else flies in my place. Somebody dies doing my work. Covington died to teach me that. Ah, Cov! Lieutenant, the Army never told his wife he was dead. Did you know that? Pinky could have gone on from now till Doomsday morning thinking he was 'missing.' A hundred men could swear he's dead, but nobody told her. I almost didn't have the heart to tell her he died flying my mission. Sir, I don't want to have to tell anybody else's wife that. No one can be a pacifist when his friends are dying. If I'd gone to Dustoff, I'd at least have been sharing the load. But I'm not going to ground myself while I can still fly a ship. Death will still be there if I wash my hands of it." He stood up, pulled on his cap, and turned to the others in the hooch. He looked them over one by one and then chortled to himself, almost like the Bear of old, and said with a shake of his head, "I don't know why I go to all this trouble for *you* guys." He went out and down the ramp toward the flight line. After a moment Arp went out and walked swiftly after him.

Atterburn said after they had gone, "That Bear sure is a crazy bastard."

Cripps lay on his cot and stared at the roof. After a long time he mumbled, "They never even told her he was dead? How could they not tell her?"

Handy went to the door, but seeing Arp and the Bear on the ramp he went back to his table and began oiling the stock of the Thompson. "Cripps," he said, "tell me if they get done down there. I got to get some oil on the miniguns."

"Who'll ever get a chance to use them?" Atterburn snorted.

Handy shook his head sadly. "You don't never know, sir," he said. "He could be the old Bear yet." But Handy sounded dubious. He added, too low for even Atterburn to hear, "But sharin' a ship with him *is* gettin' to be like livin' with las' year's woman."

Arp caught up with the Bear near the first ship on the ramp. He caught him from behind the arm. "Don," he said, "you're going to go to the flight surgeon."

The Bear turned to face him. He had the melting eyes of a llama. "No," he said, "I'm not."

"That's an order, Don."

Bear laughed again. "Court-martial me," he said.

"Oh, Christ, Don!" Arp said in disgust. "You know I can't! But you can't take a crew down with you, just to spite Blood and Baker! Or even to ease your own conscience!"

"Oh," Bear said, as if awakening from a puzzling dream. "Is that what you thought? No, I can't do that. And I won't. I'm going back to being a gunnie. That's what I meant. Somebody's going to do it anyway, and I can't ask someone else to be executioner for me, just to keep my hands clean. So I'll do it. I'm no better than the rest of humanity, taken as a whole." He grinned weakly. Seeing the doubt behind Arp's eyes, he added, "I mean it, sir. I won't let you down."

Arp knew he had no right to feel let down now, by the mere fact that one of his officers—one of his friends—had said no more than that he would do his duty, would do what others did, what Arp himself did, daily. Yet Arp heard the words with regret, as one recognizes the passing of an unreturned love, or looks back on the loss of the faith of his childhood years. It was better so. And yet . . .

"All right, Bear," Arp said.

11

To those who learned of it in their newspapers, or those who woke in city villas to the sound of rockets falling, Tet of 1968 may have come as a shock. Farther from Saigon and the pleasant hotel rooms of the war correspondents, the attacks of the Viet Cong and North Vietnamese came on as imperceptibly as a change of seasons or a change in tides. The four-day holiday itself was only the peak of a storm that had wandered the length of the land for years not to be counted without heartbreak. For a few weeks before and after Tet, men killed one another at a rate somewhat greater than usual. That was all.

But for the Bear, it was a time of despair. Daily, almost hourly, as the old year neared its end, his words to Lieutenant Arp were thrown back at him by grinding circumstance. After Hill 473 his return to flying had been a return to hours spent on mildewed cots, in the rain-spattered hooch at Chu Lai or in a baking tent on the asphalt helipad of a fire base, dreaming of Alice and waiting to fly and reliving minute by minute the flaming fall of Covington's ship into the relentless sea. But not killing.

But now was not a time for thought or dreams, good or ill. It was a time to survive, and to keep one's friends alive. To survive meant to pull the trigger, to touch the thumb to the red button. Whenever he did it he felt the light caress of death, touching him back. He had not thought, when he spoke to Arp, that there could be so much killing. He wondered sometimes who brought home the word to the wives of the North Vietnamese soldiers.

The sound of the scramble horn became a horror to him. He went about leaden-eyed: but, as others were leaden-eyed from want of sleep, he supposed no one noticed him, and he preferred that. Arp, it was true, watched him closely, but more with the regret of one who has seen a fall from grace than with the admiration of one professional killer for another. Arp's strange notions, however, were not shared by many, probably by no one at all except Wolcheski, to whom Arp spoke once when their paths crossed at a fuel dump at Hill 63.

Arp came aboard while Wolcheski's helicopter was being refueled. He plugged his headphones into the ship's intercom, and they talked through the nervous system of the helicopter about things far removed from the war. The ship was too noisy for conversation outside the intercom, and Wolcheski did not have the time to shut down. Before leaving he asked after the Bear.

"I think," Arp said, "the Bear has come to worse than dust."

"Maybe dust is worst of all, after all," Wolcheski said. "I've seen enough of bodies for the day." He put his visor down, not with the finality of one cutting off the subject, but only because the crew chief had withdrawn the fuel hose and it was time to go for still more bodies.

"What did that mean, *Trung-úy?*" Guiterrez asked after Arp was gone.

"It meant that the legendary beast is still flying his gunship—and killing."

"Shoot," Guiterrez said, "I told you a long time ago that deep down he was attached to his guns."

"You've told me a lot of things I don't believe, Primo," was Wolcheski's reply.

But there were those who did believe. Alice was with Dr. Rawlinson in the officers' club that night when Guiterrez came in. "I heard news of the friendly neighborhood Bear today," Guiterrez remarked with elaborate casualness. His quick grin was for the way Rawlinson stiffened, and not for Alice's sudden uncertainty that would not let her quite meet his eyes nor let her look away.

"I hope he's all right?" she said hesitantly, for she had not

261

heard from him since that night he had found her on the beach, although he had promised this time to keep in touch.

"Oh, I think he's fine. Very fine. But he's gone back to his first love. You lost him."

"I don't 'own' him," she said, with a shrug of her shoulders but not her heart. She added, on an impulse, "I hope he's happy with her."

"Oh, it's not a *her!*" Guiterrez answered. "I just meant he's decided to go on killing Charlies. I knew he wouldn't give it up. Remember?" He left behind another grin for Rawlinson.

She did remember. She would not have believed it then. Although she would have liked him for his company alone, the kindness of his heart was what she had valued in the Bear. She did not think the less of any man for being a soldier: she had, in the abstract, no convictions against one man's killing another. It was only in the flesh that she found it repulsive. But hiding within her was a feeling that could be found as well in nurses outwardly more cynical than she—that it *was* worthwhile to try to limit human suffering wherever it was found. It was why they were nurses. It was why she was a nurse.

She might have loved someone who lacked the tenderness she thought she had seen in the Bear; but in caring for one who showed it, she became unable to accept less from him. And what she had not believed before, she believed now, because he had not tried to see her nor sent word to her, as he had promised, and because it was the easier to believe as the flood of wounded from both sides swelled daily through the ER.

"If you've lost *him,*" Rawlinson said after a silence that was more awkward for him than for her, "you might fall back on me."

She placed her hand on his, with a laugh that she hoped was sparkling, and told him, "You're nice, Danny, but I couldn't ever love you."

"So you've said. But I don't see why not. I'm so much handsomer than your warrant officer, and you're *crazy* about him!"

She smiled. "You are handsomer than he is," she agreed, "but I'm not 'crazy about him.' I just can't love you. I'm sorry. I tried to when you were so kind to me right at first, and I just couldn't."

"And you do him."

"I *could* him, perhaps," she said. "But I don't." She said it with more certainty than she felt, and began making plans to cross him out of her heart.

Whatever glee or disappointment Baker and Blood felt at the Bear's return to military righteousness, they did not communicate it. Probably they felt neither the one nor the other. It would not have occurred to either of them that the Bear had ever wanted more than to escape his past or their presence, unless it was really to join his nurse girl friend. Neither one had lost his dislike of the Bear, but action on that could await easier times.

Some in the company looked on the assault from Duc Pho as a turning point. That was a small view of the war, though not unlike those from Saigon or Washington or Hanoi in which the Tet offensive which came immediately after was seen as a great change in the direction of the war, for better or worse, if one knew which was which. For the company the assault from Duc Pho brought a change of command, a loss of a commander and executive officer, at the moment that the fighting swelled and the deaths mounted. The "old days" came to mean the time before Baker and Blood were in command—a better time altogether. Only Atterburn ever showed resentment when someone noted that they "wouldn't have had this shit in the old days."

The complaints came chiefly over company operations. There had been few large operations in the old days; but the missions that came down were flown well, and the crews were given credit for knowing their jobs. Under the new regime, briefings increased, always beginning with the assumption that no one knew anything, because nothing had yet been told him by the present command structure. Among aircraft commanders with more time in country than either the commander or his executive officer, that did not go down easily. Worse yet, extra duty alert times were scheduled, beyond those assigned by Division. "Bad enough to work an eighty-hour week!" Griggs thundered through Operations. "But then to get stuck for an extra twenty hours of sitting on your ass in the company area, just so the BBs can suck up to the brass! Jesus!" For once no one thought Griggs was being a complete ass.

But that was at the end of those days before Tet, when tempers were already short. Then the slicks flew combat assaults daily, and pieced in the spare hours with resupply, while the guns waited from hour to hour for fire missions.

By Tet three men were gone. One, a crew chief named Hobbs, was killed in a mortar attack on the fire base where his ship was standing by. He had always been late getting to the bunkers. The fact that he had once, when drunk, slept right through an attack gave him a feeling of immortality that remained with him up to the moment the round dropped on the tent pole and caught him stretching and yawning. Even after his bunk was dragged outside, the smell of blood was so strong in the tent that the other crewmen sat outside weary-eyed in the dawn rather than go back to bed.

The second and third were Bear's friend Carter and his copilot, the new guy Williams. They were flying number ten thou, whose smoking engine finally did fail as they were racing home alone low level under a ragged sky, hoping to beat rain and nightfall into Chu Lai. They were flying low level—inches above the treetops, or a few feet above the new rice in the paddies—because the cloud base was too low for them to fly above the Dead Man's Zone. Slicks forced to fly in the Dead Man's Zone flew as close to the earth as possible, twisting and turning and hiding behind every ridge and tree line. The earth is every aviator's enemy, but in war it is only his second-worst enemy, and its presence offers some shelter from his worst enemy so long as all goes well with his aircraft. When their engine failed, Carter and Williams did the only thing that could be done—they landed the ship straight ahead. Straight ahead was a Vietnamese graveyard whose round stone tombs reached up to tear them from the sky. Nightfall beat them into Chu Lai.

The maintenance warrant officer, Burgess, had made a flight that day to Cam Ranh Bay, halfway down the coast toward Saigon, to pick up parts. His ship came in just after dark. It whistled down the hover lane and wound down under the eyes of the crew chief while Burgess hurried up to Operations.

"Burgey, I ain't seen you move so fast since somebody put that cobra in your bed," Rauch said to him. "What's up?"

"That's what I was going to ask you," Burgess said. "What's up? Something big's going on, man! Everyplace I tuned in the radio, all up and down the coast, they had an attack going! I couldn't even get into Nha Trang to go to the PX! The tower said aircraft were taking fire in the landing pattern! What the hell's going on?"

"Partyin'," Rauch said. "Didn't you know? Tet started today. You ought to read the intelligence reports I sent you. Or read *Stars and Stripes*. It'll tell you everything that's in the G-2."

"If you'd mark your stuff Top Secret, I'd read it," Burgess said.

"I do, Burgey, I do! Your sergeant's probably been throwin' 'em in your desk drawer again. Clean out that rat's nest once in a while, huh?"

"Top Secret in a desk drawer!" Blood exploded from behind Rauch's filing cabinet. He was checking Rauch's files to see that they conformed to the latest Division directive on filing. "Who's putting Top Secret documents in a desk drawer?"

"Just a little joke, sir," Rauch said calmly, winking at Burgess.

"That's nothing to joke about," Blood grumbled. "There's a war on, Rauch." He added to Burgess, "Don't let a little gunfire scare you. We'll kick Charley's ass around some, and he'll get tired quick enough. You ought to get out and see some real shooting."

"Ask *them* what's going on," Rauch suggested, nodding toward Arp and the Bear coming in the door. "They been out killin' Charley like he was goin' out of style. How many today?"

"Thirty," Arp said.

"Thirty!" Rauch took the reports they had filled out, scanned them, and tossed them into the sergeant's tray. "Only thirty ain't worth *my* time."

"Maybe they're running out of Chinamen," Arp said crossly. He knew Rauch was joking, but he did not think it a subject for jokes.

"I hope they last at least till I'm gone," Rauch said. "I wouldn't want to leave you fellas with nothin' to do when I'm gone. Did you know I was short, Bear?"

"I heard that somewhere," Bear said.

"Didn't know if I'd told you yet today. Listen, you guys didn't see number ten thou out there anywhere, did you?"

"Carter? I heard him on the radio about sixteen hundred," Arp said. "He was on artillery resupply up the Que Son, wasn't he?"

"Yeah, but he ain't come in yet. He had a seventeen hundred release time, too."

"Divarty always gives you just one more sortie," Arp said. "Especially when the ceiling's low."

"Jesus, get him back!" Burgess interjected. "The longer they fly, the sooner we have to tear them down."

"If Carter don't get his rear back here soon," Rauch said, "he's goin' to find this place closed. I'm plannin' to get my shit down to that bunker and pull the door in after me. I'm too short to be sittin' around this office after dark, the way Charley's been tearin' around. I don't aim to get caught standin' in the door tryin' to hook my static line when the jump light comes on."

"Charley won't hit here," Blood said. "Division's had patrols out for miles in every direction all week. He might lob in a few mortar rounds. The only way to stop that is to tear up that island hooch by hooch. And that's just what I'd do, if I was running this division. But if you don't want to disturb the Slopes, why, Rauch, you just can't let a few little mortar rounds bother you. There won't be anything big in here, I can tell you that. Nobody's called a red alert for tonight, that I know of."

"Just the same, I think I'll move down to the bunker. Damn, where is that Carter anyway?" He paced from one window to another staring out onto the ramp.

"He's going to be into periodic by the end of the week again, if he keeps piling on the hours," Burgess complained. "And it's going to be a bugger. He needs an engine change, if we had an engine."

"Keep 'em flyin', Burgey," Rauch said. "Keep 'em flyin'."

Burgess followed Arp and Bear out the door. "What do you think *is* going on?" he asked. "This was a wild day!"

"That's like asking a pickle what the sandwich looks like," Bear said. "You'd better take Blood's word on what's going on."

"Don't ask a man for opinions on his night off," Arp told Burgess. "Bear's been like that all day. Listen, Bear, do you want to take the three-quarter-ton tonight? You can haul the fair Alice off to one of the clubs. Eat, drink, be merry."

"For tomorrow you may kill."

"And tomorrow and tomorrow. But for tonight . . ."

"She could be on duty tonight for all I know," Bear said. He was not sure he could see her again; but he did not want to explain, even to Arp.

"In a minute you'll have me feeling sorry for you for having the night off," Arp said.

Once he was beyond Arp's shepherding eye, the Bear ambled toward his hooch with his head bowed. Killing was bad enough business, without having to look as if he could do it forever.

He turned on the light in his hooch. His bed was tightly made, as it had been for the last two weeks. Several days' mail was stacked on it. He ruffled through it and tossed it back on the bed. There were clean fatigues in the locker. At least Suzie and Yan had been at work. He had not seen them, either, in more than a week. He had heard of minor fighting around the villages outside Chu Lai. But there was no way to know what was true and what was not. He could not answer Burgess's question. The fighting he saw, he knew had happened. The rest might or might not be true. Major battles appeared, in fancy dress, in *Stars and Stripes*. Some of them he had been in himself without knowing. But you knew men died when you killed them yourself.

Bear drew a pan of warm water from the maintenance officer's shower—a tall plywood box topped by two jet-fighter drop tanks with burners under them—and began to wash away the Vietnamese countryside from his face. "What an ugly bastard you are," he said to the face in the mirror. The face said the same back to him. And well deserved, too, he thought. The face did not seem to be interested in trying on amusing expressions. He moodily began to shave. The mirror insisted on fogging over, and he cut himself. "That's the first blood I've drawn from *you*," he said. "Serves you right." The face mistily returned the compliment.

The platoon three-quarter-ton truck was parked beside the alert hooch. The crews on standby were spread over the steps of the hooch, except for Atterburn, who was seated on one fender of the truck. "I suppose you expect me to move, Bear," he said, climbing down slowly, "just because you want to go see your nursie-poo." Atterburn was an aircraft commander now, and the less inclined to give quarter to anyone.

"I'd let you stay," Bear said, "but you make a hell of a hood ornament."

"A night off for Tet," Atterburn commented: "that takes real suck with the platoon leader. I just want you all to know," he announced, turning to the others, "that tonight's the night the Bear gets to the promised land. I hope nobody told him that last night I took his nurse friend out, though. Did you know she does it for savings bonds, Bear?"

"I know that it's a big rooster that has a pecker as big as its crow," Bear called down from the truck. "Bk-bk-b-*gack!*"—the imitation of a chicken with strep throat floated behind as he put the truck in gear and roared away down the ramp.

As he pulled up in front of the hospital a helicopter pounded in over the ridge and whirled to a halt on the main pad outside the emergency-room entrance. He stopped the truck far down the road from the pad. Before he could switch off the engine the helicopter was surrounded by a swarm of litter-bearers who poured from the building at a clumsy run. They snatched the long litters from the racks at the rear of the cabin, at a pace that somehow fell from frantic to deliberate without losing any of its speed. Within seconds the last litter was pushing through the swinging doors. When it had vanished inside, the helicopter rose up and hovered to the parking ramp, where it sat swishing its blade at flight idle as the engine cooled down. The rotating beacon flashed a moving band of red around the inside of the revetment and under the flickering blade.

The Bear remained in his truck until the engine was shut down and the blade had swung to a halt. The crew dismounted. He recognized Wolcheski. He stepped out of the truck then and went down to the aircraft.

"Ah ha," Wolcheski greeted him. "Strange creatures walk the night in these parts. It's the very Bear himself, Primo."

"I bet he's only down here because he ran out of targets," Guiterrez said. "When there's nothing else to do, he comes to visit here. Just often enough to spoil the water for everyone else."

Wolcheski ignored the remark. He extended his hand to the Bear: "It's good to see you again. We've been worried." He sat down in the cargo door, making room for Bear beside him. "If you're waiting for Alice, you may as well sit down. She's in there." He nodded toward the ER. The cold light of the fluorescent lamps fell from all the windows of the room. The bottom panes of the windows were painted out, so that nothing could be seen through them; but sometimes a swiftly moving shadow fell across their translucent surface.

"Who were they?" Bear asked. He meant the men on the litters.

"I don't know. Just another company out in the boonies. One platoon was overrun just before nightfall. That's what we could find of them. The rest are scattered all over hell, or dead, or gone."

They sat without speaking, watching the shadows move across the glass and vanish. "Six was all?" Bear asked at length.

"That's all we found. They had the radio. Platoon leader was dead. Some more will show up in the morning."

"God, I hope so."

"They could have done with some gun support," Guiterrez remarked.

"Do you want me to go tell Alice you're here?" Wolcheski asked.

"No. I won't bother her on duty. I didn't know whether she'd be off tonight."

"If she was . . ." Guiterrez began. *If she was, there's a doctor who'd have her busy,* he was going to say; but Wolcheski saw that coming, and cut him off.

"She's not on duty," Wolcheski told Bear. "But she's always there for a mass cal, and we had two big loads early this evening. I'll tell her you're here," he offered again, "so she'll know to come out when she can. I go off standby in an hour. Swensen and I will stand you to dinner. I think it's steak-and-shrimp night at MAG Thirteen."

"All right," Bear said. "But let me tell her I'm here. It's all right if I go in there, isn't it?"

"If you want to." There was an edge of doubt in Wolcheski's voice.

"I don't," Bear said. "But I will."

"I'll be up at the ready room."

Bear walked up the hill toward the light-streaming windows. The cold light of that place repelled him with the force of falling water; but he forced his way against it. Outside the door he stopped to collect his breath. Then he pushed the door open.

Alice was the first one he saw. She was standing directly opposite the door, facing him from the other side of a litter. She looked up as the door opened. Her eyes were heavy and dark. His eyes did not stay on hers. They went to her hands, her arms, which were red with blood to the elbows. She was retwisting a tourniquet that had slipped from what remained of the leg of a soldier.

She frowned at him. He signed to her as best he could that he would be outside waiting. She nodded, still frowning, and went back to her work.

When he let the door close behind him, he realized he had been holding his breath the whole time. He leaned against the outside of the building to wait for his pulse to settle. While he was leaning there, four men burst from the ready room and went racing toward the helicopter ramp. "Bear!" Wolcheski called. He was one of the four.

Bear ran for the ship. The blade was already turning when he reached the side of the cockpit. "We're going on another trip!" Wolcheski called down, shouting to be heard. "Won't be long! If you want to go ahead, leave word with Swensen where to go! She's in the bar!"

Bear gave him a thumbs-up sign to show that he understood, and stepped back from the ship. It rose straight up out of the revetment and climbed out across the cliffs and northward. He watched it until the beacon was gone.

It was a long time before Alice came, but she did come at last. He approached her shyly. What had been between them had been so tentative and new, he was not sure it could be rebuilt. He did not know even if it had been between the people they had become in that short time. He did not know about what Guiterrez had told Alice, nor of what she felt; but if he had not changed in that way, he had changed. Nothing lasted.

They halted, two yards apart. She looked at him guardedly. "Hello," he said. It was with a feeling of something breaking that they moved together at the same instant. It was gone in a moment. She embraced him, but dodged his kisses. "I'm a mess," she said. "Let me change."

"Of course."

They started toward the nurses' quarters. "I don't even know if you're free this evening," he said apologetically.

"I'm not on duty," she said. "As for 'free' . . . I hope there's no need for my help for a few hours. Sometimes we need everyone in the area. After all, I can't spend *all* my off-duty hours just waiting for you." She smiled, but it was only a small smile.

"I meant 'free' to include 'not going out with somebody else,' " he said.

"I'm free." She said it with finality. But she added, as if it were a whole new idea, "I just wish I knew, when I'm waiting, whether you were alive or dead. But I suppose when you're dead I'll see you sooner than when you're alive, won't I?" The matter-of-fact way she said it invited no reply. But when there was none, she said next, "I see such a wide sample, you'd think one would look just like another: but I'll know when it's you."

"I suppose not many walruses wash up on your beach," he said.

She would not be diverted. "I'm not surprised at anything that comes in the doors now," she said without a trace of a smile.

She left him at her door while she changed. She returned shortly, still in fatigues, but freshly laundered ones, and smelling distantly of perfume. "Where?" she asked.

"Wolcheski wanted us to go with him and Janet, someplace. But he went out on a mission just after. Do you want to go on?"

"Let's wait."

Swensen was in the club with two doctors. She left them and came to meet the Bear and Alice. She kissed the Bear on the cheek. "The famous beast!" she bubbled. "I'm so happy you're back."

"That's at least two of us," the Bear said, bemused.

"Two of *us*," Swensen corrected him, taking Alice's arm. But she appeared to know what he meant. She said, "Alice thinks nothing will go right in the ER if she's not there. She's been absolutely haunting that place for weeks! Those doctors were just telling me she was there again tonight. Alice, I went to see if I could help, but there absolutely wasn't anything for another nurse to do. So I came right here and drank to that." She said to Bear, "That deserves a drink in its honor, doesn't it?"

"More than one."

"It might if the day were over," Alice said. "Ski has gone out for another load."

"Has he gone? The louse is supposed to be taking me out for dinner."

"People do die at the most awkward moments," Alice said.

"They certainly do," Swensen agreed, ignoring the irony. "Well, I'll drink my first dinner while I wait for him, then. Will you two join me?"

"Wolcheski already invited us to join you for the second dinner," Bear said. "We may as well take in the first, too."

"This may be the only one for me," Alice said. "I don't think I should leave. We can eat something here, Don."

"Oh, come on, Alice," Swensen said. "You haven't been off the hospital grounds in weeks."

"We could wait and decide when we see what Lieutenant Wolcheski brings in," Bear said.

"Spoken like a true compromiser," Swensen told him. She patted him on the back in an almost masculine way. "Let me play the barmaid. Alice has been waiting on people hand and foot for days on end. Everyone loves her for it, as long as we don't all have to keep up with her. I'll tell myself I'm making up some of it by bringing your drinks. What can I get you?"

"Nothing but a soft drink," Alice said. "I may have to go back yet tonight."

"Alice, you are disgusting, after the speech I just made. Bear, be a dear and drink something to keep me company. If *you* have to go back to work, it'll release your inhibitions and make the bullets go straighter."

"It had better be a double something, then," Bear said.

"Spoken like a true killer, dear." She patted him on the back again.

As Janet walked away from them, Alice made a brief sour face which Bear pretended not to see.

They sat in embarrassed strained silence while Janet was gone. Neither wanted to ask the other what he or she had been doing since they had last been together; but what they had been doing loomed like a dark shape in the night blotting out the constellations of things they had so recently thought they shared.

Eventually, with a feeling of surrender to hard circumstance, Bear asked whether she was still on the same ward.

"The same by number at least," she answered.

"Is Mother Courage still there?"

Alice shook her head.

"Where did she go? They couldn't have released her?"

"No. I don't know where she is. They're all gone: they have been for a week. There aren't enough beds now, you see. One day they were just all gone. No one could tell me where. I would have gone to see Mother Courage. I think she liked me, in her fierce old way. But no one could tell me where. Maybe I can find her at the prisoner camp, if there's ever time. The ward wasn't empty more than a half hour. Now it's full. It's full for the third time this week, with different patients." She rested her elbows on the table and propped her chin on her fists. Although she was on the edge of tears, it was not from weakness. Sadness had only tempered her determination to relieve whatever wretchedness the war might throw her way. Although her eyes went limpid, her face took on the angry defiance that disease had carved on the face of Mother Courage herself.

"Alice, for a girl who hasn't seen her friend for weeks," Janet said, sitting down next to the Bear, "you're not exactly the picture of seductiveness. You two are sitting here like an old married couple. Cheer up! Make hay while the sun shines, as Ski's Polish grandmother would say!" She handed Bear a glass. She was just tipsy enough to be aggressive but not unpleasant. "There's a double something for a thirsty warrior. But it seems to me that Alice needs it more than you do. Alice, can't I get you something better? After all, it's a holiday!"

"What holiday?"

"You're the friend of the 'indigenous personnel,' aren't you? You should know that it's Tet!"

"Happy New Year," Bear said, raising his glass.

"I'll drink to that," Janet joined in. "Alice? You won't be any fun if you don't keep up with us."

Alice paused before she raised her glass with a smile and a shake of her head. "I hope it is a happier new year," she said softly.

The sound of the helicopter coming in to the hospital pad

brought Alice to her feet. "Sit down," Janet insisted. "At least let me go see who they've brought in now. This poor man needs company as much as anyone else does, Alice."

"We can both go," Alice said. "He'll understand."

"If I'm going to be lonely anyway"—Bear shrugged—"I may as well get credit for being noble, too. Go do your duties." In fact he was pleased that Alice wanted to go, however disappointed he might be. "You nurse them," he said, "and I'll nurse this." He had hardly touched the drink. He knew how Alice felt, for there was no easy way down from two weeks of continuous readiness. Inside he was still listening for the scramble horn. Whatever a double something might have done for his inhibitions or his aim, he knew what it would do to his coordination, and he could only sip at it uneasily.

"I'll send word if we'll be long," Alice said. "I am sorry."

As she walked toward the ER, Alice thought of the way her feelings ran in gyres. While he was gone, they had spiraled off into a tenuous sympathy for all the broken figures who drifted under her hands, and she convinced herself that what she had felt for the Bear was no more than the focus of that sympathy. She could force herself not to think of him, except for instants when a medevac helicopter stood before the door and she waited to see who would be on the litters it had brought. She could never keep him from her thoughts entirely then. She always expected that sooner or later he was going to appear without warning on a litter. Sometimes she could convince herself that she had no special dread of that. Sometimes her first night in the emergency room came to mind, and she played at wondering whose hand had been on the trigger when the bullet sped out to shatter this bone, when the rocket fell that had mangled this limb. But when he stepped back into her life, all the feelings so carefully sorted out were emptied in a pile on the floor of her heart.

When he stepped into the ER, she had been startled and then annoyed. For an instant she had thought, as when she had seen him first, that he had come in as a walking wounded. When she saw that he was whole, it annoyed her to have him come between her and her duty. He was not coarse and blundering about it, as a killer should be, but polite and sensitive as always, motioning that he would be waiting when she had time for him. And he did not even apologize, for having been gone, for not having tried to contact her, for having defected so easily from the high image she had of him.

She was still imagining these accusations against him when she saw the bodies come off the helicopter. There were aviator's wings on the first uniform. The emotion she had only imagined so often suddenly struck her in reality; with a catch at her heart she forgot for an instant that she had only now left him sitting in the club. The face above the wings was mangled, for it had struck the array of knobs on the panel when the seat was torn from the floor by the force of the crash into the tombstone. But the body was too slender to be his, and the name was wrong. Carter, the name tag said. Her grief drained away at once. Even that saddened her: it seemed wrong to be glad that one man had died, instead of another. But she was glad. She was glad and, suddenly, eager to be with him.

Seeing Janet and Alice outside the ER, Wolcheski tried to wave them over to the helicopter. They could not see him. He gave the ship to Guiterrez to shut down and climbed out.

"Where's the Bear?" he asked Alice as he came up to the two of them.

"We left him in the club," Janet answered for them both. "Alice thought maybe we could help. But they won't need us for only three."

"Two of them are dead," Wolcheski said. "Do you know who they were?"

"No."

"Don't say anything about this to the Bear. They were his friends. Let him be happy for tonight." He went back to his ship to sign off the mission.

Bear was surprised that the girls came back almost before the helicopter had shut down. "Nothing?" he asked.

"Wolcheski is slipping," Janet said. "They don't need us for just three." Alice sat down without saying a word. Bear took his cue from her mood and asked no more questions.

Wolcheski came in just behind them. He threw his cap on the table and sat down without removing his pistol belt. "Janet, my

275

love, fetch us a drink," he said. He sounded tired. Bear gathered that it had not been a pleasant mission for him.

"We're going out, remember?" Janet said. "These two are coming with us."

"I don't think we are," Bear said, "but Happy New Year." He raised his glass. He was startled when Alice said suddenly, "Let's do go somewhere, Don." He looked at her with a question in his eyes. "We have few enough chances," she said. Her hand was cool and steady on his arm.

"Gather ye rosebuds and so forth," Wolcheski advised Bear. "Or whatever passes for rosebuds in this land."

The club alongside the western runway did business as usual on the first night of Tet. There was no local alert, and short of an attack on Chu Lai proper, outbreaks of fighting in the cities of South Vietnam had little effect on the Marine Air Group to which the club belonged. The pilots there flew Phantoms, and commuted north to a different war. Day and night the club was rattled by heavy jets going out on afterburner. But that and the beat of passing helicopters were almost the only sounds that penetrated the building. Outside in the stillness between takeoffs returning aircraft could sometimes be heard. Overhead in the darkness Phantoms trimmed for landing made weird creaking wails. Inside, the band, singing, shouts from the craps game in the side room, covered all small sounds. It was steak-and-shrimp night at the club, and the war was locked safely outside.

It was easier to be together there, at first, where not to talk was no embarrassment because talking was possible only in the band's intermissions. But Alice felt herself slipping closer to him simply by being with him; her feelings rearranged into the old pattern.

Wolcheski and Janet were off somewhere and the band was resting. She could see the words forming in him long before they came to the surface: his face went through a series of expressions, all serious but all different. He said, "I want to tell you why you haven't heard from me."

"You don't have to. I didn't mean to be nasty about it. I didn't know what had happened to you, Don, and I heard . . ."

"You heard . . . ?" he prompted.

276

"It doesn't matter."

"It matters to me." He thought he knew what she was going to say. Wolcheski had picked up Major Hart's body, and Captain Martin's, after the assault from Duc Pho. Bear feared at once, without stopping to wonder how Wolcheski might have known it, that Wolcheski had told her how they had come to die.

"I heard you had gone back to your 'first love.' " Because she had taken it seriously then, she said it now as if she were teasing.

At first there was only relief; but then slow puzzlement slid across his face, so evidently that she laughed.

"You shouldn't tease an old trooper," he said stoutly.

"You asked what I heard, and that was it. And it *was* enough to make me want to throw you over." She could admit that, so long as he wouldn't know it was true.

"Then it was a deadly slander and a base canard. And besides, it isn't true. Who told you I ever had a first love?"

"Guiterrez," she admitted. "He said your first love was . . . flying gunships."

Bear mulled that over with a physical chewing motion. "Maybe it was," he said at length. "Once upon a time."

"I know."

"Do you?" he asked. "Then, why did he say 'back' to my 'first love'?"

She shook her head.

"I want you to know all the bad things about me," he said. "To counteract my notorious deadly charm." He said the words lightly—as lightly as she had spoken of his first love—but his eyes were serious.

"Well, for my own protection, then," she agreed, smiling in an attempt to match his light outer manner and turn back the darkness in his eyes.

"It was why I didn't write or send up a smoke signal or . . . something," he began. "I wanted to see you. But I thought I was going to be free of gunning; and I wanted to wait until then." He went on to tell about the transfer; but not about Major Hart and Captain Martin—not yet. "And then, since it fell through . . . it's been a busy time." He was dismayed at how inconclusive those words sounded.

277

"It's terrible of your commander to tell you he'd let you go, and then not do it," she said. "How could he?"

"It's a different commander, you see," he said softly. "The major and Captain Martin . . ."

She laid a hand on his arm.

"They were both killed."

"Oh, Don, I'm so sorry! I shouldn't have said anything against your commander, not knowing . . ."

"It won't hurt him now. Though, God knows, there's nothing bad should be said about Major Hart. Or Captain Martin. But what did hurt them . . . what got them was a weapon I should have put out of action."

"It can't have been all your fault!"

"You sound like Lieutenant Arp. 'Not your fault, Bear,' he tells me. 'Nobody else got Charley first, either.' I don't know. Could I have got Charley first, if I'd been ready? I don't know. But I wasn't ready. I didn't want to hurt anybody, so I wasn't looking for someone to kill, and so I didn't *find* someone to kill. Instead, two good men died. Those things I know for sure.

"Now you know all about me," he said at the end, with a short laugh. "I wish I had better excuses to make for myself. Hey, don't cry! People will think I beat you! There come Janet and Wolcheski. Let's act friendly and surprise them."

She took his hand suddenly and wiped her eyes with his fingers. "You don't owe *me* any excuses," she whispered.

"I don't know that game," Wolcheski said, "but it looks like fun. You must teach me how to play it, Bear." He and Janet sat down beside them.

"Don't be cruel to Alice, naughty Bear," Janet said. "Not even if she likes it."

"We're going to learn that game, Swensen," Wolcheski said.

"B.S., as your Polish grandmother'd say."

The music began again. A Marine major came and asked Janet to dance. He asked the band for something slow and spun slowly with her crushed against him. "Let's hope the poor thing doesn't suffocate," Wolcheski said. "In a more civilized time there'd have been a war over less than that. I think there's more sense in fighting over women than over ideas. Now we both try to cram our system down the other guys' throat, and when it's over no one's got anything but the exercise. Of course," he added, "the same could be said about dancing. Dancing is war by another means, originating in an acting out of victory over the enemy. That poor Marine doesn't know he's only acting—that all he's going to get is the exercise." He sighed. "Bear, why are you wasting your life listening to me talk, when you could be dancing with Alice?"

"That's what I was wondering," Alice said.

It was awkward at first, like all their meetings. But the touch of the music drew them both back into what had been, as if the weeks past were only minor dreams. There was still room in their lives for small corners of happiness. This, at least, was a moment saved from utter loss, until the music faded and their dance dissolved into the blue-lit, smoke-washed stillness that lurked behind the music.

The end of a set found them near the door. It had been left ajar to let in the night wind. With the band silent, the talk hushed for an instant, there edged in at the door a foreign sound, faint and shy, no sooner heard than gone. Music and voices closed over its track. But they both had recognized it. It was the distant wail of a siren.

They followed the music again without a word. What the sound had meant there was no way to know; but they feared they knew. Yet they turned away, as if by their refusing acknowledgment, it could be made not to exist.

The music, and their hopes, were cut off in midflight. A Marine major came to the microphone in front of the band. "I just want to let you know," he said, "that there's a mortar attack on at Ky Ha. Those of you who are nervous types can start for the bunkers now. For the rest of you, Happy Tet, and drink up!" He raised his glass, to a round of cheers from his audience.

The words broke away the shell of happiness that the thing itself had not been able to pierce. "Let's go," Bear said quickly.

Wolcheski was leading Janet across the floor toward them. "You were marv'lous, silly old beast," Janet said to the Bear. "Just marv'lous! Look, he's having a good time, too, Ski. He doesn' want to go! Alice doesn' either."

Bear and Wolcheski spoke together for a moment. "We'd better do it," Wolcheski said, nodding. They started for the door.

"We can't go back now!" Janet was protesting. "We can't jus' go driving back into it, with ever'one else in the bunkers, and there we come driving up big as you please."

"It will be over before we get there," Wolcheski said, "and then they may need some untouched bodies to help out."

The four of them were loudly applauded by those near the door as they left. "Going to the bunkers with the nurses," someone said loudly. As the door closed behind them, the music was blasting out and Marines were singing lustily, "We gotta get out of this place,/If it's the last thing we ever do. . . ."

The lights on the main runway were out, but all around its borders the clubs and hooches still glittered. The blackout order from Defense Control, if there was an order, had not yet filtered down below the major commands. They set out in the truck around the south end of the runway on the main post road. As they crossed the end of the runway, the lights came back up. "It must be over," Wolcheski said. The moment he spoke, a heavy *boom* rolled down the runway. Bear could feel it through the steering wheel of the truck. A second followed almost at once. "Get over!" Wolcheski said. "Get off the road!"

"What is it?" Bear swung the truck down into the ditch and fought to a stop.

"Rockets!" Wolcheski spat out the word as if it had a bad taste. He had Janet out the door before the truck had jolted to a stop in the bottom of the shallow sandy ditch.

Bear saw the third rocket impact. It struck halfway up the runway. The explosion printed a dazzling dandelion-head of fire on the night, a three-quarter sphere that laced out to the whole width of the runway, and, at its full size, vanished entirely. The shock wave followed; it struck him in the chest as he came out of the truck. He took Alice's hand and dived for the inner edge of the ditch.

The next rocket they heard coming before it impacted. It came in a long hissing sigh that continued after the fiery bloom of the warhead. The fire was already gone before the hiss was cut off in a heavy shuddering blast. "They're a half mile off," Wolcheski said. He had counted the seconds between the visible impact and the arrival of the blast.

A siren began to wail from the direction of the helicopter

companies on the southern perimeter. Another answered from the direction of the club the four of them had just left. The lights on the runway were gone again. This time the lights in the buildings along its flanks began to wink out as well.

Another rocket came in behind them, in the direction of the helicopter companies. "Charley's a darn poor shot," Bear said—"or he's got the whole place bracketed." They pressed flatter against the sandy bank, grasping at roots of grass in an attempt to pull themselves nearer to the earth. But, though the nearer explosions shook the solid earth, few rockets fell at all near. They dropped in a leisurely rhythm up and down the runway and eastward toward the second runway along the sea. Between explosions there was absolute silence except for the mixed chorus of distant sirens.

The Bear peered cautiously over the top of the ditch bank. A fire up along the runway was sending a plume of dense fire-tinged smoke northwestward on the light wind. As he watched, another rocket flashed among the hooches beyond the fire. He rolled onto his back. The low clouds were beginning to glow with the light of many fires. A rocket passed high overhead and fell into the hooches crowded among the dunes behind the beach. They could hear it all the way across the sky. He was glad to be outside, free of the stifling uncertainty of a bunker. He did not want death to find him in some black hole as it had poor Jones. Better for a pilot to die under the open sky. "I wonder if it's true," he said, "that you don't hear the one that hits you."

"Don't talk about it!" Janet insisted suddenly. "Please, just don't talk about it!" She continued to clutch at the earth, and Wolcheski lay beside her talking to her in a low voice. Alice took her hands and tried to comfort her, but she continued to lie face down, sobbing to herself.

Off to the south the slow beat of a helicopter blade arose. Another joined in quickly. Bear sat up, and he felt Alice's hand on his arm. "Gunships," he said nodding.

The helicopters went out to the south and turned back toward Chu Lai along the beach. They could not be seen against the clouds. The rockets continued to arrive in a slow rain from the west. "Where are they coming from?" Janet asked in a small, shaking voice.

"Nui Ong," Bear told her. "The big mountain."

"But it's so far away!"

"Not more than five miles. That's close enough for rockets."

"If . . . if they're gunships"—she looked up toward the sound of the blades over the beach—"why don't they go out there?"

"There must be artillery out there by now. I doubt they can get through it." Now that he thought about it, he could even hear it— a low, intermittent roll like surf that crashed in waves about the feet of the mountain. Concentrating on the sound of each rocket as it fell, or waiting for the next, he had not noticed that sound; but he knew now that it had been present for some minutes. North and south, too, artillery muttered and grumbled. The uneasy sleep of the whole coastal plain had been broken. But the rockets continued to hiss and boom along the edges of the night.

Janet's body was shaking with silent periodic sobs. "Can't we please go somewhere?" she asked toward the ground. "There must be a bunker someplace! Why don't we go?"

"We're not going to move," Wolcheski said quietly. "Nothing but a direct hit can get us here. Charley can put all the rockets he wants to out in the open fields."

But Wolcheski was wrong. A rack of bombs, on their way from the ammunition bunkers to the arming line, had been left standing when the first rocket came in. The bombs were unarmed. They were not dangerous, left alone. Their explosive was insensitive. They could be kicked, rolled, dropped, or burned without exploding. Only the shock of another explosion would set them off. For that purpose they would be armed with a fuse of more sensitive explosive.

The rocket that fell among them took the place of a fuse. Its detonation took the bombs with it, and the concussion from that blast raced down the arming line and through the ammunition bunkers, through earth and through air, through sandbags and steel doors, waking bombs that had slept soundly through the height of the attack, and would have slept on until they touched the foreign earth.

The Bear was looking up the runway when that rocket fell. He saw the blast coming. It was a sharp line that defined a dome of fire, a swelling orange hemisphere that raced outward as if intent on engulfing the universe. Its outer surface raced through the low scud clouds, and they vanished. Bear threw himself on the ground, pulling Alice down with him. The shock wave hammered over them. "Get up now!" he said urgently. "Get under the truck!" He was on his feet and running; but Alice was not with him. He turned back. Janet was still stretched on the ground. Alice and Wolcheski had her by the shoulders and were shaking her fiercely. She would not move. "Get her up!" Bear shouted. "There's going to be all kinds of stuff falling here!" Even as he said it, he heard the first pieces thudding around them: broken concrete, shards of steel plank, five-pound lumps of lead bomb fuse. He ran back. "Let me take her!" He tore Alice's hand from Janet's shoulder, picked Janet up, and got her arm around his neck. "Come on, Ski, let's get her moving!" As they turned her around, his eyes met Alice's. "Happy New Year!" He laughed.

She would have loved him forever, for that if for nothing more.

There was a brilliant flash and an instant concussion that staggered him. He was looking into her eyes, and the flash printed her features on his memory like a photograph, forever. "Go on!" he said, shaking off the impact. She took her hand from his arm.

When they reached the truck, when he turned again, she was lying on the ground.

"What's the matter?" Bear said—cried.

"Something hit her," Wolcheski said. "Maybe it's not much."

But she was unconscious when they got her under the truck. Given a task she understood, Janet threw off the spell which had seized her; but too late. "I can't do anything for her!" she said. "She's all shocky!" Janet was crying still: no longer senseless tears, but no less in vain. "We've got to get her to a hospital!"

The steel rain had ceased. Janet helped them get Alice in the back of the truck. She and the Bear rode in back, holding Alice on one of the benches along the side, while Wolcheski drove.

There was no one else on the road. South of the perimeter a few artillery flares were now dropping. They threw a faint yellow glaze over the passing scene. Everywhere buildings had been thrown down. Those still standing leaned away from the center of the bomb dump. One steel maintenance hangar had a dark hole that gaped over half the roof, obliterating the proud sign painted on by its makers: BETTER BUILT BY CB-12. There were no lights anywhere. There was no one moving.

Wolcheski drove madly. The truck skidded and nearly left the road on the sandy washboard corner near the prisoner compound. Even on the straight stretches Bear could hardly hold Alice on the jolting bench. He shouted for Wolcheski to slow down, but Janet shouted in turn, "We can't slow down! She won't last if we do!"

The rockets were falling at longer intervals now. Most of them were back near the bomb dump. Once a smaller secondary explosion ripped the dump; but by then the truck was roaring up the twisting road over the ridge that was the spine of the Ky Ha peninsula.

The hospital was blacked out. Wolcheski slammed the truck to a stop outside the emergency-room door and ran for a litter. When the doors opened, the cold light fell out and across Alice's face. Bear thought it was the color of the light that made her face so pale, until he saw the blood spreading on her fatigues.

The litter-bearers appeared almost at once, with Wolcheski behind them. Bear expected them to say something, because they knew her; but they accepted her silently. Janet and the Bear helped them move her onto the litter, and they took her through the doors. Janet went after her. Bear started to follow, but Wolcheski caught him by the arm. "Why don't you wait out here, Bear," he said.

"I'm no good to her here." He struggled against Wolcheski's grip.

"You're no good to her there, either. They'll take care of her. You don't have to see it."

Bear broke free and pushed through the doors.

The ER was seething. Up and down the floor a double row of trestles bore two ranks of men. The rags of their uniforms were caked with red clay mud: they had not been wounded in the attack, but were grunts in from the field. Most of them lay untended—some bloody and groaning, some impassively studying the ceiling. A few dangled IV tubes. One of those rolled his eyes up as if trying to read the number inked on his forehead. Activity bubbled around six or eight centers in the room, where gowned or fatigue-shirted figures clustered around a man on a litter.

Between these a handful of orderlies strolled aimlessly or stood about. Or so it seemed to the Bear. He had not seen a mass casualty in its early stages and could not place this scene in the stream of scenes as the mass cal developed. He did not know that the triage was just over, and that those who needed aid most urgently were receiving what aid there was to give.

Alice was on the litter on trestles just inside the doors. A man in a gown detached himself from one of the groups, glanced briefly at Alice, and went to another of the groups, as if to a point of greater interest. He spoke in passing to a young black spec-five in jungle fatigues who disappeared instantly down the back corridor.

Bear stood beside Alice's litter. Above the collar of her jacket her skin was like marble. It looked the paler because the jacket was soaked from the collar down with blood. It had been cut open down the front, but the flaps had been pulled back over her. She was breathing. He could see that she was breathing.

The spec-five returned rapidly pushing a cart. There were several plasma bags on it. All but one were taken by another corpsman. The spec-five brought the cart and the last bag over to Alice. The other corpsman came up to help him lift the litter onto the cart.

"Where is she hit?" Bear asked. The spec-five spared only an instant to stare at him. "I don't know, man," he said. He started away with the cart.

Bear followed him to the end of the ER. The spec-five pushed the cart under an overhead bar there and hung the plasma bag overhead. He began to uncoil a plastic tube; but before he had well begun, someone shouted to him from down the room. He looked up, startled, then took down the bag and hurried away with it.

"Where are you taking that?" Bear called. The man hurried on. "What are you doing? Somebody's got to take care of her!" Bear caught a nurse by the arm from the closest group. "It's Alice Porter!" he insisted, pointing. "Somebody's got to help her!"

"Someone will," the nurse said. But she made no move to go herself. He looked wildly about the room, looking for Janet. He saw her at last where she had joined one of the other clusters about an earlier casualty. The spec-five had gone there with his plasma bag. Bear ran up the line of litters and edged between two of them, brushing aside the hanging IV tubes. "Isn't anybody going to do something?" he demanded. "There must be a doctor who can look at her. Do you need so many standing around here?"

Janet bit her lip and appealed with her eyes to the gowned man opposite her. It was the one who had stopped beside Alice. "Doctor Rawlinson?" she said. Bear understood that it was for his benefit that she had addressed the man as doctor.

"Yes, we do need so many standing around here," Dr. Rawlinson said without looking at the Bear. "And I did look at her. So did Dr. Kant. She's dying. Now get out of the emergency room." The spec-five was hanging the plasma bag on the bar above the soldier on the litter between Rawlinson and the Bear.

"Dying!" Bear stared up at the plastic bag, full of clear fluid, glittering like a crystal under the fluorescent tubes. "Dying? You son of a bitch, she's dying and you're going to let her lie there and die?"

The doctor had a scalpel in his hand. He threw it down and looked up at the Bear. No one else except Janet looked away from the soldier on the litter. "No, I am not going to 'let her die'! There is no way I can stop it!" He rubbed the bridge of his nose between his thumb and forefinger. It was a gesture Major Hart had often used when he was tired, or under a strain. Bear forced himself not to feel sympathy because of that coincidence. "You were going to give her blood! You took that away!" he shouted.

"We had three chopper loads of casualties ten minutes before she came in," the doctor said evenly. He glanced up and down the row of trestles. "We've had fifty others through here today. We're all but out of blood, and we have to save it for those who have a chance to live. She doesn't have a chance. Anything we do for her will be thrown away. I was going to throw away an IV, just because I can't help hoping sometimes. But *this* man can live, if he gets blood!" Now the doctor shouted, too, as he jabbed a finger toward the soldier between them. "Can you get that through you thick ugly skull? I thought a lot of Alice, too, but this man can live, and *she can't!* Now will you get out of here?" He nodded to Janet.

Janet took the Bear's arm and steered him away. She had changed from the frightened girl who could not force herself to stand up in the open air. When she stepped back into her familiar professional setting, some compound of training, habit, and professional pride took charge of her fear. "I'm sorry, Bear," she said. "He really did try."

Her words would have enraged him if they had come from anyone else. But he did not have in him even then the cruelty to say that it was her fault Alice was there at all. He could see that she was bitterly aware of it, as far as it was true; and how was *he* to lay blame at the feet of another for any such thing?

He went back to where Alice was lying alone. No one looked his way. He ghosted about the litter, sometimes looking at her, sometimes not. He could not tell whether she was breathing now.

The ER began to clear out. Soldiers were wheeled off on carts down the back corridor toward the operating room. The clusters of medical people broke up, reformed at different stations, broke and reformed again. During one of these permutations Dr. Rawlinson came back to where Alice lay. He put a hand on her wrist for a moment and shook his head. He looked at the Bear then. "Go on home," he said. He added, with a glance that took in the Bear's clothing from ankle to shoulder, "I take it you're not wounded?" Bear realized for the first time that he was covered with Alice's blood. "No," he answered. "I'm not hurt at all." The words were bitter on his tongue.

The doctor vanished up the back corridor among the stream of patients. Bear did not go until the spec-five came to push Alice's body away.

He found the truck outside the hospital. He went looking for Wolcheski, to tell him about Alice. But Wolcheski had gone out on a mission, to replace a pilot who had taken a thirty-caliber round through the chest while hovering in the dark above a rice paddy looking for wounded grunts. The pilot was the man who had lain between Bear and the doctor; but there was no one to tell the Bear that.

He drove down the ramp to the company. The sirens had been shut off. Patches of dim light stretched and slid over the helicopters on the ramp where the maintenance crews were out checking for damage. In some revetments there was no need for a light to see by: one ship sat broken like a straw, its tail boom angling to the ramp at one end and its nose touching at the other; another revetment contained only a pile of grey papery ash with the ends of a rotor blade sticking out—a direct hit by a mortar shell had set off the fuel in the tank, and eventually the magnesium alloys of the structure itself had burned like a torch. The Bear passed all this, slowly, without looking to either side.

"Bear, you missed all the excitement!" Atterburn appeared to have been waiting outside Operations just to find someone who had not seen it all, so that he could tell all of it again. "It was Suzie's Revenge! Those mortars walked up and down the ramp— boom, boom, boom! One every ten yards, and then over to the next row of revetments! They must have had it measured down to a gnat's eyebrow! Jesus, was the old man pissed!"

It was the first time Bear had heard anyone call Baker "the old man."

"They got four ships cold," Atterburn went on, "just totaled them. And put six more down, that we know of so far. They didn't get the gunships, though. We're still in business, Killer. Too bad you missed it. Did you hear the bomb dump go up, or whatever the hell it was? Jesus, there must not be anybody alive over there!" A long silence as he followed the Bear up the hill among the hooches finally seemed to give rise to an idea that the Bear had not been suspended somewhere during these events, and Atterburn asked, "Listen, where were you anyway? I bet you were down in some nice quiet bunker with your nursie-poo all the time the shit was coming down, weren't you? Jesus, what a life you have, Bear."

They were in the middle of the officers' area. Bear stopped, and Atterburn stopped beside him. There was no one else in sight, nor any sound of human movement. "How many casualties did we take?" Bear asked. He could not imagine where everyone might be.

"Casualties? Oh, hell, not a one. Not a damn one! Except the usual—sprained ankles and stubbed toes. The Operations clerk busted a finger. He was typing a report when the first round landed right outside, and he just shoved his hand right through the keys. All Suzie's work went for nothing." He laughed. "They missed everybody."

"Where is everybody, then?" He ignored the part about Suzie.

"All down on the perimeter. Captain Blood and the old man

288

think there might be a ground attack coming. Captain Blood's got me up here coordinating. We've got some people down on the beach, and I'm in charge of them. I had to come up to Operations to report in." Reminded now that he had command duties, Atterburn said, "You better report to Captain Blood, Bear. We need every man we've got."

"This is my night off," Bear said. He turned away and went into his dark hooch.

Atterburn followed him. "What the hell are you going to do in here?" he demanded.

"Go to bed, or hang myself. I haven't quite decided yet."

"You got to be shitting me! You mean you're going to just come in here and go to bed?"

"No, Atterburn. I told you I might hang myself instead."

"Bear, what's your nursie-poo been giving you to drink, anyway? You got to be drunk to talk about going to bed tonight!"

Bear lay down on his bunk in the dark. "That's right," he said. "I'm drunk. And you know, Atterburn, that when I get drunk I step on all the shit I come across. So if you don't want a waffle tread on your ass, get out of my hooch."

Atterburn sputtered out the door. Beyond his quick footsteps on the metal walk, the deep thump of the bombs in the ammunition bunkers continued to roll over the ridge.

He heard Blood coming within two minutes. The steps rang sharply, as if Blood had somehow contrived to square off the very sound in a military manner.

A light flicked on beyond the Bear's closed eyelids. "What is this?" Blood's voice demanded.

"This is a man lying on his bunk and minding his own business," Bear answered without opening his eyes.

"Are you drunk?" Blood snapped off the end of the question between his teeth.

"Sir, when I'm drunk, I step on all the shit I come across. Do you feel anything?" The words had worked so well with Atterburn that the Bear tried them again as an incantation. If they rid him of Blood for the moment, he did not care what else might follow. He did not really expect them to rid him of Blood; but Blood snapped off his light and walked out. Bear felt neither surprise nor interest.

Blood had never paid enough attention to his underlings as persons to be surprised that the Bear should be drunk; and it never occurred to him that anything else could make a man insult his superior directly. Blood rather liked the idea of the Bear drunk. It was an ordinary weakness. Let him sleep it off where he was. Maybe a rocket would fall on him.

For hours the Bear did lie there, listening to the war go on around him. It went none the worse for his absence, so far as he could tell. A machine gun along the perimeter chattered uneasily, and flares popped beyond the wire. Another weapon took up the cadence, and then another, and soon a whole sector of the perimeter was wild in defense against shadows. After several minutes it all died away. Over the ridge the fire the bombs had begun continued to gnaw its way through the ammunition bunkers, intermittently flinging out with a roar the artifacts of war it uncovered. The muffled explosions went on until near dawn, when a light north breeze sprang up and with a puff of its breath chased the sound back over the Ky Ha ridge.

The breeze poured wraithlike through the screen above the Bear's bunk. Its cool hands passed over him. Bear came near to weeping.

12

There was a soft step on the porch outside the back door. The door opened and Arp came in, followed by the grey light of dawn. He stopped at the foot of the bed. He stood looking down at the Bear, but he said nothing until the Bear spoke: "I'm alive, if that's what you were wondering."

"That's not exactly it," Arp said. "I heard this strange report that you were blasphemously drunk, and I had to see it for myself. How's your head?"

"About like my heart," Bear said. "Empty."

Arp went to the end of the hooch and switched on the light. Bear's eyes were full of the darkness: he threw an arm over them. "It's for your own good," Arp said, laughing. He came back toward the bunk. The laugh was abruptly cut off. "Good God, Bear, are you all right?" He leaned forward, stretching a hand toward the bloody fatigues the Bear was still wearing.

"No. I'm not."

"Those asses! They didn't even ask if you were hurt, did they?" Arp stormed. "Stay there! I'll get the truck!"

"No need," said the Bear. "It's not my blood."

Arp had already started. He stopped, his hand on the door, and turned back.

"It's Alice's."

"Alice's?"

"She's dead, sir." He could not keep a little tremble from his voice.

"Oh, God, Don!" Arp switched the light off, as if to cover up in darkness what he had said, his joking tone, his stupidity. He came back to stand beside the bed. "I'm sorry, Don. Forgive me!"

"For what?"

Arp had no answer to that. "Is there anything I can do for you?" he asked helplessly, knowing there wasn't.

"Yes. You can keep me from cutting Atterburn's tongue out when he lets it run off today." He said it as if joking, but then he sat up on the side of the bed and buried his face in his hands. "Atterburn is going to have more smart remarks about her than I think I can bear, with her in the hands of strangers."

"I'll take care of him," Arp said.

"Thank you."

All the ships that were combat-ready went out that morning on a combat assault. There was no advance planning, as there had been for Major Hart's assault. At 0730 word came down from Division that the assault would go. The ships that had already departed on missions were recalled. At 0900 they were to assemble at Hill 69, across Route One in the foothills north of Nui Ong.

The event swept the Bear up with the rest. When he took his helmet to the ship, Ruth had already preflighted. He climbed aboard without so much as looking at the main rotor—nodding to Cripps, who stood tongue-tied with the blade hook in his hand—plugged in his helmet, cranked the engine, called the tower and his second ship, and flew away.

As the ship crossed the main runway, Ruth called Chu Lai tower for traffic, but there was none. The main runway was closed. At the far end plumes of white smoke trailed away to the south.

Helicopters littered the tiny pad at Hill 69. The guns parked down along the fence overlooking the rice paddies, and the officers walked up to the briefing at one corner of the pad while the enlisted crews tied down the blades.

There were ships from two understrength aviation companies on the pad. Baker was to lead the flight. He strode importantly beside his helicopter while the pilots gathered.

292

Those around the Bear looked sidelong at him, or mumbled and edged away. Even Ruth fidgeted in silence beside him. Bear did not care. It was not a sorrow he wanted to share. He could see that the word had spread beyond Atterburn; but Atterburn stayed away. Blood, however, did not: he came down to greet the Bear: "So, how's the head this morning, eh? Bothered by the noise of a few helicopters? If you want to play, you've got to pay, soldier." It was the first time that Blood had ever spoken to the Bear in what passed for a friendly way. "What, nothing but sour faces?" he went on. "I thought you'd be a real tiger today, after your vacation last night. The sun's not bright enough for you this morning, I guess. Nothing but a sunshine walrus after all, ha ha."

"Sorry I couldn't get to everybody," Arp muttered behind the Bear as Blood turned away.

There was no sun that morning. Over the coast there was a high thin overcast, but low clouds shrouded Nui Ong. Men looked up uncertainly toward it as Baker began the briefing from the door of his helicopter.

"This morning," Baker said, "Charley is up there on the mountain grinning; but he ain't going to be grinning long, because we're going to cut his ass off and keep it for a trophy. Our mission is to pick up an infantry company here"—he pointed to his map and gave the coordinates—"and put them down here, on the west slope of this little peak." Ho Cong was its name. It was one of the subpeaks of the big mountain. "Whoever fired the rockets into the main post last night is going to be running west for the jungle. This company is going to cut them off at the pass." While Baker was talking, Blood paced impatiently beside the helicopter. When Baker had finished with the details of time, place, and radio frequencies, Blood jumped onto the step on the helicopter skid. "I reckon I don't need to tell you," Blood said, " 'cause Major Baker said it, that this is an important mission. We're goin' to get out there and romp and stomp, and the eyes of the whole Division are goin' to be on us. Maybe the eyes of the whole country, or the whole world." (Blood could not know that in the avalanche of attacks which had taken place around the country, the journalists would not have an attention span sufficiently broad to extend beyond those closest to their native haunts, the press bars of Saigon and Da Nang. A mortar shell close to home is always more

293

interesting than a rocket in some remote province.) "Now, this could be a hot LZ. The slick drivers are gonna expect some good support from you gunnies, and they deserve to get it. I know what it's like to fly support in a really hot landing, and what it's like to need it, too, 'cause I've flown both ends. The guns are gonna have to work close and put those tubes right down Charley's throat before they fire, even if it means facin' down some heavy-caliber weapons. Now . . ."

Blood would have waxed eloquent, except that Baker announced that pickup time was in one-five minutes and he would be pulling pitch for the flight to the PZ in zero-five.

The guns went out early and orbited while the slicks trickled out of the pad to join up in the air in the initial formation for the pickup. There were thirteen slicks and three light fire teams of gunships—the two led by Arp and the Bear, and one from the other company. The slicks were barely in formation before they reached the PZ and Baker's anticollision beacon flashed the signal for landing.

About the mountain itself clouds still hung below the peak. The flight path would have to follow back around the north slope. It was empty, jungle-choked country.

The guns orbited upwind from the PZ waiting for the slicks to load. At each circle the dark bulk of Nui Ong swept across the windshield and vanished astern. "Nice day for an RF," someone muttered sourly on the gunship channel. Otherwise there was no chatter on the radios.

The flight started north along the foothills to the west of the Chu Lai perimeter and swung into the broad but rapidly narrowing valley on the north side of the tumbling mass of mountains that was Nui Ong. Few of the crews had come this way before. American units did not often patrol the jungles beyond the head of that valley. The Bear had last come this way on his last flight into Hill 473. The landing zone for which the flight was bound was halfway to that hill, above the peak called Ho Cong. ("Do you reckon," one of the slick pilots from the other company had said, "that's because nobody's out there but Uncle Ho and the Viet Cong?") The clouds lowered as the flight penetrated the valley. Soon, at the elevation of the LZ, the ships were scraping the cloud base. While Ruth flew, the Bear studied the ground. The broken valley floor on the right held a narrow stream slashing a streak of daylight through the treetops. On the left the steep flank of the mountain, a wall of black treetops, curved out of sight ahead. They crossed the first, lower, saddle beyond Ho Ngon, into the land where the streams ran north rather than east down to Song Ben Van and the sea. Baker led the formation along the lower slopes, over the almost hidden jungle village of Trung Chanh, and turned upstream above the silver thread springing from the heart of the mountain.

The valley pressed in on both sides. The gunships, which had been flying on both flanks, were forced in below the formation or ahead of it. "Where do you want to be?" Ruth asked on the intercom. He was staring up at the bellies of the slicks two hundred feet above. The rocky streambed was rising below.

Bear came on the controls and edged the ship out to the right until his rotor was slapping at the treetops. "Vere's going to be noffing but clouds in a minute," Ruth said. At the same instant Arp came on the UHF. He was well ahead of the formation, leading the first fire team. He called to ask Baker, at the head of the formation, if the LZ was yet in sight.

"Negative yet," Baker answered. He sounded annoyed.

Ruth had picked up his chart. "It's in ve clouds," he said. "We're at ve LZ altitude now." The slicks were scudding in and out of the rags of cloud that looped down from the overcast. The air became turbulent. The main rotor banged through vertical gusts.

"Is that cumulo-granite out there?" an anonymous voice asked over one of the radios.

"It's only a little stratus," another answered.

"Strato-granite?" asked the first.

"This is Coyote Six," Baker's voice said vehemently. "Cut the chatter."

Arp's call slashed urgently across the banter: "Six, Wolf Lead is making a one-eighty. There's no place to go up here." Bear saw Arp's fire team a half mile ahead break to left and right in hard driving turns that barely cleared the treetops at the sides and bottom of the valley. The two ships came whirling back toward the formation.

"I have the LZ in sight," Baker announced. His beacon came

on. His ship nosed up into a decelerating attitude, but did not descend.

"Negative on the LZ!" Arp called. "The LZ is in the cloud!"

"Stay off this channel, Wolf." It was Blood's voice this time.

The formation was then a half mile from the spot where Arp had turned back, groping forward at sixty knots. There were at most thirty seconds before Baker's error became irremediable. Probably there was not half thirty seconds, for although one helicopter might grope through the murk at a near standstill, and so find a way safely back to the clear air below and behind, a formation of thirteen could not. In the cloud the formation would dissolve into thirteen mutual unseen enemies each wielding a deadly blade. But where Arp had turned back the valley was already too narrow to turn the whole formation. And ahead in the clouds the rocks climbed on three sides, perhaps faster than a loaded helicopter could climb.

Bear saw what was coming. He broke instantly to the left and below the formation, then pulled in power to accelerate away from Arp's fire team arrowing down the streambed toward him. He did not see what happened behind him, but he heard Baker call: "Six going around. Execute bad weather break."

Baker had not briefed on bad weather procedures. He was not planning to fly into cloud, not with a formation of slicks behind him. But sure of himself, sure of what he thought he saw, sure of the need to put the troops on the ground where Division demanded, he did fly into cloud, with a formation of slicks behind him.

Even without special briefing, every pilot in the formation would have known what had to be done. The bad weather break was a standard flight school exercise, designed to separate three ships which had lost sight of one another. The lead ship in the V was to climb straight ahead, while those on either side turned right or left away from the flight path in a standard-rate turn and at a five-hundred-foot-per-minute climb to the right or descent to the left. With three aircraft this would provide vertical and horizontal spacing while the pilots sorted out what to do next. With thirteen ships in close formation and rocks rising on three sides, it could not be done. Every pilot in the formation would have known that, too. For that reason only the first six aircraft entered the cloud. Those at the rear still had room to turn and dive away, bursting into a startled swarm in which they all maneuvered frantically to avoid striking rocks or trees or one another. All but one managed that. That one turned directly into the path of Arp's gunship. The gunship's main rotor struck off the tail boom of the slick, whose cabin nosed inexorably over and dived into the rocky stream. The gunship's blade, shattered and hopelessly out of balance, tore itself free from the airframe and went pinwheeling through the formation. ("It looked like a telephone pole whizzing by," one pilot said.) The fuselage dropped through the jungle canopy without leaving a mark.

Atterburn, flying a hundred meters behind Arp, shot through the melee and came untouched out the other side calling out that Arp and another ship had gone down.

Bear turned back instantly in a violent pull-up that shook the aircraft but brought it back to cloud base, above the other ships and headed back up the valley. "Is Ward still with us?" he called on intercom.

"He's coming up, sir," Cripps said. It was the first thing Cripps had said all day.

Ward's was the only other ship Bear was responsible for now. Knowing that it was still in the air, he dived away behind the formation to where the cabin of the slick lay cracked open like an egg on the rocks. A body was rolling slowly down the foaming stream. As it bumped and rolled from pool to pool, the limp arms waved meaningless signals to the gunship overhead.

The air at the head of the valley was suddenly empty; but the radios were cluttered with frantic calls as the slicks in the cloud tried to announce their movements to one another. They seemed to cease trying at the same moment, and into the ensuing silence a single word erupted: "Mayday!" The silence closed over the word.

Baker came back on the UHF: "Aircraft calling Mayday, identify yourself." There was no answer.

Baker had not heard Atterburn's call on the gunship channel. In the cloud himself, he had no time for those who had managed to stay clear. He tried now to gather the ships still in the cloud: "This is Coyote Six. Any aircraft now IFR, climb to at least forty-five hundred feet and fly a heading for the coast. Contact Chu Lai radar for a steer. The rest of the flight, reassemble at the PZ. Anyone in the cloud who breaks out, return to the PZ. Now, I want all aircraft to check in . . . ah, by your position in the formation. This is lead. Number two?"

Two checked in. So did three and four. There was a long wait. Baker broke it at last: "Five? Number five, do you read?" Number five failed to answer. Baker called at last for number six, who said quietly, "Six here. We're in the clear and joining the rest of the formation, in sight."

While Baker was counting his lost slicks, the Bear had been on the gunship radio, asking where Arp had gone down.

"Left side of the valley," Atterburn answered. He, too, had turned back and was picking his way through the tangle of slicks.

"There's smoke up there," Handy said.

A thin trail of white was oozing up from the trees on the valley wall. Bear flew slowly up toward it, through it. The ship was too heavy to hover there. He flew a slow figure eight upslope from the smoke. Even as he did so, the smoke increased. The shock of a heavy explosion rocked his own aircraft, and a ball of fire belched through the treetops. It left a ragged black patch of withered leaves, but the ground still could not be seen. "We can't get to vem wifout a winch," Ruth said.

Blood had been flying the last ship in the formation. He called to Baker now, "Six, Coyote Five here. We have a flight of six up, and one more in sight. Number twelve is down. Will check him and proceed to Papa Zulu to wait for you. Break. Flight, this is Coyote Five, moving from Tail-end Charley up to lead. Number seven, move back here, and number six, you can join in at the rear. Break. Wolf Lead, what's your status?" Blood's voice was choked with emotion—the voice of a man who has just won the Irish sweepstakes.

Bear watched Blood's ship slip below the truncated formation and bob up again at the front. "Coyote," he radioed, "be advised that Wolf Lead is down."

"He lost a blade and went into the trees," Atterburn called. Atterburn was making slow passes over the wreckage of the slick.

Blood acknowledged. "Any survivors in either ship?"

"Negative survivors in view," Bear told him. "Request a medevac with a winch." The formal phrasing of radio procedure was a great relief to him at that instant. It left no room for emotion. The words had a fitness of their own. They embodied action; and action, even when hopeless, was at least something— something to keep futile despair at bay. Coldness was better than tears. If he could have announced Alice's death over a radio, perhaps it would not gnaw at him so.

They slid into the pickup zone and shut down to wait for the rest of the slicks to come down from the overcast. Two of them had already landed. The others were soon there, except for one that had wandered far to the south and descended over the plain halfway to Quang Ngai. While they waited, Baker had earnest discussions with the infantry battalion commander, who arrived in a jeep only minutes after the flight landed.

Bear looked around to see who was missing. Something was wrong, but he could not decide what for a long time. He got it at last. "Where's Carter?" he asked Ruth. Had it been Carter's ship in the stream? Bear asked in sudden fear, "He wasn't flying number five, was he?"

Ruth looked at him strangely. "No, he wasn't flying number five."

"Where is he?" Bear asked. He saw the way Ruth was looking at him.

"I fought you knew—his ship went down last night."

"Carter?"

Ruth nodded. He knew the state Bear was in, and he wanted to say as little as possible.

"What happened to him?" Bear saw that Ruth was trying to avoid an answer. "Is he dead?"

Ruth nodded again. "He went down just at dark."

Bear remembered then. "He was medevacked, wasn't he? Him and two others." There had been three on Wolcheski's helicopter. "Who were the other two?"

"Williams—ve new guy, you remember?" Already, Rufe was calling someone else a new guy. How quickly they went! "And Rensdorff, the crew chief."

"Dead?"

"Williams was. Rensdorff is up at ve hospital. Ve gunner wasn't hurt," Ruth added, trying to end, at least, with better news. "He stayed wif ve ship until vey hooked it out. But I fink a mortar hit what was left of it, on ve ramp last night." He laughed a little nervously.

Bear shouldered the loss of two more friends and went back to his ship.

Blood came there as soon as all the slicks had landed. The other Wolfpack pilots had already gathered there. Bear was now the senior officer in the platoon, and they expected him to lead the three remaining gunships. "We're going back out," Blood said. "There's a new LZ if the other one isn't in the clear yet." He showed it to them on his map. "You'll have to form a heavy fire team with your three ships. Atterburn, you'll be the lead ship."

Atterburn's eyes were like a pinball machine.

"So the Burn gets a promotion," Ward said before leaving for his ship. "And he's never led even a fire team. How does Blood figure he can take Arp's place?"

"He'll never take Arp's place," the Bear said.

The alternate LZ was not needed. By the time the formation—eleven ships now—reached the area once more, the primary LZ was in the clear. The formation overflew the crash site. Dustoff was there with a winch, hovering along the stream collecting bodies.

There was no sign of ship number five. It was a ship from the other company. After the second sortie, all of the aircraft of that company returned to search the slopes of Nui Ong for any trace of wreckage. But there was no emergency radio transmission, no signal flare, no scrap of metal on the rocks, no tear in the jungle canopy to mark a grave. The trees on Nui Ong stretched a hundred feet from base to crown, and a ship that went through the canopy would leave no trace unless it burned. If it burned, everyone aboard would die swiftly. If it did not, then injured men might linger for days in the wreckage; but they would never be found.

The sky was dark in the east. The long waves broke slowly on the shore, leaving trains of foam-bubbles that winked out in random order or were crushed by the next wave. The coarse sand slid away beneath his feet and slid back. The sea wind smoothed it into place once more, and his steps were gone. Stars climbed out of the misty edge of the sea and glittered faintly overhead. All around, the land lay under the brief truce of evening. He did not smell the sea, nor feel the wind, nor savor the stillness of the land. His heartbeat raged in his ears, and his thoughts were driven down the wind from a wider sea.

Wolcheski found him there on the shore.

"Sometimes I wish I could vanish the way you do," Wolcheski said. "Your Operations doesn't know where you are."

"If they need somebody killed, I'll be there," Bear answered.

"I wish you had come to us," Wolcheski said.

"It's not what you want that makes you fat."

"My grandmother used to say that," Wolcheski said. He and Bear both smiled, but there was no joy in either smile.

Bear stuffed his hands in his pockets and worked his boots into the sand. "Anyway, I'm afraid if I was in your business I'd see too many people I know. Carter . . . Arp. It can't be that much fun carting in your friends' bodies."

"It ain't much, but it's the only war we've got."

"I suppose it beats killing. Lots of things beat killing. Maybe dying does. I don't know. I've only tried the one."

Wolcheski grasped his arm above the elbow. "Listen, Bear, promise me you won't do anything rash, eh?"

Bear shook the hand away. "You're starting to sound like Arp. Jesus, what would I do without somebody to worry about me? You do know about Arp, don't you?" He looked at Wolcheski for the first time.

"Yes. One of our ships went out for him."

"Why is it the people you like always get it first, Ski?"

"I don't know. That's the way wars are arranged, I guess. 'The good die first, and they whose hearts are dry as summer dust burn to the socket.'"

"Yeah. Why couldn't *I* have been born with a golden tongue, instead of a puckered asshole? Well, don't worry about me, Ski. I'm not going to drown myself. But I'm just trying to decide why it is that I'm not. Can you tell me?"

"Because you're the only Bear we've got?"

"And I'm not the Bear that I once was. I'm empty, Ski. I've had good friends, more good friends than I'm worth. And they're all

301

gone, or going. It's the people that matter to us that give us substance. If *you* go, maybe I'll just crinkle and blow away in the wind. I'm light-headed already."

"You've got plenty of friends, Bear. More than you know."

"Maybe I'll have one less enemy, at least. Baker's been scampering around Division, trying to head off an investigation. Isn't that grand? Blood's grinning from ear to ear. If he grins any more, the top of his head will fall off." They had begun to climb the trail up the cliff. Bear stopped near the top, near the roll of concertina. The vine now had covered it; but the barbs were still there. Bear shook it idly with his foot. "I hope you can stand my rattling tongue," he said. "I don't know what I can do, Ski. I really don't." They had talked all around Alice. He saw that Wolcheski was not going to mention her if he did not. But there was no need to say her name. He turned his face seaward once more. "What's out there? Tomorrow, coming up out of the sea, bringing nothing but more killing or more dying. As far as I can tell, neither one is worth a rat's ass."

"More living, too, Bear."

"Is there? I wish I knew that."

For answer, Wolcheski only pointed. He was pointing at the wire that Bear was shaking. The vine that had covered the concertina was putting forth flowers. They fell in pale cascades over the rusting coils of the wire.

Bear pulled at a spray of blossoms. The petals stripped free and fluttered away like snow. He shook his head.

"Bear, if things get rough, you can call on me."

"You bet your golden tongue on that, Lieutenant." He laughed, but it was a dark, mirthless laugh. Wolcheski's offer, an offer of nothing but friendship, moved him; but he dared not let it touch him. He could not clutch at another straw caught in the wind. He turned the offer to its other, unintended, meaning: "I've got your call-sign on my kneeboard. You'll be the first to know when I need to be carted in from the field."

"I was right!" Atterburn crowed. "She didn't come back to work!"

"Who?" Bear didn't look up to ask. He kept his face buried in

302

his pillow so that Arp's empty bunk couldn't stare him down. Besides, he knew who.

"Suzie. That's who. I *told* you it was her, Bear."

"All right, you told me." Atterburn's name for the mortar attack had spread through the company. To every man it was already "Suzie's Revenge." But today, the day after Tet, was the first day the hooch-maids would return to work, and they had all been waiting.

"Yan came back," Ruth said, after he had waited for Bear to speak again.

"What's that prove?" Atterburn demanded.

"Well, she's Suzie's daughter."

"She's probably hanging around to get more information for the next time."

Bear walked out of the alert hut and through the company area. Yan was in his hooch. She was ironing a set of fatigues. When he came through the door, she dropped the iron. "You not hurt?" she gasped. She had washed out the fatigues with Alice's blood in them.

"No, I'm not hurt," he said. "I'm number-one GI."

"I see here"—she raised the fatigue jacket—"I think you *bị thu'o'ng*—wounded." She turned away and took something from behind the end of his bunk. "I bring you," she said, extending her hand shyly. "For Tet." She had brought him a tiny basket of flowers. He took it and turned it in his hands, unable to say anything. She looked away and said in a lower voice, "I bring for *Trung-úy* Arp, too. You see him?"

He made himself look her in the eye as he answered. "*Trung-úy* Arp *bị thu'o'ng,*" he said. "No—*tu'-trận.*" He said, "killed in action." He did not know the Vietnamese for just "dead."

"Ai! *Trung-úy* Arp!" She folded herself onto the bed behind the ironing board and began to weep. At length she wiped her eyes into one of his handkerchiefs and asked unsteadily, "What happen him?"

"Death happen him. That's all. He's gone. *Tu'-trận!* The dark angel took him! Christ!" He did not know how to tell her in her own language, and he hated the bastard Army patois that was all the hooch-maids understood because it was all that was spoken to them. He thrashed incoherently among the stubble of two languages, unwilling to reduce Arp's death to the ridiculous, unable to raise it to the sublime or even the comprehensible.

"Mama-san be sorry," Yan quavered. "She think *Trung-úy* Arp number one." She began to sob again.

"Isn't your mama-san here today?" Bear asked.

"*Khong biết?*"

"Mama-san no come to work today?"

"Mama-san sick," she said. "She no come work. She no come work again."

"What's the matter with her?"

"*Khong biết.*"

"Why she no come work?"

"*Khong biết,*" Yan insisted, crying harder than ever. It was all she would answer—that she did not understand the question.

Each time he had thought he grasped some piece of truth, it slipped away and left him holding out an empty hand. Now he felt even his old anger on Suzie's behalf slipping away. Surely she would have chosen another day to stop coming to work, if there were any truth in what Atterburn implied? Or did she want them to know? But then, would she send her daughter back? And with flowers? And Suzie *had* liked Arp—he knew that was true. But what would she do, if duty called her?

He dropped the matter from his mind. What difference could it make? Either way, where was Arp now? And Alice? He picked up the fatigue jacket which Yan had dropped on the bed. It was clean. There was no sign of the life that had drained into it. How long would it be before they were all gone from his heart?

13

Cripps rolled over on the sour-smelling, mildewed sleeping bag. The Bear was seated on the next cot, his legs crossed and his hands cradled palm-up in his lap with his thumbs not quite touching. He raised his eyes. They met Cripps's own, and stayed for a moment. "Cripps," he said, "you sleep like a pig in clover. I wish I had your dreams."

Cripps blushed. "They ain't much to write home about, sir," he muttered.

"No? From the look of you when you were asleep there, I'd have said your momma would have been pleased to hear about them." The ghost of his old gentle smile touched Cripps, faint but warm as candlelight seen through a frosted winter window.

"I'm not so much for writing home," Cripps said with a slow shake of his head. "Not like Mr. Covington was. He was the one, wasn't he, sir? I don't guess it does any good to talk about it, though?"

"Maybe it's a good thing to talk about old friends," Bear said. "Do you think we could keep him alive for a while, if we talk about him?"

"We could use him now, sir."

"You speak the truth, Cripps."

"Not that I don't like Mr. Ruth, you know, but . . ."

"Rufe is good folks," Bear said. "But new friends never quite fill the void."

"I guess that's it." After a long silence Cripps added tentatively, "Do you ever hear from . . . Pinky, sir?" He hesitated before using her name. He would have called her "Mrs. Covington"; but he had never heard her spoken of except as "Pinky," and he always thought of her so. He had seen her picture. It was hard to say "Mrs. Covington" about a girl no older than himself.

"I wrote and told her about Cov," Bear said. "I guess you know that. I haven't heard from her since. Maybe she didn't want to know, Cripps, not really? Maybe I should have let her think, well, somewhere he's alive. Maybe the Army knew best. But I told her." He sighed. "What do you think, Cripps? Was it wrong for me to tell her?"

Cripps was flattered that the Bear would ask his opinion on anything. He did not hesitate to answer. He had the answer ready in his heart. "You did right, sir." He would have told her himself, had she written to him. But probably she did not know his name, or even that he existed. "You did right."

"Well, one time out of a hundred probably won't spoil my reputation," Bear said.

"Maybe you ought to write again, sir," Cripps offered. "If you haven't heard from her, you don't know that she got your letter. And you don't know that she didn't write back if she did get it. You remember I got just that part of a letter from my momma when that C-130 carrying the mail got hit by a rocket at Da Nang?"

"Cripps, I love your faith. You restore my soul."

But the words were empty. He knew it. He did not believe anything would restore his soul. He would not write the letter. He was afraid that she hated him because Cov had died flying in his place.

Cripps knew that, too. Bear said nothing about it now, but Cripps remembered.

There was no memorial service for Arp and his crew. Major Baker did not want their end remembered. An investigation of the mission had not materialized, but the wraith of it hung always about the orderly room, and Baker lurked in his back office listening for its first footsteps on his floor. He said little about combat missions now, and made sure that Blood did not, either, at least

306

where he might hear of it. Blood hated losing the combat assaults this way; but he did not say so, at least not where Baker might hear. He did complain discreetly in the officers' club, the alert hooch, the Operations shack; but Baker, if he knew, did not dare to take notice.

Blood had a growing fear that without combat assaults to fly, not only was there no chance for glory, but no chance that Baker would be killed. He might drag on as CO forever, or until the end of Blood's tour of duty.

And Atterburn became acting gun platoon commander.

"Atterburn! God help us!" Ward groaned.

"You say it should have been the *Bear?*" Handy said to Cripps. "What are you, crazy? Suppose he was to take another spell of not firin' his weapons? How many Charlies would still be alive to shoot up your ass another day? He ain't the Bear he used to be, you know. I admit, he was somethin' to watch, in the old days. I seen him put a dud rocket through Victor Charley's belt buckle at a thousand meters! Sure, he's been all right here lately, but you can't count on him. He ain't the Bear he used to be."

Atterburn began by pasting on the alert hooch wall a chart showing the running total of kills for each fire team. He personally inspected the weapons of every ship daily. He spoke of applying for a commission. "Captain Blood thinks I ought to do it," he said, as if seeking the wise advice of others on that hard question. "But I don't know. It's a lot of responsibility. Look at Captain Blood—he's got a lot on his shoulders."

"Not to mention his conscience," Ward muttered.

"Vat's right, I wouldn't do it," Ruth said. "Once you get to be captain, vat's ve end of your flying. Noffing but desk jobs. You wouldn't like ve responsibility. Don't do it, Burn."

"A lot you know about it, Rufe!" Atterburn answered indignantly. "You think just because you don't mind being a flunky all your life, nobody else minds. If you want to get ahead, you've got to grab for the brass ring."

"Well, if it's what you want, ven do it!" Ruth said, perplexed. "You'll probably like sitting behind a desk."

"I don't think I could stand it if I ended up just sitting behind a desk," Atterburn said, shaking his head. "What do you think, Bear?"

What Atterburn really wanted was for everyone to be aware of the magnitude of the problems facing him. But he also yearned for the Bear to show some envy. By date in grade the Bear should have been acting gun platoon commander. Atterburn was determined to smoke out the hard feeling that must be inside him.

"I think you ought to follow Blood's advice," Bear said. "After all, he used to be a sergeant, and look at him now." He smiled blandly and scratched his rear.

"You don't have to worry about spending your life behind a desk, Atterburn," Ward told him, "so you might as well put in for a commission."

"How's that?" Atterburn asked. Visions of general officer rank danced in his head.

"If you outlast the war, you're going to get riffed out anyway."

Atterburn grinned uneasily at the laughter around him. They would be slower to laugh once he had his commission.

The numbers on Atterburn's chart grew rapidly. Those under the Bear's fire team grew as rapidly as any. The tide of killing that had begun to flow weeks before Tet was past its crest, but often the guns were out all night long. Bear, coming in after dawn to throw himself on his bunk, would turn away from Arp's empty bed, turn his eyes from the hospital buildings down the ramp, try not to dream of the figures caught in the wire under the fevered light of the flares, caught in the fiery web of the tracers.

One night outside LZ Ross they left a hundred bodies hanging in the wire when their ammunition gave out and they turned for Hill 63 to rearm. A Mustang fire team came on station behind them. Before the Wolfpack ships had gone five miles, one of the Mustangs called out that he had taken a round through the transmission and was going down. The pilot's voice was as calm as if he were announcing a stroll in the park. The ship landed outside the wire, within a hundred yards of unreachable friends. When the Wolfpack returned, the helicopter was standing there in the light of the flares, looking as if it had been parked, except that the blade was not tied down. The next afternoon one of the pilots walked into a firebase three miles away, dressed only in his OD undershorts and T-shirt. He had stripped off his uniform to look more like a farmer out in his fields. He was almost shot by a sentry for his efforts. But the rest of the crew were never seen again. Were they still alive somewhere, Bear wondered, in one of the secret jungle prisoner camps the VC were said to keep; or did only their names now wander the earth, to the torment of their families, kept moving because the Army permitted no empty tombs?

Bear defeated Arp's empty cot by occupying it. As the numbers on Atterburn's chart mounted, he could not bear being where it always met his eye, and Arp's old place still stood empty in the corner. He was not superstitious about the cot. He liked it better than being under the eye of the monster.

He was lying on Arp's cot one morning—he supposed it was a Sunday, for the chapel bell had rung an hour before—when Cripps appeared at his feet. It was one of those silver days into which the monsoon expires, a cool still day with the mountains awash in haze. The shutters were up. The hooch was bright with refracted sunlight, so that Cripps's untanned face floated against the remnant of darkness hiding above the rafters. Cripps was grinning.

"You look like the cat that ate the canary," Bear told him. "Do you know something I don't but wish I did?"

Cripps blushed, mumbled, and held out his hand with an envelope in it. "I got your mail for you" was all he said.

"Cripps, you don't have to do that every day. You're turning into my personal servant lately."

"It's okay, sir."

Bear sat up and took the letter. Cripps stayed at the foot of the bed, beaming. Bear looked at the return address. He knew the hand even before he read the words: "Covington." It was from Pinky. He looked up at Cripps and then opened it.

Dear Bear [she wrote], I hope you'll forgive what must seem my unforgivable thoughtlessness in not thanking you for your letter to me. I did answer it, but my letter must have gotten lost somewhere between me and you, for I had a note from Sp. 4 Cripps (Doesn't he have a first name? I've written to him asking if he won't write again and tell me, but please you tell him, too) saying that you hadn't received it. I hope this will make up for it. I don't want you to think I'm angry with you for what you told me. You only told me the truth about Wes. It was what I asked, and it was what I wanted to know. I'll always be grateful to you for having the compassion to break the Army's rules (and thank you for explaining them to me—I hope their effect isn't always so cruel as it seemed to me) and share the hard truth with me. I know that Wes's death was hard for you to take, too. All of his letters showed how close he was to you. But you can't blame yourself for his death. You said he was flying your mission; but I know that's not true. If you had been flying, I would only have lost you both. That was why I didn't write to you sooner—not because I didn't think of you, but because I knew that you and Wes always flew together. Every time I thought of you I was terrified that I might write and learn that you weren't there, either.

Dear Bear, I wish you would write to me again. I know Wes asked you to be the godfather to our child, and that you agreed. I'm going to hold you to that. I so much want you to be that. I hope you won't think it silly of me to say that in that way it will seem that some part of Wes will still be coming home to us. Please stay whole for us, dear Bear, and write to let us know that you are.

"Stop grinning, Cripps," Bear said roughly, as he finished the letter. "You know I can't stand a show-off."

"Yes, sir," Cripps answered, grinning.

"The proper answer to that is 'No, sir.' "

"Yes, sir. No, sir."

They both began to laugh. Bear felt that his heart had flowered.

"Share the joke," Atterburn demanded as he came in the door. Atterburn could never rid himself of a fear that unexplained laughter was aimed at him. "What's the joke?" But the two of them only laughed the harder, until he wandered off to mull over the numbers on his kill chart.

310

14

The carefully nurtured plans of Baker and Blood bore fruit after the sowers had ceased to tend them. The slick pilots no longer treated special standby as anything more than a formality. They read their names on the list and wandered away in the evening to the movie at the officers' club. The only reason there was a full complement of crews available when the call did come from Division for a quick-reaction assault was that the call came at three A.M. The duty officer had some trouble locating the list of standby crews; but by 0330 pilots were beginning to straggle in to Operations with helmet bags and pistol belts in their hands and sleep in their eyes.

The fire team on standby was called last, because the gunships were already preflighted and set up to fly, and also because the duty officer in his distress forgot that gunship escort had to be provided. The crews in the alert hooch slept on uneasily as the mission took shape around them.

Marching feet moved through the Bear's dreams. Dark shapes passed him in the darkness. They bore weapons and carried helmet bags under their arms as they trod inexorably down the hill to where the helicopters waited. He searched among them for a face he knew, but it was not to be found. Every face was turned from him, and there was no reply to his questions.

A low mound of sandbags rose beside him. He turned to it and began to climb. As he climbed a wind arose from the sea. The rain streamed over him. The sand ran beneath his feet, and the faster he climbed, the faster it flowed away. The red star before him winked in time to his footsteps. With each step he took toward it, the star moved farther off. "What's the joke, anyway?" Atterburn asked him. The star fell heavily into the sea. He sought it up and down the rows of drawers. Each drawer had a name on it. He could not read the names. The drawer handles were cold to his touch. He rattled and pounded at them in vain. They would not open. The clerk laughed at him: "Why do you seek the living among the dead? He is in his tomb." Below the cliffs the sea cast spray into the white dawn. "Go back," he said to Alice. "I have to find it alone." "You can't," she told him, "it doesn't exist alone." She walked heavily beside him. Her pregnancy made her clumsy on the rough path, but she went on, cool and white as the dawn that trailed its fingers down the sea. "Look," she said, "it's still there. You can see it." He did see it. The dawn cleared the mist from the sea, and in the space where the mist had been, the space where heaven and earth flowed into one, he saw it. The island floated there, mirrored between sea and sky, a part of both and of neither, untouched by the storms of war—Cu Lao Re, the rock in the void, the dream of peace beyond the bleeding land.

A burning light drove the image from his eyes. Was it the sun that had leaped into the sky? "Wake up, Bear, wake up!"

The lights overhead had been turned on. "Time to get a move on. There's a briefing."

"There goes my night vision," Ward was grumbling. "Who turned that on?"

"I did. Get your night vision on your own time." It was Captain Blood. He was going down the row of cots, jolting men awake with a kick at the foot of each cot.

The scramble horn or an incoming round would have brought the Bear to his feet wide awake in an instant; but he was not tuned to wake to a human voice. Groggy and disoriented, he buckled on his pistol belt and stumbled across to Operations. "What's ve matter, B.?" Ruth asked. "You look like you saw a ghost." Bear shook his head, but he could not shake off the dream. The night was clear and chill, but the cold air did not clear his head.

The Operations hooch was filled to the corners with dark-eyed pilots. They talked in low tones among themselves. There was none of the horseplay that preceded most briefings. "I just can't get up to operating rpm three hours before get-up time," Carlisle said. No one laughed.

Rauch was drawing on the plastic overlay to the large-scale area chart. Blood paced nervously behind him, three paces to the right, then three to the left. At each end he consulted his watch. He stopped when Baker came down into the hooch.

Baker smiled about the room at the dim ranks of men in the unlighted rear half of the hooch. His forcibly steady smile bordered on being a grimace. Rauch met him beside the chart and began gesturing toward the Tam Ky coast while Baker shakily lit a cigarette. He blinked off the glare of the match and nodded his head as Rauch spoke to him. When Rauch had finished, the major made an expansive gesture toward the chart with one hand, as if offering the territory all to Rauch, and sat down abruptly on the nearest chair.

"Y'all want to have a seat, and we'll get this thing on the road," Rauch said. The room subsided into silence.

"As some of you prob'ly know," he began, "you folks are all on standby for a quick-reaction force tonight. Well, tonight we're goin' to quick-react—even if not *too* quick." He glanced at his watch. "Division says there's a big shootout goin' on up here"— he gestured toward the chart of the coast north of Chu Lai—"at about three-six-zero, two-eight-zero. There's supposed to be an NVA company, more or less, in contact with an ARVN company. Division wants us to cut off their escape to the north by puttin' two platoons of grunts down on the beach between this here little river—that's a *big* river on the ground, in case you never noticed it —this little river and the ocean. We pick up the grunts north of Tam Ky, right here at three-zero-zero, two-five-zero, at oh-four-thirty, so we got to do some fast travelin'. Ground frequency is fifty-one-hundred on the Fox Mike. C and C will be on company UHF. You got eight ships, formation will be V's of three, and the basic load will be six packs—it's nice and cool out there tonight. Even ol' seven-six should be able to cut it." Seven-six was a notoriously weak-hearted ship. On a hot day it could not be got off the ground with a half load of fuel and two passengers. "Any questions?"

"What about lights?" someone asked.

Rauch shrugged and looked toward Baker. "Sir?"

"Sure, we'll use some lights," Major Baker answered loudly. There was a scattering of laughter.

"You want position lights on dim in formation?" Rauch suggested. "No beacons, except to signal liftoff and landing?"

"Sure," Baker said agreeably. "Soun's great. Ask Blood there. Blood knows what we want."

"That's fine," Blood said. His voice was neutral; but his eyes sparkled.

"Sir, you got anything else?" Rauch asked the major.

Baker teetered on the edge of his chair. It seemed only a matter of chance whether he rolled forward to his feet or back against the chair back. Finally, he lurched forward onto his feet and took the pointer from Rauch's hand. Jabbing the tip of it at the floor, he stood leaning against its frail length with both palms down against the handle. "Gen'men," he addressed them gravely, "as L'tenan' Rauch said, this is a very importan' mission. Division gave us this one on a ver' short f-f-fuse, and they gave it to us b'cause they know this is the bes' ou'fit in the Division. I expec' you all to do a good job on this, hol' right in there tight while it's dark, you know, an' . . . an' . . ." Unable to think of anything further to say he at last asked if there were any questions. If there were, they went unanswered, for at that moment the overstressed pointer, which had been bowing under his weight, gave up the struggle and snapped in the middle. Baker jigged two steps forward and came upright against Captain Blood sitting in the first row. He straightened up with a shake of his shoulders, grinned around the room as if he had done it all for their entertainment, grinned down at the shaft of the pointer still clutched in his right hand, and threw the shaft on the floor.

The briefing broke up in silence. The pilots drifted down the ramp among the dim blue lights marking the hover lanes. Across the muffled tread of boots on the ramp came the clatter of a blade hook dropped by some crewman. Cargo doors slid open with a hollow rumble. Blades were swung out to the side for starting. Overhead, the luminous stars hung heavy in the sky.

Bear had seen and heard all of it a hundred times before, but tonight it all seemed strangely foreign. He looked around, bemused by the dark shapes passing him. "Hullo, Bear," one said.

314

It was Carlisle. His face, too, looked strange in the distortion of the shadowy darkness. His bare scalp glistened pale as a death's head as he swept off his cap to wipe sweat from his forehead with the back of one arm. Bear felt it was all still part of his dream. "Wasn't Baker rare?" Carlisle said. "I hear he just got back from the club an hour ago. If you ever want to know what it's like to fly with a drunk, ask me when we come back for breakfast."

"Are you flying with him?"

"Somebody's got to do it." They came to the tail of the Bear's ship, and Carlisle turned aside. "Luck, Bear."

"You too, Hitch. You need it more."

Cripps was beside the tail boom, waiting to untie the blade. He greeted the Bear with a smile but no words. The Bear climbed into the cockpit and strapped himself in. Ruth was already there. Lights began to flick on up and down the ramp as aircraft was ready to crank. The whirr of the first starter rose up from a revetment. The Bear reached up to turn on his ship's position lights and nodded to Ruth. "Clear!" "Clear, sir." Those were the only words he heard from Cripps.

The formation hung off the left flank of his ship, no more than a faint constellation of colored lights, as motionless and unreachable as the stars themselves, which were splashed undimmed across the heavens. Over Song Ben Van the steel sheen of open water stretched below; but after that only faith could affirm that anything at all remained. Not a candle showed from the dark earth until the flight passed Tam Ky. Then, far to the northeast, there arose the distant flicker of artillery.

Two quick flashes of red from the head of the formation signaled that Baker and Carlisle's ship was descending. The cluster of lights dropped slowly away below the horizon. The Bear pointed down for Ruth to descend along one side of the formation's approach to the pickup zone. They were close to the ground before he could make out the faint triangle of lights that marked the PZ.

While the slicks were loading, the guns cast a wide circle around the pickup zone. Then the constellation of lights within the circle extended, turned, condensed once more as the formation left the earth and turned east toward the coast. The formation climbed, and Bear found that while he had been turned away, dawn had insinuated itself over the horizon. At first it spread in a long narrow line on that far edge of the world as if, without touching either heaven or earth, day had dawned in that uncertain space where in the long haze-blued afternoons the horizon hid itself. Then it spread slowly down the sea toward the dark shore. The marshes and sandy waste directly below seemed to feel it before the shore itself: they glimmered up faintly, the merest suggestion of solidity, as if the light afar had called them into being from nothing, but only half succeeded. Ahead, the waters of Truong Giang were dark behind the dunes at the sea's edge.

The artillery had gone out. The shells had been falling from the west until they could no longer be fired without endangering the helicopters. From a distance the shore was peaceful. But as the formation drove steadily closer, the impression of peace was proved false. The remnant of night that hung in the dunes beyond Truong Giang was torn by streaks of fire. The angry flashes spit back and forth in ever-changing patterns. Had not the malice behind them been known, they would have seemed as random as the paths of lightning.

The artillery strike had left a pall of smoke hanging over the dunes. On the windless air it thinned slowly, flowed with the chilled air down the shallow draws and valleys, billowed above the breath of dying men. It thickened and spread where the predawn chill spun a veil of mist over water and sand.

There was a fishing village on the landward side of Truong Giang. Beside the water its dark houses loomed like peaceful shaggy beasts sleepily contemplating the battle that raged on the far shore a half mile distant. Cooking fires within made the houses steam like cattle in a foggy meadow. Nothing moved within the village. The boats were drawn up on the shore, up-ended.

On the opposite shore men could now be seen moving. Who they might be, no one could tell. They waded the chest-deep fog slowly, sometimes plunging over their heads only to reappear farther on. As Ruth swung the aircraft toward them, they vanished into a deep pool of the mist and were seen no more.

"Were they Charlies?" Handy asked. Bear shook his head to

show that he did not know. Up and down the dunes now tracers cut through the deepening mist. But they were fading as the light of dawn reached landward.

As the slicks turned north toward the landing zone, Bear ranged out over the dunes. Machine gun fire rippled up and down the evergreen scrub where two armies of Vietnamese drove one another over the sand. Sometimes he could see the men. Intent on killing one another as they were, none fired on him. He could not say which were friends and which foes. Nor, perhaps, could they. Once a smoke grenade was set off below him. It stained the velvet mist a bloody purple that spread and thinned and ebbed away into the valleys to melt into the remaining darkness. He could not tell what it was meant to mark. He prowled the marsh, the dunes, the edge of the sea. Bodies were bobbing in the low surf. They were dark-haired, uniformed, uniform in the equality of death; and whether they fought for north or south he could not say. Nor could they.

And always, always, the day crept up the sky, and down the sea. Not over the horizon—there was no horizon. But from wherever it was stored, from that eternity where sea and sky did not quite meet, day came back to try again. It was so like the dream, he almost expected to see the island there. He could not see it, but he knew it was there. Cu Lao Re was out there. There were things worth perceiving that the eye could not see. Visible or not, it was there still, the dream of peace. And home—that was there. Lost in the same uncertainty, but there nonetheless, it seemed suddenly close at hand. There was nothing between himself and home— only the curve of the sea, and time, and they were nothing at all.

He turned back to catch up to the formation. Baker had set the final approach path directly over the village. "He should have gone farver norf," Ruth said, "so he wouldn't have to overfly ve village." The landing zone was nearly a mile farther north in a narrow marsh between the tidal channel and the dunes.

As Ruth spoke, a broken stream of tracer bullets darted from Baker's aircraft toward the dark roofs of the village. "Wolf Lead," Baker's voice said from the company radio channel, "Coyote Six is takin' fire from this village. Reques' to fix 'em. Flight, open up." His voice, instead of urgency, contained a sly gaiety.

"Not another Mustang trick!" Bear kept Ruth's hand from the

317

arming switches. Only one of the other slicks had opened fire—
Blood's, at the rear of the formation.

The roof of one of the houses began to smolder. The slow
general seep of cooking smoke from within changed to a dense
white cloud boiling from one side near the ridge.

"Six, where's the source of your fire?" Bear asked quickly.

"Down in this village. Lay it on 'em, Wolf."

"Did you confirm visually?"

"You damn bet! There was tracers all roun' me!" Baker
laughed.

Bear made a swing over the village; but he knew Baker was
lying—there had been no tracers. The formation drove steadily
downward over the channel, out of range of the village. "They
were them invisible tracers," someone said. It might have been
Carlisle.

The roof of the house had broken into open flame; but still no
one appeared outside. They might not dare, with a helicopter
circling overhead. Bear cursed into his silent microphone and
turned to follow the slicks.

Baker had already taken the flight into the thin ground fog that
undulated over the marsh. The ships hovered heavily as the
troops on board hesitated before plunging into water of uncertain depth. As they hovered, two things happened together: bullets ripped through the formation from the low evergreens clinging to the surrounding dunes; and the mist suddenly began to
thicken.

Bear heard Baker's voice on the radio: "Get 'em off! Get 'em
off!" He saw crew chiefs and gunners sending troops out the
doors with the palm of their hands. With the first few out, the rest
followed. The water was only knee-deep, but the bottom was soft.
Slow, sucking steps took the troops away from the helicopters.
Those on the dune side of the ships fired toward the sand dunes
without knowing where they were firing. Those among the helicopters could not do even that. They waded slowly, slipping into
the reddening water, while the whole world slipped away into the
fog.

Baker's voice sounded high in his throat as he called out,
"Coming up!" With the horizon vanishing, the ships could not be
hovered over water any longer.

318

When he saw that Baker was taking the flight down into the ground fog, Carlisle got on the controls and then sat as still as he could. He tried to slow his breathing to nothing at all, to keep his pulse from racing. All the instincts of battle had to be suppressed. He did not want to be excited: he wanted to be steady. He knew he would need it. But it was no use: when the fog blanked out the horizon, his heart raced. Still, his hands were steady. Baker's control movements were erratic, going that fraction of an inch too far and then searching back. Carlisle steadied the controls.

The ship came to an uneasy slipping hover. Carlisle could not settle the ship down. All of the world that could be seen was a half-circle of undulating marsh grass and wind-whipped water. It was not enough to steady a helicopter against.

Someone called out that his ship had been hit; then a second called.

Baker did not wait to be told that the troops were off. He called for departure and pulled pitch. Troops were jumping from the skids. To give them a chance to get off, Carlisle tried to hold the collective down. The collective jerked up against his hand before he was ready. As he groped for that, the cyclic got away from his right hand. Baker had jerked the helicopter into the air and shoved the nose down in an attempt to force his way to flying speed. The overloaded engine would not respond so fast. The main blade began to slow. The low rpm warning went bouncing through the earphones.

Carlisle, leaning on the collective with all his weight, could not force it down against Baker's grip. "Get off it! Get off!" Carlisle demanded; but Baker had frozen on the controls.

The marsh grass began to spin away to the left. The blades had lost so much speed that the tail rotor could not counter the torque of the straining engine. The ship was in a slow turn to the right. When it came broadside, its speed fell off, and it ceased to fly. The marsh grass spun up across the left windscreen and crashed through Baker's door.

Bear saw a helicopter blade burst through the top of the fog. The ship was not going to fly. It was sideways and pitched steeply

319

down. It slid back into the fog. When it appeared again through a thin patch farther on, the blade was slashing the water.

The aircraft shuddered to a stop under the rolling white blanket. The crew were coming out over the upturned side. Tracer bullets twinkled against its belly. One of the crew fell, but he rose again and followed the others as they waded off to the north.

Other helicopters burst from the fog and climbed away over the channel. Blood's was the last. His ship crossed low over the thin patch and turned toward the downed aircraft as the crewman fell. Then it turned away. The ship left a telltale puff of black smoke as the power came back on.

Bear, still racing in from the village, thought that Blood had not seen the crew get out. He called urgently, "Five, they're wading north!" At first there was no answer. Then, Blood's voice: "Wolf, we can't get in."

"Ve bastard!" Ruth said.

Bear dumped the ship into a power-off slipping dive. The crew, if not picked up at once, did not have long to live. The turbulence of the formation landing had mixed the shallow layer of cold misty air near the ground into the next layer above, producing the much deeper layer in which fog was now forming. The downed ship was already vanishing. The other ships had got out; but landing was harder, with the cold water waiting for any mistake. But if it were not done at once, it could not be done until the fog burned away. And the sun had only touched the horizon.

Carlisle dragged Major Baker free and started the crew moving northward, trying to keep the fuselage of the ship between them and the machine gun until they could get out of sight in the fog. He propped up the gunner, who had broken his ankle in the crash. The crew chief stopped to return the fire with his own machine gun. His foot slipped in the mud, and he fell. He came up sputtering and choking, without the weapon. He could not find it in the ooze under his feet. The other machine gun on the helicopter was buried under the left door. Carlisle fired back with his pistol as they moved off. It had no effect, but it expressed his feelings.

Baker, once they got him started, moved quickly enough and was soon ahead of the others. When Blood's helicopter passed

320

low overhead, he stopped and waved frantically; but when it turned away he plunged on without a backward glance for his crew. Bullets geysered the water at random throughout the marsh. A low sand dune swelled from the water ahead. Baker surged toward its cover. He was far ahead of the others when the Bear's ship beat down through the mist.

The world narrowed suddenly to a hundred-meter circle, with the broken hull of the other ship the only reference mark. The voice of the machine gun was suddenly loud. Handy's weapon answered. "Where the devil are they?" Bear growled.

"They're coming, sir!" Cripps sang out. Three men were coming toward them in a great flurry of water. The two on the outside ran with the third between them. Bear turned to hover to them. They went down as he did so. Bullets slammed against the ship. A hole appeared in the windscreen before Bear's face. The bullet had come in the open side door, passed between him and Handy, and exited through the windscreen.

One of the men was up. It was Carlisle. He began to stagger toward the ship, dragging one of the others. Bear swung the ship to a halt beside them; but Carlisle could not lift the crewman aboard. Handy dropped his weapon to help. A little way off, the third crewman was face down in the water.

"You've got the ship," Bear said to Ruth. Ruth had been following on the controls. His face was white, and his gloved hand was rigid on the stick. Bear unbuckled his harness. "If I don't come back, get out while it'll still fly. And take care of my crew." He unplugged his phone jack before there was an answer. "What a fate, to become a grunt at this stage of my career," he said—to the ship, since no one else could hear. He patted the ship's door, and waded off.

Carlisle had got the gunner aboard and was starting slowly back for the crew chief. Bear started in that direction, too; but beyond that, at the edge of the hundred-meter world, Baker appeared. He was running in high splashing bounds, waving an arm and shouting. The return sweep of the machine gun cut his legs from under him. He came up again to his hands and knees, his head just above water. Bear waved at Ruth, signaling him to fly the helicopter toward the crew chief. He himself started to run

321

toward Baker. His feet sank deep into the sucking bottom. He lost a boot to the mud, but he got his knees up and kept moving.

Blood was pouring from Baker's nose and mouth when Bear reached him. "You might have told me you were going to die anyway," Bear said roughly. He took the major by one arm. "Come on, let's not waste my effort now."

A tremendous blow to the chest knocked him on his back. The dark water closed over him. It tasted of salt. Cov's tomb. "Death," he thought. Just the word: death. But the air touched his face once more. As he came to his feet he saw that it had not been death knocking after all. The bullet had struck the center of his armor plate. The plate was cratered, but the bullet had not come through. He lifted Baker once more.

Something hit his back.

This time no thought carried the message through his brain. Although the armor did its patient work, he was facing away from the weapon, and the armor was on the wrong side of his life. The bullet passed through the body and shattered against the inside of the armor. Its companions snuffed out the life in Major Baker and hammered at the sides of the helicopter hovering over the crew chief. Ruth, seeing them fall, seeing no hope, did as he had been told and took the ship out while it could fly.

The ship with the red cross came down out of the sun in a tight circle. The pilot was careful not to stray far from the secure area close around the American unit. The battle had pushed back to the south, but stray bullets had still winged around the ship on his previous trip in. The risk had been acceptable then, with live casualties to evacuate. But he did not want to die for a dead man.

He took the wind direction from the thin plume of smoke drifting inland from the burnt hooch in the village across the channel. He set his final approach directly into the onshore breeze, well north of the village. He touched the ship down just beyond the edge of the marsh and, after testing the solidity of the spot, put the collective down quickly to let the storm of sand settle back through the blade.

The detail of grunts waited for the sand to fall before they came with the bodies. "We've got no ponchos for these two!" one shouted up apologetically to the corpsman on board. "They

322

came without!" None of the living wanted to give up a poncho for the dead.

"We'll take 'em, wrapped or not," the corpsman answered. Bodies no worse than these he was glad to get. He signaled thumbs-up to the aircraft commander. As the grunts scattered out of range of the sand, the helicopter lifted up over the dunes, across the beach, and out to sea to climb to a safe altitude.

"Hey, Lieutenant Wolcheski," the corpsman remarked over the intercom, "a couple of these guys have wings."

Wolcheski had seen that they were pilots when the grunts carried them out: one of them, though missing a boot, was still wearing a chest plate. Wolcheski supposed that the bodies belonged to the dead slick lying down in the marsh. He turned the controls over to Guiterrez now, and looked back.

Baker's face was still bloody, but the Bear's looked quite at peace. Only the mobility was gone from it. The walrus was nowhere to be seen.

"Something wrong, *Trung-úy?*" Guiterrez asked him.

"No. I always feel like crying on days like this."

Guiterrez glanced quickly into the back. "Ah," he said. He added, in what Wolcheski knew was meant to be sympathy, "Well, it ain't much, but it's the only war we've got."

"It ain't much," Wolcheski said.

After a while Wolcheski took the controls back from Guiterrez. Still heading south, he put the ship into a slow, steady climb.

"Were we goin', *Trung-úy?* You lookin' for angels?" They were at five thousand feet and still climbing.

"Tryin' to keep the meat cool," the corpsman suggested.

"I was looking for an island," Wolcheski said.

Guiterrez looked at his chart, then out to sea. "Cu Lao Re? Yeah, I've seen that. Kind of neat."

"I've never seen it," Wolcheski said. "He told me about it; but I've never seen it."

"Well, you ain't goin' to see it today. Too much haze."

"I'll see it."

The gold thread of beach unspooled out of the haze below them, vanished again behind. To the west the mountains climbed from the plain. Beyond the paddies green with new rice they rose, range upon range into the west, while ahead the wide Song Ben

323

Van sparkled around the crescent island. Ahead were Chu Lai, Dong Xoai, Quang Ngai; behind him the villages Phuong Tan, Vinh Giang, Hoi An; out on the plain Tam Ky, Khanh My, Que Son, whose names the Bear had loved. But to the east the ocean closed with the sky, and if the island was there, he didn't see it. Wolcheski looked and looked, but he didn't see it. He wished he could see it, for the Bear's sake; but he didn't see it.